DANCE WITH THE DEAD

Donal has been banished to the Cold Case Unit for the past six months, investigating the unsolved murders of several prostitutes. So when another woman's body is found in North London's red light district, Donal leaps at his chance to get back on the Murder Squad. The police suspect a serial killer at work, but Donal uncovers evidence that points to a notorious gangland boss. As the body count rises, can Donal keep his personal demons at bay long enough to convince his superiors that he's right?

DANCE WITH THE DEAD

DANCE WITH THE DEAD

by

James Nally

Magna Large Print Books
Long Preston, North Yorkshire,
BD23 4ND, England.

British Library Cataloguing in Publication Data.
_____

A catalogue record of this book is
available from the British Library

ISBN   978-0-7505-4457-3

First published in Great Britain 2016 by Avon
a division of HarperCollins*Publishers*

Published in Large Print 2017 by arrangement with
HarperCollins Publishers Ltd.

Magna Large Print is an imprint of Library Magna Books Ltd.

Printed and bound in Great Britain by
T.J. (International) Ltd., Cornwall, PL28 8RW

Acknowledgements

Thanks Ed Wilson, my literary agent at Johnson and Alcock, for your energy, wisdom and lacerating wit.

Thanks Kate Ellis and Natasha Harding at Avon for coaxing and cajoling this book out of me with such chutzpah and guile.

Thanks editor Donna Hillyer for painstakingly weeding out the chaff.

Thanks Caroline Kirkpatrick of Avon for all your encouragement. Thanks Helena Sheffield, Avon's digital and marketing guru, for so ingeniously spreading the word. Thanks Louis Patel for so expertly handling the production side. Thanks cover designer Andrew Smith for capturing the essence.

Thanks Kate Stephenson, Avon's Commissioning Editor, for making all this happen with such verve and passion. I truly don't deserve any of you fine people.

Thanks literary agent Ben Mason, now in the US, and Katy Loftus, now at Viking, for believing in this series from the very start. I miss you both.

Thanks reviewers, reporters, editors and writers for heroically backing my debut, *Alone with the Dead;* including Raven crime reads, Anne Cater, Deirdre O'Brien and my dear friend Nigel Atkins of the *Mirror,* my old mucker John Sturgis and the brilliant Boo Findlay of the *Sun,* Brook Cottage Books, Killing Time, Killer Reads, Writing.ie,

Books and Writers, Rachel Millard of the *Brighton Argus* and Eilis Ryan of the *Westmeath Examiner*.

Thanks Brighton contingent for all your ongoing support, including Matt and Clare Crosby-Adams, Bob and Sally Sherlock, JP and Sally Hamilton-Savory and Peter Roemmele.

Thanks fellow TV troupers Bruce Goodison, Paul Crompton, Emma Shaw, Jeremy Hall, Andrew Mason, Laura Jones, Andy Wells, Alex Wood, Kathryn Johnson and Laura Dunne.

Thanks old friends for inadvertently providing so much priceless raw material. Step forward Fleet Street legends Ian Gallagher and Dennis Rice; Dublin media stalwarts Frank Roche and Vincent Cribben; Tom Larkin; David Hayes and the Bracken clan from the town of Moate and Alison Clements of Brighton.

Thanks indomitable in-laws, the McGraths, for your Trojan backing; Jim and Anita, Rebecca, Philippe and Raphael, Mike and Laura, Brian and Meaghan.

Special thanks to the Nally clan – Jim, Bunny, Helen, Jacqui, Claire, Lee, Greg Woods – and our myriad extensions for rowing in behind this project ... it really means a lot. Even more special thanks to my sister Claire for single-handedly doubling sales of the debut.

Thanks daughter Emma Nally, aged one and a bit, for instilling new drive in my tired old bones.

Thanks son James for all your ingenious ideas, energy and positivity. It means the world.

Thanks finally to my soulmate and backbone, Bridget McGrath.

Jim and Bunny Nally
Thanks

Prologue

Let's get one thing straight – I'm not a 'psychic cop'. I can't predict the future. God knows if I could, I wouldn't be in the mess I'm in right now.

Nor do I possess some macabre ability to contact the dead, and I feel nothing but contempt for those chancers who claim that they can. You know who you are ... psychics, mediums, men of the cloth.

But something's not right. Every time I get close to the body of a murder victim, they appear to me in the middle of the night. I'd like to say they turn up in my dreams. That would neatly explain it away. But they don't. They appear when I'm awake, and engage with me. At first, it scared me half to death. Until I realised they were trying to tell me something.

They're always trying to tell me something.

It's got to be my subconscious mind, right? Presenting clues to me in a novel fashion? To a devout sceptic like me, anything else is unthinkable.

I told three people about my 'visits' from the other side. My brother thought I'd 'lost it'. My shrink almost destroyed my fledgling cop career. My ex-girlfriend tried to kill me.

So I'm not telling anyone else. If this cursed 'gift' helps me crack more murder cases, then I'll

13

reap that benefit in secret.

No one else needs to know about my occasional Dance with the Dead.

Chapter 1

Manor House, North London
Saturday, April 10, 1993; 13.30

The Woodberry housing estate's basketball courts heaved, the thudding of balls and squealing of trainers sounding like a massacre at a school for mice. A car alarm's shrill whistle pinged about the tired old tower blocks, like the yelps of a seagull strapped to a high-speed propeller. A souped-up, blacked-out Ford Escort growled past, its drum 'n' bass heart spreading Kiss FM and fresh defiance.

As I got close to my car, two large men in dark clothes appeared. One leaned against my driver's door while the other walked towards me.

'Donal Lynch?'

'Not me,' I lied, veering sharply to my left and taking a route between two rows of parked cars.

The car leaner read it well, heading me off where the final two vehicles stood off, face to face, like duelling cowboys.

So did we...

Behind him, a large, blacked-out jeep pulled up. The back door ghosted open.

'Get in,' his strong Dublin accent insisted, and

14

I found myself hoping to God this was the IRA. At least I had some leverage with the boyos.

But the acid sizzling my gut told me these were Jimmy Reilly's grunts, and that he'd dreamed up something diabolical for them to do to me today.

Chapter 2

One week earlier...
Arsenal, North London
Saturday, April 3, 1993

My drunken mistake hadn't been falling asleep fully clothed – God knows I'd survived that often enough – but forgetting to remove the pager from my front left trouser pocket. Its sudden vibration sent an electroconvulsive blast through my piss-filled nads, forcing my unconscious mind to perform a urethral emergency stop. I woke to the sound of my own desperate yelps.

'*Tom, Brownswood Red-Light Zone N4 – Check MO*' flickered the blunt paged message. My clock radio's Martian digits glowered 0754. Below me, a stricken wine bottle spewed red across the cheap laminate. I saluted Shiraz, my fallen night nurse, for delivering almost three whole hours of sleep.

My grudging slumber had been broken only once, by a recurring nightmare that hadn't afflicted me for weeks. Why did it come back last night? Was he in some sort of danger?

To banish my angst, I flicked on the radio.

Lost in the Milky Way
Smile at the empty sky and wait for
The moment a million chances may all collide

The Lightning Seeds' 'The Life of Riley' seemed way too excitable for this time of day. I padded into the bathroom. Murdered prostitutes, or 'toms' to use police parlance, had become my area of professional expertise these days. Anyone would think I was trying to save their souls. But I had a point to prove about solving their murders. A career-salvaging point, I hoped.

Having spent the past six months on the Cold Case Squad dealing with long-dead stiffs, I comforted myself that at least this body would still be warm. Maybe she'd come to me tonight, like those murder victims had two years ago. Before all the trouble...

I'll be the guiding light
Swim to me through stars that shine down
And call to the sleeping world as they fall to earth

Or maybe those weird, inexplicable episodes had run their course. A large part of me hoped so. In the meantime, I decided to find out all I could about this local vice hot spot that had slipped below my radar, and knew just the man to help, so I cranked up the radio full blast.

So, here's your life
We'll find our way
We're sailing blind
But it's certain, nothing's certain

'Turn off that shite,' roared Fintan from his room. I knew he'd have to surface for a piss now too. He'd been in a worse state than me, having spent all day with his cop contacts, slumped over some bar like slugs in a saucer of booze.

We'd wordlessly devised a morning routine that kept us apart, leaving our hangovers free to fester in peace. But my older brother's success as a crime reporter owed much to his unabashed familiarity with London's carnal underbelly. 'Vice Admiral Lynch' they called him. And worse.

So, as he staggered out of the gloom, squinting like Barabbas and scratching his expense-account gut, I seized my chance; 'I suppose you know that Finsbury Park has its very own red-light district around Brownswood Road?'

'Well, I thought it best not to tell you–' he yawned '–I've seen your patter with the ladies. I didn't want you getting knocked back by a Skeeger. That could push you over the edge.'

'A Skeeger?'

'Yeah, you know, a raspberry. A toss-up. A *rock* star.'

'Sorry, Fintan, I don't speak Snoop Dogg. What are you on about?'

'Crack hoe?'

'What, the city in Poland?'

'No, ya fucking eejit. Crack whores. That's what they are down there. They sell sex for rocks of crack. Desperate skanks really.'

'Ooh.' I heard myself blanche.

'It's small scale, probably about a dozen girls. I can't believe you don't know about it.'

'I'm not a vice cop,' I protested. 'It's never been mentioned in any of my cases.'

'All I know is it's the scrag end of the game. Guess what the going rate for full sex is?' he

17

asked, hosing down the porcelain.

'I wouldn't have the first idea,' I said. 'Hey, this is like a sordid version of *The Price is Right*, you know, higher, higher...'

'Or "The Vice is Right", except my advice would be lower, lower. Fifteen quid for full sex. Fiver for a blow job. Ten without a johnny. I mean, sweet Jesus, most of them don't have any teeth left. Can you imagine?'

I couldn't but, as he vigorously shook his cock, Fintan seemed to be having no trouble at all...

'Putting your unbagged member into one of those scabby gobs? Jesus, you'd have to be one sick pup. Or desperate.'

'At least the men have a choice,' I said.

'Ah, don't give me that old liberal shit,' he harrumphed, rinsing his hands. 'Why slave on your feet in McDonald's or a factory all day when you can earn a fortune lying on your back? They know the dangers. No one forces them to do it.'

'Violent pimps?' I felt tempted to say but I knew it'd be pointless. Fintan's binary outlook on life was crucial to his job. In a world where everything had to be explained in 300 words or less, black and white barely had space to tangle, leaving no room for tedious grey.

'Are they all crack heads then?' I asked.

'Jesus, you'd hope so. What else would reduce them to that? Anyway, why are you asking?'

'They've found a body near Brownswood. They want me to take a look, see if it tallies with any of the unsolved cases I've been looking at.'

'What, you mean the other whacked hookers?'

I bristled. 'The women who were murdered

18

who happened to be on the game, yes. They're still human beings, Fintan, you know ... somebody's sister, somebody's daughter.'

'Yeah, but let's not idealise these girls. None of them were in the running for Nobel Prizes, were they? Or doing charity work? Most of them ended up on the streets because they got kicked out of even the scuzziest massage parlours for stealing from the other girls, or punters or taking drugs.'

'Jeez, maybe you could say a few words at this girl's funeral.'

'Well, at least it's a fresh body for you, Donal. At last...'

'Yep,' I said dismissively.

'Your first since...'

'Yes,' I cut in again.

'Wow,' he said, his tone of false wonder mocking me, 'I wonder if you still have *the gift?*'

'That stuff's all in the past,' I snapped at his hatefully-curled top lip. 'I had the treatment. I got the all-clear. End of.'

But Fintan could never resist twisting a well-anchored knife: 'But what if she comes to you, you know, after you see her body this morning? What will you do then?'

'Well, I won't be telling you or anyone else about it,' I spat.

'God, you still believe in it, don't you?' he laughed. Then, all serious: 'Just make sure you don't start spouting off about spirits again. That whole thing was a real fucking embarrassment. For all of us.'

'Like I said, nothing to see here.'

19

'Good. Give me two minutes and I'll drive you over. I haven't had a decent show in weeks and, as it's on our doorstep, well ... you never know.'

'Don't worry Fint, I could use the walk...'

'Two minutes...'

That was Fintan these days, walking, talking, plotting faster than ever. No time to take 'no' for an answer; feeling real heat. God knows what he'd promised to secure promotion to Chief Crime Reporter at the *Sunday News*. But now he had to deliver, scoop after scoop. 'Exclusives' were his crack fix. The pimps on his news desk knew just how to keep him hooked, hungry and hounded so that he'd do anything for the next hit.

What a time to suffer his first barren patch. I sensed every fibre of him rattling, like a desperate junkie. Random parts of his body had taken to pulsating, hinting at imminent combustion; that vein on his left temple, his cheek muscles, a restless right foot.

'You're only as good as your next story,' he'd started to joke, which is why I felt confused right now. The murder of a street hooker – no matter how spectacularly blood-curdling – would never make it into Britain's bestselling weekly. The *Sunday News* revelled in its own cheerful, saucy-seaside-postcard venality, boasting a weekly roll call of randy vicars, love-rat footballers, showbiz/royal tittle-tattle, and bingo. Had this victim been a high-class call girl with a black book of celebrity clients, I'd understand his enthusiasm.

I had to assume he was sizing it up purely on spec, out of sheer desperation. And a desperate

Fintan spelt atrocious tabloid capers. Last time, it nearly cost me my job. And my life.

'Come on,' he barked from the front door of our little rented house in North London. His pallid head protruded from an oversized, crumpled brown mac, bringing to mind a bottle sticking out of a drunk's paper bag. He smelled like one too.

'Jesus, you look rougher than a knacker's arse crack,' I said.

'Couldn't sleep,' he frowned, aggrieved that such a thing could ever bedevil his conscience-light mind.

'Everything okay?'

'Yeah, of course,' he snapped, so I backed off.

He aimed a key at a spanking new red car, which shot back a wink and a robotic whistle.

'Woah, what is this?'

'Chief Crime gets a company car. The new Mondeo. Two litre. Sixteen clicks. Fresh off the forecourt.'

'Wow, did you pick the colour?'

'Yeah. Hot Rod red. Pretty striking, eh?'

'Had they ran out of Baboon Arse scarlet then? Jesus, they'll be able to spot you from space. How will you go incognito on some council estate in this? You'll stand out like a London bus.'

'Why are you so begrudging ... Jesus. Get in, it's unlocked.'

He beamed, his restless hands unsure what to show off next.

'It's got a built-in car phone. A CD player. Air-bags.'

'And you drove home in this last night?'

'I know nearly every senior cop in London,

Donal. If I get bagged, I just have to make a phone call.'

'It's not you I'm worried about. You could barely walk you were so hammered.'

'I probably still am. Now, do you want a lift or not?'

'Can we try out those airbags?'

'They're for when you crash, you bollocks. They pop out on impact.'

'Oh, right,' I smiled, gratified by his low aggravation threshold these days, 'they should have put some on the front as well.'

'What?' he growled.

'You know, so next time you're driving around, pissed out of your mind, you don't pulverise some poor fucker.'

We set off in silence along Drayton Park, turning right onto Gillespie Road. Everything I saw reinforced the absurdity of a vice hotspot nestling in this white, middle-class quarter of London.

Even on a Saturday morning, city types thrusted towards Arsenal tube station, all dreaming of that property upgrade to nearby Islington – two miles up the hill, two hundred grand up the housing ladder.

Along Gillespie Road, slim 'yummy mummies' yanked precocious blonde toddlers out of vast 50 grand jeeps.

Even ropey old Blackstock Road, with its tumbledown newsagents, plastic-appointed greasy spoons and sketchy boozers seemed a world away from crack houses, *pimps 'n' hoes*.

We turned right into Brownswood Road and a scatter of Rover Metro Panda cars. Through twitching blue crime-scene tape, a sprightly forensic tent glared fiercely white, sucking all the pale sunshine out of the sky.

'Oh dear,' said Fintan, 'The guts gazebo. It must be bad.'

Beyond the marquee of misery and more fluttering tape, tired parents dragged their nosy kids away, incapable of even beginning to explain what had probably gone on here.

'All part of their London education,' quipped Fintan.

'I couldn't imagine bringing up kids in a big city,' I said, 'So much madness to explain. Mam and Da never had to warn us about paedophiles or nutcases.'

'No, they sent us to be educated by them instead.'

'How is Da?'

'Why do you ask?'

'I keep having these weird dreams about him. I don't know. I'm starting to wonder if something's wrong.'

'You need to lay off the sauce for a while, Donal. He sounds his usual self to me. Come on,' he said, opening the driver's door, 'it's bad manners to keep a lady waiting.'

We walked towards the crime scene ghouls gathered at the tape. The streets around us groaned with elegant three-storey Victorian homes peering out over tree-lined pavements. You'd expect to score nothing more toxic here than a slice of Victoria Sponge.

'I can understand why there's a red-light district in King's Cross,' I said, 'It's busy and it's a dump. But this looks like a nice, local neighbour-hood. The roads don't go anywhere! They're all cul-de-sacs. How does a vice trade flourish here?'

'The council put up metal gates at the end of these roads a few years back. They figured that forcing punters to perform a series of tricky three-point turns would put them off. But the punters still come here because the girls never left.'

'Because crack is easy to source locally.'

'I'm told it's a "one hit and you're hooked" kind of drug. A pimp finds a vulnerable girl, gives it to her for nothing for a few weeks. Then, when she's addicted, tells her he's been keeping score and she owes him two grand. They take her out to "work", beat the shit out of her if she resists or tries to escape. Most of the girls don't bother. They can't run away from the crack.'

'Where do they, you know, do the business?'

'They get the punters to drive them round the back of Texas Home Base up Green Lanes, get this, because it doesn't have CCTV. They don't give a shit about their own safety, just getting the next hit. If they emerge unscathed with their £15, they get the punter to drop them off at one of the local crack houses. A 500-milligram rock, funnily enough, costs £15 and lasts between 30 and 50 minutes. An hour later they're rattling and desperate to avoid the comedown. And the shits. Until you score again, you've no control over your bowels. It's a grim scene.'

'A grim scene about which you seem remarkably knowledgeable...'

He snorted glumly.

'Last year I got a tip that the wife of some hot-shot city broker was hooked and working out of one of those DSS hostels opposite Finsbury Park. The source is a good one so I checked it out. I didn't find her but I came across lawyers, plumbers, bankers, cops, all sorts, popping in and out of these crack houses. Some of the wealthier guys would spend four or five thousand on two-day benders, smoking their rocks and doing all sorts of sick shit to the girls. Take crack and you lose all control. Honestly, it makes *Scarface* look like *The Muppet Show*. If they really want to educate kids about drugs, they should take them to a crack house. No water, heating, toilets, food, furniture. Just blood-stained sofas and sheets nailed over the windows.

'Anyway, you better get inside that tent before the circus leaves town.'

I weighed up the crime-scene tape and elected to take the manly route over the top. After all, this was my crime scene now.

I lofted my left leg towards the tape just as a WPC approached.

'Can I help you, sir?' she demanded.

Her scent made something cartwheel inside my chest, knocking me off my stride, quite literally. I realised now that the tape was higher than I'd thought and struggled to get my left foot over the top.

'DC Lynch,' I warbled, my standing right foot now buckling under the strain, so that my upper body jerked about violently, like some sort of sick Ian Curtis tribute. 'From the Cold Case Unit,' I somehow managed to add between lurches as my prodding left foot failed to locate *terra firma* crime side of the tape.

'That looks a little awkward,' she said, her worried eyes moving down to the piano wire-taut tape just as it flicked up into my crotch, 'and a little uncomfortable.'

'It's fine,' I gasped, yanking the tape down with my right hand and springing off my right foot onto my left.

One leg over.

'Perfectly fine,' I panted, leaning forward now to swing my right leg over the tape behind me. But no matter how far forward I lurched, my right foot refused to clear this damned tape which, at the very second she looked down at it again, sprang back up into my balls.

'Really, it's no trouble,' she giggled, mercifully lowering my polythene nemesis.

Desperate to get my right leg finally over, I swung too fast. I felt my left leg buckle and my arms flap like a penguin in an oil slick. Too late. As I slumped helplessly onto my back, I saw only sky and a pretty face etched with alarm.

'Smooth,' cackled Fintan with undisguised glee, my humiliation complete.

'Who's in charge?' I babbled, springing up instantly, as if the whole thing had been a pre-planned manoeuvre.

'DS Spence,' she managed to squeak through suppressed laughter.

She clamped her hand over her mouth and nodded towards a wiry little man strutting about in a tight mac.

'The one with the short legs,' she wheezed,

about to burst.

'Does he bite?'

'Sometimes,' she chirped through her muffling hand, 'but I'm sure you'll get over it.'

Laughter exploded from so deep within her that she had to bend over to cope.

'Sorry,' she said finally, hauling herself back upright and sleeving her wet eyes.

Her expression had changed but the tears kept coming.

'It's just been such a horrible morning. I really needed that. Sorry if ... no offence.'

'None taken,' I deadpanned. 'With my talent for slapstick, I should be working in family liaison.'

'Thanks for not being a dick about it,' she said, her sad watery smile somehow reducing the earth's gravitational pull on me a second time.

'I think I've been plenty dick enough already,' I smiled, walking on.

'I hope you've got a strong stomach,' she called after me. I turned to register her worried round eyes, instantly bringing to mind Holly Hunter in *Raising Arizona*.

'It's really horrible,' she added.

Her stark warning set my heart on a club-footed gallop around my chest. Sudden shocks of any kind – physical, mental, even a really good joke – could cause me to suffer total collapse. It's called Cataplexy, a rare side effect of insomnia and narcolepsy. An attack turns my bones to liquid; I simply capsize like an Alp, fully lucid but unable to move anything except my eyeballs.

I gave myself a stern talking to: *You've already fallen at the first today. You can't go over again.*

27

They'll label you a total flake.

I galvanised myself by studying DS Spence's dour, pinched face. He looked about as forgiving as a scalded hornet.

He never stopped stomping about. Underlings had to build up to his ferocious pace, then fall in beside him to talk, veering and turning as he did in a surreal crime scene speed tango. When, finally, they left him alone for ten seconds, I set off in pursuit.

'DC Lynch, sir, from the Cold Case Unit. I've been sent by my supervising officer, DS Simon Barrett, to take a look at the killer's MO.'

His lifeless, powder-blue eyes locked sullenly onto mine.

'Is that a statement or a request?' he barked in paint–peeling Glaswegian.

'Sir?'

'What is it that you want, Constable?'

'I'm analysing the unsolved murders of prostitutes in the city over the past few years, sir, establishing links and connections between cases.'

He squinted at me in irritated disgust. 'We don't even know who she is yet.'

'I only need a few minutes, sir, maybe a chat with the pathologist.'

'Why didn't you just say so?'

He continued to pitilessly survey my face, then laughed sourly. 'I doubt if you could link this to another murder on the planet, son. It's outta this fucking world.'

Two gore warnings had me snorting air like a rhino with the bends. I stole one final lungful, banked it and pulled back the forensic tent flap.

It felt like someone had just yanked open my rib cage and let my heart topple out onto the grass. All the blood in my head went south as my misfiring brain struggled to register the horror. I shifted from foot to foot, subconsciously trying to earth the shock. But it just ricocheted about my insides like a charged cannonball. I breathed in and out hard, willing the head swoon to pass.

'Christ,' I finally managed.

A pathologist and a Scenes of Crime officer padded about in white overalls, shoeless and joyless, taking swabs and snapshots. I reached for my black, Met Police-issue notebook and pen. Jotting down the date, time and location steadied me. Falling back on training and routine, the clerical somehow formalised the grotesque chaos that lay at our feet. I reminded myself of my task here – to record the facts, not comprehend the crime.

Her naked body, flat out on its back, had been sliced in two around the waist. The lower half had been positioned about a foot away from the torso and head. I started at the top.

Jet black hair. A troubled forehead. Wide, thick eyebrows that looked like a four-year-old's attempt to draw two straight lines. Tiny, narrowing, vivid grey eyes that looked puzzled. Early 20s. A ringer for actress Juliette Lewis. The corners of her mouth had been slashed right up to her ears, giving her a grotesque, purple 'Joker' grin, known as a Glasgow Smile – the city's blade gangs had patented this sick ritual during the 1920s. You make a little incision in each corner of the victim's mouth, then hurt them so that their screams do the rest.

Her arms had been raised over her head, her elbows at right angles.

Her breasts and stomach sported spoon-size gouges, red-rimmed. The lack of blood anywhere confused me.

My eyes moved down to her spread-eagled lower half. Her intestines had been tucked neatly beneath her buttocks. Her pubic hair trimmed into a 'landing strip'. More spoon-size gouge marks around her thighs.

I watched the pathologist insert a thermometer into her rectum and wondered why anyone would choose such a profession. Especially this woman. Mid-40s. Sculpted blonde hair. Strong nose and chin. Imperious, rigid, poised, she clearly hailed from Britain's 'red trouser and Land Rover' country elite. I could picture her astride a stallion sipping a pre-hunt sherry, or flagellating the local magistrate with a bullwhip. Yet here she was, crouched at the business end of a murder victim's arsehole, the Last Judgement in a florid, shoulder-padded jacket and pearls.

'Right,' she said brightly, springing up, 'let's pop her into a bag and get her back to the mortuary.'

Peeling off her polythene gloves, she turned to me.

'Dr Edwina Milne,' she announced, 'and how may I help you, young man?'

'DC Lynch,' I said, offering a hand, 'from the Cold Case Unit.'

She gave my outstretched arm an arched eyebrow.

'I don't think so, DC. Not where my hands have been. Besides, they get very sweaty in these things.'

She sealed the gloves in a transparent plastic pouch. She then squirted pungent splodge into her palms, rubbed them vigorously together and looked at me with a hint of impatience.

'I'm analysing the unsolved murders of street girls from the last ten years, ma'am. I need to report to my chief today about any possible links between this and the others.'

'Oh please. Ma'am makes me sound so bloody ancient. Edwina, if you can stand the informality.'

'Donal, if you can stand the name,' I said, wondering why so many upper-class British women seemed to be saddled with androgynous Christian names. I'd never met a working class Henrietta, Georgina or Jemima. Was there some sort of unspoken but institutionalised aristocratic distaste for femininity?

Edwina's hand rubbing slowed to a hypnotic, almost suggestive dandle: 'Cause of death is, as yet, unknown. As is time of death. All I can say for certain is that she's been dead for more than ten hours but less than three days. Hopefully I'll be able to ascertain more after a full internal and external post-mortem.'

I glanced over at the body, fly-tipped here like a busted fridge. Now the final indignity: every organ removed, analysed, bits of her sent away in jars for further tests. The rest of her poked and prodded, her most intimate parts photographed, scraped, swabbed or cut open. Body fluids, fingernail dirt and pubic hair sealed in plastic glass in the hope

31

that it will trap her killer. But I knew from all the other unsolved cases that prostitute murders are notoriously difficult to crack. Street girls don't talk. When you find a way to make them talk, their chaotic lives and suppressed memories make them unreliable, easy to discredit. Punters are too ashamed to come forward. The media sees no value in publicising the death of 'a desperate skank'. Family or friends rarely come forward, pressing for answers.

And so the girls lie in refrigerated cabinets for a year until the case is quietly shelved and what's left of them swiftly buried in unmarked municipal graves. I wondered if this woman had family searching for her. Anyone who cared? Was there a person on the planet willing and able to identify her body?

Edwina's erotic hand motions stopped suddenly. 'She has two perfectly round indentations on her skull which were delivered with moderate force. These blows didn't kill her; they subdued her. I'd say almost certainly from the rounded head of a ball-peen hammer.

'If you look closely at her ankles, wrists and neck you'll see ligature marks. The marks are red, so the ligatures would have been applied when she was alive. She was held somewhere else, tortured, killed, cut up with considerable expertise. Her body was drained of all its blood prior to being dumped here, probably sometime between 3 and 5 this morning. There's no grass discoloration beneath her. She hasn't been here for very long.'

Two young men in forensic overalls burst in,

the second dragging a black plastic body bag behind him like a sleigh.

'*Dedwina!*' they cried.

'Oh Christ,' she muttered, 'these clowns.'

'We're like the DHL of death,' the first explained to me.

'Dead Haulers of London,' beamed the second.

'Oh look,' said the first, pointing to the dead woman's face, 'it's the Joker.'

'It's me, sugar bumps!' called the other, imitating Jack Nicholson's star turn in the *Batman* movie.

The lead man got in on the impromptu Jack/Joker tribute: 'As my plastic surgeon says, if you gotta go, go with a smile.'

'Stop this at once,' snapped Edwina, flashing the steel beneath her cultivated cosiness, 'Show some respect for the deceased.'

She resumed her appraisal: 'You can tell your Chief that this woman wasn't a drug user or a streetwalker.'

She registered my surprise, and seemed to enjoy it.

'She was a fit, healthy young woman. Good skin and teeth. Manicured hands. Very toned legs, I'd say a sportswoman of some kind, or a dancer.'

'So how did she end up here?'

'I think that's your department,' she said, a little sharply.

The corpse couriers stood between her two halves, taping transparent plastic bags around her smooth hands and painted feet while humming a tune I recognised but couldn't place. As they bagged her head, the humming got louder. Finally, as the chorus arrived, they took one shoulder each and sang into the dead woman's face: 'Stuck in the middle of you.'

Edwina planted balled fists against her hips and sighed. But her dominatrix stance and whip-crack tuts failed to chastise our madcap crime scene gagsters.

'I hope we haven't mortally offended you?'

'This is how we get through our day,' protested the straight man, and I could see his point.

They rolled both halves of Jane Doe up in a large plastic sheet, gaffer taping it shut as you might an IKEA return. They hefted the load into the body bag, zipped it shut and hauled it away like a condemned old carpet. I almost expected them to break into a chorus of 'Heigh Ho'.

'There's scant enough dignity in death without it being reduced to panto,' harrumphed Edwina.

She looked at me conspiratorially. 'Now, let's turn our attention to the notable features not for public consumption. You may have noticed the penny-sized gouges on her fleshier parts. At first I thought she had been hacked at by something very pointed, like an ice pick. But on closer in-spection, I could make out very tiny but very sharp serration marks. I've only ever seen wounds like this on a drowned body, when fish have nibbled at the flesh. I need to do more tests but it's very strange.'

'Maybe they kept her body somewhere with rats or mice?'

'I'd recognise rodential incisions. Also, she bled from these wounds,' she said, looking at me gravely. 'She was alive when they occurred.'

She throat-coughed back her composure: 'There

34

are a few other elements that may interest you, detective.

'We removed very tiny fragments of unidentified matter, deep red in colour, from inside those hammer wounds to her skull. They look to me like flecks of paint, but are almost certainly too minute to test.

'We removed an A3 battery from her anus. The significance of its insertion is not my department. However, my assistant reminded me that we came across the same thing about three months ago. The victim on that occasion had been a street prostitute named Valerie Gillespie.'

She fixed me with a hard stare and sighed. Pathologists are natural storytellers. She'd been building up to this final twist.

'Between the clasped thumb and index finger of this woman's right hand, we found human hair, just a few strands.'

I couldn't stop my mind skidding across assumptions like a well-hurled pebble: 'This has to be the hair of her killer, surely Edwina? Or someone party to her murder? An accessory?'

She eyed me as you might an over-exuberant toddler. 'Hair identification isn't an exact science. Far from it. There could be hundreds of people out there whose hair follicles would appear very similar to these under a microscope. However, it may prove useful for confirming or eliminating a suspect.'

'I see,' I said, nodding solemnly as if mentally storing her points. But I'd already drawn my own cast iron conclusions. The victim here had clearly known her killer. The hair belonged to someone in her circle. Find the owner of the hair clasped between her stiff dead fingers, and we'd find her killer.

Chapter 3

Brownswood Road, London N4
Saturday, April 3, 1993; 11.10

As I emerged from the tent's gloom, the mid-morning glare scored my tired eyes and tasered that dormant hangover back to life. A familiar knot of aching dread tightened behind my navel. What if I'd missed the chance to catch this killer before he'd struck here? With merciless certainty, my gut was telling me I must have.

This woman may not have been a streetwalker, but she'd met a wretched, protracted, depraved end just like the others. It had to be connected.

'The Others'.

That had become the Cold Case Unit's by-word for the unsolved female murders that no longer had an incident room or an officer attached. In other words, the cases that had been quietly wound down. Of course, *officially* Scotland Yard doesn't close the file on any unsolved crime. But these particular investigations had clearly been shelved, the victims forgotten, all ties cut. Only a walk-in confessor, a knockout new witness or a DNA breakthrough could reboot these cases now.

Not that anyone was bothering to explore any

of these possibilities…

I stumbled across this stash of 'dead' files while reviewing unsolved female murders in the capital over the past decade. It felt like uncovering an unmarked mass grave. I couldn't understand how this could happen – until I met the victims.

They were all young women estranged from their families and communities, often just out of care or prison or a mental institution. Most had been hooked on smack or crack, lost souls with nothing but their bodies to sell. *Desperate skanks.* Nobody noticed they were gone until their bodies turned up; rent asunder like the carcasses of Christmas turkeys. No witnesses, no murder weapon, no DNA, no media interest, no relatives making noise.

No motive.

I also discovered scant will to catch their killers. The murder of a tom somehow didn't count, especially a crack-head street cat. *They knew the risks.* As if somehow their grim demise had been inevitable. Deserved. Without the other standard pressures – raucous relatives, meddling media, panicking public – these investigations had been expediently binned at the earliest opportunity.

After all, resources were stretched and Scotland Yard could divert much-needed detective brain-power elsewhere, to serve more pressing political agendas. Like the highly publicised murders of middle-class, 'respectable' women.

However, when I analysed these 'dead' case files, I made a series of alarming discoveries. For starters, the sick tableau of depravity endured by 'The Others' proved that a number of woman-hating killers were on the loose in London right now, who would kill again soon.

I raised the alarm with my boss, DS Barrett. He didn't listen.

I drew up a list of men who frequently used streetwalkers and had convictions for violence against women, explaining that any one of these cretins could escalate to become tomorrow's notorious serial killer.

He didn't listen.

Then, a few months back, a notorious crime that had grown into a national media event changed everything. Michael Sams had been convicted of the kidnap of estate agent Stephanie Slater, who police managed to free after a sensational, high-profile manhunt.

Sams confessed that, a year earlier, he'd carried out 'a dry run' by abducting 18-year-old Leeds prostitute Julie Dart and forcing her to write a ransom note to her boyfriend. Sams knew Dart's family couldn't afford to cough up the 150k demand, so he killed her anyway. But the case proved my 'canary in a coalmine' theory – that dangerous men were willing to 'practise' their most carnal desires on easy-meat prostitutes first.

DS Barrett suddenly realised that the men we'd failed to catch for these prostitute murders may strike again – and they might not restrict their depravity to crack-addled streetwalkers next time.

Now he listened.

He set me a task: comb through every one of these 'dead' files, highlighting all potential suspects and links to other cases.

He then set me another: if a breaking female

murder appears to share any link or connection to an unsolved case, attend the crime scene.

It hadn't happened, until today.

Now I felt convinced that whoever tortured and killed this poor woman had struck before. He'd escalated to this. That blade of dread twisted in my guts. What if I'd failed to spot him in the old files, leaving him free to kill her?

What if I'd missed the chance to stop him?

It felt a strong possibility. After all, I'd spent months poring over those old case files yet failed to level a criminal charge against a single suspect.

I must have missed him...

My angst turned to agitation at the sight before me; Fintan at the polythene perimeter, chatting animatedly to the crime scene officer I'd fallen head-over-heels for earlier. Even from this distance, I could tell he'd turned on the old charm cannons full blast.

'Here he comes, Dick Fosbury,' he called towards me, and she cackled mercilessly, shrivelling my insides. I knew I had to hit back, so faked a serene smile while scrabbling about desperately for a witty riposte.

'I think you'll find I'm no flop,' I heard myself declaring to the suddenly silent planet. That wiped the smile from her pretty face. Fintan glared at me aghast.

'Donal, this is Zoe from the Forensic Science Service. I've been telling her all about the important work you do, for the Cold Case Unit.'

I checked to see if he was taking the piss. Had the flirting couple decided to gang up on me again, for another cheap laugh? I wouldn't be falling into their trap this time.

'I'm doing my best to get the hell out of there, to be honest,' I mumbled, clearly wrong-footing both of them.

Fintan ploughed on, undeterred. 'Zoe's been telling me what happened to that poor girl in there. We've just been saying, whoever did this isn't a first-time offender. As this is a red-light zone, he's probably targeted working girls in the past.'

'That's speculation,' I protested.

'So, I've been explaining to Zoe how you've spent the past few months analysing unsolved prostitute murders, and that you may well have a head start in tracking down the person responsible.'

I would've disputed this too, had I managed to get a word in edgeways.

'I've asked Zoe here to page you as soon as she gets a confirmed ID for the victim and to keep you abreast of any forensic developments. That way, you can crack on right away linking the MO here with these other unsolved cases you've studied, which could save a lot of time. And let's face it, we're in a race against the clock here to find this maniac before he strikes again. I hope that's okay with you both?'

I thought about asking him outright, there and then: 'What angle are you playing here, Fintan, because this murder still doesn't seem newsworthy to me?' But Zoe had my pager number now, her smile toasting me like a marshmallow. So I defied my gut and rolled with it. Whatever 'it' might turn out to be...

When Zoe's smile turned quizzical, I realised I'd been frowning all this time. That's what trying to keep up with a Machiavellian brother does to you; like playing speed chess against Gary Kasparov. So I released all my anxieties in one multi-coloured party balloon by declaring: 'I think that's a great idea.'

Zoe turned serious then, almost solemn. 'Fintan tells me you've come down here of your own accord, just to see if you can find any connections.'

'Well ... not exactly,' I reddened again. 'I got paged and...'

Fintan interjected: 'I told you he'd be mortified.'

Zoe put her hand on my arm, stopping my heart stone dead: 'Well, I think that's so admirable, and on your first weekend off in months ... amazing.'

'Er ... thanks, Zoe,' I flustered, the feel of her name tingling my tongue.

Fintan hoisted up the police tape: 'It's the low road for you this time, Dickie.'

Before I had time to utter another word, he bundled me under the tape and away in a virtual headlock.

'Don't forget to stay in touch,' he called back over an impressively executed mobile half-nelson.

'What the fuck was that all about?' I muttered.

'Can you just button it until we get round the corner?'

Fintan led me into the fake wood-panelled Star café on Blackstock Road: 'Don't worry. I'll give you a lift to work. You've got plenty of time.'

'What's going on?' I asked as he lit a cigarette

41

and took an enormous drag.

'Well?' I demanded.

'Donal, you haven't been on a proper date in months. I could tell she took a shine to you. So I decided to take the initiative and intervene.'

'And, thanks to you, the first thing I tell her is a pack of lies.'

'Did the trick though, didn't it? She thinks you're some tortured soul in solitary pursuit of the baddies that hurt fallen women. She's got your pager details now so even you can't bottle out of it.'

I cast my most disapproving look.

'She's cute though, right?' He smiled. 'She reminds me of Holly Hunter. I was almost going to ask her "why the long face?" but she didn't look in the mood.'

His aloft eyebrows demanded a reply.

'If she's so cute, why didn't you stake a claim?' I said. 'You're not normally slow in flinging yourself forward.'

'She seemed a bit emotional to me. Or highly strung ... definitely brittle.'

'Maybe she just cares, you know, possesses normal human feelings?'

'Well, there's something not quite right there,' he sniffed, 'so, hey, you two should be perfect together.'

'I knew you couldn't do it,' I smiled.

'What?'

'Just do something nice for me. I knew you'd have to ruin it. It's in your DNA.'

The waiter arrived, his apron suffused in disturbing red stains that had clearly defied repeated washing.

'It's Sweeney Todd,' muttered Fintan under his breath. 'Imagine the fucking DNA in that.'

I couldn't face flesh after what I'd just seen, so opted for fried eggs, toast and tea. As ever, Fintan had to both top me and go off-piste, ordering scrambled eggs, baked potato and tomato 'not out of a can'. He then flummoxed the waiter further by saying no to tea *OR* coffee.

'You off the hard stuff then, Fintan?'

'Have you ever looked at the mugs in cafés? I mean really looked? Or at the knives and forks for that matter? I'll only eat somewhere like this now if I've got these.'

He leaned into his satchel and produced a packet of wipes.

'Jesus, you're turning into Howard Hughes.' I laughed. 'Shall I order some peas for you to arrange in size order?'

The tea, knives, forks and paper napkins crash-landed.

'Go on,' he urged, 'take a really close look.'

'Later,' I said, 'tell me first the real reason why you went to all that trouble back there with Zoe.'

He put out his cigarette, plucked a wipe from the packet and set to work on a fork.

'Well, you're always complaining that the press never covers any of these prostitute murders,' he said, polishing away, 'that the cases are, how do you always put it, "starved of the oxygen of publicity". Where did you get that by the way? On one of your training courses in Bramshill?'

'Where else?'

He lifted the fork to his eye to examine it: 'This

43

time I'm really going to try.'

'Why?'

'Zoe told me how this girl had been cut in two and had her face disfigured.' He placed the fork carefully on one of the napkins and looked up at me. 'I've got a feeling about this story. There's more to it.'

I couldn't believe Zoe had been so indiscreet.

'You didn't tell her you're a hack, did you?'

He shook his head. 'She didn't ask. If there's one thing this job has taught me, it's to act like you *should* be there. People presume the rest.'

'Christ, wait 'til she finds out. That'll fuck every-thing up.'

Fintan set to work on the knife.

'The thing is,' he said, 'your best chance of cracking this case is if it gets lots of publicity. But for me to get it into the paper, I'm going to need your help.'

I shifted uncomfortably in the screwed-down, plastic seat. For a split second, I recognised my eye glinting in the knife's reflection.

'I need you to tell me all you know, and tell me the girl's ID when you get it.'

'Because...'

He placed the gleaming knife down beside the fork.

'The more I know, the better chance I have of getting a good show in the paper. The better the show, the more likely I get a call from someone with information which I can then pass to you. Think about it ... if you work with me on this, we might just get you back on a murder squad.'

'What do you get, Fintan?'

44

'A scoop. Let's just say my gut instinct is telling me that this girl was no skanky torn. In fact, I'd wager she's an actress. If she's an actress of any note, this story will go big. Very big. It's all about celebs these days, even minor ones. That's what sells papers.'

I tried not to look shocked or impressed. But my mind was throwing bouquets at his feet; how in hell had he figured this out?

'What makes you think she was an actress?'

'I'll give you a clue,' he said.

'I don't do riddles, Fint, you know that.'

'Okay, well, if you change your mind: A black flower, six letters. Sounds like the surname of your ex.'

The gruff waiter dropped my fried eggs with such ferocity that they scrambled on impact. He informed Fintan that his order would be 'many more minutes'. Clearly the culinary ambitions of the Star didn't stretch to the baking of potatoes or the sourcing of real tomatoes.

Or, for that matter, to the cleaning of knives and forks. Under duress, I agreed to examine my cutlery before tucking in. Sure enough, both bore the microscopic debris of previous meals, including a rock-hard yellow speck on the inner rim of the fork's central prong that had to be congealed egg.

'They'd have to fucking carbon date that,' said Fintan.

'It's probably older than the chicken who laid it,' I agreed.

He handed me his polished cutlery, but the

45

damage had been done. I pushed the plate away.

'Happy now?' I said.

He shrugged. 'If you look at anything closely enough, for long enough, you'll find its dirty little secret. The thing is, Donal, without publicity there's far less chance that they'll catch this woman's killer. So why don't you help me, just this once?'

'I don't know, Fintan...'

'For her sake. I mean come on, you don't want her winding up in some clerical bin like the others, do you? Or was that all just talk?'

As he re-appropriated his sparkling cutlery and – when it finally arrived – picked at his bespoke meal, I unloaded everything that Edwina had told me. Well, almost everything.

I held back the detail about the strands of human hair found between her thumb and finger. I didn't want this to become common knowledge; it could yet prove our secret insurance policy, our suspect-clincher.

I concluded with the pathologist's certainty that the victim hadn't worked as a street hooker, news he greeted with unbearable self-satisfaction. I could tell the rest didn't really matter to him now. So long as she wasn't 'a desperate skank', he could 'get the story away'.

As he put it: 'If she's a looker and not a hooker, it's a double-page spread.'

'So her murder now merits a story?'

He frowned, genuinely perplexed that I didn't view the world through the twisted scope of his news desk.

'The thing is, when a prostitute is murdered, no

one is surprised. None of our readers relate to it because it's happened to a prossie, not to a normal woman. Prostitutes and pimps and crack are not part of our readership's world. It's different when a "good" woman is murdered ... that creates a threat to all women. That sells papers. All I need now is a sit-down with the parents and selects.'

'Selects?'

'That's the trade term for family photos. Some less scrupulous hacks have been known to swipe them from the mantelpieces of grieving relatives. I know one woman who always asks to use the upstairs loo so she can perform a quick sweep of the bedrooms.'

I sighed. 'And now I'm aiding and abetting the same scurrilous press.'

'Hey, I don't do stuff like *that*.' He glared at me, wounded. 'Jesus, give me some credit.'

He pushed his virtually untouched meal away and lit another cigarette. I cringed: 'You are aware that Sweeney Todd has access to sharp implements from the kitchen?'

He didn't even hear me. 'The question now is, why did they dump her body here? Clearly they're sending a message to someone. But to who? There's a bigger play here. Much bigger.'

My pager buzzed.

Below a mobile number, the message read: Hi Donal. Victim ID confirmed. Please call, Zoe.

I grabbed Fintan's fat mobile and dialled.

'Hi Zoe, Donal Lynch, we just met at the crime scene.'

'Hi Donal. Turns out this girl was on the Met's

47

Missing Person file. We're pretty certain we know who she is.'

'Wow, that was quick.'

Fintan's eyebrows shot skyward.

'We haven't confirmed it yet but she has a very distinctive rose tattoo on the back of her shoulder with her initials beneath it. And there's a scar that matches too. The height, weight, it all tallies. You got a pen?'

Fintan's notebook and biro stood to attention.

'Yes. Shoot.'

'Elizabeth Phoebe Little, Date of Birth 29/7/70. Single. Originally from Armley in Leeds,' I repeated after her as Fintan whipped out his laptop and inserted a floppy disc.

'The most recent address we have for her is 14a Princess Road, Richmond. No previous convictions. Profession: Actress.'

'Actress eh?' I said, as Fintan's smugometer almost exploded.

'Can't say I've heard of her,' I added, in an attempt to puncture his euphoria.

'Me neither. That's all we've got so far.'

'That's so helpful, Zoe. I can't thank you enough.'

'Not a problem. If it helps catch the bastard who did this to her, I'll feel a little better about today.'

'I'll do what I can.'

'Good, and you've got my number now. Don't hesitate to call if you need anything else.'

'I will, Zoe. Thanks.'

'Oh, and Donal?'

'Yes?'

'I hope it's okay to ask, but can you let me know

48

when you catch him?'

'Of course I will,' I said, as long-dead butterflies rose and fluttered about my chest tickling the edges of my hopeful heart.

I couldn't decide which was wilder, Fintan's driving or his underhand journalistic techniques. As his Mondeo sped us away from Brownswood Road, he made six calls in a row. The first, to his office, went like this:

'John, I've got a phone number here for a Rodney and Jean Little in Armley. I want you to call them, say you're Phil Blackman from the *Mirror*, tell them you're contacting them because their daughter Elizabeth has just landed a role in *Eastenders*. Fillet them for all you can. Don't give them your number at the end. Got it?'

'What the hell?' I asked. 'How did you get their phone number?'

'I've got a floppy disc with electoral roll and phone numbers, all perfectly legal and above board.'

'What if they've already heard the news?'

'That'll be John's problem. He's work experience so it'll do him good.'

'Jesus.'

'Look, the cops won't call them until they have something concrete like dental records. At least I'm not making him break the news.'

'Why did you tell him to say he was from the *Mirror*?'

'They'll be Northern working-class stock, won't they? So they're bound to be Union members and lefties who read the *Mirror*. When they get the bad news and realise that the *Mirror* behaved so appallingly, they'll be putty in my hands. Oldest trick in the book.'

'You're despicable,' I spat.

He dialled another number.

'Yes, hello showbiz desk. Fintan Lynch here. Listen, grab your red pages and tell me who the agent is for an actress called Elizabeth Little.'

He memorised the number, hung up and dialled again while tackling a roundabout.

'Hello, Roger Alsop please?'

'Hi Roger. My name is Neil Jordan. I'm an Irish film director. You may have heard of me,' he said in a ridiculously posh Dublin accent.

'Ha ha, well that's terribly kind of you, Roger. Bob Hoskins gave me your number and says hello,' he gushed, giving me a wink.

'Ha ha yes, dear old Bob. Wonderful. Yes.'

'Well, it's a little delicate, Roger. But I'm told I can count on you being discreet. I'm casting for a new film and I've heard great things about a young actress called Elizabeth Little.'

Fintan listened for a very long time.

'Before I do that, Roger, is there any chance I could get hold of a show reel and some quality photos, you know, studio shots.'

'Excellent. I'll have an assistant pop round within the hour. Thanks, Roger. Ciao.'

'Do you think Neil Jordan says "Ciao"?'

'They all fucking do, don't they?'

'Well, what's she been in?'

'She had a bit part in *The Bill* last year.'

'That's it?'

'Well, it'll be a major part by the time I'm done.'

50

He was dialling again.

'Who are you calling now?'

'The picture desk.'

He held up his hand to shut me up: 'Jim. I need a VHS of an episode of *The Bill* from last year featuring an actress called Elizabeth Little.'

'No idea.'

'Call them then.'

'Yes. It's very fucking important.'

'Now I've got to get our Northern stringer out of the pub,' he said tapping out another number.

'Bob, you fat Northern git.'

'Yeah, not bad. Listen, you and your monkey need to get outside an address in Armley and wait for my call. I'll text it but start heading there now. And be discreet.'

'Actress. Murdered.'

'*The Bill*. Stage mostly.'

'It'll be massive, Bob, trust me.'

'I can't say. Look, the *Mirror* have already harassed them today so be gentle.'

'Exactly, as soon as it's official, I'll call you.'

'Get them on a train to London ASAP.'

'I don't know. Offer them a ferret or a pair of fucking clogs or a year's supply of ale. Whatever it takes.'

Another call: 'Dennis. Pull everything you can about Elizabeth Little, date of birth 29/07/70.'

'Princess Road, Richmond.'

'The Full Monty.'

'Talk later.'

'Who was that?' I asked.

'A helpful ex-copper.'

'Let me guess, the Full Monty means her bank

accounts, health records, criminal records?'

He nodded: 'Best of all, phone records, everyone she's called in the past year and the five personal numbers on her "friends and family" deal. That's where the gold is, everyone who knew her best.'

'And I suppose you're going to insist that this is all perfectly legal?'

'It's not illegal. Like I've told you before, this is all information held on systems that anyone who works for banks, building societies, debt collection agencies or private investigators can get legitimately. Sometime next week, Dennis is laying hands on a floppy disc containing the names and dates of birth of everyone in Anonymous groups in the whole of the UK. He doesn't collect the data but he can get hold of it and pass it onto me. That's not illegal.'

'And I suppose morality doesn't comes into it?'

He pulled up outside the Cold Case Unit's non-descript annex off Albert Embankment, just south of the Thames between Vauxhall and Lambeth Bridge.

'You want my help on this story, right?' he said. 'You want to find her killer?'

'Not if it involves pulling people's confidential records ... that can't be right.'

'You do know that there are sales companies out there who routinely access all of our records – financial, medical, everything. There are City banks who employ private investigators full-time to dig the dirt on people. If it's on a computer system, it's being sold on.'

I suddenly felt hot and irritable.

'Look, let me do the journalism. I'll shake down this story and then you can run with whatever we get out of it, your conscience clear. Okay?'

I opened the passenger door, hauled myself out: 'Where are you off to now?'

'Princess Road, Richmond.' Fintan smiled. 'With any luck, I can talk my way in and get hold of her post.'

'Jesus.' I sighed, slamming the door of his blood red Mondeo and wishing to God I'd never set foot in it.

Chapter 4

Vauxhall, South London
Saturday, April 3, 1993; 13.20

I walked into the library-like silence of work and smiled to myself: that's what they call us out in the real world – the Cemetery. Wind up in the Cold Case Unit and your career is truly dead and buried.

Unusually for a Saturday, a couple of the dirty dozen were in, slumped, brooding, in various states of drink-fuelled disrepair.

The Cold Case Unit seemed to serve as a last refuge for the knackered, disgraced or discredited. By the time of my enforced exile here six months ago, I ticked all three boxes, thanks to a now infamous episode the previous year, 1991.

That summer, plodding the Clapham/Battersea

beat in South London, I'd stumbled across my first freshly murdered body. The victim, Marion Ryan, came to me that night and, in the course of scaring me half to death, acted out what I later recognised to be a key clue to her killer.

Of course I didn't 'get it' right away. I was too busy fearing for my mental wellbeing. So she came again and again, until I felt haunted and cursed. The fall-out proved catastrophic, costing me a girlfriend, my job and very nearly my life.

Eventually Marion's nocturnal charades led me to her killer.

Sounds bonkers, I know. As a devout sceptic, I refused to accept that a dead person could reach me from 'the other side'; that something supernatural might be occurring. Then it happened again...

I blamed it on my insomnia and an over-active subconscious. A psychologist agreed that the visions had to be coming from within me, attributing them to a rare hallucinatory disorder called Sleep Paralysis. Sufferers of this condition sometimes can't 'snap off' the dreaming segment of their brain after they wake up, creating a phenomenon known as 'waking dreams' that seem terrifyingly real.

My refusal to accept this prognosis failed to prevent the ambitious shrink publishing a paper about it in a leading science quarterly. There was little scientific about the tabloid-newspaper follow-up, which labelled me a 'self-proclaimed psychic cop'.

After that article Commander John Glenn summoned me to his eighth-floor office at New

Scotland Yard. 'No doubt as you will have foreseen yesterday,' he sneered, 'I want your warrant card now.' By the time I'd left him sprawled across his antique desk gasping for air, Heckler & Koch had a bead on all three ground floor lifts. Like Ann Frank in that annex, I came quietly.

I expected to be charged with assault and sacked on the spot. Instead they suspended me on full pay and assigned me to Darius, a Police Federation solicitor who turned out to be dodgier than most criminals I'd dealt with.

A week or so later, over several pints at the Feathers, Darius asked me to tell him exactly what had happened. 'Don't worry,' he assured me, 'what you tell me will never leave these four walls. In an exercise like this, the truth is merely our starting point.'

I switched into 'victim' mode – a skill I'd learned from petty criminals while in uniform. I explained how Commander Glenn had summoned me to HQ on the back of a 'malicious and libellous' Sunday newspaper article which had 'degraded and humiliated me'.

'Of course I'd never made any such claim about possessing psychic powers,' I bleated on. 'My mistake had been to confide in a trainee psychologist about the vivid dreams that plagued me after I'd attended a series of gruesome murder scenes.'

'*Caused* by attending a series of gruesome murder scenes,' corrected Darius, jotting down my juiciest revelations in an archaic moleskin notebook. 'Classic symptoms of Post-Traumatic Stress.'

I nodded gravely. 'Next thing, they're cracking

gags about me in the papers and on TV and radio shows. I couldn't leave the house for months.'

I next described Glenn's 'unsympathetic and dismissive' attitude to 'my crippling sleep disorder'. I finished up with the comment that had caused me to snap: Glenn's assertion that, as an Irishman, I should know all about miscarriages of justice. Darius seized upon this last line like a drowning man.

'He said what?'

'He was explaining how any suggestion that I'd used "psychic powers" in my police work would give grounds for appeal to anyone whose case I'd ever worked on.'

'Yeah, I get that. But what did he say specifically about you being Irish?'

'He said words to the effect that, as an Irish person, I should know all about miscarriages of justice. I remember his last line: "Haven't you read about your compatriots, the Guildford Four and the Birmingham Six and what not?" I just lost it.'

Darius blew hard out of his mouth: 'Any witnesses?'

I shook my head.

'Did he record it?'

'I don't think so.'

'Well, guess what–' dodgy Darius grinned, a gold tooth glinting beneath his leering top lip '–it's your lucky day.'

I tried not to let his Romanian-beggar oral chic put me off. After all, I needed him to get me back to work. But I couldn't stop staring at it, or wondering if any personal affectation on the planet could make him look less trustworthy. A toupee

56

perhaps? Or a glass eye. No, the gold tooth still triumphed.

'The Commission for Racial Equality has just announced it's backing a test case brought by a machinist from County Antrim against his former employer. He's claiming that Irish jokes on the shop floor made his day-to-day life intolerable.'

'That's ridiculous, he lives and works in Ireland.' I laughed. 'Anyway, how could he hear all these hurtful gags over the racket of his machine?'

'I know.' Darius shrugged. 'But it's going to happen and with the Commission's support, he can't lose. If I hint to the Met that we're talking to the Commission about your case, and specifically Glenn's near-the-knuckle racial stereotyping...'

'Hang on a minute, Darius. He wasn't being racist. If anything...'

'You want to get back to work, don't you?'

'Is this the only way?'

'It's the best way.'

'So you ... we're playing the race card?'

'The race card's the ace card, baby. You only have to show it and the other side folds.'

While Darius set about rigging the disciplinary deck, he insisted I attend a consultation with one of his preferred psychologists.

'We need to deliver a clean bill of mental health,' he explained, 'and this man will help. All you need to show is that you're not mental now, and he'll report that whatever episode you suffered in Glenn's office had been a one-off. He's even got a name for it, *Bouffe Delirante,* which translates as 'a

57

puff of madness'. Bollocks, I know, but because it sounds exotic, they fall for it every time.'

'Right, so I won't have to go into anything else then, like my insomnia or childhood or any of that stuff?'

'Not unless you want to.'

Dr Swartz proved to be everything you'd expect from an ageing quack winding down an undistinguished career in leafy Finchley, right down to his Einstein tribute grey thatch, hairy ears and bumbling, distracted disposition.

I told him that I couldn't remember anything of the Glenn incident, which seemed to suit him no end. What I hadn't considered was how we'd fill the remaining 55 minutes of our appointment.

Like a newborn snuffling out nipples, wily old Swartz instinctively located my crippling insecurities, one by one, then latched on.

I wouldn't mind but I knew the psychology mating dance pretty well by then, having tangled with that trainee shrink a few years' back. They use questions like pawns to manoeuvre you into a vulnerable position, all the while reassuring you that you're making these moves all by yourself. It goes on and on until, cornered, you run out of patience and invent a fit-all conclusion of your own, just to get the hell out of there.

'What about sleep?' came his opening gambit, 'do you get restful, unbroken sleep each night?'

'Who does?' I quipped, fighting fire with fire.

'How many hours?'

I suddenly remembered Fintan's proclamation that he could never trust anyone who is incapable of lying. Now I understood what he meant. Swartz peered imperiously over his double-glazed reading glasses, wordlessly breaking me.

'I've never been a great sleeper, to be honest, doctor. Four or five hours a night is plenty.'

'Why obfuscate, young man? How much sleep do you get, on average, each night?'

I pictured a puff of madness swirling about the room like a mini-tornado, waiting to pounce.

'Three hours,' I muttered.

'Would you say that's down to a specific anxiety, or a more general malaise?'

'I had it down as insomnia, sir. I've had it all my life, off and on.'

He shuffled uncomfortably in his leather seat.

'Have you read Percy Pig?'

I looked at him in amused disbelief.

'I thought they just did sweets, sir. Do you mean the back of the packet?'

He frowned. 'No ... *Pirsig*. In his book, *Zen and the Art of Motorcycle Maintenance*, Pirsig writes: "It's a puzzling thing. The truth knocks at the door and you say 'go away, I'm looking for the truth'. And so it goes away. Puzzling." I'm asking you, Donal, why don't you answer the knock on your door?'

'Interesting hypothesis,' was all I could think to say, playing for time.

He smiled in satisfaction, as if we'd just shared some sort of intellectual in-joke: 'Very good. I suspect you're toying with me now.'

I smiled back, because I felt it would anger him less than looking bewildered.

He stood suddenly, making me start. 'Damned seat. There's no purchase in the leather. I have to

59

perch upon it, like I'm sitting on the blasted lavatory.'

'If you can suffer another hypothesis, Lynch,' he declared, flouncing off towards his Georgian window, 'I introduce clients with sleep troubles to my old friend, the worry worm, that niggling little creature that burrows its way into your brain at night and wriggles about so that you can't drop off. The W–O–R–M in my worm stands for work, old or overweight, relationships and money. When it comes down to it, one or more of these is the source of almost all human anxiety. So allow me to dissect your little wriggler. This work incident ... clearly you suffered insomnia long before it, so I'm discounting that. You're not getting old or overweight, so that rules out the "o". It's got to be either relations or money. Are you in debt?'

'No, thankfully.'

'In a relationship?'

'No, and I'm tempted to say I'm thankful for that too.'

'How did you lose her? The last serious one?'

I felt cornered. 'She cheated on me. Twice.'

'How long ago did this take place?'

'Almost two years ago.'

'Her name is?'

'Eve Daly.'

'Have you seen or spoken to Eve since?'

'No.'

'What about your family? Are you close?'

'I'm close to my mum. Or at least I was. Now it's a bit more complicated.'

I suddenly felt found-out, checkmated. He sensed it, almost jogging back to his slippery black throne to home in for the kill.

'And why is that?'

'My father is a rabid Republican. When he found out I'd joined the British police force, he made it known he never wanted to see or hear from me again.'

'When did you last see your mother?'

'Eighteen months ago,' I croaked, my throat dry with shame.

'How were relations with your father before that?'

'Not good.'

The silence demanded filling.

'I never seemed to be able to please him, you know? At best, I embarrassed him. I'd try to help out on the farm but just end up annoying him. I had this ability to make him blind with rage without even trying, and I mean apoplectic. Anything I did angered him, basically.'

He knew there was more, the misery-milking, sorrow-sucking fuck.

I sighed in resignation. 'I found out recently that my mother almost died during my birth and that we'd both been very ill afterwards. She couldn't bear any more children after that, I'd say physically or mentally. Over those first few years, I didn't sleep very much and she got prescribed tranquilisers. She's been hooked on them ever since. So basically I ruined my dad's life, and he's hated me for it ever since.'

There you have it, you nosy little prick. Happy now?

'Any siblings?'

'One older brother. Of course, he's brilliant at everything. I could never outshine Golden Boy.'

61

The bitterness with which I imparted that last line shocked me. Did I resent Fintan? Had I been holding him responsible all this time?

Swartz breathed in and out hard through his nostrils, sated.

'What do you think your mother would like to happen?'

'Well, obviously she'd like me and Da to patch things up, get on.'

'Do you think you can ever find inner peace while you have this impasse with your father?'

'Well, it's not like we used to be best buds, is it? I've borne his disappointment all my life. Now's no different, it's just more … official.'

'What do you think is the cause of your insomnia?'

'With respect doctor, that's like asking me "What do you think is the cause of my fuzzy hair?" Your hair is just fuzzy, like Shredded Wheat. There's nothing I can do about it.'

He studied me thoughtfully, caressing his Shredded Wheat beard. I sat there absently, wondering why they all felt compelled to sport beards. Some sort of academic Beard Pressure?

'I can't sign you off until you at least attempt to address your insomnia,' he announced, finally.

'But that's got nothing to do with why I'm suspended,' I protested.

'It's got everything to do with your mental health, Donal. If I sign you off and you blow up again … well, they could wash their hands of both you and me.'

'I've seen specialists about it. No one can help.'

'You have to help yourself. You need to address

the worm. Sort things out with your father. Or at least try to. Do your bit, see what happens.'

I shook my head and shot to my feet: 'It's not that simple, doctor. Besides, like I say, that's got absolutely nothing to do with the reason I'm here. I'm afraid I'll be seeking a second opinion.'

As I walked to the door, that puff of madness found me.

'Let's not forget Swartz,' I raged. 'I've been sent here because of a single provoked incident, a moment of madness. To drag some random issue from my personal life into it, then use it against me ... well, it's outrageous...'

He didn't even look up.

'I had a son like you,' he said finally, quietly.

That shut me up. They never talk about themselves.

'He joined the army just to spite me really. He was a bloody musician, not a soldier.'

His eyes studied the carpet, softening.

'You always think you have time to sort these things out, but you don't.'

He sighed sadly. 'He got killed in 1982, in the Hyde Park bombing.'

I shuddered at the memory. The IRA had planted two devices. The first, a car bomb, killed three members of the household cavalry. The second exploded under a bandstand in Regent's Park, killing eight soldiers as they played songs from the musical *Oliver* to a crowd of lunching workers and tourists.

He looked up, his eyes manic now, hunting for understanding.

'He was 22, same age as you.'

63

'Oh Christ,' I whispered, shame flooding me, 'I'm so sorry.'

'The idiot boy who planted the bomb was also 22. He'll spend the rest of his life in prison. They say now the authorities ignored a warning. They let it go off.'

He shook his head, his gaze somehow peering inwards.

'It'll be eleven years in July. His mother has never got over it.'

'And you?' I said, unable to resist turning inquisitor on a shrink.

'I've forgiven them, Donal. She hates me for it, but I don't see any other way.'

Those eyes flashed agony.

'Anyway,' he sniffed, snapping back to the present, 'wasn't it Wilde who said always forgive your enemies, because nothing annoys them so much?'

He laughed. I sensed it was that, or cry.

'I couldn't forgive.'

He didn't react. 'Well, we hear now that the government is talking to the IRA, trying to thrash out a ceasefire. If I can forgive, and they can sit and talk peace, then surely you and your father can give it a go?'

'I tried before, several times,' I protested.

His wet eyes begged mine, like a starving dog's.

'I'm still seeking a second opinion, doctor,' I said.

'I just hope you get a second chance,' he said flatly, looking away to release me.

That night, two vivid dreams terrified me awake. Those same nightmares have been haunting me ever since.

64

At least I hope they're nightmares. Because if either of them is a premonition, Da's in grave danger. And I'm the only person who can help him.

Darius looped the holes and I got my badge back. But we'd been sneaky, petty and the Met wouldn't let it go. They agreed to reinstate me so long as I didn't work on 'live' cases. After all, that had been the root of 'all my trouble' last time around. And so they buried me here in their Cemetery with full Acting DC honours. Now it was my job to break out.

My arrival made us 'The Filthy 13'. But our odd-numbered battalion of outcasts didn't follow a granite-souled pilgrim like Lee Marvin. No, we fell in behind a kindly old duffer named Detective Superintendent Simon Barrett – known as 'Claret Barrett' on account of his poorly disguised drink problem, or 'Carrot' Barrett because of his red hair and crippling inability to ever wield the stick. But Barrett's soft-touch leadership made him an ideal boss for what had become the Force's cushiest number. After all, the Cold Case Unit had recently acquired the most effective stealth weapon in criminal justice history.

The development of 'genetic fingerprinting' in the late 1980s had turned 'DNA' into *the* byword for belated justice. There was no place you could hide from DNA – it was all conquering, infallible, omnipotent.

As the dispensers of Justice's indomitable new truth serum, our Unit had recently cracked some of the country's most iconic unsolved murders. Of course the media – tireless proponents of a flat, black-and-white earth – depicted us as a dynamic squad of avenging angels, hoofing down doors and meting out justice to the worst kind of killers – the ones who'd beaten the system and 'gotten away with it'.

The truth was rather more mundane: DNA fingerprinting proved to be pretty much *all* we had. And so we approached every unsolved case in the same way. We'd take DNA samples from either all of the suspects in the original case or every man of a certain age in the local area. Meanwhile, we commissioned the Forensic Science Service (FSS) to re-test all of the original exhibits using the latest DNA fingerprinting techniques. When the results arrived, we cross-referenced them against DNA records. If we got a match, we made an arrest.

When that failed, we still fell back on the almost mythical power of genetic fingerprinting. We'd reveal to the national and local media 'a positive new lead' or 'significant new information' about a particular case, and that this fresh twist was being subjected to ground-breaking DNA techniques.

We peddled this white lie for good reason: it rattled the perpetrators and any witnesses who'd lied to protect them. We then paid them all a visit and acted as if we'd finally worked out the truth – we just needed the imminent DNA results to confirm it.

The prospect of 'having to go through it all again' made many dodgy witnesses and even hardened killers break and confess. Few have the stomach for it, second-time round.

There was a downside to all this, of course. No matter which route we took – testing new science

66

or knocking old doors – we had to inform the families of the murder victims. The effect tended to be two-fold negative. Firstly, by 'bringing it all up again' we were forcing these people to re-live the darkest episode of their lives. Secondly, to flush out twitchy witnesses or repentant suspects, we had to play-up our certainty that, this time round, we would get justice for the victim, thus raising expectations that we couldn't always meet.

Either way, there was little actual 'investigation'. We spent our days cross-referencing the new with the old, be it science or statements, making our work almost entirely clerical, soulless and solitary. And so the alcoholics in the unit drank more. Those prone to depression or other unspecified illnesses got signed-off more. Whatever dastardly deeds the rest of us had committed to end up here, only the Met's internal disciplinary board truly knew. But I was the most desperate to get away, to swap cold for hot, to get back on a murder squad.

Now the murder of Elizabeth Phoebe Little presented me with my first real opportunity. If I made a good impression on DS Spence, he might just scout me. I needed to go back through all the unsolved cases and unearth some solid potential leads to present to him.

A chill slithered around my neck. Until now, my work at the Unit had been as a revisionist, correcting history, back-dating justice. Sure I'd helped hunt down killers, but they weren't active, mid-spree like this maniac.

Forget the usual DNA 'fishing' or the bluff for buried secrets. This was a murder hunt. I was looking for someone who'd struck before and would almost certainly kill again, soon.

I needed to fillet, dissect, treble check and treble challenge every single detail in our unsolved files that could be pertinent to this murder. If I missed a suspect who then went on to kill again, it'd be on my head.

The air tingled, charged. The lilting plants rallied and those empty white boards pined. I'd found my purpose, my road to redemption.

I reached for a floppy disc marked 'Unsolved Female Murders – Live'.

The first disappointment: how few of these killings shared characteristics with the Liz Little murder. I thought I'd be spoiled for choice. Instead, only one case screamed out. At first glance, I felt convinced it *had* to be the same killer.

I scolded my tearaway mind: *treble check and treble challenge every single detail.*

Eighteen months ago, 43-year-old Helen Oldroyd had been found slashed and stabbed to death at the wheel of her racing-green Jaguar XJS in the car park of a leisure centre in Brentford, West London. That morning, she'd left the family home in Marlow, Bucks at 9.40am, telling builders renovating the property that she was running late for a 10am appointment. She'd been expected at her place of work – a Bureau de Change she co-owned in Paddington, West London – between 10.30am and 11am.

No record of this 10am appointment had been found in her diary or detailed notebooks. She hadn't mentioned it to her husband, Alistair, colleagues at work or to any friends.

Two swimmers turning up at the Fountain Leisure Centre at 11am noticed the distinct green jag parked at the very perimeter of the car park, facing into an eight-foot-tall hedge. They assumed that the woman sitting in the driver's seat was taking a nap. An hour later, they came out to find her in exactly the same position and raised the alarm.

Officers found the keys in the ignition. On the console between the driver and passenger seat sat a sample of blue wallpaper and a six-inch piece of wood. Across the back seat of the vehicle, a variety of carpet tiles had been laid out as if on display or up for discussion. Her handbag sat untouched on the floor.

The pathologist reported that Helen had been stabbed 50 times with a knife three to four inches long and an inch wide. Ten of the wounds were slashes to her hands and arms as she fought for her life.

They found no weapon or signs of sexual assault.

The pattern of her wounds showed that the killer launched his attack from the passenger seat, then got out of the car, walked around to the driver's door, opened it and finished the job.

Detectives interviewed more than 800 people who'd parked at the leisure centre that morning. None of them remembered seeing anything suspicious. Officers were baffled – the attacker must have been covered in blood and either walked to another car to drive away, or left the car park on foot. They'd never know because neither the car park nor the road outside was covered by CCTV.

Helen had lived in a £600,000 detached house with Alistair, an estate agent, and their children Luke, 12, and Martha, 9.

Alistair was interviewed at length and eliminated as a suspect. He insisted his wife couldn't have been conducting an affair as they were 'completely open' with each other. He was unable to offer an explanation as to her presence in Brentford that morning, or who she might have been meeting. Helen had simply indicated that she would be driving to work as usual.

He speculated that she must have received the call to attend this mystery assignation after he'd left for work at 8am. However, the builders working inside their home from 7.30am that morning insisted that the landline hadn't rung. She didn't own a mobile.

The wallpaper found in her car was a small sample of a roll brought to her home that morning by the principle contractor. None of the builders had left the Oldroyd home at any time between 7.30am and 4pm.

When news of the murder broke, a man who drove through Brentford that morning claimed that he saw Helen's Jaguar travelling slowly and erratically along Chiswick High Road, south of the M4 flyover, at about 10am. When he overtook the car, he saw the woman driver wrestling with a man in the passenger seat. It had been a fleeting glimpse, he felt unable to provide a description. Assuming it to be a domestic, he sped on. Intriguingly, he said that at least five more vehicles held up by the Jaguar overtook at the same time, just as it pulled into the leisure centre car park.

The report pointed out that the Fountain Leisure Centre couldn't have been on any logical route Helen might have taken to work. The centre's visitor book had no record of her ever attending. They found no swimming costume or towel in the car.

My brain ached. I reminded myself of the goal here: to establish if both women could have been killed by the same man. There were obvious similarities; Helen and Liz had both been savagely attacked with a knife. They had known their killers. Their bodies had been left exposed in public places.

But there were key differences too. Helen hadn't been held somewhere, tortured or cut up. She'd died in what appeared to be a spur-of-the-moment frenzy, whereas Liz's murder seemed meticulously pre-meditated.

In fact, Oldroyd's murder had been so messy that her racing-green Jag interior must be chock-full of DNA. After all, she and her attacker had wrestled for a matter of minutes. She must have grabbed hold of some skin, hair or even clothing fibres that might seal her killer's fate. She kept herself fit; maybe she managed to draw blood. Perhaps the ferocity of her defence is what caused her killer to 'flip out' and stab her in such a blind frenzy.

There had to be evidence of him *somewhere* in that car.

My finger trembled as I dialled the incident room number.

The meek 'Mavis' at the other end took my name, rank, badge number and insisted on calling me back 'on a secure landline'.

'DS Hobbs, Oldroyd incident room. How can we help you?' stated an impatient male voice.

I explained our initiative and the similarities between the cases, wrapping up with an offer to finance a fresh forensic sweep of Helen's car.'

'I'm afraid that's not possible,' barked Hobbs.

'I'm sorry?'

'The forensic side of things has been fully explored, constable. I can confidently say there is nothing more to be gained from examining the car.'

'With respect, sir, I can confidently say there's been a lot of progress in genetic fingerprinting over the past 18 months. They can work with much smaller samples now ... microscopic samples.'

He sighed. 'I am aware of forensic developments, constable.'

'Excellent, so you know where we're coming from then, sir.'

I could sense his brain grappling.

'Look,' he said finally, 'you may as well know. The officers at the scene let the undertakers remove the body from the car before forensics arrived.'

I couldn't speak.

'It was the summer holidays, don't forget. The place was packed with families, kids. By all accounts, it was a horrific sight.'

The full impact of his revelation took time to sink in. Removing Helen from the car not only contaminated the crime scene, it tainted anything connected to her body – skin, hair, fibres, even blood splashes. Just one body part could possibly be deemed exempt from this human contamination.

'Did you send her fingernails away for examination?'

'Yes,' he said, his voice dry and tight, 'but it didn't throw anything up.'

'I'd like to request them, sir, put them through the ringer again.'

'I'm afraid not,' came his irritated response.

'Sir?'

'They've been mislaid,' he squeaked.

'Mislaid, sir?'

'Lost constable. The fingernails have been lost,' he spat bitterly.

'Christ. So what now?'

'What now? We need a bloody miracle.'

Chapter 5

Vauxhall, South London
Saturday, April 3, 1993; 17.00

My only hope now of connecting the murders of Liz Little and Helen Oldroyd would be to identify a common enemy with murderous potential.

But that would have to wait.

Having exhausted the 'live' unsolved female murder files, I needed to dredge those 'dead files' for potential connections, suspects and leads.

Time to revisit 'The Others'.

The folder for 1992 – last year – contained four surreptitiously jilted prostitute murder investigations. Considering the Met Police boasted an overall murder detection rate of 90 per cent of about 170 homicides, this failure spoke volumes. Then I remembered how '92 had been dominated by two of the most high-profile Met Police manhunts of all time; Stephanie Slater's kidnap and Rachel Nickell's murder. With finances already stretched to breaking, something had to give. And nobody in the national media had written a single word about the deaths of these 'desperate skanks'.

The first three didn't appear to have any links to Liz's murder: Karen, 26, spine crushed, nose broken, asphyxiated, dumped in the Lea River; Carol, 32, sexually assaulted with a blunt instrument, bled to death, buried at a concrete works; Mandy, 23, choked with a ligature, found 'posed' in a disused warehouse, wearing just a demonic facemask and a pair of Mr Men socks.

And so I discarded those poor women, just as society had in life and the Met Police did a matter of weeks after they'd died.

But the fourth unsolved case needed to be flagged.

In December last year, three boys fishing the Wood Green reservoir near Alexandra Palace hauled a heavy-duty black plastic bag out of the water. But the bag wasn't nearly as heavy-duty as the contents … a woman's severed body parts.

A specialist forensic team hooked three more bags from the depths. The victim was an unidentified Caucasian woman in her 20s – a mystery not helped by her missing hands. When dental records failed to unmask her, the pathologist had a moment of inspiration. Good old *Dedwina* discovered that the dead woman had 'double D' breast implants, and that each pair came with its own unique pin code. Via manufacturer and surgeon, police learned that they'd been paid for by one Philip Armstrong, with an address in West London.

What a way for the 63-year-old property magnate to discover that his former lover, 22-year-old Valerie Gillespie, had been murdered.

A few months earlier, sugar daddy Armstrong had pulled the money plug on his ex-call-girl lover, for reasons that didn't seem adequately explored. Valerie's 'good life' dining at the Ritz and shopping in Bond Street came to a sudden end. She hit self-destruct, then rock bottom, working the strip behind King's Cross railway station to fund a £150 per day crack habit. Sugar Daddy, drug dealers, clients and co-workers were all interviewed and eliminated. The investigation fizzled out. I was about to re-ignite it.

Valerie's murder had already been linked to Liz Little's earlier today, when Edwina revealed how both women had been anally assaulted with an A3 battery. Similar killer MO, similar victim injuries ... I had something to present to DS Spence.

I trawled back through '91 and more unspeakable acts against the only women desperate enough to get into cars with strange men. As ever with prostitute murders, most of the girls had been murdered swiftly, before any sex act had taken place. Usually, all that stuff came later – proving that, for this particular category of killer, it was all about wielding power and control over a woman.

Another case leapt out. Melinda Marshall, 19, from Bristol had come to London in May 1991 to find work as a model. Within months, she'd signed up to the Diplomat agency as a 'high-class escort', meeting men in West End hotels for between £300 and £500 per night.

Within weeks, she'd earned enough to rent a luxury two-bedroom flat in one of Chelsea's smartest streets, for cash. She shared with a friend and fellow escort, Kim Morley, 21, also from Bristol.

On the morning of January 1st, 1992, Kim found her flatmate naked, stabbed and beaten almost beyond recognition on the floor of her bedroom. She'd been raped and sexually assaulted.

Because there had been no forced entry or robbery – £100 in cash was found close to her body – detectives assumed she'd been murdered by 'a client' or someone she knew. The report went on: 'The last person to see Melinda alive had been a minicab driver we failed to trace, who dropped her off outside her flat just after 2am.' I couldn't help thinking how such lazy thinking typified the general apathy towards these victims. The last person to see Melinda alive was the man who murdered her.

The manager of the Diplomat Escort Agency revealed that her last booking had been a 10pm supper date at the Langham Hotel, near BBC Broadcasting House on Regents Street. At 10.30pm, Melinda called the agency from the hotel foyer to report that the client – a Syrian businessman and frequent customer – hadn't shown. They never heard from her again.

Forty minutes later, at about 11.10pm, staff at the swanky Waldorf hotel on the Strand turned her away. The concierges of London's five-star hotels wielded vast influence; working girls of any class only gained entry on their say-so.

Diplomat's manager couldn't offer any explanation for her Waldorf cameo, but guessed she'd been 'moonlighting' either alone or for another agency.

Reluctantly – and only after the threat of a court order – Diplomat handed over the details of Melinda's clients during her 14-week stint on their books, including the final John who'd failed to show. Each of them had been quizzed by detectives; each had a rock-solid alibi for what was, after all, a night when we tend to have rock-solid plans: New Year's Eve.

Unusually, Melinda's murder did get widespread media coverage, making me realise that newsworthy loosely translates as *fuckworthy*.

The fact she'd been a 'high-class' call girl helped. As did her recent work as a model – especially those racy but tasteful portfolio shots of her in lingerie and thigh-high boots. The newspapers' trickiest editorial challenge had been finding a way to justify publishing this copyright-free soft porn. They all managed it admirably, even the broadsheets.

Melinda's parents knew nothing of their daughter's secret life.

'She wasn't even blonde,' her bewildered dad, Jack, told one newspaper, 'she was a redhead. We

77

didn't even recognise her in those modelling shots.'

In another: 'I just can't believe that she got herself involved in something like that. She was so shy that she'd send for someone else to order for her at a café.'

But her flatmate and fellow escort Kim offered a very different perspective: 'Sometimes businessmen say to me "You're smart. Come and work for me as my secretary". But why would I swap the tube at rush hour for a chauffeur-driven Rolls Royce at dawn? Why would I make tea for a man when I can get him to buy me £300 glasses of champagne?'

I wondered what Melinda would have swapped at the moment she first saw that knife. I blocked it out, stuck to the facts. Similar MO, similar injuries... Melinda made it onto the list of murders that could be connected to Liz Little.

I'd just started dipping into the previous year's file when my office phone rang.

'I've got some very interesting news for you,' Fintan teased.

'Please tell me that "very interesting" also means "very good". I need some.'

'Ah, Jesus, you're not still falling in love with all those dead hookers, are you?'

'I'm reading about men who have sex with dead hookers, Fint. Honestly, I don't think I'll ever get the horn again.'

'And what a devastating loss to London's womankind that would be. Usual place, six-ish?'

'Why do we always have to go to that kip?'

'Trust me, it'll be worth it.'

Chapter 6

Soho, London
Saturday, April 3, 1993: 19.00

The Coach and Horses in Soho felt like stepping into a faded 1970s Polaroid photo, all nicotine yellow and cancerous tan. Especially the cadaverous regulars. They were the worst kind of pissheads – arrogant drunks with an image of themselves as rakish intellectual mavericks. Beware the self-proclaimed 'local character', or anyone who works so hard to appear eccentric. The Coach was full of them – clinging to the bar and their own high opinions of themselves, an exclusive club validating each other's kamikaze drinking habits and boorish wit.

I resented these Peter O'Toole wannabes in their tweed jackets and cravats, wafting their imported Gauloises cigarettes, affecting the louche deportment of drunken professors.

They seemed to be either overpaid voiceover artists (failed actors who'd peddle any product for money), overpaid columnists (failed writers who'd peddle any opinion for money) or people who 'work in TV' (whatever that meant).

Of course, Fintan loved it. The Coach plugged him into the glorious Fleet Street of yore, when charlatan hacks drank, whored and rabble-roused while occasionally bashing out award-winning nuggets of copy.

He arrived in customary style: inexcusably late, mac on, fag on, game face on. Buzzing with mischief.

The pint I'd bought him three rounds ago now looked like stale piss, but he downed two thirds in one go, sleeved his mouth and said: 'I hope you've got plenty of paper cash with you.'

'Why would I need paper cash?'

'Because, last time I checked, G-strings don't hold pound coins.'

I cringed. Taking me to a strip club felt akin to tying up a starving hound outside a butcher's shop window. There was a very real chance I'd lick the glass and howl ravenously at the carcasses.

Of course, I came up with a more mundane objection. 'And why would I want to tuck the best part of a week's salary into the knickers of a girl who isn't even interested in me.'

'Because, my bold, intrepid, swordsman of truth and justice, you can find out all about Ms Elizabeth Little. Same again?'

He skipped to the bar, schoolgirl-giddy and beaming. Tonight he had a scoop rocketing through the printing presses and a series of juicy follow-ups baking in the oven. For once, he could relax. He returned with three pints – two for himself to catch up – and a chipped bowl of gnarly pork scratchings.

'Come on, Fintan, don't make me beg.'

'Well, if begging's your thing, lover boy, I'm sure we can find a lady to cater for your wanton, unmanly needs at the Florentine Gardens hostess and erotic dance club, just off Regent's Street. Of course, we're going there purely on business, you understand?'

'How did you find out she worked there?'

'She filed a tax return, invoices, the lot. Though I suspect she declared about a tenth of what she actually earned blowing fat Arabs and the like, certainly judging by her flashy pad.'

'What, so hookers are paying tax now?'

'Well, Donal, funnily enough she didn't describe herself as a hooker on her tax return. Jesus, can you imagine? Annual turnover: 300 men...'

'Current assets: pert tits and arse.'

'Fixed assets: horny old men. No, as far as the taxman's concerned, Elizabeth Little is a professional dancer who invoiced the Florentine for 24k in the last tax year.'

'I still don't understand why someone in the black economy would declare themselves to the taxman.'

'Well, they got Al Capone for tax evasion.'

'What?'

'Maybe the owner of the Florentine wants to make sure it's legit, at least on paper. Think about it, Donal, it's the perfect business for laundering money. It's all cash, isn't it? No man's going to risk having a payment to a glorified whore house on his credit card bill. And because it's officially legit, the owner can rinse his dirty money through the club's accounts.'

'And that owner is?'

Fintan didn't speak for a moment. Behind me, the ancient cash register dinged and spat out its clunking metal drawer. A knot of people to my right laughed way too hard.

Fintan's words were as dry as chalk, as if they'd sucked all the moisture from the air.

'The club is owned by Jimmy Reilly.'

It felt strange hearing the name spoken aloud. Hardened gangsters melted at the mere mention of it, refusing to talk about him even in hushed or reverential terms. Newspapers, including Fintan's, refrained from printing his name for fear of reprisals.

Unlike cartoon 1960s villains the Krays, Reilly eschewed fame and limelight. But amongst criminals, police and the media, his reputation for creative violence – which he preferred to carry out personally – made him an almost mythical bogeyman figure.

I learned all about him a few months' back when our Cold Case Unit had been struggling to cope with a mounting number of unsolved gangland hits. DS Barrett hauled in Scotland Yard Intelligence to supply us with a 'who's who' of London's criminal underworld. Reilly won that particular beauty pageant hands down.

They described him as one of a new breed of ruthless and sophisticated 'godfathers' who'd completely overhauled the way criminal gangs worked – so that bringing bosses like him to justice proved all but impossible. They listed on a whiteboard the differences between this 'new wave' of crime lords and the 'pavement-crossing, sawn-off shotgun merchants' of yore. Some stuck in my mind.

• They acquire legitimate businesses and use them as a front for their illegal activities.

• They employ top accountants, lawyers, barristers, financial advisers to make this happen.
• They are willing to deal with any group globally, including terror organisations.
• They are surveillance aware, tech savvy and shun fame. Photographs of these people do not exist in the public domain.
• They are willing to kill or punish people personally rather than employ others to do their dirty work, to eliminate the risk of blackmail or betrayal.

Officially, Reilly made his money in security, recycled metal and waste management – the classic gangster's holy trinity of Slap, Scrap and Crap. But as the Scotland Yard spooks explained, his rise from nowhere came about through the far more dubious trio of gold, protection rackets and E.

The youngest of 12 kids, he'd been brought up on London's meanest streets in Canning Town – an irredeemably drab and pitiless slum near the Royal Docks on the river Thames. The East End of his childhood pre-dated Canary Wharf, City Airport, Docklands Light Rail and fancy apartment blocks, performing instead as London's coke-caked arsehole, the watery outlet for miles of ironworks, chemical factories and filthy gasworks.

By the time Reilly left school in 1975, aged 15, any docks that hadn't been shut down were closing. Rampant unemployment led to a thriving black market and the emergence of local gangs like the Snipers and the Inter-City Firm (ICF), soccer hooligans who'd attached themselves to local club West Ham United, aka the Hammers.

Like five of his brothers before him, he was recruited by the Snipers and got involved in lorry hijacks, armed robbery, protection rackets and muscle for established local criminals.

By 21, he reputedly headed the Snipers and ran his operations out of the Duke of York pub on Freemason's Road, at the edge of Canning Town. He'd terrorised the landlady into giving over the lease even though her name was still above the door.

That same year, 1981, after a shooting at an illegal drinking den in Homerton, detectives raided the Reilly family scaffolding business and seized stolen goods, a sawn-off shotgun and ammunition. Reilly was convicted of handling stolen goods but escaped prison, receiving a nine-month suspended sentence – his only conviction.

This brush with justice spurred Reilly to identify less risky, more profitable criminal enterprises in which he didn't have to get his hands dirty. He muscled in on local massage parlours, taking a cut of the profits. He invested in an amphetamine sulphate factory ran by major league East End criminals with distribution networks all over the country. He set up a security firm supplying bouncers to clubs and pubs, employing his old pals from the ICF and the Snipers. This proved an ingenious ruse as he could 'charge' drug dealers to work inside, barring anyone who refused to pay the going rate.

Then, in November 1983, a robbery near Heathrow airport set Reilly and his 'new wave' criminal contemporaries on a whole new trajectory. The five-man gang who pulled off the

'Brink's Mat robbery' expected to get away with £3 million in cash. Instead, their overloaded getaway blue Transit van trundled up the A4 weighed down with 6,800 bars of gold in 76 cardboard boxes, a three-tonne booty worth £26 million.

This jackpot altered the British criminal landscape forever.

Police nabbed the robbers and put tabs on any major criminals with the clout/contacts to move/melt such a large amount of precious metal. So the major criminals divided the gold and delegated the moving/melting to trusted fledgling gangsters or specialists on the rise. Men like John 'Goldfinger' Palmer, Kenneth Noye, the Evans brothers from Islington and to James Declan Reilly from Canning Town.

These criminals became masters in a new art – laundering or cleaning dirty money so that it couldn't be traced back to criminal activity. Reilly hired dodgy expertise to rinse his filthy lucre through property, clubs, bars, restaurants and a waste recycling plant. He shifted yet more into untraceable offshore accounts.

By the late 1980s, he'd become something of a criminal venture capitalist, investing in the importation of ecstasy from Holland while his 'muscle' forcibly took over nightclubs where it could be distributed. He also set up chemical companies to develop 'designer drugs', substances that could replicate the effects of E and cocaine while avoiding the illegal classification.

But he still wasn't afraid to get his hands dirty, especially when it came to dealing with people who crossed him.

Reilly's flair for innovative savagery under-pinned his fearsome reputation.

First, they quoted a statement made by criminal Paul Clarke who'd borrowed a car from a dealership controlled by Reilly in Barking – only to have the vehicle seized by creditors. When Clarke returned to the showroom and broke the news, Reilly explained how he 'couldn't be seen to let something like this go' and produced a four-inch knife. Clarke thought he was about to be stabbed. Instead Reilly pushed the knife up through Clarke's chin then pulled it all the way to his left ear. Clarke described 'this terrible scrap-ing noise' and 'feeling as though the skin on my face was flapping'. He made the statement after receiving 45 stitches and life-saving treatment at the local accident and emergency ward, then promptly withdrew it the next day.

Just before Christmas, Reilly carried out a ruthless double hit on a couple in Epping Forest, Essex. Terry Golden, 39, and his girlfriend Marlene Anderson, 28, were found slumped in the front seat of a black F-reg Mercedes on an isolated forest track, blasted to death by a sawn-off shotgun. Police could prove that Golden, an accountant, had been managing the accounts of a string of clubs and pubs connected to Reilly. But they couldn't prove much else.

Golden had been siphoning off funds when Reilly invited him to an emergency meeting at the Good Intent pub in Upshire. Golden brought Marlene along, believing this would protect him from any extreme censure, at least for now.

Reilly waited for the couple in the pub car park,

climbed into the back seat and directed them to the spot on a lover's lane where they were later found riddled with lead. Apparently, Golden had protested: 'You can't shoot me in front of my girlfriend.' So Reilly shot her first and said, 'Well, you're not going to die in front of her now.'

But the most infamous example of his pitiless streak took place three years ago when he learned that an old associate, Bobby Atkins, had been a police informer.

Reilly instructed his son and daughter, aged 11 and 15, to invite Bobby's unwitting nine-year-old girl Amy over for a party at their outdoor swimming pool. Later that sunny afternoon, medics found Amy on the second step down to the wading pool, arse clamped to an uncovered suction drain so powerful that it had already caused a two-inch full rectal tear and drawn out a foot-long section of small intestine. Trans-anal intestinal evisceration is the technical term. Loss of blood caused her to go into hypovolemic shock. Paramedics performed a blood transfusion at the scene.

Over the following weeks, she underwent small bowel, liver and pancreas transplants. Her body rejected one of these imposters and she died.

When questioned by police, Jimmy blamed the 'accident' on a Portugese pool attendant who'd removed the drain cover to carry out general maintenance and had failed to replace it. Officers didn't get a chance to quiz 19-year-old Christiano before he vanished. Most suspected he ended up at Jimmy's waste recycling plant in Dagenham, incinerated with the rest of his rubbish.

Reilly topped it with a typically twisted touch. He had the drain cover turned into a wreath and delivered to Amy's funeral.

'He has an especially psychotic hatred for two types of people,' one of the spooks had explained, 'grasses and sex offenders, and has no qualms about killing anyone he even suspects of being either.'

Fintan returned with pints and whiskey chasers. I downed my Jameson in one.

'So let me get this straight,' I said, still reeling, 'we're going to a strip joint owned by London's most notorious gangland psychopath to ask questions about a girl he's probably just whacked.'

'Jesus, don't make it sound so formal.' Fintan laughed, a little nervously, gnashing away on his scratchings. 'We're just a couple of punters asking after our favourite dancer. You never know what one of the girls might let slip, especially after a few cheap champagnes. I've looked at every facet of Liz's life today. Her death has to be connected to that club.'

'But what if one of the girls cottons on and tells Jimmy's apes? Jesus, imagine what they'd do to a prying cop?'

'Knowing Jimmy, he'd put you on the payroll with all the others. Look, the girls don't even know she's dead yet, do they? Why would they find it suspicious? But this is our only window. Once our first edition drops then everything changes. There'll be journos swarming all over the story. But it isn't even news yet...'

'Journos swarming all over a dead hooker? Why will Liz's murder be such a big deal?'

'Let's just say I've uncovered a few juicy angles...'

'Don't tell me, you managed to get a clip of her from *The Bill?*'

He nodded.

'Much of a role?'

'Blink and you'd miss it. Well, that would be my advice anyway.'

'Not very convincing?'

'Let me put it this way, Donal, you won't see more wood in the Florentine tonight. But this makes her a celeb, so that makes the story up-market sleaze and the advertisers get a real stiffie over that, not to mention our porn-mag reading, woman-hating demographic. The *Daily Mail* will go crazy for it Monday, their lower-middle class readership loves a good hate. This one could run and run.'

As Fintan devoured his third pint, my eyes seized upon the last few pork scratchings in the bottom of the bowl. I'd never noticed before how these leathery, wrinkled circular snacks look like mummified arseholes. I couldn't stop myself imagining my insides being sucked through one of them and shuddered.

'Jesus, Fint, I don't know. It feels like we're walking right into trouble. What if we're rumbled...'

'Oh, for Christ's sake Donal, you've been banging on at me for months about having no excitement in your life and not being "a proper detective". I'm telling you now, this is going to be a massive case. It might be the best chance the cops ever have of taking down a major league villain like Reilly. You didn't choose this job to act like a fucking politician. You need to take risks. One break tonight – a lead, a potential informant – and you're in the box seat, indispensable to the murder squad. They'll be practically begging you to join.'

He scooped up the last scratchings, shovelled them into his mouth and crunched: 'I mean really, what have you got to lose?'

Chapter 7

Soho, London
Saturday, April 3, 1993; 21.40

As we set off up Greek Street, I felt instantly reassured by Soho's drunken school-playground vibe. Outside the pokey, sticky-carpeted pubs, drinkers clumped obediently between territory-marking velvet ropes; hemmed-in lives cutting loose, drinking, smoking, talking and laughing too hard.

It all happened here. We were just another pair of pissheads who'd run out of pleasure, innocently seeking more.

As we turned left into Old Compton Street, Fintan pointed out a semi-derelict three-storey building on the corner.

'Reilly owns that place now. A few months back, he sent his heavies in, demanded the deeds, got the deeds. A year or so ago, a similar place on Berwick Street resisted his approaches and got burned to the ground.'

90

'A turf war, over a cattle shed like that?'

'If you look closer, there's a clip joint in the basement, an unlicensed sex shop on the ground floor and three or four prostitutes on the first and second floors.'

I turned to see a red door open to a bare wooden staircase. On the flaky wall, a garish square of pink card announced 'Models' in black marker pen.

I couldn't imagine how any man could take that stairway to farmyard sex with a spent, cowed slave. The very existence of these fleshy wank stations had to be about male power and control: a King Kong, chest-beating, 'me Tarzan' fleeting reassertion of authority for men emasculated by modern life and equality. Or maybe they were just horny as hell and this had to do.

Either way, Soho had dozens of these so-called 'walk ups'. It would be the 'walking back down again' I couldn't handle. Maybe it was the Catholic in me, but how could you face the outside world again after your sordid deed, burning with guilt and shame? What if – blinking into the sun, sticky and dishevelled – you bumped into someone you knew? How could you ever explain away your behaviour? And Soho really is that small.

'Talk about putting yourself in a vulnerable position,' I said. 'Presumably as soon as your keks hit the floor, some muscle jumps out of the wardrobe and robs you.'

'No, those girls are the real deal,' he said, and who was I to argue with the Vice Admiral.

'There's a menu of services on the wall,' he went on. 'You get what you pay for, albeit with varying degrees of skill and enthusiasm.'

'You seem to know an awful lot about this, Fintan.'

'I've very good contacts in the Vice Squad. And they maintain good relationships with the pimps and the girls, mostly. The cops know they're never going to get rid of it so they try to make it as safe as possible for all involved. Most of these places have CCTV in the hallways now and covert cameras in the bedrooms. They set it up to protect the girls but it's helped them in all sorts of ways that they hadn't bargained for.'

'How do you mean?'

'Let's just say men of influence don't like being caught with their trousers round their ankles. Especially married ones.'

'I trust a thorough, conscientious journalist like you has insisted on seeing this footage.'

He laughed: 'Let's just say it made me feel very conventional. Boring almost.'

'I don't understand why a multi-millionaire, semi-legit gangster like Reilly would get involved in something so ... tawdry.'

'According to my snouts in Vice, two reasons. His place back there pulls in two grand cash a week, and he gets to road test all the fresh meat.'

'Sounds like a fucking animal,' I said.

The seedy, decrepit underground sex hovels soon gave way to Old Compton Street's colourful gay sex shops, pubs and clubs – so clean, overt and unashamed. I wondered what this contrast revealed about male sexuality.

We stomped on through more neon-lit alley-ways, past joints promising peeps and teasing strips. Under the archway announcing Raymond's

Revue bar in Walker's Court, a dread-locked man mumbled offers of crack, his hamster-like cheeks storing the rocks, ready to swallow if police swooped.

Brewer Street's porn cinemas, weirdo publishing outlets and sex shops eventually gave way to the innocent white-bulb signs of legitimate theatre, and to the trendy restaurants of Glasshouse Street – bouncers on the door, celebrities inside, paparazzi on the pavement.

Finally, we crossed the grand, sweeping, traffic-heaving Victorian vista of Regent's Street.

'Okay, don't stare, next street on the left, four or five doors down, red canopy. That's our place.'

'Aren't we going in now?'

'For God's sake, Donal, we're high rollers! We don't go anywhere on foot. We'll hail a black cab.'

'Damn, if only you'd brought your Hot Rod Mondeo. They'd be laying their black bomber jackets over the puddles...'

'Shut up and stick this on.'

I felt something pushing into my hand, opened my fingers to find a silver watch with a comedy-large red face. Fintan was already strapping what looked like an alarm clock to his wrist.

'That,' he said, nodding over to my scarlet arm-candy, 'is a Paul Newman Rolex Daytona 6565, worth 200 grand. I'm letting you have the flashiest watch because you're most in need of sprucing up.'

'Gee, thanks ... 200 grand? For a watch?'

'Yeah, bonkers, isn't it? Then they have the gall to complain when they get mugged. Only Father fucking Time himself knows these are fakes, so make sure you flash yours towards the apes on the door. And, later, at the mutton inside. They're experts at wheedling out real money from time wasters. So keep your sleeve high and the hoes will come a running. It'll be no change for you really, will it?'

'What do you mean?'

'Relying on your right wrist for sex!'

He hailed a black cab and we dived in.

'Here,' he said to the driver, handing him a tenner, 'take a loop round the block, then drop us outside the Florentine. Keep the change.'

I could never summon up the chutzpah for an enterprise like this alone. But Fintan thrived upon it. Although this probably confirmed my long-held suspicion that he was a fantasist, it also made him an ideal wingman. He didn't so much get into character as transmogrify. Like that time he posed as a restaurant critic for the *Irish Times*, earning us a three-course meal at the trendy new Atlantic Bar and Grill in Piccadilly. He'd even insisted on inspecting the kitchens.

'Hey,' smiled the scoop monger, mission-high, 'this'll be the closest you've got to a piece of female ass since, ooh let me think, your actual birth?'

'Very good, Fint. I must tell that one to Mam. She's so proud of you already. You know she's stopped going to the local shop altogether now? Too embarrassed by all your sordid "bonking bishop" exposés.'

That wiped the smirk off his face.

'Imagine,' he said, shaking his head sadly, 'there's men of the cloth out there who are getting

94

more sex than you.'

The taxi driver pulled up a door down from the Florentine. A sudden twang of dread strummed my nerve endings. I'd confidently pictured myself inside the club, talking the talk. After all, how intimidating could these hostesses-cum-hookers be? And they didn't even know that their colleague Liz had been murdered. Not yet.

What I hadn't prepared for was 'walking the walk' past the leering row of bouncers outside. This small army of enormous dead-eyed Slavs had probably disposed of Liz's body earlier today. What if they guessed from my haircut that I'm a cop? What if, while I'm inside asking awkward questions, they found a way to *confirm* I'm a cop?

'Get out of the fucking car,' hissed Fintan from the pavement.

I let him lead. Fintan's streetwise swagger imbued him with confidence, whereas my metronomic stomp screamed *farm labourer or escaped village idiot.*

The bouncers' pitiless eyes had already fastened upon us, seeking out hidden truths. I imagined them with Predator style infrared vision, peering into our very souls. I wondered suddenly what I'd say if they stopped me. We hadn't made any plans for that. And I'd always been hopeless at lying.

I took a quick scan of their faces: glum, hateful, exhausted. Small wonder; it can be wearing work halving, disemboweling and draining a hooker. Terrible hours.

I'd heard about these Eastern European muscle men, how easily they could make people disappear before vanishing themselves. I pictured

95

their homelands brimming with gaunt, ravenous, psychotic replacements.

I thought about spinning on my heels and fleeing. They'd never catch me. But Fintan was already level with the first two members of our unwelcoming committee. This was it.

As I winced through their glowering death stares, I couldn't help bracing myself for unexpected impact – as you might walking through an open gate at an automatic tube ticket barrier.

I checked my 'millionaire alert' timepiece more often than a Chechen suicide bomber, but none of the goons clocked it. Surely just one well-aimed shimmer of Rolex would mark me out as a youthful captain of industry 'slumming it' incognito for the night. In desperation, I faked an itchy forearm and wafted it in front of their faces, back and forth, like a lighter at an Aerosmith concert.

'Excuse me, sir?' came the gruff Soviet-baddie command and I leapt fully four inches off the red carpet. I landed but my heart remained lodged somewhere around my Adam's apple, beating so hard that I couldn't speak. I nodded, mouth open, like a halfwit.

'We will need to see ID, proof of age.'

Fintan turned back, a well-rehearsed picture of surprised innocence, while my mind performed a rapid-fire inventory of everything on my person that proved my 23 years.

'As you can probably tell, gentlemen,' Fintan gushed, 'we're on a very low-key night out. Neither of us expected *this* to happen. Though I can tell my 23-year-old friend over there is absolutely thrilled.'

Fintan threw me a look that said: 'Snap Out of it now. TALK!'

'You are both Irish?' asked the Russian.

Fintan nodded.

'Then we require ID for you too,' he said, his darkening eyes letting Fintan know he wasn't swallowing any of his old blarney, 'and we must frisk you.'

'May I ask why?' Fintan laughed, a little too desperately.

'Oh, let me see,' said Russki, his heavy-lidded, hateful eyes somehow managing to convey both tired boredom *and* latent violence, 'last October you blow up Sussex Arms, in Covent Garden; last November, Canary Wharf; last December, the city centre of Manchester...'

'Say no more,' said Fintan, reaching into an inside jacket pocket and producing his driving licence. Russki barked something at his under-lings. One began writing down the licence details while the other introduced Fintan's inside legs to what looked like a black table tennis bat with lights.

My insides collapsed in horrible realisation. I had only one piece of picture ID on me. And I didn't want any of these men to know I was a cop.

'I haven't brought any ID,' I announced flatly.

Russki looked at me balefully. 'Close up, you look older. We just search you.'

'No need to bother,' I said, hands-up, taking a step back, 'I can go home and get it, be back in half an hour.'

I took another baby step back and trod on a foot. I turned to apologise, only to nuzzle a great wall of chest belonging to another bouncer – and he wasn't moving.

'I'm sure you have nothing to hide from our friend Yulian,' said Russki with a smile. 'We do a quick search, you go in.'

My eyes locked onto Fintan's, relaying the bad news. Through some inexplicable sibling sympatico, he read it instantly.

'Hang on one minute there,' he piped up. 'If he says he wants to go, then he's free to go. And after this harassment, I'm leaving too.'

Russki's enormous left hand reached out to Fintan's chest, shutting him down. Yulian palmed mine like a zombie on a first date. He reached into my inside pocket and whipped out my warrant card. He blankly absorbed the contents before handing over to Russki.

'Why didn't you tell us you are an officer-of-the-law?'

'You didn't ask,' I said brightly, matter-of-fact.

'If I know this, I let you straight in. Why you not show me?'

'Look at the card,' I said, suddenly emboldened by the memory of a small detail that I never thought would come in handy. 'It has my name, photo and number. What's missing?'

Russki surveyed it, his narrowing eyes dragging his brow into a full-on frown.

Suddenly I felt in control. 'It doesn't have my date of birth, does it? That's what you asked me for. ID for proof of age. That doesn't provide it.'

Russki handed it back to me nodding.

'I see,' he said finally.

'Besides,' I added, still a move ahead, 'we're not

encouraged to broadcast the fact we're cops, especially on a night out. It can put us at unnecessary risk.'

'When he says we...' blurted Fintan, 'I'm not actually a cop of any sort.'

Russki ignored him.

'You will be safe here tonight, detective,' he said solemnly, standing aside, 'I can assure you of that.'

These words sounded about as reassuring as the last rites.

As I walked through, Fintan turned to Russki and said, 'You do know that every single ounce of Semtex in the world comes from your old Eastern Bloc. Ironic, isn't it, that it's now shitting you all up here in London.'

I floated down the ornate staircase on a current of relief, into the carnal-red, cabaret-style club. Fintan quickly caught up, riding a very different wave.

'Fucking hell,' he gasped, 'I can't believe you brought your warrant card on a job like this. What were you thinking?'

'I hadn't planned on showing it to anyone, Fintan. Did you think we'd get searched? Of course you didn't.'

'Yeah, but I didn't bring my press card. I'd never take it with me on a job like this. Because I'm not a fucking idiot.'

'We could've walked away until you opened your big mouth,' I pointed out.

'What?'

'They could smell your bullshit. That's when they started getting heavy. Until that point, we could've turned around and walked off. Instead they made you produce your driving licence.'

'Yeah, but if you'd shown them your driving licence, instead of your warrant card, we'd be in the clear now. They'd have our names but no idea what we do for a living. Now they know you're a copper, they'll be watching our every move. They're probably on the phone to Reilly right now, as we speak, telling him about you and some other professional busybody turning up at his club.'

We both stopped dead in our tracks. Until now, neither of us had dared to properly acknowledge what we might be getting ourselves into here. Suddenly Jimmy Reilly felt too real, too close.

'What if Reilly turns up?' I rasped, 'Starts asking questions.'

Fintan's cheek muscle flickered. He squinted to see things clearer in his mind.

'We're safe until the first edition lands,' he said, 'but when they see my by-line on that story, then our cover is blown. He'll realise we came here to check him out.'

'What time does that happen?'

'The first batch lands at King's Cross around midnight. That gives us almost two hours. But we need to be out of here literally on the stroke of 12.'

'I'll come and find you Cinders,' I said.

'No, you won't,' he muttered, 'we leave separately, and not the way we came in.'

He felt my confused glare.

'Check out the lenses,' he said, his eyes shooting up.

About a dozen pillars propped up the ceiling, each one a four-eyed CCTV monster.

'Forty-eight cameras. I bet there are 48 tables, one trained on each,' he said.

'Makes sense,' I agreed.

'They can watch us all night. If we both get up to leave suddenly, they could intercept us in the foyer for another chat. No thanks. Don't look now but there's a fire exit about 50 feet to the right of the toilets. Before it gets to 12, tell the lady you're with that you're going to the loo. On the way, veer right, go through that door and don't stop.'

'Until...'

'We'd better not hang around the West End. All the nightclub and taxi radios are on the same bandwidth. The goons here could have every bouncer and cabbie in Soho looking out for us in seconds. Head to Tottenham Court Road but keep north of Oxford Street. Those roads will be quiet by then. I'll see you at the Troy on Hanway Street, about 12.30.'

'Why don't we just scarper right now?'

'Will you quit staring at that fire exit? Check out the stage instead. Everyone else is. Then let's try to look like we came here for a good time.'

The club's focal point was a glass platform about the size of four snooker tables, shimmering three feet above a sparkling blood-red floor. Little red circular tables, each dimly lit by a single lamp, jostled hungrily around it, like piglets around a sow's nipple board. Silhouetted men sat alone in scarlet retro armchairs, waiting for the next floor show, studious, smoking and bereft.

'10.09pm and not a cock in the house stiff,' announced Fintan. 'Bit gynaecological sitting that close, wouldn't you say, Donal? Jesus, they might as well put them in stirrups.'

'Ringside, quite literally.'

'I think we'll do better over here.'

He led me around the island of ground-level tables and chairs, up two steps to an elevated area, also wall-to-wall red velveteen.

'Good job we didn't wear red,' he quipped, taking a seat at a front table, 'they might never have found us again.'

I took the chair next to him as a waitress swooped in. 'What can I get you gentlemen?'

'The house champagne will be fine tonight, thank you,' said Fintan, trying to sound like he usually quaffs the Dom Perignon.

'Anything to eat?'

'Just a portion of fries please, for now,' he said, uncharacteristically frugal for a man who loved nothing more than splashing out on expenses.

'Jesus, look,' said Fintan in wonderment, nodding towards a dark corner behind the stage, 'the livestock, in their holding pen.'

Inside a roped-off zone, a dozen or so fake-tanned, black-eyed girls sat bored and restless in their scanties, waiting to splay their orifices to the assembled pervs.

'They all look orange, like Sooty puppets,' he said, shaking his head.

'By the looks of it, tan isn't the only fakery going on.'

'Hey, looking on the bright side, you still get to ram your hand up their holes later.'

'Jesus, Fintan! They might just be dancers. Maybe that's all Liz did here.'

'Why do you always have to idealise women? It

102

must be because you've never actually known any, not properly. Listen, if dancing is all Liz did, then she must've been better than Anna fucking Pavlova, to rent a flat like that.'

'Why didn't she scale down, rent somewhere cheap, then she could've stopped working here?'

'They get hooked on the lifestyle. A lot of these women have several properties, kids at private school, membership to Chelsea health clubs, all achieved without a husband or a partner. Once you get used to earning a thousand pounds a night, how do you give all that up?'

I couldn't believe what I was hearing: 'A thousand a night, for dancing and sleeping with one person?'

'Some of the Arabs leave with three or four girls, and don't even fuck them all. They still pay the ones they don't touch just for sitting in their tent.'

'*In their tent!* Jesus, Fintan, you can't say things like that.'

'What?' he protested. 'In the weeks before and after Ramadan, wealthy Arabs flood into London to shop, eat and shag, get it all out of their systems. Some of the poshest hotels erect tents on their roofs, supposedly so that the Arab men can enjoy their traditional shisha pipes without smoking out the hotel lounges and bars. At least that's how the hotel explains it away to the other guests. The tents are for smoking alright, smoking hot hookers and drugs and booze, but well out of sight of their devout Muslim mums, wives and families. These men are the wealthiest in the world. It is almost a matter of honour that they party harder than the next richest man in the chain.'

He frowned and turned to me: 'You have brought some money here with you, Donal? Or a credit card?'

'I don't have a credit card. I took out 70 earlier. I've got about 50 left.'

'Fifty quid?' he whispered, eyeing me in disbelief, 'Jesus, Donal, I've just ordered the cheapest bottle of plonk on the menu and that was £120. You're expected to buy two of these before a woman will even sit with you.'

'I'll just eat then.'

'The chips are another 50.'

'Fifty pounds! For a portion of chips? You can't be serious.' He pushed a menu towards me. I scanned it without bothering to disguise my disgust.

'This is ... obscene. We still have time to buy perfectly adequate £2 pints in any pub down the road.'

'For fuck's sake, you can't go now,' he muttered, reaching into his inside jacket pocket and whipping out a black wallet.

He set to work beneath the table, then tapped my knee and hissed: 'Five hundred quid, fully sanctioned by accounts.'

'I can't do that.'

'Like I said, it's been signed off by accounts. Relax and have some fun.'

'How would this look to anyone on the outside? A cop taking 500 pounds cash off a reporter, who is also his brother, to spend on hookers? I could get the sack just for having this conversation with you.'

'I'm a little more concerned about us getting our legs broken if you try to leave after ten minutes,' he growled. 'I've had my hand under this table now for fully two minutes. In the name of all that is holy, will you take the fucking cash?'

I took the fucking cash, pocketing it seconds before the waitress bounced a wine bucket, two glasses and a bowl of fries off the cloth-cushioned table top. The fries remained steadfastly rooted to their receptacle because they were soggy McCain oven chips costing three pounds each. The champagne failed to fizz enough to flow out of the open spout, because it was lukewarm sparkling wine from Kwik Save. I suddenly didn't feel so bad about taking the newspaper's money. This felt about as luxurious as Ryanair.

'Here,' he said, pushing the wine bucket towards me, 'take this, go sit over there, and get your enormous Rolex out for the girls.'

By 11pm, foreign businessmen flooded the Florentine; wealthy wallflowers coaxing out the honeybee hostesses in their black leather mini-skirts and orange tans.

Let's get this straight – every female in the club had been officially rated since birth as 'way out of my league'. Pretty, slim, lithe and glowing – they were the kind of textbook beauties dangled daily in the media as an example of what all women should strive to look like.

Maybe it was just me who didn't find them sexy. Over-tanned, over-toned, overbearing – like their rictus smiles, their entire personas seemed dehumanised and robotic, designed for a photo-shoot rather than real life.

But maybe the finer things in life are wasted on me. I'd tried criminally expensive whiskey and chocolate, but found them bland and character-less. I've ridden in a Bentley and driven a Jaguar – both felt too smooth and insulated. No fun. As for food, I'd take a carvery over caviar any day.

Beer, bangers and boilers all the way for you then, Donal, I told myself.

My jangling nerves had a thirst on, polishing off bottle one in no time at all. Bottle two came with bottle-blonde Lenka, a Slovenian who proved every bit as bitter sweet as the Margarita she insisted I buy her.

'So nice to meet you, Dunnell,' she smarmed, making my name rhyme with Sally Gunnell.

'You too, Lunka,' I replied, wondering whether it was the sulphites, sugar or pesticides in cham-pagne that always drove me slightly loopy.

'Nice watch,' she purred.

It was all I could do not to whip it off, hand it to her and declare: 'It's yours Lunka' – just for the joy of imagining the chop-slap she'd suffer tomorrow morning when getting it valued at a jewellers.

'Thanks,' I smiled, 'as you can see from my clothes and drink, collectible timepieces are my only vice.'

Her sapphire eyes flashed 'timewaster'.

'Apart from beautiful women, of course,' I bolted on. She nodded uncertainly. *Wow,* I thought to myself, *I'm actually blowing it here WITH A HOOKER.*

To fend off the ignominy of prostitute knock-back, I got down to business: 'There's a girl here who I've come to see. A brunette called Liz?'

Her face visibly warmed, as if to say: *Aw, poor love-struck schmuck.*

I pressed: 'Do you know who I mean?'

She scrunched up her face in thought – her first spontaneous act in our five-minute relationship, and the first time she looked beautiful, at least to me. She shook it finally: 'I can't think of a Liz.'

'Looks like Juliette Lewis, you know, the actress. I think she said her surname was Little.'

Her bottom lip dropped a fraction, almost imperceptibly, but her eyes remained icy, impenetrable.

'I don't know her,' she said quietly, shaking her head gravely. Her gaze lowered, her pupils twinkling red, reflecting the crimson floor. 'I don't know anyone like you describe,' she said blankly, getting to her feet. 'Sorry.'

'Lunka!' I called after her, 'what about your 75-pound Margarita?'

Black-haired, green-eyed Belarussian 'Kate' could've doubled for Betty Boop – if she put on two stone, shed 20 years of wear and tear and learned to smile. Her autumnal green eyes immediately triggered memories of Eve – my ex, the One, until she cheated on me with a man she subsequently killed. Cue a *grape-fuelled* outpouring about my disastrous love life. Kate's eyes grew bigger, kinder, sadder as I ran her through Eve's cheating, sundry rejections and my recent failure to 'get it up' during what should have been my first one-night stand.

I wrapped up to find her eyes inspecting me with a mixture of pity and contempt.

'Jeez,' declared the 40-something, emaciated, trafficked East European hooker, 'yer life is fuuucked.'

That sobered me up. I ordered a pint of tap water, took a trip to the loo. Time to straighten myself out. On the way, I took a good look at that fire exit and asked Paul Newman the time; still only 11.20.

The kindly toilet attendant let me borrow a flannel. An ice-cold cat lick to face and neck coaxed my sobriety up off its stretcher to stumble. As I headed back to my table, I failed to pick out Fintan from the sharp-suited throng. A paranoid certainty slapped me back to pin-sharp lucidity; the fucker had already scarpered.

Ah well, I thought, as I sat back down, may as well be hanged for a sheep as a Lambrusco; I'd be 'doing a Cinders' and quaffing criminally over-priced bad plonk right up until the twelve bells.

'Hey, I'm Tammy,' boomed a typically nasal American female voice, and I cringed instinct-ively, 'like the harlot from the Bible.'

'Hey, I'm Donal.' I smiled, vowing that if she started banging on about her Irish roots, I'd word-lessly get up and walk straight out the nearest door.

'Thanks for not making a wisecrack about standing by your man,' she said, taking the seat next to me. 'Trust me, Donal, that's refreshing.'

'So is having someone pronounce my name properly.'

'Donal like Zonal right? Or *Bonal?* Can't our erstwhile conquerors manage that?'

'Apparently not,' I said, thinking *what's Bonal*

... the plural of Boner, perhaps?

Everything about Tammy seemed tiny. Five two tops; fine, almost pinched nose, chin and cheeks; girl-next-door brown hair. The exception: her all-ball, no-snow, brown Bambi eyes, whip-smart, knowing, a little dirty. Think Sandra Bullock in *Demolition Man*.

'What's *Bonal?*'

'Oh it's like a sickly sweet wine. What the French call an *aperitif,* which makes it okay to get pissed before dinner.'

'You seem very cultured, Tammy.'

'Lord no! I was a bartender, you know, a proper one. Got kind of obsessed with cocktails.'

Great, I thought, *now she's going to hit me for one of the £90 'Florentine specials'.*

'I wouldn't bother here though,' she said, leaning forward conspiratorially. 'They've got a couple of kids decanting supermarket spirits into expensive bottles. They're charging Japanese businessmen £300 for a bottle of £6 supermarket Scotch. That's how they make the real money.'

Tammy's willingness to share this dark Florentine secret suggested she was her own woman, ballsy and indiscreet. If anyone was going to spill about Liz Little tonight, it had to be the gobby yank.

'You know, Donal, this is like a really expensive place to be bored.'

'I'm not bored,' I protested, way too much.

She smiled. 'The second I saw you I thought "he doesn't fit here". I've been watching you. You seem determined to finish your overpriced drink and escape.'

'I'm just a fast drinker. Why did you come over then?'

'I don't know. I'm intrigued I guess. And I get tired performing like a seal. I figured I'd get a rest with you.'

'Wow, an attractive woman like you has to perform for them? I thought you'd just stand there and let them drool.'

'Where would be the fun in that?'

'Performing like a seal is fun?'

'I said it was tiring, not boring.'

'Now I'm intrigued. So who does "fit" here at the Florentine? And how do you keep it interesting?'

'Well, they're all wealthy, successful, achievers.'

'No wonder I stood out.'

She threw me a slightly amused, mostly disapproving look and I marvelled at how even the most worldly Americans don't quite get self-deprecation. It should be listed as an un-American activity, alongside Communism, small portions and winning wars solo.

She resumed her hostess club deconstruction: 'Every guy in this place could book a hotel room and order up a girl like a pizza. But they come here instead because it makes them feel like real players. They let themselves believe that all these hot women find them irresistible.'

'They're all the same?'

'No, you've got three basic categories. First you've got the "can't get enough" guys – sex at home or anywhere else, status at work, gratification. For them, buying a girl off-the-shelf presents no challenge so they come here to seduce a

110

'IT girls?'

'It stands for International Travellers. She and a few of the girls go abroad. A lot...'

She stopped talking, suddenly transfixed by events behind me.

'Mr Lynch,' came a foreign male voice over my left shoulder, 'our manager would like you to join him for a glass of Krug in our VIP area.'

'I have to go,' said Tammy, getting to her feet.

'Tammy, hang on,' I said, but she didn't even look at me again before vanishing.

'This way please,' ordered the voice.

I turned to a pair of supersized suited men standing way too close. I looked up and smiled: 'Gentlemen, I came here to meet girls, not the staff.'

'He's opened the '88. One drink, Mr Lynch, then the boss will be happy to introduce you to any girl you please.'

As I got to my feet I stole a quick glance at Paul Newman. 11.20. Still. The fucking thing had stopped. Fuck! The fake watch was dead. My insides crumbled like chalk cliffs into a raging sea. I was dead. The boss? Did he mean Reilly?

'What time is it?' I demanded, flustered.

The lead goon checked his watch.

'12.25.'

'Shit. I've really got to go.'

'Come,' he smiled, gripping my left elbow, 'the '88 is a very fine vintage.'

Fintan's words drifted around my fuzzy head like champagne ache:

When Reilly sees my by-line on that story, then our cover is blown. He'll realise we came here to check

113

him out.

As the goon guided me towards the foyer, my mind rattled and bounced like the little white ball on a spinning roulette wheel. Scenarios clattered past. Jimmy Reilly had seen the first edition of the *Sunday News* and was waiting for me. Or he'd learned about it and instructed his men to keep me here until he arrived.

Red or black, odd or even, it didn't really matter. No one could stop this wheel now. We'd been rumbled. I suddenly pictured a knife effortlessly slicing off the side of my face as if it were ham. My chest tightened. A swill of burning, bitter wine gurgled up into my throat. I held my breath and swallowed hard.

He ushered me through a coded security door just off the foyer. It closed slowly behind us, muffling the club's joyous cacophony to an irregular heartbeat thrum. It then slammed deafeningly to silence.

I climbed a spiral metal staircase ahead of him, our clanking feet a lonely chain gang of two.

I needed an escape plan.

Deny all knowledge.

Blame Fintan.

Bluff them into thinking my boss at work knows I'm here. This visit is semi-official. Surely they won't risk doing anything to me then? I'm a serving police officer...

Of course there was always a chance he'd do as Fintan had predicted – offer to put me onto his payroll. I'd have to say no. But would he take no for an answer?

Maybe that's how other cops wound up entangled in his web. Perhaps Reilly deliberately manoeuvred them into compromising positions, until they reached a point where they couldn't say no to him.

That's how I felt right now.

The top of the stairs opened to a red mezzanine. Each side hosted a small, circular, mirrored stage with a pole, a bar and a couple of sofas. All empty.

At the far end, a figure stood statue still, silhouetted by sound-proof glass overlooking the dance floor.

Fuck. It had to be Jimmy Reilly.

'He's waiting,' hissed the goon behind me.

I walked towards him, unable to feel my legs now, or the carpet beneath my feet. I'd somehow moved beyond terror into a trance-like state of fatalistic doom. This must have been how those soldiers felt during The Great War, I suddenly thought, when they left their trenches to go 'over the top'.

Somehow, as the silhouette turned towards me, I knew that my life would never be the same again.

As I got closer, he seemed larger than I'd imagined, squat almost, with no neck and hardly any hair.

'Sit down,' he said, in a strong Birmingham accent.

This isn't Jimmy Reilly!

Somewhere deep inside, a hard-wired survival instinct jolted me out of my self-induced stupor into a state of 20/20 lucidity. I'd never felt sharper, more sober or alive.

There was still a chance I could make it out of

here unscathed.

I sat. On the little red circular table in front of me lay a folded up *Times* newspaper, the cryptic crossword half complete, a walkie-talkie and a pair of remote controls.

He turned to me. 'I'm Bernard Moss, the manager. You can call me Bernie.'

He turned back to the glass. 'Name your drink, officer,' he said, 'and later you can name your girl. All on the house, of course.'

'I'm happy to pay for my own drinks, thanks all the same Bernie. And girls too, if it comes to it.'

He laughed.

'Fuck's sake, have a drink at least,' he said, still addressing the glass, 'no one's gonna know. We've got champagne here from before World War Two that you can't put a price on.'

Suddenly, he gave the glass an almighty slap, raising me an inch off my seat.

'That fucker's getting it,' he roared.

He marched over to the table, grabbed the radio.

'Table 16 ... he's at it again. That's the third time. Get him the fuck out of here.'

He glared at me: 'I've already sent staff over, twice, telling him not to put his cigarettes out on Jimmy's precious floor. Twice he's told my staff to fuck off. I don't care who he is, he's leaving, if there's one thing I can't stand it's people being rude to waiting staff. It drives me mental. That and cruelty to animals.'

I recalled the advice of a hostage negotiator on TV: keep your captor talking and address him by name.

'What's so precious about the floor, Bernie?'

He turned to face me. 'It's terrazzo, priceless apparently, over half a century old, and Italian, which Jimmy loves. Makes him feel like Don Corleone. It's so rare they slapped a preservation order on it so it can't be removed. Jimmy literally worships it. He gets down on his knees every day and fixes the cigarette damage himself.'

'Well, you can keep your priceless champagne, Bernie.' I smiled, digging my right hand into my trouser pocket. I pulled out a tenner and placed it on the table.

'Any chance we can send your goon to an off-licence?' I said. 'I could murder a bottle of Heineken.'

Bernie smiled. 'Good shout. I can't stand that fizzy piss either. But I'm getting them. Surely you're allowed to take a drink from me personally, if you're not on duty, like?'

'I didn't swallow the rule book, Bernie. Why not?'

He stood, summoned the meat over and placed his order. 'Make sure they're cold,' he called after him.

'Honestly, these muppets ... if I didn't say that, he'd come back with warm ones off the shelf.'

He stared down at me hard. 'So, how can a copper afford to come to a place like this?'

'I can't really. It's just a one-off. A special birthday treat.'

'Where did your brother get to?'

My heart caved in. They knew.

'That's the thing, Bernie, I'm supposed to be meeting him in Chinatown right now.'

'I suppose your boss from Scotland Yard will be

there too.' He smiled, the clever bastard.

'No, but he knows I'm here,' I lied, my cheeks in full bloom.

He turned to survey the dance floor.

'The thing is, we already look after some of your lot. If they find out that you've come here, sniffing about ... well, it puts them in a very difficult position. It totally undermines our arrangement.'

I didn't see that coming. 'Arrangement?'

He turned to me. 'You've left yourself completely exposed here, on both fronts. We've got video of you accepting cash from your brother and consorting with women of ill-repute. I told Jimmy we should hand this over to our friendly coppers. They'd deal with you in their own way.'

Please don't, my mind silently begged, *I'm on my final warning.*

'But Jimmy doesn't like to be devious like that. He prefers to deal with matters head on.'

Fuck. What did that mean? Please tell me he's not on his way...

Blame Fintan, deny all knowledge.

'Who's Jimmy?'

He turned away again, his malevolent smirk reflected in the glass. 'You'll find out, soon enough.'

That imaginary knife glinted cold against my hot cheek as dread clawed at my guts.

Footsteps lumbered up the stairs. I squeezed my eyes shut: *please don't let it be Reilly.*

'Look at Mary Quant swinging that fucking bag,' muttered Bernie. 'I hope you like your beer shaken *and* stirred.'

The moody goon dumped a bag of cans on the floor, change on the table.

'I asked you to get bottles, you thick cunt,' Bernie roared. 'Fuck off out of my sight, Slob, before I kick you down them fucking stairs.'

He leaned into the bag, pulled out a can in each hand, deftly peeling both open in one smooth move. The beer fizzed up and spilled over the edges, somewhat spoiling his 'sharp shooter' cabaret. He handed one to me and raised his. *'Slainte!'* he said, then gulped wide-eyed, like a goldfish.

I badly needed a hit so set to work. My only hope: Fintan. He must've realised by now that something's gone very wrong. So why hadn't he come back? I suddenly pictured him holding court in the Troy, bullshitting some foreign girls, tucking into the pint he'd bought for me earlier. I swallowed hard and told myself: he'll get here before Reilly, and then he'll think of something.

He always thinks of something.

'Alcohol is the anaesthesia by which we endure the operation of life,' declared Bernie. 'One of your lot said that.'

'I prefer the Sammy Davis line,' I said, 'that alcohol gives me infinite patience for stupidity.'

He glared. I panicked.

'Because of where I work, Bernie,' I blurted, desperately.

'Which department?'

'The Cold Case Unit,' I said, wiping my mouth and wondering what I could add that might help me, 'unsolved murder cases, at least two years old. Nothing current.'

Bernie nodded approvingly.

'So, do you get stick at work, for being Irish like?'

119

'A bit,' I said, 'not so much from English people. Some of the Northern Irish can be fairly hostile.'

'Bitter Prods. Tell me about it. I served in Northern Ireland. The Paras. First time I realised I was Irish!'

I latched on; bonding with Bernie might be my only ticket out of here.

'What are your Irish connections then, Bernie?'

'I'm not, obviously, but me mum's from Mayo, dad Leitrim. He's a right pisshead. Used to beat the shit out of us, so I joined up to annoy him really. I ended up in Belfast during the Hunger Strikes. Of course like most rational people, I had some sympathy for the prisoners. Next thing I'm being called an IRA-loving left footer and getting into punch-ups about it. I nearly got kicked out, twice. That's how I got this,' he said, pointing to the lump missing from the top of his left ear.

'I wouldn't mind,' he smiled, 'but that's me good one. The other one's fucked from shooting.'

'At least your dad must be proud that you made a stand. Mine's ex-communicated me.'

'He doesn't know anything about it. We haven't spoken since. Even when I had kids, he couldn't bring himself to let it go.'

'He sounds just like mine, armchair IRA man, professional drunk.' I paused. 'I wonder what makes them so ... unforgiving.'

'Well, they were the men of the house, weren't they? What they said went, unchallenged. Women wouldn't stand for it today.'

'How did you end up working here?'

'After the army, the only work I could find was in security. And even then I had to take jobs on doors in places like Basildon. It's like the Wild West out there: gangs, guns, drugs. I got into some right scrapes. Jimmy took over one of the joints and told me to clean it up, which I did, eventually. After a fucking war. He sort of took me under his wing after that.'

We both swigged hard.

Bernie belched, placed his spent can on the table and sat opposite me.

'Jimmy trusts me. I can help you here, Donal. But you have to tell me the truth. Right now, in confidence, man to man. Why are you and your brother asking about Liz Little?'

I swiftly flicked my mind through a multitude of angles, like a wing mirror, trying to read the situation. Bernie didn't seem to know Liz was dead, let alone murdered. Or was he just playing me?

Blame Fintan, deny all knowledge.

'Look Bernie, my brother's a reporter. He offered me a free night of booze and beautiful girls in exchange for coming here and finding out all I could about a girl who works here called Liz Little. That's all I know.'

'You've got a choice here, Donal,' he said, leaning back, all statesmanlike. 'You can either let me help you, or accept the wrath of Jimmy Reilly alone. You're a cop. I know you know who Jimmy is. He's on his way here to deal with you. I don't fucking care either way but, if I were you, I'd take any help I could get right now.'

'I've told you everything,' I said.

'This shitty business has taught me two useful lessons,' said Bernie, leaning forward again. 'One, how to read people. I know when someone's going to throw a punch before they even clench their fist. I deal day-to-day with professional liars – criminals, hookers, successful businessmen. I know you're lying to me.'

Bang! Empty cans and remotes obeyed his slammed fist and scuttled to the floor.

'Tell me the fucking truth.'

I shifted in my seat.

'Liz Little is dead,' I said. The words seemed to hang between us like ghosts.

Bernie blinked twice, too quickly.

'How?' he said, quietly.

My throat felt drier than a dead cactus.

'We found her in North London this morning. She'd been tortured. Fintan's got all the gory details in tomorrow's paper.'

He sighed. 'To think an evil cunt like me is still here, and she's gone. Fucking hell.' He smiled bitterly.

I tried to read it. Guilt? Regret?

He leaned down to the shopping bag and pulled out two more cans, handing one to me.

'Thanks,' I said.

'To Liz,' he said.

'You said that by telling you the truth, you could help me, Bernie.'

'Yeah, well, that's the second lesson I learnt in this business,' he said, getting to his feet. 'Don't believe a word anyone tells you.'

We drank in silence but my mind set off on a frantic hunt for leverage. Fuck it, I thought, I've nothing to lose now.

'You clearly have feelings for Liz,' I said, 'maybe you can help me find her killer.'

He snorted bitterly.

'Couldn't you protect her, Bernie?'

'Fuck off, cop.' He laughed. 'You've been watching too much *Cracker.*'

His radio suddenly spluttered into life, the shock almost ending mine. The deepest, fuzziest voice I'd ever heard gabbled against a backdrop of piercing banshee screams.

'…outside the toilets,' was all I could make out.

'Copy that,' said Bernie, turning and frowning down.

I stood up and walked towards the glass.

Outside the ladies' toilets, three women clutched their faces and caterwauled.

'What the fuck…' muttered Bernie.

More women staggered out of the toilets, weeping and hawking. People nearby covered their mouths and ran away.

I wondered if Fintan had come back and taken a massive dump. That would be his style.

'Get Slob up here,' Bernie instructed the radio, 'everyone else, evacuate the club. Repeat, evacuate the club.'

Goons emerged from all angles, urgent, pumped, rehearsed. Within seconds, they too were stumbling about, bewildered apes clawing at their own faces.

As Slob arrived, screams began to pierce the thick gallery glass.

'Listen to me, Slobodan, don't let him out of your sight,' ordered Bernie. 'If you need to go outside, take him with you. But only leave this building as a last resort. I'm off to check the dogs are okay.'

123

Bernie bolted to the stairs.

'There's mayhem in the club and he's checking on some dogs?' I said to Slob.

'That's Bernie. Loves animals, hates people.'

The house lights blazed on to reveal revellers crawling about on the floor, gasping for air. Others were racing to the exits. Incredibly, a cluster of people had formed an orderly queue at the cloak-room hatch; unflappable Brits, no doubt.

I suddenly remembered the remote controls that Bernie's fist had scattered to the floor.

'Okay if I get another beer, Slob?'

He watched me all the way to the bag. I lifted it onto the table, took out a can, handed it to him, then opened another and sat down. He turned back to watch the action below, gulping greedily.

I sneaked my left hand down, picked up the white remote. Sure enough, it controlled the air con. I cranked up the fan, clamped my mouth shut and held my breath.

Within seconds, my eyes stung. Someone had released some sort of toxic substance in the ladies. Fintan?

Slob turned to me, his gurning face a turnip of tears. Suddenly, puce face in meaty hands, he slid down onto the floor. I stood only to feel his enormous hands clamping my ankles.

I grabbed the plastic shopping bag of cans by the neck, spinning it around until the contents formed a solid lump. I raised it over my right shoulder then, with my left hand, pushed Bernie's little table over.

Slob looked up at me, crying, somehow knowing, as I brought a half-dozen unopened cans of Heineken crashing down onto his thick skull. He moaned, his hands falling away from my ankles like freshly sliced meat.

'Reaches parts other beers can't get to.' I wheezed, tears now rolling down my cheeks too.

I snapped the fan off, wiped my eyes and walked back to the glass. Below, four uniformed police officers strode about, checking on the stricken and directing people outside.

Bernie and Jimmy can't touch me now.

As I turned to leave, I had an idea. I grabbed Bernie's copy of *The Times* and the cans both he and Slob had drunk from, then bounded down those stairs.

'Please, don't run,' came the futile order as I hurdled bodies on my way to that fire door.

I got out, looked left to see Bernie on the other side of wire mesh soothing a pair of Alsatians, then right to flashing blue lights. Police cars and fire engines hurtled to a stop outside the main entrance. I couldn't figure out what was going on so I just ran. A couple of hundred yards later, I recognised Fintan crossing Regent's Street towards me.

'What the hell happened to you?' he shouted. 'And what are you doing with that stuff?'

I felt too furious to form actual words, so emitted a primeval growl instead.

'Fucking hell, Donal, all you had to do was keep track of the time.'

I whipped off the Rolex and hurled it in his direction

'What time does it say on your stupid watch?'

He checked it. 'I told you they were fakes. It's

almost half one now. What have you been doing all this time?'

Unloading brought home to me just how close I'd come to real harm tonight, hurtling me into a post-traumatic low.

'It's a miracle I got out of there. A fucking miracle.'

'Yeah, alright, Billy Graham. Steady.'

'You sneer all you like. I could be strapped to a chair right now, getting a Jimmy Reilly smiley.'

He nodded. 'I know, I know. How do you think I felt, sitting at the fucking Troy, wondering what the hell had happened to you?'

'Oh poor you,' I spat bitterly.

'By ten to one I thought "Fuck it, I'm not taking any chances here", so I headed to a phone box, put on my best Ian Paisley and rang a coded warning into the *Today* newspaper. I wouldn't even have thought of it only for all that shit the Russian gave us going in.'

'How do you know the code word?'

'Everyone in newspapers has to know it. We're the ones they call. What the hell happened in the ladies?'

'I don't know, but that's what really saved my arse. I never would've got away from Bernie.'

Fintan sighed. 'I still don't understand how you got yourself into that mess in the first place.'

'The watch was working when I last checked.'

'You drink too much, Donal. Admit it. That's why you fuck up.'

'Well, I shouldn't drink champagne or any white wine for that matter. It doesn't agree with me at all.'

'Anyway, thank Christ you're okay,' he said, 'and I can promise you now, I'll never rope you in to something like that again. It nearly did for the fucking both of us.'

Chapter 8

North London
Sunday, April 4, 1993; 02.00

Our unlicensed minicab stopped on Holloway Road so that Fintan could grab a couple of early editions.

'BILL STAR SLAIN' screamed the *Sunday News'* front accompanied by a photo of Liz looking demure, sophisticated.

Underneath, a 'screen grab' from an episode of *The Bill* showed her in a scene opposite the soap's most popular character, DS Tosh Lines.

'Black Dahlia copycat-killing baffles police...' added the sub-heading.

'Great,' I bristled, 'we're baffled already, less than twenty-four hours after her body has been found.'

'Are you or are you not baffled, Donal?'

'We're all fucking baffled, aren't we?'

'Well, there you go then.'

I had to marvel at his ability to spot the iconic 'Black Dahlia' angle. It's one of those cases everyone's heard of, even if we don't all know the gory details. He had single-handedly turned the murder of an unknown dancer-cum-hooker into a major news event. I read on:

'A rising TV starlet has been savagely murdered just weeks after landing a breakthrough role in prime time hit series *The Bill*.

'The mutilated body of Liz Little, 22, was discovered just yards from a primary school in North London. Her murder bears disturbing similarities to the infamous "Black Dahlia" killing which rocked Hollywood almost 50 years ago.'

The splash was accompanied by a 'spread' inside, aptly named as it consisted mostly of studio snaps of Liz lounging about in lingerie. I wondered if all young actresses had to bare their assets to find work. It didn't seem fair somehow.

'Now that Liz is dead,' I said, turning the 'spread' his way, 'surely these photos are bordering on, I don't know, snuff porn?'

'Her parents took the money and signed it all off.'

'They've been paid?'

'Not yet. One of our junior reporters will be sent up there next week to renegotiate the contract.'

'What do you mean, renegotiate. You said they signed.'

'Yeah, but the paper always beats people down before they cough up. Standard practice.'

'Jesus,' I gasped, unable to comprehend how anyone could be so callous.

Below the soft porn, an interview with Liz's 'devastated parents' carried the headline: 'Our Liz Dreamed of Hollywood'. At least in death, they'd given Liz the fame that had eluded her in life.

Another piece gleefully revealed the 'string of

128

uncanny similarities' between this crime and the murder of Elizabeth Short – 'The original Black Dahlia' – in 1947.

'Apart from sharing the same Christian name, both victims were 22, five foot two and budding actresses. Like Liz Little, Short was found mutilated, her body sliced in half at the waist and drained of blood.'

'You've said nothing about her working at Jimmy Reilly's club?'

'Well, you know the rule Donal, build 'em up, then knock 'em down. This week, Liz is the tragic victim. Next week, we'll reveal her saucy secret life as a high-class call girl in a club owned by a notorious gangster. The old one-two. It's always worth holding something back when you can, give yourself a little edge.'

'Right, so you haven't bottled it then?'

'No danger. But the thing is, Reilly doesn't technically own the club and it isn't technically a knocking shop. We'll need concrete evidence before we can run any of that.'

'Won't the daily papers beat you to it now?'

'They don't even know she worked at the Florentine. If they do find out, they'll face the same legal headaches we do. The dailies don't have the time or resources to deal with all that. We might not be able to stand it up ourselves in time for next Sunday.'

As soon as the cab sped away from our house, Fintan lit a cigarette and asked: 'Did any of the girls say anything tonight, about what Liz might have been up to?'

'I sensed two of them knew something,' I said.

129

'The first got very defensive as soon as I described Liz and just walked off. Then this American called Tammy seemed about to talk when those bouncers showed up and took me to the VIP area. I wish I had five more minutes with her. What about you?'

He shook his head. 'One girl said Liz went abroad a lot, for weekends, often with some of the other girls. Nothing concrete.'

'Yeah, that's what Tammy said. Is there a way of pulling her travel records?'

'I'll find out.'

A breeze came from nowhere, chilling me into a stark realisation: 'Jimmy Reilly could come for you or me at any time, now he knows we've been sniffing around.'

Fintan took a monstrous drag on his Rothman cigarette, then flicked it hard into the pavement, sending sparks flying.

'He might want to shut me up before next Sunday,' he said, 'and that's why we've got to prove he did it.'

'Aren't you concerned for your own safety?'

'We can't just let him get away with murder.'

'But we don't know for certain it was Reilly. If we did, that'd be different. As it stands, we've got nothing on him.'

'You know they never caught The Black Dahlia's killer?' he said, following me through the garden gate. 'They think they know who it is now. A man called Mark Hansen.'

'So?' I said, unlocking the front door and pushing it open.

'So back in 1947, Elizabeth Short worked at

Hansen's nightclub in Hollywood. Guess what it was called?'

He closed the door behind him as I shrugged. 'The Florentine Gardens.'

Fintan hit the bed as I took up my customary position, propped against the arm of the sofa, bottle of Shiraz to hand, Sleepless in Arsenal.

A few months back, I had to leave South London and my shared flat with Aidan 'Stalker' Walker in a hurry. Aidan – stressed-out, underpaid psychiatric nurse – had taken to smoking weed at night and leaving his keys in the front door in the mornings. They were swiped, of course, and, we feared, sold on. A few nights later, while watching TV alone, I could hear the rustling of a key in the front door. Key purchaser had come to redeem his investment. As the key scrabbled about hopelessly in the changed lock, I felt gratified that the £120 we'd been fleeced out of had been worth every penny, after all.

I banged a few saucepans together, to let our prospective robber know someone was in. I figured that even a rattling junkie would appreciate the guiding principle of burglary – best done when the occupants are out. He'd just have to come back later, despite the inconvenience.

But still the key kept scratching and scraping, so I flashed the hall light on and off. When lightbulb Morse code failed to deliver the message, I gave the door a few kicks and yelled a manly 'fuck off'. The key stopped rattling. Then it started again.

I knew 'Stalker' kept a 'Big Bertha' golf club behind his bedroom door that could scalp a hippo, so I grabbed that, samurai-style, and told myself 'today's the day you man up'.

I crept to the door, club clutched in my right hand as that old key still clattered away, each manic metallic jab ratcheting up my terror. What kind of relentlessly demented head case stood on the other side of this door?

I swallowed the fear, raised Bertha, turned the lock and pulled the door open hard. I had to look down at the key bearer, because he couldn't have been more than 12 years old. He glared up at me in shameless, fearless disgust: 'Fuck, he sold one to you as well?'

'I *live* here,' I said, brandishing the club's meatier end, 'unless you want me to use your neck as a tee, fuck the fuck off.'

'You can't speak to me like that,' declared Arnold from *Diff'rent Strokes*, 'I'll be back later with my brothers.'

'Oh yeah, and who are they?' I taunted, 'the fucking Drifters?'

'No, the fucking Dentons.'

I packed immediately – in other words, filled three bin liners. I rang Aidan at work, ordered him home to do the same. We were out within an hour. I'd seen how Jamaican/Irish family the Dentons treated anyone who 'crossed' one of their own. A few months earlier, they'd set their tormented, feral fighting dogs on an old man called Malcolm after he'd complained about the constant partying upstairs. As medics stitched him up in hospital, the brothers kicked in his front door and dragged out his paltry belongings, setting them alight in the car park. A real Bonfire of the Inanities. The only

132

items of value he owned, his World War Two medals, were never seen again. Neither was Malcolm, but we learned a valuable lesson from that noble old war hero ... as soon as you get any Denton Attention, scarper.

Neither of us could face the prospect of new flatmates, so Aidan agreed to join me north of the river. Meanwhile, the palatial isolation of London's trendy new docklands had started to grate upon hard-living Fintan, for whom 'every evening felt like a Bank Holiday Monday'. To make matters worse, the police had just erected a counter IRA 'Ring of Steel' around the City of London, which Fintan had to negotiate daily to get anywhere. Bored of 'being treated like some Palestinian farmhand', he snapped up our third bedroom and, lo, the hack, quack and insomniac were as one.

Even now, 'Stalker' still needed a nightly 'toke' to wipe away the horrors of the day, and stored his little balls of brown cannabis in an old Cuban cigar case on the mantelpiece. I got up, grabbed the tin and set to work.

Any Cuban would've been proud of my Petit Corona, rolled as it was against the thighs of a virgin. I popped into the kitchen, liberated another Shiraz and flopped back onto the couch.

Two years ago, I'd discovered that supplementing my nightly quota of Shiraz with a big fat joint made my encounters with the recently whacked less terrifying. It was irrational, an affront to logic, scientific heresy, inexplicable. So I stopped trying to rationalise it, lit up, sat back and zoned out.

I'd been next to Liz Little's body this morning.

133

Would her deranged spirit appear to me tonight? If so, could I survive all that terror and torment again?

Was I ready for another Dance with the Dead?

Those slate-grey eyes emerge from the shadows, unblinking, dry, foggy, like old grapes.

I see now the outline of Liz's head and bare shoulders. She sashays towards me. Seductively? Menacingly?

'For one night only,' a clipped British voice announces, 'exclusively for your pleasure ... a Dance with the Dead.'

What is that gloriously ramshackle, stomping, off-kilter tune? Something by Tom Waits?

Her perma-alarmed, straight-line eyebrows look like knocked-over exclamation marks, trying to scrabble back upright.

'Oh my God,' I tell myself, 'she's trying to wake.'

She smiles, letting me know she'll be the one making that decision. Then she tilts her head, curls her top lip into a malignant grimace and flexes her cheek muscles.

I notice now it's only her top half swaying from side to side. She's a glove puppet without a hand. A bundle of dirty green cash falls out of her. Then another. As roll after grubby roll drops to the floor, she starts to collapse, deflate. I must stuff the money back in.

I dive to the floor to grab it, but the cash isn't there. The floor isn't there. I free fall into thick red metallic goo. It swallows me greedily. Holds me under. I feel pin-sharp jabs to my body as my eyes and chest bulge to bursting. I'm drowning. As I fight this liquid hell, I realise the surface above me is solidifying.

Hell is freezing over. What is that damn tune?

I look up through the red glass-like surface to see more red flowing out of two neat round holes in her skull. It cascades down her neck and shoulders, dripping onto the impenetrable transparent plane above me. Plop, plop, plop. Hardening instantly. Trapping me. Devouring me. I must break free. I must break free.

Stars bounce across my vision and implode. A blinding tunnel spins open. Oh my God, so this is what it's like to die.

Chapter 9

Arsenal, North London
Sunday, April 4, 1993; 09.20

I woke in my bed and crept down to the sitting room, like a killer returning to the crime scene.

Please tell me it didn't happen... that I didn't sit on this couch last night and see Liz Little.

The stubbed-out joint confirmed my recent presence; the drop-kicked wine bottle my violent reaction to an episode. Shit.

The red light on the answerphone flashed two missed calls. I pressed 'Play'.

'...oh I hate these awful things ... I need more time than that.'

Mam must have started speaking before the beep.

My heart raced. Mam *never* rang. Something must be seriously up.

She nailed it second time. 'Hi lads, I don't want

135

to worry you but I need to talk to you about your father. Give me a call as soon as ye can. God Bless. Oh, it's your ma by the way. And it's a quarter to nine on Saturday night.'

I jabbed re-dial. It went straight through to their answer machine. I guessed she'd be at Mass... I'd try again later. I wondered what the hell was going on. I sensed Fintan knew something, but was holding back. I decided not to mention the missed calls. I'd tap Mam up later, free from his prying.

I headed to the kitchen. The ashtray told me Fintan had been up for hours. The supplement-strewn kitchen table confirmed he'd already ransacked that day's newspapers. I couldn't imagine the strain of constantly chasing news, second-guessing events, scouring between the lines for fresh angles. He was obsessive. I figured you'd have to be.

'Well,' he said, looking uncharacteristically gloomy, 'how was your wine-induced coma?'

'Deep,' I rasped, 'but all too brief. And yours?'

'I slept a bit better. Liz Little has taken some of the heat off me, at least for now.'

'I'm sure she'll rest more peacefully knowing that.'

I filled a grubby cup with tepid tap water and drank. My sand-blasted throat would've happily sucked it out of a pothole.

'Any sweet, case-cracking dreams?' he asked.

'No,' I said, re-filling the cup so he couldn't read my face.

'Nothing at all?'

'Not a dickie bird. Whatever was going on in my head back then has obviously passed.'

'Obviously,' he said. 'That must've been some other Liz you were screaming about at half past five this morning.'

'I don't remember that at all. Sorry if I woke you.'

I scanned the papers. They'd all followed up on his Liz Little scoop. A rival tabloid even had the gall to label their front page story 'Exclusive'.

'Isn't that outright theft?' I asked.

'Not really. They managed to track down the actor who plays Tosh Lines and get a few quotes out of him. My editor won't be happy about that.'

'Yeah, but you broke the actual story.'

'You don't know my editor.'

He sighed. 'The only reason it made the papers at all is because she'd been on the telly. This is the only currency that matters now: celebrity. There's not one proper crime story in our paper today, or in any of the tabloids.'

'Doesn't exposing randy vicars count?'

'We've got three million unemployed, schizophrenics who should be locked up murdering people on our streets, IRA bombs going off, a war in Bosnia, corrupt cops, the Tories flogging off the nation's assets to their grubby pals, gangsters like Jimmy Reilly on the loose and all we feed people is shite about soap stars and the latest tiff between Charles and Di.'

'Maybe that's what people want, a little light relief.'

'It's not about what people want. It's about what people get, whether they want it or not. Our owner has just forked out a quarter of a billion pounds on TV rights to the football. All he'll let us write about soon will be what's on his TV channels. Or to destroy anyone or anything that gets in the way of his plans for world domination.'

'Oh, come on.' I laughed. 'That's a little Orwellian.'

'Trust me, if he and his ilk get their way, newspapers will be dead in ten years. You'll all be force-fed entertainment 24/7 on your TVs, computers and mobile phones, no escape, leaving the powerful free to do whatever the fuck they want. Investigative journalism will be dead.'

'Not much point risking your neck pursuing Jimmy Reilly then, is there?'

'I said in ten years. We hacks might be drinking in the last-chance saloon, Donal, but it's still our duty to cause lusty, democratic mayhem. Besides, I need a big one. A really big one. The inside track on the taking down of Jimmy Reilly would make me. There'd be half a dozen scoops in that, maybe as many awards. Not to mention the documentary, even a book. Now that newspapers are doomed, I've got to get out there and flash my wares. A scoop like this would make me high-class Florentine Gardens game, as opposed to Finsbury Park gristle.'

'No matter which path you choose, Fint, your depthless humanity will doubtless shine through. What's your relationship like with the man in charge of the Liz Little case then, DS Spence?'

'Non-existent,' he said glumly. 'He doesn't drink or smoke, a real dour Scot. Oh, and he hates the media, especially after the kicking he got a few years back when a major drugs dealer won an appeal. Turns out one of his men illegally bugged

138

a hotel room. He now insists on personally hand-picking his team.'

I visibly sagged.

'That's good for you though. He's desperate to even the score by nailing another major criminal. If you can deliver hard evidence against someone like Jimmy Reilly, he'll welcome you on board with open arms.' He jumped to his feet. 'Which reminds me, forensics aren't finished at Browns-wood. Shall we take a stroll that way, just in case?'

'Just in case of what?'

'Doe-eyed Zoe might be back. And let's face it, bro, you have a solid track record in crime-scene romances, having once seduced the Black Widow herself, Eve Daly.'

Not too long ago, the mere mention of her name would've triggered an internal meltdown. Sometime recently – I couldn't quite pinpoint when – this had cooled to a sort of wounded confusion, a familiar ache I'd almost miss. I was getting over her.

Ready to move on...

Having tangled with that crime-scene tape yesterday, and lost, Zoe looked at me with a curious mixture of amusement and worry, as you might a drunk staggering across a busy street. I feared getting to know her and provoking the mild contempt that my flimsy confidence seemed to engender in any woman I'd met since, well, Eve Daly. I wasn't sure I could handle another knockback.

But I had an in-built defence with Zoe. Before I had the chance to fuck things up emotionally, I needed a professional favour from her, right now.

My pursuit of Liz Little's killer depended upon

139

her saying yes.

As we walked past Arsenal's Highbury Stadium, Fintan pointed to the £10.50 match ticket price.

'It was 9 last season. My pal in sport reckons it'll cost 30 by the Millennium.'

I baulked. 'No one in their right mind is going to pay 30 quid to watch a game of football, I don't care who is playing.'

At the Blackstock Road junction, the squealing brakes of two number 19 double-decker buses battled with a clattering Kango for sonic supremacy. A panicking couple in smart suits overtook us, darting across the road and waving furiously at the bus drivers.

I turned to see a trio of road workers – soggy rollies clamped between their pursed, bloodless lips – wearing the expressions of men jack-hammering to hell. Every main road in London was being turned inside out so that cable TV and the Internet could clasp onto us all.

I watched the second number 19 bus groan off in convoy with the first, ignoring the frantic, door-bashing appeals of the two suits.

I shook my head. 'He only had to open the doors for three seconds.'

Fintan hadn't noticed ... too transfixed by that freshly dug hole.

'Surely this Internet shite can't catch on,' he muttered. 'I mean who in their right mind wants to sit glued to a screen all day?'

We crossed Blackstock then bore right into Brownswood Road, a winding cut-through fashioned from the butt ends of grander side roads.

Grubby garden walls and gable ends stretched unbroken around the first bend, making it feel like a drained brick canal. Past the second junction, cellophane-strangled flowers huddled abjectly beneath the quivering blue tape, like nuns flinching under a gyrating Chippendale: Fintan was right: forensic officers were still combing the scene. My eyes instantly located Zoe, striking even behind a white facemask, her gloved fingers erotically teasing crime-scene grass. She glanced up at us and scowled, those Holly Hunter eyes squinting into bitter little almonds.

Fintan bent down to read the dedications on the flowers. I refused to stoop to such shameless voyeurism. Instead, I closed my eyes and allowed the sombre Sunday gloom to envelop me.

What did Liz's dance mean last night? She'd come to me as a glove puppet, stuffed with cash which tumbled out beyond her control. Had she lost a lot of Reilly's money? Blood had run from her skull and trapped me beneath a red floor ... cash, blood, skull wounds, a floor. Jimmy's precious floor?

Just as the maddeningly abstract charades of previous murder victims eventually led me to their killers, I felt certain that these images would prove critical to her case. But I craved more, to placate those birds of confusion flapping about inside my skull.

Last night, thanks largely to the pot, I had embraced the terror and let her in. I'd do so again, in exchange for precious clues. So, with all my mental strength, I summoned Liz's spirit. I visualised her taking a foothold in my psyche, treading the boards of my subconscious, rehearsing for tonight's second performance.

Poor Liz: the girl who dared to dream. She'd come to London wide-eyed, ravenous, desperate not to fail. She could never go back and admit it hadn't worked out. She'd rather not go back at all.

How proud her parents and friends had been of her TV debut. How careful they were not to dwell on its fleeting insignificance. Liz had explained over and over; it wasn't about the role or the screen time. It was about getting another acting credit towards that all-important Equity Card, and raising her profile. She might just get spotted by someone of influence, and plucked from obscurity, Lana Turner-style.

But her agent had received no follow-up enquiries or offers. Her savings dwindling fast, Liz needed paid work. So did three million other skint, unemployed Brits.

Why slave on your feet in McDonald's or a factory all day when you can earn a fortune lying on your back?

Of course, that's not how it would've been sold to Liz Little. She knew or met someone who worked at the Florentine Gardens, heard how they were always on the lookout for accomplished, trained dancers. Performing in London's West End had been all she'd dreamed of since those first ballet lessons aged four – to follow in the footsteps of her heroine, Audrey Hepburn.

That, in turn, was how she'd sold it to her parents, Duncan and Audrey. She just had to hope that no one from Armley would ever turn up at the Florentine. What a shock they'd get. But that seemed highly improbable; they didn't serve bitter or ale, and charged a week's wages for anything else.

I could only guess at how she'd squared it with her own conscience to prance about naked for the gratification of strange men, then have sex with those who promised to 'take care' of her. But that was her business. Above all else, Liz was striving to make it as a professional actress. Maybe she treated this as her latest role: get into character, get on with the job. Northern grit. I bet she used her classical training to be the best damn dancer in the joint.

Maybe one day, Prince Charming would appear and sweep her away, never to return to the Florentine. He'd provide the security she needed to fearlessly pursue her true ambitions. In the meantime, Holly Golightly entranced rich and powerful men who showered her with expensive gifts and fancy meals. As Truman Capote said of the original, 'not a prostitute, but an American Geisha'.

How then had she upset Jimmy Reilly? Had he fallen under her spell, only to get knocked back? The other theories I liked less. She'd said the wrong thing to the wrong person at Jimmy's expense. About his small cock, big hands or hairy back. He seemed typical of the type – egocentric to the point of God complex. It wouldn't take much to earn the full-set, ten plagues of his biblical wrath. Or, had Liz uncovered some dark secret about Reilly? Was she trying to play him? I needed to find out if she could be that greedy, that naïve.

Whatever she did to earn her wretched end,

Reilly was sending a clear message to the other girls: *Fuck with me and you'll end up either butchered or working the streets.* The Black Dahlia tribute had to be a chilling postscript, designed to reassert his omnipotence: *you all know I did this, but none of you will ever touch me for it.*

'Hey, check this out,' said Fintan, his forefinger pulling out the bottom corner of a hand-written card, attached to a single white lily. I had to bend and lean in close to read the microscopic, feminine writing: *Beautiful Liz, so graceful, elegant and warm. The prettiest flower in the garden. How we'll miss your mischief-making and humor. How I wish I could turn back the clock. Join you one day on one of those trips you so loved, T xxx.*

Fintan didn't even wait for me to finish: 'See the way she's spelt *humor?* The rest is too eloquent and precise for that to have been a mistake. T is an American. It's got to be Tammy, that girl you met at the club.'

My heart sank. I knew what he'd be angling for next; me going back there to tap Tammy up.

'This note doesn't actually tell us anything though, does it?' I said.

'Really, detective? Why does she want to turn back the clock? And what trip is she referring to? Whoever wrote this is a Yank and a close friend to Liz. She must have some idea about what was going on between her and Reilly.'

'Please tell me you're not suggesting we go back to the Florentine?'

'There must be another way of tracking down this Tammy?'

'I've been thinking,' I said, because I had, 'Liz

144

was new in town. Someone must have introduced her to the Florentine, maybe someone who already worked there. The only way Liz would've met someone like that was either at an audition or through her agent.'

Fintan had already locked onto my idea's flight path: 'The agent must have a file of all the women on his books. If one of them works at the Florentine, then bingo. Maybe Tammy's one of his. I'll call him first thing tomorrow, ask what Americans he represents. Maybe "T" is another American dancer. Whoever T is, let's find her, then figure out our next move from there. Going back to the Florentine has to be our last resort.'

I blew out hard to register my whole-hearted agreement. When a scoop tickled Fintan's tabloid snout, he could lose all reason, becoming gung-ho to the point of reckless. Finally, he'd grasped the kamikaze lunacy of braving Reilly's lair again. At least for now...

'Good job we came down here,' he said.

'Can we really expect T, whoever she turns out to be, to speak to us? Especially after what's happened to Liz? We can't protect her.'

'We've got to try,' he said, 'don't forget, you've got a cavalry to call on whenever you need to. They'll be impressed by what you've dug up already about Liz and her connection to a major player like Reilly. If you can deliver a witness from the club, you're well and truly back in the game.'

The Finsbury Park Tavern's front door loftily boasted its credentials as 'a traditional British boozer'. Soulless, soiled and hostile, it proved to be all that and worse. They certainly didn't need to concern themselves with the missing signs on the toilet doors. You just had to follow your nose.

The eye-watering stench of blue urinal cakes made our first 'recovery' pints hard to get down. But we persevered doggedly.

'Yet another woman shunning you after a single encounter then, Donal,' Fintan said.

'Shunning you more like. She read your rag this morning and realised you'd tricked her into talking.'

'I didn't trick her,' he protested. 'It's not my fault she made a lazy assumption and couldn't stop gossiping. She's probably just embarrassed.'

'You could have told her you're a reporter. If you had a decent bone in your body, you would have. Anyway, what are you up to later?'

'I'm meeting a couple of my friendly spooks down at Gower Street for a few jars; should be back about midnight.'

'Hope you've brought your longest spoon with you, supping with those creeps. Why are you buying drinks for spooks?'

'They're buying drinks for me, actually. They're shitting themselves that peace is about to break out in Northern Ireland. That means they're out of a job.'

'They shouldn't worry. It's only been going on for, what, 800 years now?'

'I know, right? You'd put money on Israel/Palestine getting sorted first. But they seem convinced.'

He leaned in. 'They're only telling me that an IRA ceasefire is on the fucking table.'

I snorted dismissively. 'It'll never happen.'

'That's what I said, unless someone has something very juicy on a few of the leaders. They just smiled. That's when I realised they weren't bull-shitting me.'

'So what's this got to do with you?'

'They're trying to carve out a new role for themselves, using their counter-terrorist resources to tackle organised criminals.'

'Like Jimmy Reilly?'

'They didn't mention him by name, but yes. They want me to help them write a briefing for the Home Office. Of course, I'll agree. It's a win/win. If MI5 starts tackling major criminals, I'll have two sources in prime positions inside the organisation. Meanwhile, right now, I've got the inside track on these secret talks, and an IRA ceasefire would be scoop of the century.'

'The auld fella won't be too happy about it,' I said, suddenly remembering Mam's mysterious answerphone message from last night. As soon as I opened my mouth to tell him about it, he changed the subject. 'Who knows? So you think Bernie Moss didn't know Liz had been murdered?'

I wondered why he seemed so jumpy about the subject of Da these days, and made a mental note.

'Unless Bernie's a trained actor, then no way,' I said.' 'He seemed genuinely shocked.'

'If Jimmy had her killed, you'd expect Bernie to be in on it, wouldn't you? I mean he's one of Jimmy's main enforcers.'

'Maybe Bernie hadn't the stomach to hurt her, and Jimmy knew this.'

'Are you kidding? I checked out Bernie's form

this morning. He's been a football hooligan, an animal rights' activist, a hunt sab. He's served a couple of stretches for GBH. He put one fox hunter into a coma.'

'Maybe he draws the line at women, kids and animals. Anyway, if he was involved, we'll nail him, because I've got his prints and DNA.'

He recoiled in surprise.

'Remember the newspaper and cans of beer last night? His and Slob's.'

'Brilliant. Now all you need is a good friend in the forensics department to cross-reference them for you. Mmm, I wonder who that might be...?'

'I don't know, Fint. The way she was back there... Anyway, it's not like I can just walk right up to her and ask her outright, is it?'

'Why not?'

'What do you mean "why not?" Because I'd be asking her to break every rule in the book for me, someone she doesn't even know. Jesus.' I frowned, clutching the pint to my face for comfort.

'That's right, Donal, have a drink. Sit back there and wait for everyone else in your life to take the lead. Have you ever heard of spontaneity? Taking a risk? Blowing a woman away with your verve and daring? The trouble with you is you're inert. A passenger.' He downed the rest of his pint and got to his feet.

'Another?' I said.

'Honestly, you're like a lump of driftwood, Donal, dawdling along aimlessly with no purpose. You need to make things happen in life ... see ya later.'

I ordered another pint. When a third sank easier

still, I knew I was straying into dangerous territory. Time to head home, maybe call Mam, check she's okay.

On the way home, distant church bells chimed 3pm, the homely scent of roast beef wafted across the cooling air and an ache clawed at my insides. Back home, the only time we sat as a family was over Sunday lunch. Dad and Fintan always had something on after, so Mam and me would drive deep into the Slieve Bloom Mountains, take a good hike, maybe stop in for a drink at Giltraps in Kinnitty. The more pointless and aimless our journey, the more meaningfully we talked. Dad and Fintan could never understand that.

At around 4 or 5, I'd cycle to Eve Daly's house where we'd watch MT USA and abuse her estranged dad's collection of fine malts. On summer evenings, we'd jump over her back wall into the golf course and play 'pissed and putt'. In winter, we'd snuggle up and make outrageous predictions about everyone's future.

In London, I'd wake to a house full of people, but bereft of any comfort such as food, drink or a source of heat. So I'd bunker down somewhere that did. Lunchtimes in pubs like Quinn's in Camden or the Spotted Dog in Willesden suggested many thousands of young Irish, Aussies and Kiwis faced the same dilemma. That's how 'The Church' came about.

Lonely ex-Pats needed to drink all Sunday afternoon to forget, but some archaic British law forced pubs to close between 3pm and 7pm. So in the spirit of prohibition, some bright spark hired a large venue and stocked it with cans of

149

beer which his staff gave away for free – once you paid for a ticket on the door.

With fancy dress, drinking games, strippers and a sawdust-covered floor to soak up unspecified spillages, the Church delivered debauchery on a biblical scale. To me, it felt like an 18–30 holiday set in about 1830, for sex-starved Goldrush desperadoes. Laddish, lairy and vulgar – and that was just the drunk Antipodean women. By early evening, those worshippers who'd achieved their goal of oblivious salvation looked capable only of crying themselves to sleep. How I envied them that luxury. For an insomniac, being legless at 5pm came with a massive drawback – I was awake for the 10pm hangover. And so, after three or four ultimately doomed pilgrimages, I never set foot in the Church again.

Sunday afternoons continued to render me antsy and anxious. I'd decided they were good for one thing only, romance. I just needed to find somebody to share them with.

'Fuck it,' I declared to no one in particular, fishing around for a 20p piece. I found a phone box on Blackstock Road and dialled Zoe's mobile.

Perhaps I should have rehearsed this, I thought, as her answer machine's shrill tone demanded instant ad-libbed sentiments.

'Hi Zoe, Donal Lynch here, the man who fell head over heels yesterday at the Liz Little murder scene. Not *for* Liz Little, of course. I didn't suddenly like fancy her or something. Jesus, that'd be weird. I just tripped over the tape, like I'm tripping over my tongue now. I'm sure you remem-

150

ber who I mean. *Sniff.* Er, me. Anyway, can I say sorry firstly for my brother's behaviour. He's a very underhand and devious character. I sometimes think that we can't actually be related...'

The tone beeped and I cursed loudly. But I hadn't finished or given her a number to call, so I dialled again. As her greeting repeated its demand for a brief message, I vowed to supply just that, as unruffled as possible.

'Zoe, sorry, I was going on a bit there. Anyway, you asked me to let you know when we made any progress with this case and I think we have. In fact, I think we know who did it, the difficult part will be pinning it on him. But I have a few ideas on that score, as I'm sure you will. So I was wondering...'

The beeping caused me to scream hysterically and slam the receiver hard into the dull silver metal of the phone, over and over. 'Fucking technology,' I howled. When a knock sounded on the glass, I felt my eyes bulge to bursting. *This fucker's gonna get it...*

'What the fuck is your problem,' I bellowed, dropping the receiver and spinning around. Zoe had that worried/amused look on again. I'd already committed to hoofing the door and it now cracked against her shoulder with some force, causing her to tumble backwards.

She managed to stay on her feet, barely. Her eyes screamed wounded bewilderment, like I'd just reversed over her dog for a laugh. My face literally steamed red, like a microwaved Santa.

'Zoe, I'm so sorry,' I protested, 'I was just leaving you a message...'

'What is the matter with you?'

'I'm an insomniac,' I said pleadingly, without thinking.

'What's that got to do with anything?'

'And I've got sleep paralysis,' I added meaningfully, as if that explained all that had gone on here, with plenty to spare.

'Is that why you were ... vandalising the phone?'

'Like I said Zoe, I was trying to leave you a message. Please don't listen to your messages.'

She scowled. 'What?'

I realised I was panting – it's never a good sound. Or look.

'I'm – going – to – go – now,' she said, enunciating each word slowly and loudly, as if talking down a nutter.

'How did you find me here?' I smiled, sounding just like that nutter.

'I didn't *find* you,' she snapped, shaking her head in disbelief. 'I saw someone trashing a public phone and decided to intervene. Vandalism is my pet peev.'

I nodded solemnly, mouth pursed.

'Mine too.'

The laugh came involuntarily, from somewhere low in her throat, seemingly catching the rest of her off guard. It burst through her nose as an alarming snuffle, causing her to clamp her hand to her face. She quickly caved in to it, bending to let those hysterical peals of laughter pour out of her.

I tried to laugh along, out of embarrassment mostly.

She recovered, finally, wiping her eyes and

shaking her head in apparent disbelief.

'Can we start again?' I asked.

'I think we'd better,' she gasped, helping herself to a good gulp of breath.

'But please don't listen to your answerphone messages.'

'Are you kidding?' she said, 'I can't wait.'

Out of the corner of my eye, I could see the neighbourhood's dullest pub preparing for its Sunday afternoon lock-in. I knew this was my chance.

'Zoe, do you remember asking me to let you know when we caught Liz's killer?'

She nodded urgently, eyes now serious and searching.

'I think I've figured out who was behind it. And I've got an idea about how we might be able to prove it. But I need your help.'

'Name it.'

'That pub over there is so numbingly dull that it doesn't even get full on match days. Yet they persist with a Sunday lock-in that feels like drinking in an old people's home. No one will ever see us in there. Can I buy you a drink and fill you in.'

'Blimey, you're a bit forward.' She smiled.

'Eventually today, I will say something right.'

'Believe it when I hear it.'

Chapter 10

The King's Head, Blackstock Road N4
Sunday, April 4, 1993; 15.20

'Whoever owns this pub loves the colour brown,' I whispered at the bar.

'I don't think I've ever seen this particular shade on a paint chart,' she gurned in mock horror, and I loved her for it.

'What do you think they'd call it?' she asked.

'Ooh I don't know. Monkey-shit brown?'

'I'm thinking more Bog-body Mahogany.'

'Nice. And spoken like a true forensics officer.'

The pub's funereal atmosphere was perfectly topped off by the barman's mournful pale face, tragi-comic comb-over and slow-witted rural Northern Irish lilt.

'Well?' he said, as if he wasn't expecting anyone at all, ever.

'A pint of Guinness for me,' I said, 'and...?'

'Same please,' said Zoe.

'I'll bring them over to ye,' he announced sadly.

'Do you do sandwiches?' she asked.

'Sure there's no money in it,' he said, shaking his head in genuine, wide-eyed regret.

The pub was all quiet corners so we just sat at a table in the middle.

Zoe had read the *Sunday News*' splash about Liz Little; including her own quotes which Fintan had

154

attributed to 'a source inside the investigation'.

'What an utter bastard,' she said, but with a sense of mild awe, 'but a clever bastard, and charming with it.'

'All part of the Irish brand.' I smiled. 'What he couldn't include for legal reasons was where Liz worked and who for.'

Zoe knew nothing of Jimmy Reilly or his monstrous criminal career so, as soon as our pints landed, I kicked off our maiden date with those gory nuggets.

Before long, she looked thoroughly sickened.

'Sorry, I know some of it is pretty gruesome,' I said.

'Oh, it's not that,' she said, 'gore doesn't faze me, not in my line of work. It's just that I really hate Guinness.'

'Me too!' I said, way too loudly. 'I thought it would make me look more intelligent, you know, with their trendy ads and all.'

'It didn't achieve that I'm afraid, Donal.' She smiled. 'It is only beer after all.'

'You're one to talk. Why did you order it if you hate it so much?'

'I don't know. It always *looks* so appealing. It should be gorgeous. But it actually tastes how this place feels, if you know what I mean.'

'Yeah, sad and sour.'

'That's what they should call this pub, The Sad and Sour.'

'What can I get you instead?' I said, rising to my feet.

'Not that kind of girl,' she said, shooting up too. 'I'm gagging for a large red wine. What

155

about you?'

'Now you're talking, lady.'

I ran her through our visit to the Florentine Gardens – the glum Slavs, vanishing Tammy, bonding with Bernie and clobbering Slob.

She wanted me to run through it all again, in detail, so I raised her round by ordering a whole bottle of red.

As the barman with suicidal puppy eyes planted the bottle on our table, I sensed Zoe shifting uncomfortably. Was I pushing it too far?

'Don't worry Zoe, I'm not trying to get you pissed,' I assured her. 'It's just my liver celebrating.'

'What has your poor liver got to celebrate?'

'Meeting the female liver of its dreams! You can keep up, hallelujah!'

She raised a deadpan eyebrow: 'You Irish boys and your charm.'

As the wine reddened her lips and softened her eyes, Zoe began asking more personal questions. I told her about my professional fall from grace – retold as a grossly unjust suspension over a slanderous news article – and how I needed this case to get back onto a murder squad.

She seemed sympathetic, but my misery memoir had killed the euphoria of earlier, somehow overshadowing my feats of derring-do at the Florentine. I needed to get her excited about catching Liz's killer again; time for my *pièce de résistance*.

'Before I got out of the Florentine, I grabbed hold of these,' I said, opening my leather bag to reveal a *Times* newspaper and two cans of Heineken, all safely stowed in sealed freezer bags.

156

She looked at my exhibits, then at me, her eyes hardening, sobering up.

'These are the cans Bernie and Slob were guzzling out of, and that's Bernie's crossword. I was wondering if you could take their prints and DNA from these items, then see if they match anything at the scene. If we can place either of them at Brownswood early Saturday morning, we can start building a case against Jimmy Reilly.'

Her forehead scrummed down into a *let me get this straight* frown. 'You want me to bring these exhibits to my boss, explain what you've just told me?'

'Not exactly, Zoe. I was wondering if you could do it unofficially, as a favour to me.'

I could sense an instinctive resistance to going off-grid, bending the rules. I'd been the same myself, not so long ago, before my crash course in the dark arts of policing. So I spoke next not to Zoe, but to my old self.

'I could go through official channels, of course, but I'd have to make a statement and admit that I didn't have a warrant to remove material from the Florentine Gardens, and that I wasn't even there on official police business. My boss didn't know I was there at all. The police lawyer would probably throw this stuff out before it would even get to a lab. And, like I said, Reilly supposedly has a lot of dodgy cops on his payroll. I'd hate for these cans to get lost.'

I couldn't tell if my appeals were tilting any of her scales. But it felt useful reiterating the reasons why we needed to keep this under the radar – if only as a rehearsal for any official enquiries later.

157

'The thing is Zoe, if you find anything that puts either of them at the murder scene, I'll take that information directly to the straightest senior cop I know. That's our best chance of getting justice for Liz, possibly our only chance.'

'I wished you'd brought me to a busy pub,' she said, 'sitting here like this makes me feel exposed, like we're in that Edward Hopper painting.'

'Nighthawks! I love that picture. I should have consulted Fintan. He's an expert at this kind of thing.'

'No,' she said, looking into my eyes, 'your brother's devious. What you're trying to do here is actually very honourable.'

'But...'

'I'm going to the loo now,' she said, a hint of a smile playing on her lips. 'Can you keep an eye on my handbag until I get back? I'd hate for someone to tamper with it.'

No matter how much Shiraz I sank or blow I sucked that Sunday night, Liz wouldn't come to me.

Instead, I had both of my recurring dreams about Da, over and over.

In the first, I walk into a sparse room to a soundtrack of 'Love, Sex, Intelligence' by The Shamen. Da's lying on a bare, stained mattress, on his front, naked save for a hood over his head. Like Liz, he disappears at the waist. I notice dried brownish blood below the right side of the hood, on his neck and right shoulder. As I get closer to the hood, I realise that it's packed full of brain, wriggling like maggots. The hood turns. As it does so, the material is devoured by the brain maggots.

'Why won't you help me?' Da's voice pleads, over and over.

In the second, he's facing our open fire at home, drinking whiskey alongside a bearded man whose face I never fully see.

'Where have you been?' he asks the man.

'Away visiting some relations,' the man replies.

They both laugh knowingly at this in-joke. The fire hisses and starts to bang. Their laughs grow maniacal, scary.

Every time I started awake, I asked Liz where she was. In the past, I only had to attend the scene of a recent murder to get a visit from the victim. She turned up last night, after my first trip to Brownswood Road. I'd been there again today – why hadn't she shown?

As dawn broke and sleep finally came for me, so did a realisation. I'd been to two places connected to her death on Saturday – Brownswood Road and the Florentine Gardens.

Sunday, I'd only been to one. Brownswood Road. She didn't die there.

Liz Little must have died at the Florentine Gardens.

Chapter 11

Hornsey, North London
Monday, April 5, 1993; 10.30

When my pager instructed me to attend Hornsey Mortuary in North London at 10.30am, I let out a little yelp of joy – it was bound to be livelier than the Cold Case Unit office.

The dismal beige bone shop sat at the end of a suburban cul-de-sac beyond a drooping traffic-barrier gate – truly the end of the road.

The receptionist saw my paged request from Dr Edwina Milne and raised me a striking, bespectacled blonde in her early 20s.

'Hi Donal, Erika,' she stated flatly, no hand offered. 'This way please.'

I could've sworn I knew her from somewhere – no man would forget this voluptuous Viking in a lifetime. But I didn't say so, for fear of sounding like some sort of weirdo knicker-sniffer.

'What's your role here, Erika?' I asked instead, trailing her up a corridor reeking of bleach, working hard not to check out her arse.

She reached a door and held it open for me with an arched smile. 'I'm an Anatomical Pathology Technologist,' she said, 'but mortuary assistant is fine.'

I made it past her into the starkly bare 'consultation room', only for my heart to trip over her

160

honeyed fragrance. I'd always been a sucker for expensive scent. In a chemically flayed building like this, she smelt sweeter than a midnight meadow of jasmine.

'Is Dr Milne going to see me here then?' I said, my voice shaky and high.

'She's upstairs, on the second of seven post-mortems booked in for today, so you'll have to do with me, I'm afraid.'

You'll do just fine, Erika, I managed not to say.

'Take a seat,' she said, addressing her clipboard and perching on the chair furthest from mine.

'Wow, seven post-mortems in a day.'

'We perform about seven hundred here a year.'

'Out of how many bodies?'

'About three thousand, so I feel pretty inured to death. As I'm sure you do too, detective.'

'If only,' I said, and she threw me a quizzical look. Before she had a chance to speak, I hit her with the most clichéd question in modern history.

'All this death must get you down sometimes though?'

'I think working in a hospital mortuary would, where it's mostly elderly and ill. But here we get jumpers, murder victims, traffic accidents. I know it sounds dark but it can be quite fascinating.'

'So what does the average day entail for an Anatomical Pathology Technologist then?'

'Helping with autopsies mostly. Releasing bodies to families. And the toughest part–' she sighed '–viewings'.

'I imagine that's about as socially awkward as it gets, asking someone to positively identify a body.'

She laughed, but kindly.

161

'Everyone says that now, thanks to American TV "Positively Identify". Like you could "Negatively Identify" someone.'

Jesus, no need to be pedantic, I thought.

'Sorry,' she said suddenly, 'I'm not very good around living people.'

'Don't you mean just "people",' I felt like saying, 'as dead people don't fucking know you're there.' But I'd been enjoying her frank insights into a very secretive world. 'I disagree,' I lied instead.

'Thanks.' She almost smiled. 'Funnily enough, it's a calm, predictable job dealing with the dead. It's only when the living get involved that it can become ... messy. Most British people don't see death close up until they're in no fit emotional state to deal with it. Grieving is not a good time to see your first dead body. We do our best to soften the blow, you know, we wire their mouths shut and put plastic caps under the eyelids so they don't look sunken...'

'Euugh, pulling open the eyelid of a corpse and sliding something in ... I couldn't do it.'

'The caps are crucial: they have ridges around the edge which stop the eyelids popping open. Can you imagine that happening during a viewing?'

My laugh earned a dazzling display of her dentistry, which looked way beyond a mortuary assistant's pay scale.

She went on: 'But we don't do hair and make-up, that's funeral parlours, so when they come here, they see this grey, rubbery mannequin and freak out.'

'Luckily, both my grannies looked like that alive.'

162

'I persuaded Elizabeth's parents not to view her,' she said sadly. 'We had her dental records. Why put them through the trauma?'

'So a closed coffin then, for her funeral?'

She nodded.

I couldn't imagine losing a loved one, and not seeing them one last time. No matter what state they were in.

'Do they not say it's better, psychologically, for grievers to see the person dead, you know, to help with closure?'

She tilted her head to one side defiantly. 'Not on this occasion, surely?'

'So what happens to her now?'

'She's in a body bag in a drawer downstairs, re-frigerated to minus-8 degrees centigrade. She'll stay there until after the inquest. As soon as the death certificate is signed, we'll pass the body over to the family's undertakers. You know the worst part?'

'It gets worse?'

'We have to invoice her family for the cost of her staying here. Fifteen pounds per week.'

'After all that, I think this pathology report might actually cheer me up.'

'I doubt that,' she said, perusing her clipboard for a place to start.

'Basically, what I've got here are extracts from Dr Milne's full report which has yet to be re-leased. She's letting you have this because she's a big fan of the Cold Case Unit. As she says, you've emptied a lot of our refrigerated drawers. I don't know how much you already know...'

'I'll have it all, thanks Erika.'

163

She listed the injuries I'd seen Saturday morning, finishing with those mysterious gouges out of her flesh.

Her soft, secretive blue eyes shot up to mine. 'Off the record, we'll be briefing the coroner that these appear to have been made by some sort of small creature, but that won't go into the report. It's too lurid and sensational. The papers would go crazy.'

Her eyes shot back to business.

'Now, internal injuries. Subject X-rayed for foreign objects inside her body. An A3 domestic battery had been inserted into her anus. Blunt trauma injury to rib cage, skull and upper right arm. Small amount of bleeding in the sub arachnoid space on the right side of the brain, consistent with blows to the head.'

She glanced up. 'The truth is, in a case like this it's impossible to isolate a single or even sequential cause of death, so we'll be recording it as blunt instrument trauma to the skull, and pretty much making up a time.'

The clipboard lured her back.

'Stomach empty so hadn't eaten for at least eight hours prior to death. Microscopic samples of unidentified red matter found inside the wounds to her skull.'

My mind flashed back to Liz's visit – that crimson-coloured liquid pouring from her head injuries.

'What colour was this, exactly?'

'Dark red it says here.'

'Can I have a sample, to take to forensics?'

'The report states it's probably too small an amount to test.'

'But it's been isolated?'

'I would think so, as it's listed, most likely on sticky tape.'

'Could I sign that out before I leave please?'

'Er, yes, I suppose you can.'

'Thanks.'

'Last thing, a sample of hair found in the victim's right hand. Microscopic examination confirmed it to be human, damage to roots indicate it had been forcibly removed from the scalp of another person. And this is where it gets weird...'

She looked up at me, her painstakingly coiffured eyebrows arching in horrified fascination. 'We were able to trace this hair to the original owner, because we carried out an autopsy on her just four months ago. We noted that the pigment distribution and the scale patterning matched. This was later confirmed by DNA. The hair in her hand belonged to a street prostitute named Valerie Gillespie.'

My jaw fell.

Erika looked surprised. 'You know the case?'

'I remember she was fished out of Wood Green reservoir in plastic bags. She was identified by her breast implants.'

'Edwina's a very smart lady.'

My mind reeled. How did Liz Little come to be clutching the hair of someone murdered four months earlier?

Erika shrugged, seemingly inured to even giving a shit.

Then I had an idea. *Hang on a minute, I'm in the mortuary, why don't I ask the lady herself?*

'Can I see Valerie's body?'

165

'She's not here,' said Erika. 'I signed her out myself.'

'Another closed casket, I suppose?'

She nodded. 'It's the implants that made her stand out, if you excuse the pun.' She smiled. 'Now I've really got to press on. Are you okay finding your own way out?'

I nodded and she bustled to the door.

'I thought the bodies in unsolved murder cases are supposed to be kept for a year?' I said, but she'd already gone.

Only my brain groaned and strained harder than the W7 bus back to Finsbury Park.

Why did Liz Little have locks of Valerie Gillespie's hair clasped in her cold, dead right hand? Her killer must have planted it there. But why? The pathologist's notes stated that the hair had been forcibly ripped from Valerie's head – presumably during her violent end. No matter which way I looked at it, I kept drawing the same conclusions.

Whoever killed Valerie Gillespie had kept a chunk of her yanked-out hair as a trophy. He then killed Liz Little and planted Valerie's hair on her body as a signature. He was letting us know that he'd murdered both women.

Why would Jimmy Reilly murder a crack-addict streetwalker like Valerie Gillespie, then boast about it by planting her hair on Liz Little? It made no sense.

I began to question why I'd been so convinced that Reilly had killed Liz in the first place. She worked at his seedy hostess club. So what? This fact alone didn't implicate him. She'd met hundreds of rich, powerful men at the Florentine and, no doubt, maintained the more enjoyable/profitable of these relationships independently of the club. Any one of these men could have had her rubbed out, for any number of reasons.

Tammy, the Yank temptress, may have had toxic intel to spill Saturday night. How did I know if any of it splashed Jimmy Reilly? Maybe she was about to unmask another suspect – a member of staff or a regular john? At the last moment, she elected not to take that risk and disappeared. After the horrors that befell Liz Little, who could blame her?

As for my extended stay at the Florentine, no actual threats had been made or force used. Bernie had even stood me a couple of cans of lager – hardly a hostile action. If questioned by police, he'd insist I could've walked away at any time. His boss just wanted to know why I'd come to his club with my gutter-press brother.

I comforted myself that at least our brief, covert pursuit of Reilly had caused no real damage to the official and, no doubt, judiciously open-minded Liz Little murder investigation.

Straight-laced DS Spence and his crack team would be painstakingly piecing together her final hours, tracking down the last people to see her alive. They'll be seizing the Florentine's interior CCTV and receipts. This week, a lot of very influential men will be fielding awkward phone calls about their nocturnal assignations. How the Catholic/class warrior in me would relish such a task. *Oh, squirm all ye Unfaithful!*

As a cop, I'd learned that the rich need constant reminding that they aren't above the law. So we'd leave messages with their suspicious, unfulfilled wives: make sure hubby calls the Liz Little incident room urgently, about her murder at the Florentine Gardens.

WIFE: *What are the Florentine Gardens, dear?*

HUSBAND: *A restaurant, I think, darling. Don't ask me, the PA books these things. I just get into the taxi and arrive.*

WIFE (TO HERSELF): *Another one for the divorce dossier, chump.*

Spence's squad will smoke out all of Liz's enemies: lovers, embittered exes, stalkers, rivals – anyone with a grievance against her, petty or grave, real or imagined.

I felt confident that the weird stuff – the unexplained bite marks on her body, the inserted battery, the miniscule splashes of red paint, Valerie's hair in her hand – would all fall into place once they narrowed down everyone who wished her harm. As my old boss Shep used to so often misquote: *The light of lights always looks upon the motive, not the deed.*

As the bus doors gasped open at Finsbury Park station, I took a belly-deep sigh of my own. Thank God I hadn't charged into the Liz Little incident room with any of our wilder theories about Jimmy Reilly. Today's follicular twist would have scalped me; what little reputation I had left ripped away more emphatically than Valerie's limp locks. As I'd found to my cost in the past, the tag of 'fantasist' is a hard one to shake.

Of course, the whole pursuit of Reilly had been Walter Mitty's idea. Fintan's fantastical theories might score A-Stars in the tabloid 'School of

Skulduggery' but, as a serving detective, I needed to wise up. Stick to the facts and consider only hard evidence.

Unless we found something irrefutably damning against Jimmy Reilly – Bernie/Slob/his DNA at the Liz Little murder scene, or the mysterious 'T' willing to testify – I wouldn't be mentioning his name again. But these two leads still lived and demanded following up. As I slid two 20p coins into a public phone, I prayed that at least one of them had delivered. If so, that would surely book my ticket onto Spence's squad.

I called Fintan first and relayed the Hornsey Mortuary headlines. After repeating the word 'fuck' several times, he hit back with news from Liz's fruit-bat agent, Roger Alsop:

- No Americans on his books; he wouldn't countenance such a thing.
- No women on his books called Tammy; he wouldn't countenance such a thing.
- No women on his books matching Tammy's appearance.

When Fintan asked if any of his female clients might also be moonlighting at the Florentine Gardens, the old queen exploded: 'That tart Liz Little has completely besmirched my reputation.'

I next called Zoe, praying that she'd turned up something, anything. Of course, she couldn't talk about her moonlighting for me over the phone, so I asked her out.

'Yes, I think I can do that detective,' she said stiffly.

'Great. Lincoln's Inn Fields in half an hour?'

'Certainly shall. Speak soon.'

She arrived late, downcast.

'You don't need to tell me.' I smiled, getting up from the bench.

'I'm sorry, Donal,' she said, slumping down on the seat, deflated, child-like.

I really wanted to give her a hug.

'I got in at seven especially,' she said finally, 'with the worse hangover ever. I had to pretend I was under the weather.'

'Can I get you something to eat?'

'I've got to get back,' she said, 'sorry. My line manager's a prick. A clever prick. He sensed I was up to something and he's watching me like a hawk.'

'Thanks so much for doing this for me, Zoe.'

She groaned. 'I feel like I've let you down.'

'That's good actually,' I said, letting her confused gaze survey me for a few seconds. 'Now I don't feel so bad about asking you for another favour.'

I slipped the transparent pouch out of my pocket and into her hands. She studied it closely.

'What is this?'

'Not sure. They found it in Liz's hair.'

'I can't see anything.'

'Tiny droplets on the sticky tape, between the glass.'

'It's virtually not there.'

'Could you get it tested? It's the only thing we've got left.'

'What are you hoping it is?'

'I don't know. They found those bits inside her

170

head injuries. It's a long shot but maybe it'll lead us to the murder weapon.'

'I doubt there's enough here to properly identify it,' she said, hauling herself back up, 'but I'll do my best.'

She turned to me, her big eyes smiling.

'I had a really good time last night, Donal. Thank you. It's been a while since I've laughed so hard.'

'Me too,' I said. 'Hey, there's some lovely pubs round here. Why don't we do it again some evening, after you finish work?'

She beamed. 'That'd be great.'

I remembered yesterday's 'seize the day' pep talk from Fintan, squeezed my fists and blurted: 'What about tonight?'

Her smile flicked to low beam. 'It's tricky. I'd have to make arrangements.'

I wondered what she meant by that.

'Let me know, either way,' I said, reaching into my pocket for a business card. 'It sounds like you can't really talk when I call. Maybe you can call me, you know, when clever prick isn't spying on you.'

'When is a good time for you?'

'With you on the other end, Zoe, any time at all!'

'I'm just going over to that bin now, to puke.'

'Hey, that's about as romantic as I get.'

'Thank God for that.'

Her smile fell away. She lingered, opened her mouth and closed it again, like a singer who'd forgotten the words.

'If it's tricky...' I started.

'No, it's fine, really,' said Zoe, nodding uncertainly. 'It's just that there's something I need to
talk to you about actually. Before, you know, we
decide if we want to ... take things further.'

'Well, as long as it's not a venereal disease,' I
chirped, immediately regretting it.

She blinked slowly, as if using her eyelids to
deflect my gross remark.

'I'll call you,' she said, raising her left hand into
a forlorn little wave. She wasn't looking at me as
she turned away and walked off.

'Fuck,' I muttered to myself, 'what's all that
about?'

Chapter 12

Cold Case Unit, Vauxhall, South London
Monday, April 5, 1993; 14.15

'Lynch,' called Barrett from his office door, 'it's
your lucky day.'

By the time I sat down, he was already installed
behind his chaotic desk, engrossed in a piece of
paper. He liked to make visitors wait, clearly
believing it reinforced his flimsy authority.

'You're keen to get back onto a live murder
squad, Lynch?' he said finally, not looking up.

'Yes, sir.'

'You've certainly made that abundantly clear
from day one, haven't you?' he added, slurring
slightly, his strained nasal breathing and flushed

face confirming a grape-fuelled lunch.

'I have, sir,' I said uncertainly, trying to weigh up how much my overt ambition had irked him. Was he now angling a chainsaw to my impudent ambition?

He looked up at last. 'How familiar are you with this Valerie Gillespie case?'

'I'd say superficially, guv, to be honest.'

His closed mouth sigh grew into a whiney hum, as if he'd swallowed a model World War II fighter plane. He drove home his irritation by noisily smacking and unsmacking his wine-parched lips, over and over.

'You've been focussing on these unsolved prostitute murders for quite some time now, Lynch.'

'Yes, sir. But I've been looking for trends, links in MO, that kind of thing. I haven't really dug down deeply into a single case.'

'That's not quite how I've sold it to the Assistant Commissioner.'

'Sir?'

'As you know, the Yard is keen on us assisting with ongoing cases. As soon as they connected Liz Little to Gillespie, they were on the phone demanding to know how we can help. I've told them you're something of an expert on the Gillespie case.'

'Well, sir, if you give me a couple of days...'

He stood suddenly and lurched past me. He flung his office door open with such gusto that the breeze rattled his picture frames and rustled my neck hairs.

'DS Spence from the Liz Little murder squad is expecting you tomorrow morning, Holloway

Road station, ten o'clock sharp.'

I stood and turned silently, my air supply zapped off.

As I walked out, his stale Claret breath hissed into my right ear: 'We're all under scrutiny here, Lynch. Don't let us down.'

I pulled up the Gillespie murder folder on my computer and checked the time – just after 2.30pm. The content amounted to less than a hundred files. I could grind through this lot in three hours – provided I kept my notes brief, which felt apt. DS Spence would want the baby, not the birth.

I didn't require motivation: make a strong impression and Spence might poach me right away. I took a look around at the tired old lions slumbering in the shade. No one else here would take on this extra workload, let alone responsibility. Not while there were bars open. This could be my moment in the sun. I needed to make it count.

I also needed to find out for myself how the murder of two women at polar ends of the prostitution spectrum could be linked. To me, it simply didn't stack up.

The pathology report made me think otherwise.

Like Liz, Valerie Gillespie had been carved up with considerable expertise, but into six parts – head, torso, two legs, two arms. I jotted down my first point – there can't be many homicidal maniacs out there with the skills required to expertly dismember a body.

Other connections to Liz leaped out.

A grade 'C' battery had been found inserted

into Valerie's anus. She'd suffered blunt force trauma to the head, which the pathologist cited as the most likely cause of death.

But there were marked differences too. Valerie's killer had used a domestic iron to disfigure her face and breasts when alive, not a knife. There were no mysterious gouges of flesh removed from her body. She'd suffered multiple cigarette burns to her arms and neck. And, whereas Liz had been virtually put on display, Valerie had been expertly weighed in water with the express intention that she'd never be found.

I switched briefly to an overview of people interviewed. They'd checked out the usual suspects in Valerie's life: exes, relatives, old friends. All had been eliminated from the enquiry, including her 62-year-old sugar daddy Philip Armstrong. Everything pointed to a punter.

I knew only too well how easy it was for someone to murder a streetwalker. The tricky part ... getting rid of her body. I returned to the pathology report to note all the key facts relating to her disposal.

Body changes showed she'd been dead for about a week, but the insects present suggested she'd been exposed to air for just two or three days. Her killer had stored her dead body somewhere, for a matter of days.

No mention had been made of hair ripped from her head. Perhaps it didn't seem significant at the time, especially in light of her other heinous injuries. But now two murder investigations hinged on this bizarre little detail. I noted this at the top of my page, circling it twice.

According to witness statements, the last people to see Valerie alive had been a couple of street-walkers at King's Cross, ten days before her body had been found. CCTV captured the trio engaged in a ferocious catfight. When questioned, the women accused Valerie of encroaching on their territory. Valerie's 'big mistake', they explained, had been to tout for business without a pimp. The same CCTV alibied the pair; their punishing *punter/crack score* routine accounted for virtually every hour of their days and nights throughout that time.

As far as I could see, scant effort had been made to trace Valerie's movements during the 'lost four days' between her vanishing from King's Cross and getting killed. Officers had scoured CCTV footage taken around King's Cross, found nothing and given up. Where had she spent that time, and with whom? Presumably she still needed cash and crack.

Those 'lost' days were absolutely critical to tracing her killer. At some point during that period, she'd been abducted, held somewhere, tortured and dumped. Someone must have seen *something*.

I moved onto the scene of crime reports.

The black plastic bags and bricks used to dump her body parts could be bought at any hardware store and didn't carry reference numbers.

A couple of hundred yards from the reservoir, detectives discovered a bird watcher's hut containing a transistor radio, blankets and a torch, all wiped clean of prints. Burnt pieces of wooden pallet, food cans and cigarettes were found on an outside fire dated less than a week old, again

176

minus anything evidential. Whoever killed her had been forensically aware. Experienced.

He'd murdered before.

The forensic psychologist's report drew the same conclusion. Typically, the bulk of his observations could have been delivered by anyone with a taste for True Crime.

The suspect will be aged between 35 and 50 ... he has loathed women since puberty, possibly through an unwilling early sexual encounter, possibly with a relative ... he will have sexually assaulted and raped women before, and had 'built up' to murder ... he has poor education, a menial job, an interest in porn, hunting and fishing, a record for petty crimes.

However, he added a series of general observations about sexual sadistic murders that could prove useful.

First: *Offenders subject the victim to anal rape, forced fellatio, vaginal rape and foreign object penetration, in decreasing order. The majority of offenders force their victims to engage in three or more of these acts.*

I couldn't help concluding that, as A3 batteries had been found inside Liz and Valerie, they'd suffered all four. I read on.

The primary cause of pleasure for the offender isn't these sex acts but the pain caused to the victim.

Physical violence is focussed on the sex organs, genitalia and breasts.

Sexually sadistic acts may include biting of areas with sexual associations, including thighs, buttocks, neck and abdomen.

He topped this off with personal observations of his own. The most relevant to these cases being: *The offender's vehicle will be altered for use in abduction and torture, including disabled windows and doors, sound proofing and installing police scanners.*

Occasionally, the body may be transported to a location that increases the chances of discovery because the offender wants the excitement derived from the publicity that the body's discovery generates. This is known as 'staging'.

With foreign object insertion, sexual arousal occurs most frequently with the victim's expression of pain, and is evidenced by sexual fluids or possibly defecation at the scene.

He then added a note regarding the specific object inserted into Valerie.

'The symbolism of the battery shouldn't be overlooked or ruled out. It may be an expression of what the offender considers his, as yet, untapped power. Or of the total control he believes he can exert over the women he selects. It appears to be a personation or signature and will likely feature in his next attack.'

Despite the fact Valerie had been targeted by a serial killing maniac, her case failed to get any national media attention. Fintan's brutal words chimed:

It's different when a 'good' woman is murdered … that creates a threat to all women. That sells papers.

Paucity of publicity meant a scarcity of calls to the incident room – less than a dozen in total. One of them caught my eye. A man claiming to be a Garda in Birr, Co. Offaly, in Southern Ireland, called anonymously and advised the team to check out a rapist with convictions in the Republic called Robert Conlon, in his 40s and originally from Foxburrow, near Roscrea.

An officer from the team contacted the regional

Garda headquarters in Birr and spoke to Detective Superintendent John Keegan, who claimed that no record of a convicted rapist of this name or anything similar existed.

Three days later, the mysterious Garda informant made a second call to the incident room. Once again, he refused to reveal his identity but claimed that Conlon was staying in the Camden Town area of North London and getting help from the local Irish centre. Why did the Garda not give his name? Why hadn't the squad checked out this second, specific lead? And surely a call to the police station closest to Conlon's original home in Foxburrow, Roscrea would've been the best bet for background information?

I dialled Fintan's mobile. Before moving to London, he'd been a crime reporter for the Irish Press in Dublin. If, over the last quarter of a century, a sadistic rapist called Robert Conlon had been operating in the Republic, he'd know about it.

'Hang on 'til I get outside,' he shouted above the unmistakable din of a bar. I'd forgotten how Sunday newspaper journalists spent Monday to Wednesdays getting pissed.

'You're working late,' he said finally, drawing on a cigarette.

'You're drinking early, more like. Listen, I've been asked to put together a precis of the Valerie Gillespie case for Spence tomorrow morning. Get this. The Gillespie investigation received an anonymous tip off about a rapist from Foxburrow in Offaly called Robert Conlon. Any bells ringing?'

'Convicted in Ireland?'

'Yes, of rape, according to the source.'

179

'Unless it was a long, long time ago, I'd have heard of him. Jesus, I covered that patch as a local reporter.'

'Well, it can't be that long ago. He's supposedly in his 40s.'

Had someone taken a sledgehammer to a tank, I thought, or was that the sound of a gargantuan ego being violently dented?

'Robert Conlon, normal spelling?' he asked.

'Yes, no middle name given.'

'If this Conlon exists,' he snapped, 'I'll find him. Leave it with me.'

Chapter 13

Holborn, London
Monday, April 5, 1993; 18.00

Zoe failed to call so I did, casually suggesting that we meet in the Princess Louise pub near her office. Of course it had been anything but a casual suggestion. I was already there.

I'd left work early to scope out all the local boozers for romantic potential. With its etched glass, bar lamps and dark, wooden panels, this temple to Victorian London won hands down. I'd even got there early enough to bag an intimate little booth down the back, where I battled nervous hands to pace my drinking.

She turned up with her hair down, lips scarlet and a skirt so tight it would make a dead Bishop

180

kick a hole through his coffin lid.

'Wow, you look absolutely knock-out,' I said, perhaps a little too surprised for it to be a total compliment.

'Thanks,' she smiled and I loved her for just taking the praise. In my experience, anything else can get horribly complicated.

'I see you've already got the red-wine lip camo in place,' I joked, as she slid gracefully into the seat opposite.

'You make me sound like an alky! It's just that I don't get out very often.'

'You've mentioned that before,' I said. 'Why is that?'

'Get me a small glass of red wine and I'll tell you all about it.'

I got her a large Rioja because the small one looked mean. I got me a pint of weak lager because I already felt drunk on promise.

'How's the case going?' she asked before I'd even sat down.

I kicked off with an imitation of Barrett's slurred post-lunch hospital pass, which had us both in stitches.

'I hate to bring the mood down,' she said suddenly, her hands abandoning the glass and clasping together. 'There's something you need to know and I want to tell you before I have any more to drink.'

My subconscious planted knowing hands on its hips and gloated: *See, told you this would happen. She's WAY out of your league.*

'It's okay,' I said, and she frowned in confusion. 'I know the drill. You like me as a friend but...'

181

'Oh, shut up, Morrissey. Can you let someone else provide the melodrama, just this once?'

I laughed but my ego went foetal, bracing itself for a no-doubt infuriatingly reasonable argument about how we, as a couple, couldn't possibly work.

'I've got a 14-month-old son, called Matthew,' she said.

'Jesus Christ,' I heard my voice say.

I recovered in time to bolt on... 'You'd never know it by looking at you.'

'Thanks.'

With all brain cogs locked in shock, I skidded on: 'All the women I know with kids look fucked. Honestly, I'd never have guessed.'

She hit me with her trademark worried/amused frown: 'Maybe I should be made to wear some sort of sign around my neck, you know, "fallen woman" kind of thing?'

'Oh, I'm with the Tories and the *Daily Mail* on this one.' I smiled. 'Chastity belt, facial branding, the whole hog. I presume you did it for a council flat, and that the baby's brown and the dad's nowhere to be seen?'

'Well, you got the last part right,' she said flatly.

'Oh. Sorry to hear it,' I lied, as my ego performed a series of black flips before declaring 'drinks on the house'.

'Why so?' I ventured quietly.

'He's no longer involved in any way. He's not a bad person. He just couldn't deal with the idea of settling down, so we agreed that he should go.'

'So he doesn't see either of ye, at all?'

She shook her head blankly, all emotions in lockdown. 'He's in Australia.'

I desperately wanted to ask if she still had feelings for him. Had they been in love? What if he suddenly announces he wants to play dad again? But I managed to disguise my selfish insecurities by focussing on mundane practicalities.

'How do you manage, with childcare and things?'

'My mum and dad are saints, basically. They even make me go out one or two nights a week. They're desperate for me to meet a man, of course, so that they can offload us.' She laughed, a little bitterly.

'Well, if desperation's the only qualification,' I said, raising my glass.

She smiled but suddenly looked tired, anxious – and quite a bit older.

'The thing is, Donal, you need to understand what this means. Matthew demands, and gets, most of my energy. I'm in bed by ten most nights – and up at six. I'm constantly knackered and, since he started nursery, lurching from one lurgy to the next.'

'Wow, you should make that your Lonely Hearts ad.'

'Don't joke, Donal. Any man I meet now will have to play second fiddle to Matthew. His welfare has to be my priority and will always come first. And the only clubs I'll be going to are run by the NCT.'

She softened, offering me a 'no hard feelings' look of benevolent resignation.

'You've got a great life as a single bloke, Donal. You can come and go as you please. And you're funny and handsome, in an unconventional way, of course. And you could charm the knickers off a nun. I don't want to take your glory days away from you. You'd end up hating me for it.' Her eyes smiled forgivingly, giving me the chance, finally, to properly explore them, for as long as I wanted to. I could see that they sought nothing but absolute honesty, from the very core of me, without angles or strings or conditions.

So I got honest with myself. Could I really handle the responsibility of being a surrogate uncle/prospective stepdad to a kid who didn't know me and may resent my very presence? I loved kids. They seemed to like me. But could I really do the sleepless nights, the long monotonous days, the sober weekends that parenting demanded? Of course not. Jesus.

Fintan's words from Sunday broke in again. *A lump of driftwood ... dawdling along aimlessly ... no purpose ... you need to make things happen in life...*

'I'm going to the bar now,' I announced, grabbing her fidgety little hand. 'And I'm going to buy us the best bottle of red wine they have. When I come back, I want to hear all about this fantastic little man called Matthew. And at the end of the night, right out there on that pavement, you're going to kiss me goodnight and let me fall a little more in love with you. Understood?'

Her mouth attempted to smile but was overtaken by a different emotion, one I couldn't read. When her hand shot up to her face and a tear broke through, I feared that my initial misgivings had been correct after all ... she didn't want there to be an 'us'.

184

'Thank you,' she whimpered. I felt myself starting to go, so got up and fled to the bar.

Fuck it, I told myself on the way, *for once in my life I'm just going to go for this and give it my very best shot.*

As we left the pub and faced off outside an Athena poster shop, it felt a little awkward – but then pre-planned spontaneity often does. Behind her, in the shop window, the iconic 'topless muscular man holding a baby' poster caught my eye.

That could be me, I thought, *if I worked out for a few months and got a chest wax.*

Next to it hung that famous old photo of workmen having lunch on a steel girder dangling high above the Manhattan skyline. I now knew how they felt. My forehead suddenly weighed heavy from all the red wine. I'd need a top-up soon to avoid a full-on splitter.

'I meant it when I said thanks Donal.'

'What for?'

'For not being shocked or judgemental or well, disappointed I suppose.'

'I'm actually flattered that you told me, you know, so soon. It means you're serious about us.'

'And you're not running to the hills...'

'I usually ravish a woman first, then split.'

'Wow. Do you often smooth talk your way out of romantic encounters?'

'All the time.'

She leaned in and kissed me hard. My heart felt like a shaken bottle of cola mercifully unscrewed. I'd never had a girl take the lead before. I liked it, and decided she'd have to be the one to end this kiss too.

When her mouth smiled against mine, the yellows and reds of Holborn blurred and melded into the glow of a barely dared-for dream. Zoe and me, why not? My brain embalmed the feeling for all eternity. No matter what else happened in my life, this would be making it into my deathbed clip show.

As I glided out of Arsenal tube station I heard myself whistle, then realised it was match night and stopped. After all, post soccer game in the UK is a time when any spontaneous show of emotion can result in violent death. I zigzagged through the braying drunks, chippy tat hawkers and onion-reeking burger vans towards Drayton Park and the final leg of my victory parade.

'She loves me, yeah, yeah, yeah,' I sang as I fumbled with the gate. 'Drunk on booze or love, who can tell?' I bantered the front door.

I headed straight to the kitchen, opened a bottle of Shiraz, grabbed a glass and trotted back to the sentry point to my insomnia – the sitting room couch.

I stopped dead at the sitting room door. A figure lay there grunting in the dark, mummified by blankets and whiskey. I squinted hard into the amber streetlight until the heaving lump took on human form.

I dropped the bottle on the floor and staggered back.

'What the fuck is he doing here?'

I sat in my bedroom's chilly gloom, conscious

hangover incoming. And, after my earlier handling howler, Wineless in Arsenal.

The more I speculated on what had brought my Brit-hating Da to London, the less sense it made – unless he was sinking an arms dump for the boyos...

And why did he have to stay here?

I fantasised briefly that Mam had thrown him out, but I knew her generation of Irish women never kicked out their men, no matter what they got up to. Dads almost always owned the house, and won the bread.

With divorce forbidden by law in Catholic Ireland, women had no rights. Only men could afford to leave ... for richer, for poorer indeed. Had Da now walked out on our mam? How many times had I fantasised that during my teens, when Councillor Michael Lynch heaped nothing but humiliation on us all with his very public yet disingenuous political stance of Pro-Life *and* Pro-IRA.

Following Michael's stated moral code logically, he'd be willing to die for an illegitimate foetus, but would happily kill any living 'legitimate target' for Ireland. These 'legitimate targets' included British soldiers, RUC policemen and anyone who provided goods or services to either. You know, normal people ... us. Plumbers, electricians, mechanics, bakers, candlestick makers...

They must have paid those milkmen in Belfast a bloody fortune.

If the unaborted kids of 'legitimate targets' got in the way, as 500 or so had to date during 'The Troubles' in Northern Ireland, then so be it. Sacrifices have to be made in war. Omelettes, eggs and all that...

Where he stood on aborting the foetuses of 'legitimate targets' remained unclear...

During last year's General Election in the Republic, Michael ran as Sinn Fein candidate in our home constituency of Laois/Offaly. 'The ArmaLite and the Ballot Box' had been one of their catchier slogans, making it clear that they were keeping both options open. It remains unique in political history as the only campaign promise to threaten physical violence against the electorate.

Sinn Fein's muddled take on the core principles of democracy earned Michael a paltry 432 votes – several thousand shy of his nearest rival – and cost him a hefty deposit. But even such a crushing public rejection of his core beliefs failed to detract from the singular high point of his doomed campaign.

He told Fintan that the proudest day of his life had been when Sinn Fein leader Gerry Adams travelled to Tullamore to canvass on his behalf. Dream-maker Gerry then topped this gesture by accepting Da's invitation home for a bite to eat. Mam told me how her hands shook as she served them tea and Victoria Sponge, terrified that the latter might somehow offend.

I needed to call Mam tomorrow, find out what the hell is going on.

Michael's strangled snores downstairs raged at the air like disgruntled ghosts. Whatever had brought him to our place tonight, I felt certain about two things: Fintan knew more than he was letting on, and he'd now put the three of us in grave danger.

Wildly awake in the absence of wine, I tiptoed past my whiskey-wasted dad towards Aidan's stash of hash.

'Levity of any kind required,' I thought plucking pot and papers from his trusty old tin and spiriting it all upstairs.

In less than five hours' time, I'd be shrinking beneath DS Spence's pitiless scowl so I settled on a skinny single leafer, just to pumice my fraying edges.

All night, my mind had laboured and ground like a knackered old cement mixer, turning over the same lumpen imponderables. What the hell had brought Da to London? Could I actually handle the responsibilities of being a stepdad? Why would Jimmy Reilly kill a skanky street ho like Valerie Gillespie and plant her hair on Liz Little? I banked a lungful, lay back on my bed and let the invasion of calm commence.

I sense someone in the room, watching me. The air fizzes with the certainty of imminent violence. I can hear my breathing getting faster, my heart banging against my ribs.

Had Da awoken to one of his whiskey rages, demanding to be violently expunged? Had he lumbered up here to reacquaint himself with his pathetic, punch bag of a son? I realised something startling recently … he'd never once touched me non-violently.

'Da,' I call, but it's swallowed by the dense black. I try to move but my body's rooted to the spot. Dread swallows me whole. This time, he's come to do me real harm.

A cold fluorescent light buzzes on and off, sending

steam rising. I see what looks like the lid of a chest freezer open falteringly, reluctantly.

A head rises up within the steam. The eyes are gone but I recognise Valerie Gillespie's rim-lit blue profile. Up and up that head rises, revealing a severed neck that soon dangles directly above my face. She's suspended by her long hair, so that her head swings in the wind, yet I feel and hear nothing. Suddenly, her head drops like a stone. Her hair stays where it is, blowing wildly now against my bedroom ceiling.

I look down to see her bald head wobbling above the open chest freezer door. The blue light now seeps through her empty eye sockets, buzzing, irregular.

I can't let that light go out.

It gets weaker and weaker, flickers then buzzes off.

'Hang on,' I mutter to the empty bedroom, 'I've never been anywhere near Valerie Gillespie's dead body. What the hell is going on?'

Chapter 14

North London
Tuesday, April 6, 1993; 07.40

I set off for Holloway police station ridiculously early, determined to avoid that newly assembled domestic lynch mob of two. Striding fast somehow ground the cogs of my tired mind into action. They'd a lot of catching up to do.

Firstly, I tipped my hat to Valerie Gillespie for

her grandstand cabaret performance last night. I then wondered how in hell she'd reached me. Until now, murder victims had only ever 'appeared' to me after I'd been close to their dead bodies that same day. I derived some comfort from this ... it gave me a certain level of control. If I avoided a fresh corpse, I couldn't be tormented by its spirit. *That was the deal.*

I'd never been anywhere near Valerie Gillespie's corpse, fresh or otherwise. Nor would I ever be; she'd been dead now for four months and either buried or cremated. So what happened last night? A sickening thud of dread shook my guts. Surely the scope of my dubious 'gift' couldn't be expanding? My sanity could barely cope with the old 'arrangement'.

I declared it time for a 'logic amnesty'. It didn't matter how Valerie had reached me, at least for now. What I needed to take on board were the clues she'd presented. I had to presume they were key to the identity of her killer.

I then allowed my logic amnesty to dwell on another mystery ... why had Liz and Valerie been so serene and measured during their 'visits'? All my previous imposters 'from the other side' had been vengeful and violent.

Then it clicked. Those 'angels of rage' had been killed in frenzied attacks lasting a matter of minutes. Each had fought back with all of their might. As their hearts pumped one last time, their fading brains had raged in blind, terrified furies. That's how they'd entered the spirit world, before taking it out on me.

Conversely, Liz and Valerie had suffered slow,

191

painful demises. Their deaths had come as sweet blessed relief. They weren't fighting at the end. Poor girls.

Maybe they'd ditched the 'slasher movie' approach for another reason; I didn't need shaking out of my scepticism any more. Although I hated myself for it, and wished it wasn't happening to me, I now believed.

Suddenly, I see myself in black tux and tails, stranded in the middle of a dancefloor packed with hollow-eyed, waltzing corpses, all dressed in white. I'm trapped, flustered. The odd one out. Too many couples are spinning past for me to bolt. I must wait for a girl to come free. I must accept a Dance with the Dead. It's my only chance of escape.

A corner shop's newspaper rack snapped me back to the present. Sure enough, Valerie Gillespie's murder had become newsworthy for the first time, now it could be linked to 'the sensational slaying of rising TV star Liz Little'.

I wondered how they'd gloss over Valerie's sordid final months as 'a desperate skank', only to discover that they hadn't bothered reporting any of that at all. Instead, they based the entire piece on two photos, taken well over a year ago, of the 'surgically enhanced good-time girl on the arm of property magnate Phil Armstrong at a London society ball'.

One article concluded with a single oblique reference to her months working the streets: 'Following struggles with cocaine addiction, Valerie split with Armstrong late last year and vanished from London's social scene.'

The piece then niftily skewed back to the Little case, quoting a 'co-star' from *The Bill* delivering bereavement's High Priestess of Inanity: 'Only the good die young.'

A supporting article quoted DS Spence 'denying' that a serial killer had murdered both women and was still out there, on the loose, hunting his next victim. It was a classic journalistic shakedown. As Fintan put it: 'Believe nothing until it has been officially denied.'

If Fintan can't get someone in authority to confirm something, he makes them deny it. That gets the angle or accusation out there into the open, where it takes on a life of its own. 'High Court Judge Denies Child Sex Allegations', for example. Or 'Politician Denies Plan to Raise Taxes'.

Spence would never have mentioned a 'serial killer', had he not been forced to deny it. But now the genie had been released from the lamp, the prospect of a serial killer firmly planted into the public psyche.

Spence then played further into their doom-mongering hands by warning London's women 'to use common sense, avoid walking alone at night and to remain vigilant at all times'.

But the media didn't have it all their own way. He held back the clues that connected both cases – Valerie's hair at both scenes and the A3 batteries. He would have done this for numerous sound policing reasons. Firstly, he didn't want to provoke a copycat killer to 'get in on the act'. Secondly, it deprived the killer the pleasure of glorying in his own signatures. Thirdly, if these facts were known only to the actual killer and the men hunting him, they could use it later to trip him up.

But who was that killer? Courtesy of my Liz Little apparition Saturday night and her non-appearance Sunday, I felt certain that her murder had to be connected to the Florentine Gardens Club. Perhaps lazily, I'd assumed Liz had been directing me towards Jimmy Reilly.

Now that we knew one man killed both women, I needed to think again.

The idea that Jimmy Reilly randomly picked up a crack-head streetwalker like Valerie, killed her, chopped her up and dumped her in a reservoir seemed, frankly, laughable. It just didn't stack up.

This left our mysterious Irish suspect, Robert Conlon. Perhaps he had some connection to the Florentine Gardens? Unless we tracked him down, we'd never know.

I decided to forget about both 'suspects' for now and focus instead on potential leads in each case.

With Liz Little, our best hope had to be identifying the mysterious 'T' who left that note of sympathy at her murder scene. Our only other outstanding clue came in the form of a microscopic fragment of red material found inside her head wounds. I wouldn't have bothered with this had Liz not attempted to drown me in some mysterious metallic red substance Saturday night. Her message couldn't have been clearer ... bet on red.

As for Valerie Gillespie, all I had to work with were the visuals from last night's chilling hair 'n' freezer-themed cabaret. At least one of her clues had been specific enough to pursue right away. I

194

just needed a certain someone to help, so I stepped into a phone box and dialled a number I now knew by heart.

'Guess who's on the scrounge?' I said.

'I'm beginning to think you only love me for my lab.'

'I'm sure I'll find a few other reasons to love you Zoe, eventually.'

'I'm not sure I can help you with that particular request, detective.'

'Well, for once, my other request is official and above board.'

'That's a shame. My boss isn't in today. I prefer working undercover for you.'

'Well, so long as you don't mind being my secret little lab squirrel...'

'Hey, that better not be a reference to my teeth.'

'I could've said lab rat. Come on, girl. I'm working my arse off here!'

'Okay, Mr Hot-shot Detective. Shoot.'

'I need you to re-examine the exhibits recovered from the scene where Valerie Gillespie's body was found, at the reservoir.'

'Why didn't you ask me last night?'

'I only got the idea this morning. Long story. There was a torch and a transistor radio found in a twitching den. The forensics report says they were clean. What it doesn't state clearly is whether they dusted the insides of these objects. Would they have done that, as a matter of course?'

'What, you mean the component parts?'

'No, the batteries, the bulb in the torch, anything that could have been inserted by hand.'

'I'd like to say yes, Donal. But sometimes exhibits from cases that aren't deemed top priority get delegated to less-experienced staff. I can make sure it gets done properly today.'

'That'd be amazing, Zoe. Thank you. I just feel if I can offer up some fresh leads to Spence, make a good impression … well, you never know.'

'Are you gonna mention the whole Reilly thing…?'

'I don't know. What do you think?'

'I think you've got one shot to make an impression on Spence. You should tell him. It shows you've got initiative and desire. He'd be a fool not to snap you up.'

I tried Mam next. Her message on Saturday had to be connected to Da's sudden appearance last night. When the answerphone clicked in I hung up and gave it ten minutes. Second time round, the machine's piercing beep got straight through to my guts. She never went anywhere without Da. She can't drive for God's sake! So where the hell was she?

Chapter 15

Holloway, North London
Tuesday, April 6, 1993; 09.15

I asked for DS Spence at reception, hoping that my early arrival didn't smack of desperation.

Within seconds, I found myself jogging along a school-type corridor behind a bustling, generously mulleted woman who could've stunt-doubled for Mrs Doubtfire.

As she gave the steep staircase bannister its sternest test yet, I gasped: 'I thought I was early.'

'As you're here anyway, you may as well sit in on the briefing.'

'Which briefing is this?'

'The one about how to catch a serial killer.'

'I didn't realise we were looking for a serial killer?'

'Two bodies in four months? Of course we are. But we can't panic the public. And we don't want the papers offering reward money because of all the chaos that caused last time round. So we don't speak of it outside of this building. Understood?'

My chest swelled, and not just from stair-based exertion; I'd been welcomed into Spence's club already.

She stopped at a door and nodded me through. At the top of the packed conference room, a fey little Scottish man, dapper in red rayon paisley shirt, black waistcoat and cream wale cords, was holding forth about serial killers. A caption shivering on a white projector screen announced him to be Dr Daniel Williams, Criminologist. His quick-fire recital of indisputable criminal facts told me he was taking no lip from the floor.

My short-term memory filleted the best bits:

- *The average number of people killed by a serial killer each year in the UK is seven.*
- *There would appear to be two serial killers operating at any one time.*
- *In 1986 alone, seven serial killers were active in the*

UK – the most ever recorded.

What a fun parlour game, I thought, naming those. It would certainly complete my family's Christmas afternoon.

His next subject: brands of serial killer and their particular foibles. According to the academics Holmes – not Sherlock – and his sidekick De Burgh – not Chris – there are four types of serial killer: visionary; mission; power/control; hedonistic.

Williams continued to throw out facts: *The Visionary is impelled to kill because he has heard voices/seen visions demanding that he murder a particular person or category of people. The client dialling in this homicidal order is usually a demon, or The Big Man Himself.*

The Mission killer has a conscious, self-imposed goal in life to eliminate a certain identifiable group of people, minus any voices or visions.

The Power/Control killer receives gratification not from sexual acts or violence, but by exerting complete control over their victims.

The Hedonistic killer does it just for kicks.

This list chimed uncannily with Tammy's breakdown of shaggers at the Florentine gardens. Could it be that our captains of industry share character traits with serial killers? I didn't doubt it for one second.

A man in his fifties bolted upright. Lean, steely-eyed, a street fighter, Spence didn't need any formal introduction.

'Thanks for the criminology lecture, Dr Williams,' he said in his strangled Glaswegian brogue, 'but can we please get back to your observations about the killer of Liz Little, specifically what you told me about the signatures.'

Dr Williams took three steps away from his screen, perched on a stool and adopted the manner of a man about to treat a kids' camp to a ghost story.

'The correct term is actually personation,' he almost whispered. 'That's when we find unusual behaviour by an offender beyond that necessary to commit the crime. Signature is when the offender demonstrates repeat behaviour from crime to crime...'

That put Spence back on his arse, his big old head steaming like a boiled potato.

'To the signature killer, his crime is a work of art and he wants to sign it. They want someone or a group of people to know that they're responsible for their work. They crave status and respect. They want to be considered intelligent, a cut above the norm, brilliant even.

'Our job is to interpret these clues as best as we can to decode the killer's motive and personality. After all, behaviour reflects personality and, as we say, "why plus how equals who ..." The nature of the personation can reveal a lot about the killer's personality and innermost fantasies.

'Over the years, I've read about thousands of cases involving personation and signatures.'

If his standing at this point had been for dramatic effect, it worked.

'What I've never seen, or read about, or heard of – in any other case, anywhere in the world – is for such a multitude of personations to be present at a single crime scene.

'Elizabeth Little died of haemorrhaging caused by blunt force trauma. Almost everything else she suffered had been as a result of her killer's bespoke and twisted personations. There were so many, I had to make a list...'

He returned to his lectern and rifled through some papers.

'The sexually provocative positioning of the body. The ligature around her neck – remember she didn't die from asphyxiation. This ligature would have been used to torture her. The gouge marks to her body, made when she was alive. The way she'd been sliced into two. The battery inserted into her anus. The Joker smile carved into her face.

'Even the place she'd been dumped – a notorious red-light district – carries a clear message. So what can I tell you about her killer?

'Let me get the obvious stuff out of the way first. At least three people had to be involved in this enterprise, probably more. The whole thing had been painstakingly organised, right down to the location where they dumped her body beside a busy road. They were aiming for, and achieved, maximum shock value. But only one man called the shots. You're looking for a very dangerous, violent, psychopathic man with a propensity for excessive violence.

'The less obvious stuff: he'll be powerful, wealthy, middle-aged, married with kids and vociferous about the importance of family.

'He'll be self-made. His greatest source of pride will be how he hauled himself out of the gutter to get to where he is today. He's clearly one of a new breed of sociopaths honed by the collapse of old values during the 1980s. He believes only in personal prosperity and success and pursues it at all costs. He genuinely possesses zero empathy for anyone outside his immediate family.

'He's a control freak with a massive ego, overweening pride, almost a God complex.

'He'll run some sort of an empire, possibly business, more likely criminal or a combination of both. He has lots of people under his control and he's making an example of Liz Little to them. The message, quite simply is: "Cross me and I'll fuck you up in ways you can't even imagine". Is this man a potential serial killer? I've got to stick my neck out here and say he's already a serial killer. His victims have been anyone he believes *may* have betrayed him. I say "may" because a man like this acts on basic instinct. If he feels someone's shafted him, he won't bother seeking out supporting evidence. He'll act on it right away.'

I realised that my jaw had fallen wide-open. Without knowing it, Doc Williams had just provided a chillingly accurate biography of Jimmy Reilly. And he wasn't finished yet.

'I've given a lot of thought to how the victim's injuries may reflect the reason she was killed. The "Joker smile" used to be administered to people who were talking too much. Who had Liz Little been talking to? I think this is worth exploring.

'The posing of her body in a sexually provocative manner suggests a deeply personal issue between Liz and her killer, and it's to do with power and anger. He feels that she betrayed him in some fundamental way. Again, what did she know and who was she telling?

'The staging of her body – any staging of a crime scene, in fact – often indicates an offender with a deep-seated hatred for authority. This usually stems from youth offending. This is a man who puts great store in outwitting the police and beating the system which he feels is unfairly stacked against him. Now, any questions?'

'Why do you think he's gone to such lengths to mimic the Black Dahlia murder? What should we read into that?'

'Glad you asked,' said Williams. 'This is another little game where he feels like he's putting it up to you guys, gloating, taunting, challenging you to catch him. It's driven by his hatred of authority.

'I've been reading a lot about the original Black Dahlia case. I've only just found out that police were about to arrest a suspect in 1982 – a criminal called Jack Anderson Wilson – but he died in a house fire before they got to him.

'The evidence against Wilson is strong. They, were able to connect him to letters sent to the press and police at the time, taunting them about the case and revealing information that only the killer could have known.

'The thing is – and this is why I'm glad you brought it up – after killing the Black Dahlia, Wilson went on to murder five more women. My real fear is that this is what the killer of Liz Little is telling us: that he's lined up five more for the same treatment. So you'd better catch him soon.'

Post-briefing, Doubtfire grabbed me in the

hallway – literally – and didn't let go until Spence came out several minutes later.

She shook me in front of him like a rag doll. 'Sir, this is your ten o'clock. DC Donal Lynch from the Cold Case Squad.'

He frowned while looking right through me, then refocussed and squinted into my eyes. 'Yes, of course,' he said, blinking hard, 'I'm looking forward to it, Lynch. We need chapter and verse on that Gillespie murder.'

'I'll do my best, sir,' I jabbered.

He stopped blinking to glare at me in disgusted confusion. 'I just need you to do your job son,' he said.

'Take him in to the conference room, Janet,' he ordered without taking his eyes off me. 'I'll be back in five.'

Great start, Donal, I scolded myself as I got bundled back inside. I broke free and made for a seat near the wall, just to get away from her.

'Get up,' she demanded.

'Sorry?' I said, staying put.

'He'll expect you to be standing when he gets back.'

'Really?'

'Yes, really,' she said, making a series of violent upwards gestures with her hand.

I ignored her, then reminded myself of the longer game here and stood sulkily. I needed to impress Spence. He'd just taught me my first vital lesson – don't bother with well-meaning flannel. I needed to man up, be decisive, confident, bold.

He strode back in with a mug of tea, bag still in, and a newspaper folded under his arm, open on the sports pages.

'Thanks, Janet,' he said by way of dismissing her. 'Sit down,' he said, by way of letting me know who was boss. I felt certain that his men would call him boss. Or gaffer. Or King Dong. Something red-bloodedly reverential.

I found myself instantly cowed by those cold, lifeless blue eyes. I couldn't imagine them showing any emotion other than barely suppressed rage. I pictured homeless people knowing better than to ask him for change, or ferocious Rottweilers reduced to simpering mutts before their unblinking menace. DS Spence scared the shit out of me.

'Right, Lynch,' he said, 'I need you to run through the connections between the Little and Gillespie murders for me. And, please, stick to the point.'

I rattled off the pathological connections first: blunt force trauma, expertly carved up bodies, anally plugged with Grade C batteries.

'And then of course there's the hair,' he said. 'Run me through that.'

'They found a couple of strands of human hair in Liz Little's right hand. Four months earlier, the pathologist had struggled to identify Valerie Gillespie's body. She examined her hair as part of that process. As soon as she saw the hair under the microscope again four months later, she recognised it.'

'After four months, the pathologist recognised some hair?'

'I believe so, sir.'

His glare told me *not good enough*. I either knew or I didn't.

204

'DNA testing has confirmed this hair to be Valerie Gillespie's. That is indisputable sir.'

'Well, find out precisely how they made that connection, Lynch. This is now a crucial plank of our enquiry. Had the hair found on Liz been cut or pulled?'

'Pulled out at the root, apparently.'

'Apparently?'

'Definitely pulled out at the root.'

'You're one hundred per cent certain of that, Lynch.'

'Yes, sir.'

'Why did you say apparently?'

'Figure of speech, sir. A poor one.'

'What lines of enquiry are you pursuing next, Lynch?'

'She was last seen on CCTV ten days before her body was found. The pathologist estimated she died four or five days later. The days in between are unaccounted for.'

'What are you doing about that?'

The ground disintegrated beneath me; time to sprout wings.

'Well, sir, she didn't have a pimp and that's what caused her problems at King's Cross. I'm working on a theory that she re-located to Brownswood. Lots of girls work there without pimps. I'm pulling the local CCTV, see if we can track her down.'

Of course that's where she went, I suddenly rea-lised. *She was a crackhead and they found her body up the road in Wood Green...*

'If they still have the CCTV. How many months ago now?'

'Four, sir.'

205

'Councils keep it for three.'

I could actually feel confidence leaking out of every pore.

'I'm also having exhibits re-examined that were recovered next to where Valerie had been dumped. They found a radio and a torch in a bird-watching hut. There's not much bird watching going on in December, so we're confident they belonged to the killer,' I said, hating my voice for shaking.

'What station was it tuned to?'

'Sir?'

'The transistor radio. What station was it on?'

'I don't know, sir.'

'Well, find out. If it was tuned to BBC Radio One, then it belonged to kids. Radio Three or Four, then it's most likely owned by a twitcher. But if it's on one of those talk radio stations that attracts right-wing nutters... This is all pretty obvious stuff, Lynch.'

'I'll be sure to find out, sir. One odd discovery I did make is that Valerie's body was released from the mortuary two months ago, to her ex.'

'Go see him. Find out how that happened. Maybe he'll have some ideas about those missing days.'

I smiled: 'Maybe he still held a torch for her sir, you know, all the way to the reservoir!'

He glared at me witheringly. I thought about revealing the Robert Conlon tip from the anonymous Irish Garda, then realised how flaky it sounded so shelved it. Instead, I curdled silently beneath his caustic snarl for what seemed like several minutes.

'Is that it, Lynch?' he stated, finally.

206

'That's as far as I've got, sir.'

'So there may be other leads?'

'No sir, that's it.'

'What about other unsolved cases that might be connected?'

'I'm cross-referencing all the unsolved female murders in London over the last ten years, sir. I'll report to you as soon as anything crops up.'

'I was led to believe you'd already done this, Lynch.'

'Work in progress, sir.'

'You clearly need help. Get the Valerie Gillespie paperwork over to us ASAP. In fact, why don't you send us all the unsolved case files with similar offender MO? We can take the load off you.'

No, no, no, Spence, you can't do that. This is my big chance to get onto your squad. Why would I just hand it all over to you and sideline myself?

'Sir, I'm very familiar with these unsolved cases. I don't have to start from scratch like your officers would. If you give me twenty-four hours, I'll get through the whole file and report back to you.'

'I've got more experienced officers than you here, Lynch. And they know facts about the Little case that you don't...'

'Sir, it would take my unit between twenty-four and forty-eight hours to get all this paperwork over to you. Why don't you let me go through it today? You can treat it as a preliminary exercise. I'll then bring it over myself, personally, tomorrow morning.'

'You heard the criminologist, Lynch. There's a serial killer out there butchering young women. I haven't got time for a personal ego trip.'

I should have left it there. Of course I should. But the chewed-up remnants of my pride and machismo wouldn't let me. How dare he dismiss me as too dumb or inexperienced for this role! I'd invented this fucking role!

'Despite my inexperience sir–' I heard my voice slightly wobble. '–the similarities between these cases don't seem nearly as striking to me as the differences.'

That got the fucker's attention.

'Liz had been a high-class hooker who didn't take drugs; Valerie was a crack whore. Liz had been cut with a knife; Valerie was tortured with an iron. Liz had gouges dug out of her body; Valerie didn't. Valerie had cigarette burns on her arms and body; Liz didn't. Liz's body had been laid out for all to see. We were never supposed to find Valerie's body.'

He sat bolt upright, wide-eyed, like a guard dog.

I charged on: 'The only tangible links between these murders are the MO with the batteries and that chunk of Valerie's hair found in Liz's hand. Everything else is circumstantial. What if that hair had been planted to throw us off the scent?'

He snorted in contempt. It didn't even slow me down.

'The criminologist just spent fifteen minutes describing the man who killed Liz Little. Every characteristic matched a person who knew Liz well and who has form for extreme violence.'

I took a deep breath and told myself there could be no turning back now.

'I think she was murdered by Jimmy Reilly.'

My lightning strike zinged the air. Spence eyed me warily, a dark stranger telling fantastical tales.

'There isn't a shred of evidence linking this to Reilly,' he said carefully, 'unless you know something I don't.'

Time to slay Spence with my crusading sword of truth...

'I went to his club Saturday night, sir, the Florentine Gardens, and got chatting to some of his dancers. There was definitely something going on between him and Liz.'

He leaned forward. 'I've underestimated, you, Lynch. Do go on.'

'Well, sir, Liz's death hadn't been made public by then, she'd only been found that morning, so we thought it would be a good time to do some fishing. One of the girls was about to talk ... but changed her mind at the last second.'

'When you say *we* Lynch...'

'My brother Fintan, he's a reporter. It was his idea.'

'Fintan Lynch is your brother?' he said, in alarmed disbelief. But I'd hooked him.

'Who was this girl? What did she tell you?'

'She was one of the hostesses there, sir. She didn't give me her name. She said something about Liz travelling a lot, I think she meant for or with Reilly. She was about to tell me a lot more, I could tell, when a couple of bouncers showed up at my table and she vanished.'

'Do you think they suspected her of talking?'

'I don't know, sir. I don't think so.'

'What did they want, these bouncers?'

'They'd been watching us all night, sir. They

saw my warrant card on the way in.'

His eyebrows shot up and I shut up. He didn't need to hear any more.

'This hostess woman, she must have told you something about herself?'

'Not that I can recall, sir,' I lied, my uncertainty giving me away, 'I'd drank quite a bit before Fintan came up with the idea of going there, so it's all a bit of a haze. I was off-duty, of course.'

He shuffled irritably in his seat. I couldn't tell if his agitation stemmed from my rank unprofessionalism, or blatant obfuscation about Tammy's identity. He leaned his head back and stared somewhere beyond the ceiling.

'You're probably aware that many consider Reilly untouchable,' he said softly, sucking in a lungful of air, holding it for three seconds then releasing it back to the ceiling. 'I've lost count of the officers supposedly on his books, doing his bidding.'

I nodded. He lowered his eyes down to mine.

'Playing it by the book, I have to report you right now and haul your arse before a disciplinary hearing. Not only did you put your own life in danger, you've risked the lives of undercover officers involved in covert operations connected to Reilly. Unwittingly, granted. But trust me, this provides no comfort whatsoever when your multi-million-pound undercover operation goes up in smoke. There are always bigger plays, Lynch. Always. For Christ's sake remember that.'

My insides collapsed. I'd never survive another disciplinary hearing. Not with my track record. He breathed in hard, clearly relishing the power he now held over me.

'But I'm not going to do that Lynch. Reilly's like a bloody cancer in this force. I've been trying to find a way to get into him for years. You may have just stumbled across something. So I want you to carry on with your cold case work, linking other murders to Liz Little. I've no doubt Reilly has officers here on his books, possibly even inside my team. We can't afford to have any of this leaking back to him, so please come to me personally with any developments. I'll get someone to dig out a mobile phone for you with all my direct numbers already programmed in.

'What I need from you now is a statement about everything that happened Saturday night. I've got an officer who I trust with my life who can take it from you, here in the room, once we're finished. I'll keep this statement somewhere very secure until the day we might need it, when we manage to bring a case against Reilly. You understand why I have to do this? We can't have his legal team finding out about your fishing trip later and using it against us in court and, trust me, the bastards would.'

I tried not to nod too much.

Spence fixed me with a knowing look. 'I also need the name of that hostess, Lynch, and a description. It's very noble of you trying to protect her. But she doesn't need protecting so long as we keep things between us. If we can trace this woman, we can find out once and for all if Reilly had some sort of beef with Liz Little, and that would be dynamite.'

Of course he hadn't bought my lie that I couldn't remember anything about her. But Tammy had placed her trust in me, albeit fleetingly. She wouldn't want her identity passed on to another cop. I couldn't do it to her. Besides, Fintan's words from Saturday night kept echoing through my mind... *It's always worth holding something back when you can ... give yourself a little edge.* If I spilled everything now about Tammy, Spence would have no further use for me.

'Sorry sir, I was only with her a matter of minutes. I'm not sure I could even pick her out of a line-up.'

He pursed his lips, weighing me up. 'I understand, Lynch. But just so you understand, I've dreamed of bringing down Reilly for many, many years. Your career's been on the skids. If we're smart, we can work together on this, to mutual benefit. Come up with her name, and you're on my squad. Have a good, long, hard think about that.'

Chapter 16

Holloway, North London
Tuesday, April 6, 1993; 11.25

As I left the station, frazzled and spent, my pager's buzz almost gave me a stroke. I called Zoe on my new, Met-police-issue mobile phone.

'How did it go?'

'I've just finished making a statement about Saturday night.'

'A statement?'

'Don't worry. It went really well. You were right! Spence congratulated me on my initiative and unofficially placed me on his team.'

'That's brilliant. You deserve it, Donal,' she said. 'What do you mean, unofficially?'

'Anything to do with Reilly, he wants me to report to him directly. He's worried about leaky cops. Sounds like he's been trying to nail JR for years. Please tell me you paged me with yet more good tidings.'

'Well, as the cops say on TV, I've got some good news and some bad news.'

'Well, as Van Gogh said to the prostitute, I'm all ears. I'll take the bad news first.'

'I wonder does that make you an optimist or a pessimist?'

'Only a pessimist would want the bad news last.'

'The sample of red paint you gave me, from Liz's head wound. I sent it off to the British Coatings Federation. They said it's high in zinc, so it is probably specialist, but they can't tell me any more unless they can detect the binding agent.'

'Which means…?'

'They need a bigger sample.'

'Moving swiftly on to the good news…'

'We've found a print.'

My entire top half fizzed like licked sherbet.

'Inside the torch,' I blabbed.

'Er, yes. On the bulb which must have been replaced at some point. Whoever did left one almost-complete print. How did you know?'

213

'A wild guess. Honestly Zoe, I couldn't hear better news right now. I hope to God it belongs to Reilly or one of his goons.'

'I'm getting it run through the system now ... that could take a while. But whoever owns this print has a lot of explaining to do.'

Fintan had paged me three times, so I called him next.

'Why didn't you tell me Da was coming to stay *at our house?*'

'I knew you'd overreact and I didn't want to spoil your date,' he said. 'By the way, how did it go? The fact you came home suggests not so well.'

'Never mind that. When did you know he was coming?'

'He called yesterday around lunchtime. He seemed in a bad way. What was I supposed to do? Tell my own father that he can't kip at ours for a couple of nights?'

'Why can't he book a hotel like anyone else?'

'He said he didn't feel secure booking it in his own name. Look, whatever's going on, he's under big pressure. He won't tell me what but I'm not throwing him out on the street when he's desperate. Maybe Ma knows something. Have you spoken to her?'

'No. Though she left a message Saturday night saying she was worried about him. Now she's not picking up.'

'She's probably gone to stay with one of her sisters while he's away. You know what she'd want you to do. She'd love it if you two could sort things out. Honestly, I think it would really help

214

her health-wise.'

'Don't even try to fucking guilt trip me, Fintan. He's the one that banished me, let's not forget. I was quite happy never clapping eyes on him again, ever. What am I supposed to say to him now?'

'He was asking after you,' he said. 'I got the sense he wants to bury the hatchet.'

I laughed. 'What worries me is where he wants to bury it. You need to find out what the hell is going on, Fintan, because I'm not that keen on the company he keeps. And then he needs to find somewhere else to stay.'

'I'll do my best to get him a room somewhere, okay? But if he tries to, you know, reach out to you, at least hear him out. He deserves that.'

I let my silence do the talking.

'Anyway, I can't find anything on this Robert Conlon character,' he said, exasperated. 'I've spent all morning in the cuttings library, going back through hard copies of the Irish papers, all the way to '68. I'm now cross-eyed and my hands look like Desmond Tutu's.'

'Shall I try the local paper?'

'I did that first. Called my old editor at the *Leinster Express* last night. Another blank.'

'How far back did he look?'

'He's been in that job so long, he doesn't need to look. Jesus, it's not like Offaly/Laois is a hotbed for stranger rapists. A stolen cow would make the front page some weeks. But, I'm excited to say, not this week!'

'What do you mean?'

'As it comes out tomorrow morning, I decided to give him a story.'

'What story?'

'Ah, you know, *Police in London are keen to speak to a man originally from Foxburrow in relation to a murder enquiry. Robert Conlon, believed to be in his forties* ... blah blah.'

'Jesus. I'm not sure that was very smart. I've got to tread carefully here.'

'Who's going to see the *Leinster Express* in London? No one. So I got him to put your direct number at the end of the piece. If this Garda tipster exists, then he'll know who to call now.'

As ever with Fintan, I felt two moves behind and several kinds of terrified about the consequences.

'Do you think this Robert Conlon character exists then?'

'I suppose there's a chance he was tried in a family court, in camera. You know what it's like in parts of Offaly. The only virgins are girls who can run faster than their dads. But even if it was family court, the local cops would know about it.'

'If that's the case, then *only* a Garda could've made this tip.'

'Well, you'll have to ask them yourself, I'm afraid. Take it through the official channels because I'm beat.'

Chapter 17

Islington, North London
Tuesday, April 6, 1993; 16.30

'You're the first detective to actually bother to come and see me in person,' snapped Philip Armstrong at the front door to his achingly twee townhouse offices in Islington.

Valerie Gillespie's erstwhile sugar daddy led me towards an enormous study that looked more like an exclusive private members' club. 'I trust this is because Valerie's murder suddenly matters, now that it's been in all the papers?'

I sat on a battered old leather sofa. 'I won't insult you by trying to defend anything that's gone before, sir, but, for my part, I started on this yesterday.'

He sat in the armchair opposite me, legs crossed femininely.

With his pin-striped suit, cravat, natty little hanky and brogues, Armstrong clearly worked hard to embody stiff upper-class Britishness. I could instantly picture him in gimp-masked sub-mission, taking an almighty rogering from Valerie's flapping great strap-on. Somewhere along the line, my subconscious had decreed that all posh English people are sexual deviants, thus elevating inverted snobbery to dizzying new heights. I put it down to all those tales you hear

217

about public schools...

He dry coughed more indignancy. 'The only detective who bothered to ring me seemed more interested in how we got together than the fact she'd been murdered.'

I suddenly really wanted to know how they'd got together, and wondered if there might be a way to find out without directly asking.

'I wanted to save her you see,' he said quietly, looking into the middle distance. 'I foolishly thought I had. You know, like Julia Roberts in that wretched film. But she couldn't be saved, in the end. Addicts can't, can they?'

'I'm told the only person who can save an addict is themselves.'

He uncrossed his legs and shifted about in the seat, as if to reboot his emotions. 'So what can I do for you today, officer?'

'I'm trying to establish where Valerie went after she was last captured on CCTV at King's Cross on December tenth,' I explained. 'That was ten days before they found her body. The pathologist estimated she'd been dead for between five and six days. I'm trying to find out where she spent those four missing days.'

His ruddy posh boy cheeks flared purple. 'As I told the officer back in December, the last time I saw her was in March of last year so how am I supposed to help you with that? It's blindingly obvious where she would've gone, though, isn't it? To whatever red-light district is closest to King's Cross, to score more of that ghastly crack.'

'A mortuary assistant said her body was released to you in February. Is that correct?'

'That's her up there,' he said, nodding to an ornate urn on the mantelpiece. 'Why is this relevant?'

'By rights, sir, a mortuary should keep a murder victim for a minimum of twelve months.'

'I didn't know that. They contacted me to make the arrangements. They'd already conducted the post-mortem. I can't see what else they would've wanted with her?'

'Do you remember who called you from the mortuary?'

'No, and why would I?' he said irritably. 'And what has any of this got to do with her murder?'

'I'm just trying to be thorough, sir.'

'Well, it's a bit bloody late for that,' he snarled.

We sat in excruciating silence.

'Sorry,' he said, finally, 'I've had a bloody massive deal fall through today and it's really hacked me off.'

'That's quite okay, sir. Valerie's murder must still feel very raw.'

'Right, well, if that's all,' he said, getting to his feet. I nodded.

'I'm sure you possess sufficient skills of detection to at least find your own way out,' he barked, stalking off.

I took the scenic route, stopping to take a long hard gaze into Valerie's urn. I'd never been close to fresh ashes before. I wondered again how she came to me last night when I'd never been anywhere near her dead body. I then silently asked her to come to me again tonight, if she could, to let me know more.

Chapter 18

Finsbury Park, North London
Tuesday, April 6, 1993; 19.00

As we walked past Blackstock Road's dreary Irish pubs, sketchy Albanian cafés and over-lit kebab shops, Fintan insisted he could detect any urban drug-taking hot spot simply by checking out the local newsagents'.

'Come on, I'll show you,' he said, leading me into a typically chaotic 'news, booze and basics' corner shop.

Just a half-hour earlier, I'd called him with my theory that Valerie had spent her final days around Brownswood Road.

'Let's get down there and talk to the girls,' he'd suggested excitedly. 'If she did, then someone must know something.'

Now he'd temporarily side-lined this mission to deliver a keynote lecture about 'skankenomics'.

'While I'm buying fags,' he said, 'check out the valuables locked away, somewhere near the till.'

So I did, mentally listing the random items glinting under lock, key and the proprietor's beady eye: fake roses in glass tubes; athletic socks; silver and gold spray paint cans; video head cleaner; shoelaces; spray cans of computer duster; cheap cigars; batteries and razor blades. I'd seen these items locked away in newsagents all over London countless times before, but never wondered why. On the way out, he lit up a cigarette and set about enlightening me.

'The fake roses in the glass tubes? Junkies discard the flowers and use the vases as bongs. With their bulb ends, they're ideal. Athletic socks provide the best nosebag for huffing spray paint. Silver and gold spray paint contain more solvent than others and provide a better 'high'.

'Video head cleaner is amyl nitrate, a party popper that's massive on the gay scene. Heroin junkies use shoelaces to tourniquet their arms. Those spray cans of computer duster don't just contain air, as I'd thought, but a liquefied gas that people inhale direct from the nozzle. The cigars are known as blunts, you empty the insides and fill it with marijuana.'

'What about the batteries and blades?'

'They just happen to be the other most shop-lifted items. Drugs are everywhere, Donal. Everyone is at it. They should just legalise all of it. If they did, then it would clean up somewhere like this overnight. Think about it, there'd be no profit for the dealers. The women wouldn't be desperate for money so they wouldn't have to sell themselves for sex. In the longer term, you could treat them, instead of pretending they don't exist.'

'Yeah, but you said yourself it's a one-hit addiction. There'll be nothing to stop anyone having a go and getting hooked. Jesus, next thing you've got half the population being fed their drugs of choice every day.'

'Half the population is already addicted to drugs, Donal. Most of it prescribed by our doc-

tors. Statins, blood-pressure tablets, anti-depress-
ants, painkillers, sleeping tablets. Everyone has a
drug, legal or otherwise, so we may as well legalise
the lot and get on with it. Look at Mam. She's
been taking sleeping stuff for twenty odd years.
Da's a whiskey fiend. And where would you be
without your two bottles of Shiraz a night? Jesus,
I'm the only non-addict in the family.'

'Right, so you don't count your thirty-a-day
cigarette habit?'

'I don't need fags to go to sleep, do I? Bottom
line is, the law's a joke. Crack is illegal, yet we can
walk around the corner there and buy a rock at
an inflated price and that profit goes straight to a
criminal. Where's the sense in that? Legalise it,
you make it affordable. And you make it safer. It
won't be cut or laced with shit.'

'I don't know. It feels a bit like giving away free
chocolate to kids.'

'I know it's difficult for your Catholic brain to
compute, but we all have the power of choice and
free will. No one's going to make you go to a
shooting gallery and mainline heroin.'

'So I suppose you'd legalise prostitution as
well?'

'Well, it works in Amsterdam,' he said. 'Two
prostitute murders in the last five years. How
many has there been in London in that time? A
dozen?'

I nodded. 'At least.'

Fintan flicked his cigarette against a wall. 'How
would you wipe out vice then, detective?'

'I think the problem is we prosecute the girls
for soliciting and let the johns off scot-free. I've

never understood that.'

'That's because men are dogs who'd fuck anything and we might as well just accept that fact, and it's up to the sisterhood not to go out there and let us succumb to our base needs.'

'You think that?'

'I'm just interpreting the official, legal stance.' He smiled. *If all womankind banded together and took the male path, the world would turn into one huge brothel.'*

'Ooh, very impressive. Who said that?'

'Some repressed Russian, probably.'

We turned right into Summerfield Road, the heart of the Brownswood red-light zone. There wasn't a street girl to be seen.

'You think maybe the murders have spooked them away?' I asked.

'You're joking, aren't you? They're most likely delighted that there's less competition. If we take this next left, Wilberforce, there's an off-licence at the end. Sometimes, a bunch of the girls share a bottle of vodka out front, have a little boogie round a transistor radio. The locals keep complaining about it.'

'Christ, that sounds like something out of our childhood. No wonder they've resorted to crack.'

Wilberforce proved as slavishly middle class as it sounded. Suddenly, thirty feet ahead of us in the matt-grey dusk, the passenger door of a beige parked car flung open. A black woman in her twenties leaned out and emptied her mouth onto the pavement with a repulsed 'gaah'. She'd barely swung her feet back in when the car engine gunned and it roared off. Neither of us inspected the area she'd orally bombed; we both assumed it wasn't vomit.

'Christ, she must have been rattling so badly that she blew him, there and then, without a jonnie,' said Fintan, shaking his head in wonder. 'She couldn't even hang on for the three-minute drive to Homebase.'

Further up the pavement, a skinny, pale frame of indeterminate gender fidgeted and twitched shiftily. With short brown hair, cadaverous face, loose white sweatshirt and shapeless jeans, the person's sex remained a genuine mystery until we got to within ten feet.

'Are you planning to propose or something?' came a gruff voice and I found myself thinking, *My God, that's a woman.* She raised her chin defiantly and glared at me, head wobbling in indignation.

'Oh sorry,' I stammered.

'Are you a fucking pig or what?'

'I must apologise for my brother,' shmoozed Mr WD40, 'he's only just over from Ireland.'

'Oh right, a bit special, is he?'

'I think that's a fair assessment.'

She looked me up and down. 'I don't just fuck anyone you know, you daft cunt.'

Fintan tittered. 'Strangely enough, you're not the first woman to say that to him this week.'

She turned to Fintan. 'You want business then or not? Where's your motor?'

'Actually, I'm on foot, and I'm a reporter with the *Sunday News*. Fintan Lynch.'

He held out his hand. She backed away.

'Don't worry, I'm just doing some background

research. I don't need names or photos or anything like that.'

'How do I know you're not gonna drive back down here later and photograph me after I've spoken to you. I know what you lot are like.'

I had to smile; it wasn't often you saw a street prostitute assuming the moral high ground. She enjoyed it too.

'I'm happy to pay you for your time,' he said.

She took a good bead on his eyes and sniffed. 'I'm starving.'

'There's a bagel place on Seven Sisters Road, let's get some and head into the park.'

'How much are you gonna give me?'

'Depends on how good your information is.'

'You're not mugging me off, Mr Reporter. Go away.'

'Okay, twenty quid.'

'Up front?'

He laughed. 'It's not that I don't trust you...'

'Jo.'

'Jo, it's just that we never pay anyone up front.'

'Forty then. I'm not leaving here for less than forty.'

'Alright, forty.'

'If you don't pay, I'll say you tried to rape me. Embarrass the shit out of both of you.'

'Salmon and cream cheese, okay?'

By the time we reached Finsbury Park's rotting, birdshit-spattered picnic tables, Jo had already demolished her bagel. As we took the bench opposite hers, Fintan placed his cigarettes in the middle and said, 'Help yourself.'

225

'I don't smoke,' said Jo, 'or do drugs. I get pissed most nights, mind.'

'Is that a Geordie accent?' he said, happy to lead the informal interview.

'Middlesbrough, but I'll let you off this once.'

'Is that where you started doing this then?'

She nodded. 'I used to see the girls over the border – that's what they call the rough part of town, north of the train station. They'd be standing there, outside their houses at half four every evening, waiting for the men finishing their shifts at the industrial estate. I swore I'd never do it.'

She sighed. 'One lunchtime, I was having a drink at the Zeppelin, a pub near the station, when one of the girls asked me to come out and take the registration number of this fancy jeep 'cos she hadn't seen it in the area before. I went out, memorised it. While I'm standing there, the girl gets back out of the jeep, comes over and says, "he wants to talk to you". I laughed and said "tell him to fuck off, like", and she said, "go over, he's loaded". Ten minutes later, I was back in the pub with forty quid. It's the money I got hooked on.'

'How did you end up down here?'

'I had a boyfriend who got hooked on the money as well. He wouldn't leave me alone. After a couple of trips to A and E, I fucked off out of it.'

'Wouldn't it be safer to work in a sauna than on the streets?'

'They're all controlled by vicious bastards. I've had enough of being controlled by vicious bastards.'

'Why not King's Cross? More trade. CCTV. Liaison officers, free clinic, soup kitchens...'

'Don't you fucking listen? I want to be completely independent. I don't need someone to buy johnnies for me, or give me soup. Anyway, it's safer here. It's like Middlesbrough; you get to know the punters. And some of us work together, keep an eye out for each other.'

'How does that work?'

'Same as back home. We work in pairs, memorise any car numbers that we don't recognise. I've just been stood with a lass who's gone off in a beige Datsun Cherry and I've got his number.'

'Memorised?'

'My brain's not what it was.' She grinned, bearing medieval teeth. She leaned to her left, squeezed her hand into the right front pocket of her jeans, pulled out a piece of paper and a blue bookies' pen.

'I write 'em down now,' she said, unfolding the sheet. As she flattened it out on the rain-blackened table top, I could see at least ten scrawled plate numbers, each one accompanied by a car make, model and initials.

'Do the initials stand for a girl?' I asked.

She nodded.

'Do you time and date them?'

'I'm not a fuckin' traffic cop.'

I found myself worrying why she'd taken such a dislike to me. Maybe she could sense I was a cop. She'd that kind of raw animal intuition. Of course she'd warmed to Fintan – one shameless whore to another – so I happily let him resume control.

'We're looking into the murder of Liz Little, the girl found on Brownswood the other night.'

'Posh, were she then? Went to a good school?

227

'Cos you don't give a shit when it happens to one of us street girls.'

'Our interest isn't driven by the victim,' he lied, 'so much as who we believe carried out the killing. It's really important that we catch this guy, Jo. He's a wrong'un, a real fucking brute.'

She chewed her bottom lip and nodded. Knew the type. I tried to imagine living with violent sexual murder as an everyday occupational hazard.

'Do you think any of the girls knew her?'

'I've been through this with the police,' she said quietly. 'How would any of the girls have known her? She never worked here.'

'Did anyone see anything suspicious around Brownswood that night?'

She shook her head.

'Were any of the girls around between three and six that morning, who may have made a note of a vehicle acting strangely?'

'They're mostly crack heads at that time, love. Those girls don't know what day of the fucking week it is.'

Fintan dug out a newspaper from his briefcase and laid it out in front of her. 'What about this girl, Valerie Gillespie. She worked down here for four or five nights back in December.'

'Until what?'

'Until she got killed and chopped up, possibly by the same guy.'

'I'm good with faces,' she said, unfazed. 'I've never seen that one before.'

'Could you show this picture to the other girls?'

'Could you go down there and dish out a few blowjobs? You stick to your work, Mr Reporter, and I'll stick to mine.'

Fintan sighed and leaned back, defeated. As he lit a fag, I had a thought.

'You've taken the number of that beige Datsun Cherry, Jo. Who was going to take the number of the next car you got into?'

'I can look after meself, thanks.'

'How do you know you haven't got into a car with a maniac? Because if you have, no one's taken his details.'

'I'm not desperate like most of the other girls. I make sure he's a regular. And if he's not, I know the signs.'

'The signs?'

She turned to Fintan and chuckled dirtily. 'I hope your pal here isn't looking for fucking tips.'

Fintan laughed. 'He can use all the tips he can get, Jo, for any kind of lay.'

'Okay,' she started, 'firstly, I don't know you, so that's got my bells ringing. You're not a regular. Now if you go on too much about paying me a fair amount and not ripping me off, that's a warning sign. If you're very quiet or if you try to choose where we go to do business, then I know I'm in trouble. But you know what the biggest sign of a psycho is?'

I wondered why she was addressing all this towards me.

'If you're not horny. If a guy's horny, he wants one thing. Simple. And no guy will ever attack you after he's come. You check it out. The violent bastards never fuck the girl first. So if you're not horny, and I can tell within seconds, I'm getting out of your car, 'cos you're looking for something else.'

'You must've had some close shaves,' said Fintan, taking out his wallet.

She smiled defiantly. 'What you never hear about are the girls who fight back.'

As he peeled off two twenties, he asked: 'Jo, how many of these handwritten sheets of car plates have you got?'

'Dozens,' she said, snatching the two bank notes from his hand and the sheet from mine, 'going back eighteen months.'

'I'd love to get a look at those,' he said.

'I bet you would–' she smiled '–but they're my little nest egg.'

She turned, marched out of the park and directly into the off-licence across the road.

'Ah well,' said Fintan, 'at least we know she can only drink herself to death tonight.'

Chapter 19

Arsenal, North London
Tuesday, April 6, 1993; 21.00

On the way home, we slipped into the refreshingly unfussy Plimsoll pub on St Thomas Road to discuss a more pressing matter.

'What the hell is Da doing over here?' I asked.

'He says it's best that we don't know, which has my alarm bells ringing, I've got to admit.'

'Ma won't pick up, which is worrying the hell

out of me. She knows something, I can tell. It's got to be something to do with the "beardos", hasn't it?' I said, using our code for Da's pals in Sinn Fein/IRA.

Fintan leaned in closer. 'I asked him, straight out, "is what you're doing here going to land me or Donal in the shit?" and he swore on his mam's grave that it wouldn't. And you know when he swears on that, he means it. All he'll say is it's political but nothing dangerous or illegal.'

'What the hell does that mean?'

'It's got to be connected to these secret peace talks. What else can it be?'

'Why don't they put him in a hotel then?'

Fintan sighed and raised conciliatory eyebrows. 'He says he promised Ma he'd stay with us ... and that he'd try to patch things up with you.'

'Yeah, right.'

'At least give him a chance Donal. Jesus. He's a proud man.'

He fidgeted. 'Okay, failing that, try for Ma's sake.'

I shrugged.

'Good man,' he said, 'I tell you what though, he's useless around the house. He's driving me mad. He keeps peering over my shoulder when I'm cooking and telling me 'that's done' or 'that needs another minute'. He leaves everything out, and open. There are currently three butchered cartons of sour milk sitting on the worktop.'

'Whatever he's up to, Fintan, he can't stay at ours. I'm a policeman, for God's sake. Some of his beardo pals would have me shot.'

'Yeah, but like I told you, he says he can't go

231

anywhere where he has to book in.' Fintan sighed. 'Look, I'm working on it. I should have something sorted by tomorrow, so you just need to act civilised to him tonight, okay?'

I shrugged again.

He finished his pint. 'Come on, let's head. I don't like leaving the old fecker there on his own. There's a good chance he'll burn the place down.'

'You go. I'm staying here.'

'Ah, Donal...'

'I just can't talk to him,' I said, 'and that's that.'

I picked up a couple of bottles of wine on the way home, and took my time doing it.

Da had always been an Olympic-standard drinker and sleeper, rarely making it beyond 11pm. As the church bells chimed midnight, I guessed that the coast would be clear and strolled home.

I crept silently through the front door into the hallway. Now I just needed to open both bottles and make it to my bedroom.

'Well,' came his standard taciturn greeting from the sitting room.

My heart bulged and that aching dread returned. *What if he's pissed? What if he starts?*

'Well,' I said back, and walked on to the kitchen. I opened a bottle and turned to find him standing at the door.

'You're after getting fierce stout,' he said, pulling at his shirt collar, 'around the old neck and the face there.'

'Gee, thanks, Da. I'm guessing you haven't changed a bit. More's the pity.'

232

The one thing I inherited from him is a complete inability to disguise emotions. His eyes smouldered. God, he hated my guts.

'Fintan was telling me about your manhunt. This Conlon fella from Offaly. Any luck?'

'We haven't even verified he's a real person yet,' I said. 'Why do you ask?'

'I know a lot of people back home. I could make a few calls for you. If it'd help, like.'

'You helping the British police? Wouldn't that be collaborating with the enemy?'

Those eyes blazed.

'His name rings a bell,' he said. 'I just can't put a finger on it. And he sounds like someone that needs to be put away.'

I felt my resolve sag. *He's a proud man. At least give him a chance.*

'Fintan's got a piece going in the *Leinster Express* tomorrow,' I said. 'Hopefully that anonymous Garda will get in touch.'

'I hope so,' he said.

Go now, my brain screamed, *that's enough peace and reconciliation for one night.*

'I was on the plane yesterday, watching the safety briefing,' he said. 'The woman says about the oxygen masks, always fit your own before helping a child. It got me thinking. I got married late. I was set in me ways. I always thought that I needed to sort out all the things in my life first, and once I'd done that I'd still have time to fix everything else, you know, later.'

I tried not to look confused.

He sighed. 'We're not that different, you know, Donal.'

233

My bitterness laughed before I could stop it.

'Your job,' he said, 'it's about getting justice, isn't it? Helping the small man stand up against the bully?'

I nodded. 'Sometimes.'

'When I first went to Belfast in the sixties, Catholics couldn't get jobs. They couldn't get housing. Even though they were the majority, they weren't represented in councils or in parliament. I wanted to help the small man against the bully. Like you.'

'One minor difference, Da. I don't support terrorism.'

'Civil rights is all we wanted, like the blacks in America. Things got out of hand, I agree. But I won't walk past someone getting bullied. And neither will you.'

I wished I'd poured a glass. I felt parched. Right on cue, he looked down at the open bottle of wine in my hand.

He looked back up, his smile pitying me. 'When you're Irish and you give up on religion, or it gives up on you, you're left with an awful lot of space to fill. Some people spend their whole lives trying to fill that space and they can't. I found my cause, Donal, whether you agree with it or not. I hope you find yours.'

Those dreams I'd been having about him flashed through my mind. 'Fintan and I both know this famous cause of yours has just landed you deep in the shit. So spare me the lecture about how to live my life. All I want from you is reassurance that you're not going to drag us into the shit with you.'

'I've already told Fintan, neither of ye has anything to worry about.'

234

He turned to leave, then came back.

'I'll make those calls about Conlon,' he said. 'Just keep me posted on how it's going at your end. Oh, and I put a clothes wash on for ye yesterday and it's still not done. I don't know what's wrong with that machine.'

I got down to investigate. He'd loaded it, switched on the power, poured in the powder and conditioner and set the dials. But he hadn't pressed start. *A bit like tonight's peace talks,* I thought. *When it comes to the crunch, he won't be able to quite bring himself to press the button.*

When sleep came for me, much later, so did those recurring dreams.

The final time I saw him executed on that mattress, I woke to a startling realisation.

His offer of help ... his speech ... his attempt to explain ... Mam's missed call... Da is convinced he's going to die, real soon.

Chapter 20

Vauxhall, South London
Wednesday, April 7, 1993

As soon as it turned 9am, I rang the Garda station in Roscrea and asked to speak to the most senior officer on duty.

Of course Detective Superintendent Ger O'Driscoll already knew about our hunt for Robert Conlon, courtesy of that day's lead story in the *Leinster Express* and the ever-reliable Bog Bongos.

'I can assure you, detective,' he said in a droll, nasal, all-knowing tone, 'that there is no rapist on the loose here in the Midlands by the name of Robert Conlon, or any other rapists on the loose for that matter. I don't know where you got your information from, but might I respectfully suggest you check the credibility of your source.'

I resented this bog hopper's glib dismissal and decided to let him know it.

'I can assure you, superintendent, that I wouldn't be making this call if the source wasn't credible. After all, London is a fairly busy patch, even compared to crazy old Roscrea.'

'I sincerely hope you didn't get this information from that gurrier of a brother of yours?'

'The information comes from one of your Gardaí actually,' I snapped, then kicked myself for giving this away. 'I trust all your officers are *credible*, superintendent.'

'Well, none of them are claiming to be psychic anyway–' he laughed '–which I take to be a good sign.'

I couldn't believe he knew about this.

'I'm an old friend of your father's, Lynch. I hope you appreciate what you put him through with all that carry on. I, for one, don't blame him for washing his hands of you.'

'Maybe you need to check the credibility of your own sources, superintendent,' I said, 'because he's over here staying with me right now. As for Conlon, you better be right or my gurrier of a brother will plaster your ugly mug all over his scandalous rag.'

No sooner had I slammed down the phone than it rang again; Zoe with news. The finger-print on the torch bulb didn't match any on the criminal databases, nor did it belong to Reilly, Bernie or Slob.

It now all pointed to a different killer ... and this seemingly non-existent Robert Conlon was our only suspect. Even that seemed the flimsiest of leads, coming as it did from an anonymous source briefly mentioned in a single police report.

When my phone rang again, I couldn't bring myself to answer; I'd already had enough bad news for one day.

'Lynch, you muppet! Why aren't you picking up?' bellowed a voice from the main door. 'There's a pretty young woman at reception who wants to see you.'

Cue a half-hearted chorus of wolf whistles and yelps.

'And she's a tart if ever I saw one.'

'Tammy, great to see you,' I beamed.

I didn't know whether to peck her on the cheek or shake hand so I just hovered a safe distance away.

'Jeez, you're a hard man to find,' she drawled, all liquor, sex and Blanche DuBois.

She wore her long brown hair back, a tight-fitting blue gingham shirt with too many open buttons, tighter-still jeans and cute little Western-style ankle boots. Her bright-red mouth looked a few sizes too big for her face and chewed gum defiantly. I could instantly see her as a slouching, petulant horny teenager, so busy thinking about being bad that her gum would stick to her braces.

But age and hard-living had gently forked the edges, giving her a sense of elegant decay, like a not-long-derelict Georgian plantation.

I turned to see the female receptionists gazing at her with a mixture of damning pity and undisguised envy. I couldn't help thinking how difficult it must be for beautiful women, constantly ogled by lusting men and despising women.

'Shall we step outside for a chat,' I said quietly.

'Yes, sir,' boomed Tammy, and I wondered why Americans seem incapable of going unnoticed in any situation.

Without a word, we began walking through the car park towards Spring Gardens, an ill-named, dismal patch of no-man's-land between the police buildings and spiky local estates.

'I can't believe you tracked me down, Tammy. I'm impressed.'

'When I saw the reports about Liz on Sunday morning, it totally freaked me out. But it made me realise, I had to *do* something. It took real chutzpah to do what you did and come to Jimmy's club. I remembered your name – Donal, like Bonal. I called the number at the end of the article and asked to speak with you. The guy said that they had no one on the team called Donal. So I asked if they had any Irish cop. He said no to that too so I sorta gave up.

'Then I read an article which said they were linking what happened to Liz to this other case, Valerie something. It mentioned the Cold Case Unit, so I found the address and decided to give it one more go...'

'So you came down here in person ... on the off-chance?'

'Well, I don't live too far from here. And I'd only speak to you about this one-to-one anyway. Like I said, I have to do something. So I thought "what the hell?" If you weren't here, I'd just play the dumb American. God, the Brits love that. Sorry about running out on you Saturday.'

'Yeah, what happened?'

'Rules of the house. We're all told from day one, if management offers someone a complimentary Moët, within five minutes you make your excuses and leave. If they offer Krug, you get out of there right away. But I made sure you got outta there too.'

I stopped. 'What do you mean?'

'I keep a can of pepper spray in my bag. It's the real fucking deal, like the shit they use in North Korea? So I waited until no one was looking, slipped outside to the alley and sprayed it into the air-con vents. I didn't have a clue if it would work.'

'Work? You saved my arse, Tammy. I was sitting upstairs waiting for Jimmy Reilly to turn up and torture me.'

'You certainly gave Slob a headache.'

'I feel bad about that...'

'Don't. He's a surly creep.'

'What were you going to tell me, Tammy?'

'I was in shock. God knows what I would have blurted out. In a way it's good that I've had a few days to think it over.'

'You wanna relax and start from the beginning?'

239

I said, pointing to a bench suspiciously free of graffiti and bird shit.

'Before I say another word, Donal, I need you to understand a few things. I've come to you because I trust you. I want to do the right thing, but I know what Jimmy is capable of. If he gets even a whiff of this, I'm dead meat, so I'm placing my life in your hands, okay?

'He's always bragging about how many bent cops he has working for him, so I won't be making a statement. I won't be appearing in any court proceedings. I won't be speaking to you or any other cop about this ever again. Either you agree to this and give me your word that you'll protect my identity at all costs, or I walk right now.'

'You have my word, Tammy.'

We sat. She talked.

'Okay. To be honest, when Liz first arrived last year, I didn't really connect with her, like at all. She couldn't wait to let us all know how dancing at the Florentine was beneath her, a stopgap until her acting career took off. I snapped one day and said, "you think we don't have dreams too? You think you're the only one here with talent? You think I haven't seen girls with more talent than you show up here saying the same thing?" Then I said ... oh God.'

She closed her eyes and bowed her head to let a shudder through.

'I said to her "let's see where you are in six months." I'm such a bitch.'

Her top teeth gripped her bottom lip hard. She pushed through until that loose tear somehow rejoined her moist right eye. Suddenly, a laugh

240

burst out.

'I remember her first night. She got up on that stage and started twirling around like Kate fucking Bush, all quick little tippy-toes, swaying hair and arms. One of the girls told her to save her energy and just bend over. She didn't like that.'

Her laugh lost all its heart, shrinking to a rueful smile.

'Over a few weeks, those spotlights in her eyes started to snap off, one by one. I've seen it before. She hardened, you know? Like each night she surrendered a little bit more of herself to her club persona, the one earning all the money, the dirty little girl-next-door. You have to become someone else right? That's how we get through it.'

'Well, you seem the same to me now as you did Saturday night,' I said.

'That's because only Tammy's left.' She looked at me and smiled lamely. 'Us Americans and our therapists huh?'

I smiled back. 'At least you probably attended yours voluntarily.'

We shared a look, borderline nutjob to borderline nutjob, which somehow cemented our bond. They didn't teach that at Hendon's police training college.

'She spent every penny on her dream, you know, the high-profile agent, the professionally shot portfolio, the Super 16 showreel. I know she didn't get paid a cent for that role in *The Bill*. When that led to nothing, she got involved in some pretentious art-house play that gave her a role in return for her investment. Not only did that suck up the rest of her money, she had to reduce her nights at the club to play in this thing.'

She uncrossed and re-crossed her legs under the bench.

'My God, is that a working bar?' she said, nodding over to the boarded-up, fortified and graffiti-ravaged Queen Anne pub.

'It's a strip bar,' I said. 'From what I hear, at the polar opposite end of the scale to the Florentine.'

'That's a working strip joint? My God, it looks like something outta Beirut. We've gotta check it out,' she said, getting to her feet.

Every single outside window had been replaced with unpainted chipboard. An indestructible CCTV camera eyed us from over the barred and war-scarred front door, the only indication of life inside the squat-like shack.

'Before Saturday, I'd never been to a strip joint,' I said, opening the door for her, 'now I'm walking into my second one in four days.'

'Don't give me all that "good Catholic boy" spiel, Donal. You guys are the filthiest of all.'

I stopped to let my eyes adjust. The few working ceiling lights all pointed to a tiny triangular stage to the left. Tammy led me to the right.

'I bet the cocktails here are special,' I said.

'I'll have a water, but only if it comes in its own sealed bottle.'

I risked a lager and suggested we take a table well out of earshot.

As soon as we sat, the opening beats of 'Killer' by Seal pumped through the floor. A chubby blonde woman in her late thirties mounted the stage on all fours before wobbling to full height on her six-inch stilettoes, like a newborn giraffe.

She spent half the song getting out of her cheap underwear, the rest gamely gyrating out of tune.

'My God,' gasped Tammy, transfixed.

A huddle of six men sat between her and the bar, disturbingly close to the door marked 'Gents'.

Tammy had spotted this too. 'You'd hope that rest room is for conventional relief only, right?'

'Well, I'm not going in there.'

'I might.' She smiled, and I didn't doubt her for a second.

Another very large man had somehow earned the 'Golden Ticket' – a seat behind the stage. After getting naked, the stripper backed right up to his face, bent over and waggled her arse. He returned the favour by closing his eyes and inhaling deeply.

Tammy whooped and hollered in delight. 'My God,' she said again.

Within seconds, the stripper who murdered 'Killer' waved a rusty cigar tin under our noses. Close up, she looked to be approaching 50.

'Hey, love that ass sniffing, girl,' balled Tammy, poking a fiver in on top of all the loose change. 'My friend here was wondering how he can get a seat behind the stage.'

'I can do a private show for you out the back, dahling,' she said, and I shrivelled like a nuked daisy.

The earnest opening piano notes of the Pet Shop Boys' 'Opportunities (Let's Make Lots of Money)' surged in and another scantily clad porker grappled with the edge of the stage.

'So Liz was strapped for cash then?'

'For a while, yes, until she became one of the IT girls. There's a group of them, a sort of inner core, who Jimmy sends on little holidays. I don't know how they were picked or what qualities they have that earned them a place in this clique. I've never been invited to join it and neither have quite a few of the girls I'm close to. But Liz became part of it around the start of the year.

'These girls travel abroad, a lot. Every few weeks, a group of them will be in Malaga, or Marakesh or Amsterdam, you know, druggie places. They usually travel when the club isn't open, Sunday to Tuesday. I assumed they were out there to hostess parties for Jimmy or his friends, you know, keeping clients happy.

'I got drunk with a couple of them one night and asked them outright: what's with these trips? Liz told me there was no catch. Jimmy's never there and, even though they get invited to parties, they're not expected to work, if you know what I mean. They basically have a good time at a four-star hotel for a couple of days and come home again. She said she'd try to get me in. I remember her exact words: "It's like he gets these free flights and hotels and doesn't know what to do with them, so he gives them to us." I mean who wouldn't want a piece of that?'

'They must be doing something for these free holidays. Carrying drugs or cigarettes...'

'They denied that right off the bat. Look, these girls don't need to do stuff like that. They're already loaded.'

As Neil Tennant whinnied about looks, brains and making lots of money, I couldn't help feeling that all three must have played a role in whatever caper Liz had got herself involved in.

244

'Are these girls, you know, *special* to Jimmy somehow?'

She laughed. 'I've been there almost three years and I've never seen him even talk to one of us girls. I assumed he was gay.'

'So how did Liz qualify for this club? Can you at least tell me the names of the other girls involved?'

She leaned into her pocket and pulled out a typed sheet.

'Everything I know about them is here, names, ages, some addresses, some phone numbers. When I slide this over, that's the end of me and this whole thing, okay?'

'You can count on me, Tammy, you really can. But I need to know you're gonna be okay. Is there some way I can check that doesn't involve returning to the Florentine?'

She took a sip of water and sampled her options.

'You got a pen?' she said, finally.

She folded the bottom of the sheet over, scrawled a mobile number but no name and ripped it off.

'This person knows me but nothing about me, so don't even bother trying to shake him down. If you leave a message, I'll get it.'

She stood, signalling with her hand that I should stay.

'You say you didn't much care for Liz. Why are you taking this risk?'

'Let's just say I'm planning to kill off Tammy one day soon, and I'd like her to go out with a bang, metaphorically speaking of course.'

Chapter 21

Vauxhall, South London
Wednesday, April 7, 1993; 16.10

Jacket collar up, head down, I strode out of the squalid Queen Anne as if I'd just machine-gunned everyone inside. I dreaded being spotted by a colleague, so continued my 'fleeing assassin' speed-walk away from strip pub and office towards Black Prince Road.

As I turned left towards the Thames, the sinking mid-afternoon sun scored my sight like two red-hot darning needles. My tired head pounded; how it hated those dual torments of blinding light and heat, of uncertainty and pressure.

I had a lot to think about. Firstly, could I trust Tammy? As Bernie said the other night, these girls lie and act for a living. What if she'd been sent here by Reilly, to set me up?

I didn't know her name, address or anything about her past. Of course, I couldn't blame her for wanting to remain off-grid. How many people would have the balls to make a statement against Jimmy Reilly? But I should have pressed for her real name, at least. That would've been enough to build some sort of profile, road test her credibility, excavate any hidden ulterior motives.

'Do the right thing,' she'd said. But any confidence trickster could say the same. Jingo bingo.

As it stood, I had to take her word for it, and only her word. What if she turned out to be a fantasist, a pathological liar or a scorned woman bent on getting back at Reilly? At best, I'd be a laughing stock, consigned to The Cemetery for all eternity. At worst, that laugh would be carved, ear-to-ear, into my cold dead face.

But I had to acknowledge her claim that, just by talking to me, she'd placed her life in my hands. If Reilly found out we'd met, she'd die. I felt certain of that.

As cloud rallied around the sun to protect my sore head, I decided to trust Tammy. I now had a list of women who held the key to this entire case, possibly to taking down one of London's most infamous crime lords. As I strode back through the Unit's front door, I fingered the piece of paper in my trouser pocket, certain it was my ticket out of here.

Either walking or in a box.

'Was she a tart, Lynch?' demanded Maureen, the receptionist, as soon as I got through the door. 'Tell me the truth.'

'Why is it important to you, Maureen?'

'I knew it,' she declared. 'I've got a gift for reading people.'

'Amongst myriad others, I'm sure.'

'Another very secretive Irishman called, left you a number to call him back on. He mentioned that it was urgent several times.'

'My brother?'

'Even dodgier, I'd say. And I'd trust him even less if I were you. Here.'

She handed me a 0506 number, code for Tulla-

247

more in Ireland. I got to the desk and dialled. The beeping told me I'd got through to a pay phone. After a single ring, someone picked up.

'Hello,' I said, 'DC Lynch speaking.'

'I have important information for you,' said a quiet voice on the other end, 'but I can't talk over the phone.'

'Concerning?'

'Robert Conlon.'

'How do I know you're genuine?'

'I'm a Guard. I've contacted your enquiry twice before, most recently on December 30th. And three days before that.'

'You didn't give your name.'

'I can't. If you meet me, you'll understand why.'

'You know I can't just hop on a plane to Ireland on the basis of this chat. I rang your boss yesterday and he denied that any such person exists.'

'I don't expect you to answer, DC Lynch, but does the Gillespie case feature an anally inserted foreign object or weird activity connected with her hair?'

I couldn't speak.

'Thought so,' he said. 'Give me your fax number and stand by it.'

I recited the number.

'If you're still interested, call this number again in exactly two hours.'

He hung up. At least I assumed he'd hung up. Unlike the movies, there was no dead tone, just silence. I wondered why Hollywood did that...

Twenty minutes' later, a robotic wolf whistle signalled fax incoming, followed by the familiar jerky grind. I jumped up to see a fingerprint inching through. A poor quality black and white passport photo followed. I scanned the fingerprint and forwarded a copy to Zoe. I remembered Tammy's typed list of IT girls and made a photocopy of that too.

I picked up my ringing phone.

'Ah, DC Lynch, your personal forensic lab calling,' said Zoe, sounding stoked. 'The print you just sent me is a match to the one found on the torch bulb in the twitching den. One hundred per cent.'

'Wow,' I said, my guts suddenly churning like that fax machine.

'Good news?'

'I think so. I'll tell you all about it later.'

My mind whirred: whoever this Robert Conlon is, he must have murdered Valerie Gillespie. It looked pretty certain that he then went on to kill Liz Little. Why did a serving Irish cop feel so nervous about putting me onto this suspect? Why had a senior Garda denied all knowledge of Robert Conlon earlier? If he was a known offender, how had he escaped any media attention?

There was only one way to get to the bottom of all this; meet the source in person. The faxed fingerprint would help me swing this with Barrett.

But first, I made an appointment to resurrect my career.

Chapter 22

Finsbury Park, North London
Wednesday, April 7, 1993; 17.00

Spence insisted that I meet him in the Red Rose pub a few hundred yards from Holloway police station.

'Just tell the barman you're here to see Alex,' he said, so I did.

He wordlessly poured my Stella, led me to a door at the back of the pub, unlocked it and pointed upstairs.

As I trudged up the thick red pile, the key rattled in the lock behind me. The bolt slid sweetly and clicked locked, like a bullet in a chamber. My chest tightened and my heart pumped inside my ears. I suddenly thought ... if someone wanted to execute me, the preamble would probably go something like this...

With its deep red carpet, wallpaper and leather seats, the upstairs strived to embody the pub's name, but felt more like the inside of an amniotic sac, or Cooper's dream in *Twin Peaks*. I suddenly saw Spence in a red suit and shirt, performing a jerky little backwards shuffle across the floor and laughed out loud. I then remembered Liz's red-themed appearance to me that first night and shuddered. Something about this colour pointed to her killer. What?

250

It must be connected to that sample of paint in her head wounds...

Dread clung to me like a stubborn ground mist. Yesterday, Spence had me rattling like a garden gate in a hurricane, until every last calorie of self-confidence had jounced out.

He wanted Tammy on a plate and he wouldn't stop bullying me until he got her. *Too bad Spence, Tammy is my snout, not yours.* I reminded myself not to let slip her first name. That alone could be enough for him to trace her. I suddenly felt hot and agitated. I got up and paced the room but that sense of foreboding stalked me diligently.

I needed to open a window, and marched over to inspect the closest candidate. Outside, a bus clattered through the low branches of a tree. That's what Tammy and I were to Spence now; low hanging fruit to be battered free and devoured.

As the bus cleared my field of vision, my eyes were drawn to a figure bustling out of a William Hill bookies' shop across the road. He jabbed betting slips into the inside pocket of his jacket, a rolled-up *Racing Post* into his leather satchel. I had Spence down as a self-flagellating, hair-shirted, abstentious Presbyterian ... not a man partial to a flutter. I breathed properly for the first time. I could do business with a gambler.

The clatter of the door unlocking made me jump. I stood to face the stairs and my own terror. Spence devoured them two at a time, and arrived at the top looking at me as if I might be next.

'This better be good, Lynch.'

'My contact at the Florentine has been in touch.'

251

'When? How?'

'Let's just say she's quite resourceful.'

'I dare say most whores have to be, Lynch. And...?'

'She handed me this.'

I took the photocopied sheet out of my arse pocket and handed it over.

'She said that Liz Little and the other girls on this list formed an inner circle at the Florentine who regularly take trips abroad, seemingly on Jimmy's behalf.'

'Trips for what? To where?'

'Every few weeks, a group of them fly to Morocco, Spain or Holland, "druggie places", as she put it, stay for a couple of days, then fly back. She doesn't know the purpose, but they must be up to something.'

'Surely it's obvious what he brings them over there for ... the same thing that keeps them busy at the Florentine.'

'She says otherwise. There's more to it. But that's all she knows.'

'Who is this girl? Is she willing to make a statement?'

'No, sir. And I promised I wouldn't reveal her identity to anyone.'

'You can tell me, Lynch.'

'I'm sorry, sir, I gave her my word. She won't even tell me, or give me an address or number. I genuinely know nothing about her.'

He stared again at the list.

'I'll get these girls checked out,' he said, waggling the sheet my way, 'see what comes up. Is this the only copy?'

'Yes, sir,' I lied.

'Let's keep it that way,' he said, tucking it in with his betting slips.

'Is that all, Lynch?'

'Yes, sir.'

'Let me know if she gets in touch again. I'll get to work on this.'

I nodded. He turned and walked towards the stairs. Two down, he turned back: 'You delivered like you said you would Lynch. Fair dues. You're very close to getting that seat on my team. You just need to work out what's important here. A collar like Jimmy Reilly and a promotion, or the welfare of some two-bit whore.'

I treated myself to a few celebratory pints, then rang Zoe with my news impressing Spence today, flying to Ireland tomorrow. She seemed quiet, distracted.

'Is everything okay?' I demanded finally.

'Oh, couldn't be better Donal. I've just got food to cook, a bath to run, clothes to wash, a kitchen to clean, no shopping in, bills to pay, a really grisly child and a mother who wants me to fail.'

'I can come over, give you a hand.'

'You can't just turn up in his life like that. Boom. Hey presto, here's your latest dad.'

Latest? I thought.

'Sorry. It's just ... a grind sometimes.'

'I couldn't do what you do, Zoe, and that's a fact. I think you're amazing.'

'God, you wouldn't have thought so five minutes ago...' she groaned. 'Thanks though. Nobody ever says nice things to me, except you.'

'Glad to hear it!' I said, determined to leave on a high. 'I'll call you tomorrow before I fly back.'

'Donal?' she said suddenly, just as I was about to hang up.

'Yeah?'

'This meeting tomorrow.' She sighed. 'Something about it doesn't seem right.'

'What do you mean?'

'You don't know anything about him. You're a British police officer now. You said yourself it's something you have to keep quiet about over there. The whole thing worries me.'

'It's my old stomping ground, Zoe, don't forget,' I said brightly. 'I spoke to this guy. He sounded genuine enough. We're meeting in a pub so what's the worst that can happen?'

'Just call me as soon as you're finished, okay?'

'I will,' I said, smiling at the warm fuzzy goo flooding my veins. I hadn't had someone worry about me for quite a few years.

I next dialled the house. If Da answered, I'd hang up. If he'd gone out, I'd take the opportunity to barricade myself into my bedroom until tomorrow's early start.

'Hello?' barked Fintan.

'Well,' I said, 'where is he?'

'Who the fuck have you been talking to?'

'What are you on about? Talking about what?'

'About Da being here? Who did you tell?'

'I didn't mention it to a soul. Why would I?'

'Well, someone's blabbed,' he snapped, 'and it wasn't me and it certainly wasn't him.'

'Fintan, I've no idea what you're talking about.'

'Well, you'll be delighted to learn that Dad's

not staying here any more, as that seems to be all you give a shit about.'

'What's happened?'

'Some people he really didn't want to see turned up this afternoon. I fobbed them off while he hid himself upstairs. I finally got rid of them and he bolted. I've no idea where he is now.'

'What do you mean, "some people"? Irish? Beardos?' I said.

'The guy who spoke sounded Scottish.'

'Oh great. So who were they then? Protestant paramilitaries? Spooks? Are they back to burn us out later? I told you he'd bring nothing but trouble.'

'I don't fucking know who they were,' he shouted, 'but how the fuck did they know he was here? If you told someone, you've got to tell me now. Because this is freaking me out.'

I suddenly remembered that morning's call with Detective Superintendent Ger O'Donnell in Roscrea, how I'd accidentally blabbed Da's whereabouts. Surely that can't be connected...

'I won't talk any more over the phone, Fintan, because whatever's going on here is major league.'

'Tell me about it. I've just packed an overnight bag. I suggest you do the same.'

'Fintan, no matter what's going on, you know we've got to stay the hell out of it, right?'

'How can we do that?' he said quietly, 'He's our dad.'

Chapter 23

Maynooth, Co. Kildare, Ireland
Thursday, April 8, 1993; 12.00

Frank, my mysterious source for all things Robert Conlon, refused to meet me anywhere near County Offaly, let alone in Tullamore.

'It's just too risky for me,' he said, and I snapped.

'Jesus, Frank, it's not like you're passing over a briefcase of Plutonium, or nuclear secrets.'

'You wanna bet?'

We settled finally on Maynooth, a neat little University town sixteen miles west of Dublin, and a noon rendezvous in a pub called Brady's.

'Noon in Maynooth it is so. How will I know you Frank?' I said.

'Because I'll be the only person in there,' he replied, matter-of-factly.

As I slid behind a table at the back of the pub, I realised he was almost right. One of those bone-yellow old timers propped up the far end of the bar. Pint, fag, topcoat and cap on, he sat hunched and staring into his stout, peaceful and content. Every pub in Ireland had one or two of these ancient daytime regulars, quietly basking in the stale morning air like reptiles soaking up the sun. As he took a quivering draw on his pint, I silently saluted him for doing exactly what he pleased, and felt a twinge of melancholy that these gnarled, noble islands of men would die out soon.

Frank strode in bang on 12, looking every inch the off-duty copper. Our universal 'style' could best be described as 'failed casual' and Frank had it nailed. The desert boots looked too new, the Farrah slacks too pressed and high-waisted, the striped blue shirt too 'Sunday best'. His combed, side-parted hair had been dyed a clownish chestnut so that it resembled an especially tenacious toupee.

His pale face and sad blue eyes bore the puffs and lines of a stresser. As he got closer, I could see 'w' for worrier imprinted into his pillow-ground forehead.

'Donal?' he said, right hand outstretched as his left placed a tan leather briefcase on a chair.

'We have company,' I muttered conspiratorially, nodding towards the top-coated skeleton at the bar.

Frank's eyes darted over, betraying his crippling anxiety, but he failed to see the funny side.

'Can I get you a tea or a coffee, Frank?'

'I could use a pint, to be honest.'

'Glad you said that Frank, 'cos so could I.'

It's great to be back in Ireland, I thought, walking to the bar, *where Guinness counts as a healthy snack and a pint at midday is no big deal.*

As our pints settled, I returned to the table, laid out my warrant card and laid bare my career, which seemed to settle his flaps no end. Frank Farrell told me he'd recently been promoted to Detective Sergeant in Birr having spent twelve years serving towns all over the Midlands.

As soon as the pints landed, Frank took off.

'I think it's best if we start with Conlon's criminal record,' he said, reaching into his leather case. 'I've got basic background information on all his convictions.' He plonked a grubby, cardboard file on the table. 'Ask me anything you like as we go.'

Frank paused, then exhaled a self-psyching blast of air.

'Okay, Robert Christopher Conlon, born Foxburrow, April twentieth, 1945.

'Aged thirteen, convicted of several counts of burglary and sent to St Joseph's Industrial School in Clonmel, run by the Rosminian order.'

He looked up from the file. 'Sounds like a Nazi concentration camp. The kids had numbers instead of names and were starved, beaten, sexually abused.'

'One day, the lid's gonna come off all that shit and there'll be hell to pay.'

'By the time I'm finished here, you might not feel so confident about that,' he said glumly.

He got back to the official narrative. 'Conlon returned home aged fifteen. Aged sixteen he was kicked out by his father. He lived rough in local barns and outhouses, stealing from farms and shops. One of the locals remembers hunting with his father one Sunday when they came across a farmer giving Conlon a blowjob out in the woods.'

'Jesus. What did they do?'

'His dad let off a couple of rounds, which gave the farmer such a fright that he bit down.'

I laughed out loud.

'Apparently the screams could be heard in Moneygall,' said Frank, poker-faced, before he continued. 'Aged seventeen, he was sent to an-

258

other reform school, St Conleth's in Daingean, Offaly. From what I hear, no one came out of that place right in the head. Aged twenty he moved to England, and this is where the really sick stuff starts.'

He located another sheet of paper, sliding it over for me to scan.

1964, attempted rape of a female minor, aged 6, during a burglary in Hackney, East London. Served nine days in Borstal, sent back to Ireland.

1969, attempted rape of a woman in Durham, England. Sentenced to six years, served three.

1973, rape, GBH of a woman aged 54 in Birmingham. Apprehended at Holyhead ferry port. Sentenced to ten years, served seven.

Frank spoke up. 'There's a pre-sentence report from that one. The psychiatrist described him as, hang on, "an explosive psychopath who will kill if he hasn't already", and recommended he be locked away indefinitely. He was out after seven years and on a plane back to Ireland.'

'So that would've been...'

'1981,' Frank said with a nod. 'Of course, this was before computers and sex registers, so he moved to Kilkenny city and slipped back into life anonymously. This is where his rap sheet effectively ends and a new phase of violence against women begins. By now, he'd worked out a way of getting away with it.'

'I don't follow.'

'Instead of attacking strangers, Conlon got to know his victims first, then brutalised them. And judging by his rap sheet, this new strategy worked a treat.'

259

He read my confusion, taking a few mouthfuls of Guinness to consider how best to put me straight.

'Let me explain how I first encountered Conlon. I was at the police station in Tullamore one Monday morning in 1987 when a young woman came running through the door in a terrible state, barefoot, wearing just a shirt with bright red welts on her neck.

'Her name was Anne Gahan, she was sixteen and she'd just escaped from Conlon's flat on Market Square having been held there, against her will, since Sunday morning.

'He had raped her repeatedly, in her words, "every which way" while restraining her with a rope around her neck. After more than twenty-four hours held like this, she managed to sneak out of his bedroom and creep around the flat looking for a window to open to either escape or to raise the alarm. She finally found one on the second floor, opened it, grabbed onto a drainpipe and clambered down. She must've been desperate because it was a good thirty-foot drop.

'We got round there. For starters, he was gone which I thought spoke volumes. We found her prints on the second-floor windowsill and on the drainpipe and we found the length of rope she'd described next to his bed. Medical examination confirmed she'd been violently sexually assaulted. We arrested him and, of course, he said the whole thing had been consensual. But what she told us was a real eye opener.

'She'd come out of care in Dublin. She'd no money or relations who could help and was really worried about her future. Someone at the home

260

said there was a middle-aged lady in Tullamore called Jenny Quinn who took in lots of kids from care, and she should give her a go.

'She moved into Jenny's, got a job washing dishes at a local hotel and became friends with Jenny's 14-year-old daughter Dympna and with Jenny's boyfriend, Robert Conlon. Let me quote a line from her statement here: "Bob was very kind to us all. He used to buy us cigarettes and drinks and runners, he'd take us to discos and pubs and if someone was stuck, he'd let them stay in his flat. I've never really had a proper dad so it meant so much to me." I think these days they call it grooming.

'In a later statement, she told us how he'd tricked her into going to his flat that Saturday night in the first place. She fancied a local guy who drives a taxi but felt too shy to approach him, so Uncle Bob said he'd get the fella around to his place that night and that she should pop in.

'Needless to say, the taxi driver never showed. He gave her a few drinks, she complained of a bad headache – God knows what he'd spiked them with – so he gave her a couple of pills. She thought they were Anadin but says the next thing she remembers is waking up naked in his bed with the sun shining through the curtains. He tried it on with her, and she backed away. He said something like: "You didn't have any problem with it last night." She felt a rough rope tighten around her neck and he raped her, over and over, all throughout that day.

'While she's telling us this, a senior detective at the station, John Keegan, keeps banging the table demanding to know why she hadn't escaped before Monday.

'Now he started banging the desk asking why she hadn't mentioned fancying this taxi driver before, or the drinks with Conlon. He kept saying "this doesn't look good, you take drinks from a man, you spend the whole of Saturday night and Sunday night with him, then you cry rape Monday morning." He started commenting on her denim skirt and how he'd seen her parading herself around the town in a vest top wearing loads of make-up. I remember saying "should we not have a female officer present here under the circumstances" and getting shouted down. That's when I started to smell a rat.

'Fair dues to Anne, she stuck to her story under fierce pressure. When they were finished, they told her she'd have to go back to the care home in Dublin. The last thing Keegan says to her is "if you think you're pregnant, there's a rape crisis centre up there you can call. I'm sure they'll believe you and help you get on the boat to England". She got no after-care, no health examination or psychological assessment at all. I've a daughter myself only a bit younger than her, Donal. Jesus, it could happen to any young woman, you know? You'd want your own daughter treated better than that.'

He swallowed hard and sniffed.

'Anyway, it was just as well Anne went back to Dublin. They charged Conlon with five counts of rape and one count of buggery, but granted him bail. Not only that, the judge imposed bail conditions that he must stay at Jenny Quinn's home. Bearing in mind Jenny had a 14-year-old daughter at the time who regularly invited friends around, I found this unacceptable and raised it with Keegan.

'Next thing I'm accused of getting too close to Anne Gahan and taken off the case. When I complained, Keegan threatened to leak it to the national papers. I couldn't risk it. My wife and kids ... well, you know what it's like. I applied for a transfer to Birr and got it, in record time.

'A few months later, Anne rings me in a state ... they hadn't called her to give evidence. They can't stop me going down to the courthouse. I discover that the prosecution made no mention of the rope found at the scene. The rape charges had all been dropped. Conlon pleaded guilty to carnal knowledge with a minor and received a suspended sentence. Of course, because the case involved a minor known to the defendant, the judge imposed a reporting ban. And that was that. Case dead and buried, Conlon free to carry on grooming other vulnerable young women. No one would ever know what he did to Anne Gahan.

'Two more over here?' he called to the barman.

'Why were they letting Conlon off the hook? I don't understand.'

'That's only the half of it,' he said.

'You've heard about the Kilkenny incest case that broke earlier this year?'

'I can't say that I have, Frank. I don't follow the Irish news that much any more.'

He sighed. 'You're just as well. There's a man charged with raping his daughter repeatedly over ten years and impregnating her aged fifteen. It's a scandal for all sorts of reasons, chief amongst them the fact that the authorities didn't believe her claims for many years. Even neighbours knew what was going on and did nothing. The dad was a real scumbag, used to go round the pubs showing pornographic photos of her, for Christ's sake. Anyway, I met this girl, and she tells me Conlon was a family friend. I took a statement from her. Listen to this.'

Frank picks up a piece of paper and starts to read. '"Bob used to come round to our house sometimes at night and he and my father would drink whiskey together. My father would say 'where have you been?' and Bob would say, 'I've been away visiting some relations.' Then my father would laugh. I could sense it was some sort of code. He was creepy and they were birds of a feather." I could go on but you get the picture.'

My blood froze. Those dreams I'd been having ... Dad and the dark travelling stranger drinking whiskey by our fire ... 'away visiting some relations' ... it couldn't be...

'Jesus, are you alright there, Donal? You look like you've seen a ghost.'

'Have you decent photos of Conlon?'

'Yes, of course,' he said, reaching back into his case.

He laid them out on the table and my brain went into spasm.

'Excuse me, Frank,' I managed to say before sprinting to the loo and spewing in the sink.

I blew hard and examined my face in the mirror's unforgiving white light.

'What the hell have I been seeing?' I asked my blood-red eyes. I ran the tap and swirled the water

264

until the vomit had drained. I splashed more on my hot face and let the horror sink in. I'd seen Robert Conlon in my dreams, sitting by the fire with Da, drinking whiskey. They'd been 'birds of a feather'.

I walked over to the towel, yanked down a stretch and buried my face in it. So I'd now started seeing killers in my dreams. Perhaps I was psychic after all? I took a series of deep breaths and scolded myself. Da must have known Conlon once ... somehow my subconscious unearthed that memory of him at our house. Somehow, my brain figured out he was tied up in these murders. Somehow.

Why hadn't Da mentioned it?

I walked back to the mirror to check my face and mouth for remnants. 'You've got plenty of time to figure all this out later,' I instructed my porcelain white face. 'Get back in there and hear Frank out.'

I marched back into the lounge. 'Sorry about that, Frank,' I said. 'I've been struggling with a bug. I thought I was over it.'

'Jesus, that was some turn, Donal. I thought for a second you'd recognised Conlon.'

'Christ no! Who'd forget a mug like that?'

'So, as I was saying, he targets vulnerable women and girls who wouldn't be taken seriously by the police or missed by anyone else. He realises he can do what he wants to them, that they have nowhere to turn. I have several examples here, all vulnerable young women.

'I've met most of them. They couldn't wait to tell me about his sexual kinks: cutting them and

265

drinking their blood; inserting foreign items into them, particularly anally; coming in their hair then cutting it off and keeping it as a memento. They were so fucked up that they saw this as his way of expressing his love for them, for fuck's sake.'

The pints arrived, giving Frank time to work out where to take me from here.

He swallowed a third of his in one gulp, wiped his mouth and moved on. 'Conlon has always drifted between Ireland and England, usually going via Northern Ireland. Like I said, there's no register of convicted sex offenders and he doesn't have to check in anywhere. A group of us are working together trying to keep track of his movements, so that we can warn local police. I've got people in the ferry, airline and hire car companies looking out for him too. He travels under two false names, Lesley Cahill and Thomas Koschei, believe it or not, after some mythical Slavic child killer.

'We worked out late last year that he was somewhere in the London area. When I read about the murder of Gillespie, I thought I'd better call him in. As soon as I asked you about batteries and hair, and you went quiet, I knew it was him. But at least now I know every cop in London is looking for him. That's some comfort. I've done all I can.'

I glanced up too quickly, giving myself away.

'You have flagged him. Donal?'

'I ... not yet. I didn't know anything about you, Frank.'

'Jesus, I sent you his fingerprint and his picture. You've obviously matched that print to something. What are you waiting for?'

'It's a terrible picture.'

'I could've got you a better one.'

'I had to be sure about the source, Frank. I'll call it in now, as soon as we're done here,' I said, a little defensively.

'Jesus, I hope for your sake he hasn't struck again since yesterday.'

I ignored the shudder and pressed on. I needed to get on that phone, and quickly.

'Why does he keep getting away with stuff in the Irish Midlands?'

He helped himself to the next third of his pint.

'Back in the 1960s, my uncle worked as a detective on the football corruption scandal in England, you know, when they uncovered players betting against their own teams and throwing games. I always remember one thing he told me. "No single player can throw a game. If three outfield players are in on it, they can ensure that their team loses. But if these three players can rope in the goalkeeper, then the sky's the limit, they can basically deliver an exact losing result."'

He turned to me, eyebrows raised, mouth clamped shut as if to say 'there, you have it'.

'I've got to level with you, Frank, I've never been a great one for soccer, or riddles.'

He shifted uneasily in his seat. I guessed whatever he was about to say he'd never uttered out loud before.

'Conlon has three very big players on his side in these parts, helping him escape prosecution, a senior detective, a circuit judge and a local government minister. I'm not going to name names, because I don't need to. You could probably figure out who I'm referring to in five minutes, if you still have even half an ear to the ground here.'

'And why do these three powerful men choose to help a sexual deviant escape prosecution?'

'The answer is in your question. Think parties attended by vulnerable girls still in care, some of them not yet legal age, organised by Robert Conlon and his birds-of-a-feather friends. Conlon would rent a house somewhere out in the country. They'd all tell their wives and colleagues they were away visiting some relations. That was the in-joke.'

'Jesus. That's a hell of an allegation, Frank.'

'It's a hell of a scandal, Donal.'

'And you have proof?'

'Robert Conlon has proof, video and photos. He couldn't wait to tell me all about it as soon I arrested him, show me what a big shot he is, what a big mistake I was making trying to take him down, how he'd ruin my career.'

'You've seen the material?'

'I don't need to see the material. I saw what happened to our case. He's got them by the balls alright, and they're not the only ones.'

'You said if three players can rope in a goalkeeper, then the sky's the limit. Who's the goalkeeper in all this, Frank?'

He chewed his bottom lip and shook his head. 'I can't say,' he said.

He stood, put the Conlon file back in his leather bag, snapped it shut and finished his pint.

'Oh, come on Frank, it's not like I can do anything with the information.'

He downed the rest of his pint and planted the

glass on the table. 'Good luck with it all, Donal,' he said, offering his right hand. 'I hope you succeed where we failed and put that sick fuck behind bars.'

I took it and shook, felt the slip of paper in his palm, turned my hand knuckle-down to ensure it transferred into mine. After he was out of sight, I got my stuff together, bid farewell to the barman and headed to the toilets. Once locked inside a cubicle, I opened my palm and inspected the piece of paper.

I had to check the name scrawled across it several times before I let myself believe it.

'Holy fucking shit,' I gasped, ripping it up into as many pieces as I could, flushing it down the loo and getting out of there as quickly as possible.

At least now I knew the real reason Da had come to London.

Chapter 24

Irish Midlands
Thursday, April 08, 1993; 14.15

As I bore left off the main Dublin–Galway road towards my home town of Clara, I began to wonder if springing a surprise visit on Mam now seemed such a good idea.

Her chronic insomnia and haymaker medication made her skittish at the best of times. She'd be sick with worry about Da. I didn't want my sudden appearance pushing her over the edge...

I pulled up at a phone box just outside Kilbeggan and dialled that number you never forget. When the answerphone kicked in, I imagined her pottering about in the garden. She'd hear it and come in, knowing I'd try again. I gave it five minutes and redialled. Same result. Maybe she was staying with one of her sister's, as Fintan had predicted. But she rarely spent more than a night away from home; something's not right.

I ordered myself not to panic, got back in the hire car and set off along 'bungalow boulevard' towards home.

What a morning! At least now I'd made both the Cold Case Unit and the Liz Little incident room aware of Robert Conlon. I'd even tracked down a shop in Maynooth with a fax machine and sent over several images.

Frank's outrage that I hadn't flagged Conlon yesterday had given me The Fear. He'd been right, of course. By now, every street girl in London should have had Conlon's mugshot waved under their noses. Instead, because of me, that process would only just be starting.

'Jesus, I hope for your sake he hasn't struck again since yesterday.'

I reached our place surprised to find the gates shut, so I parked up on the road.

As soon as I got out of the car, I noticed the blinds closed against the front windows. I scraped open the over-painted gate's stiff handle and crunched up the gravel towards the front door. I peered through the eye-level circular pane of ornate glass and saw that all the doors leading off the hallway had been closed. She only did this when they went away. Where had she gone?

I rang the doorbell anyway, then strode around to the back door to discover it also locked. I checked about me before making the ten-foot walk to the squat little gas cylinder box. I slid the lid back halfway and leaned in. They always kept a spare key under the bottle. Tilting the orange metal cylinder to the left while leaning down with your right could be tricky enough sober. I smiled at all the times I'd struggled to drunkenly perform this exercise and wondered how close I'd come to blowing up the house. Except today there was no key.

I slid the lid completely off and looked in. There it was, lying on the ground to the left of the bottle, dropped in a hurry. As I grabbed it, a sudden breeze rattled the shed doors and rustled the trees, prompting a murder of argumentative crows to dry-gargle the muggy, discontented air.

Something definitely isn't right.

I unlocked the back door quietly and tiptoed in. I then reminded myself that this was my home and quit the creeping. In the kitchen, every surface gleamed, uncluttered and empty. Through to the sitting room, the cushions on the sofa sat alert and plump. The TV had been switched off properly, not left on standby. There wasn't a used mug or half-read newspaper or misplaced remote control to be seen. Too perfect.

The framed Sacred Heart's 3D eyes caught mine. God, I hated that picture, the way His eyes followed you about. It was like being stalked by the fucking Bee Gees. The Omnipotent Gibb managed to look even more pitying today than usual. I suddenly sensed real eyes watching me and checked out the window. Maybe I just wasn't used to the quiet any more.

Spooked, I headed upstairs. The 'show house' charade continued as I opened door after door to manic cleanliness. At the end of the hallway, I came to that dark brown, arched, fortified oak door that neither Fintan nor I had ever crossed. Da's study, where he and his bottle of Bushmills would so often barricade themselves. He'd never left it unlocked, even with him inside. As a child, I imagined the walls sporting racks of ArmaLite AR-18s, or 'Widow makers' as his charming Provo pals called them. By my teens, I fantasised a crack team of SAS fighters hoofing down this door, hauling him and his hatred off to the H-Block for an indeterminate spell.

I felt a sudden, overwhelming urge to get through this door, to find out what lay inside Michael's hidden world. I spent half my childhood guessing where he kept the key, and concluded that it must have always been 'on him', somehow. Now, with both parents out of the way, I had an altogether more radical idea.

I rang Mick Lowry, local locksmith, and set out the problem – a lost key – and the deadline – tonight's flight. When I stressed that Michael needed something out of this room – 'a bit of an emergency, like' – he practically dropped the phone to make time.

'I see you had a bit of a go yourself,' said Mick, surveying the lock.

'Sorry?'

'You made a few scratch marks around the lock here, look.'

I squinted hard at the metal. He was right; fresh, hairline scrapes showed that the lock had been recently nibbled. Not by me, I didn't mention.

Spooks, IRA recruits and grunts are taught the basics in lock-picking and it's easy to see why. Lowry finagled the door open in less than thirty seconds. He waived the outrageous call-out fee of £50, out of fear or respect for Michael, I couldn't tell.

'Just mention I did this for him,' he practically begged.

'I can't do that, Mick,' I said. 'If he finds out I mislaid the key he'll go mental.'

'Oh,' said Mick, wishing now he'd charged me full whack and maybe more.

He stood there, waiting for me to open the door. I didn't.

'Thanks a million then, Mick. I'll stand you a pint next time I see you.'

'Grand,' said Mick, but he didn't budge.

'I'd better get on then,' I said, pointing to the door.

'Right so,' he said, backing away, the nosy bastard.

I waited until the back door slammed shut, then pushed open that study door. My hands felt clammy against the cold groaning oak, and had to call on a shoulder for backup. My eyes squinted into the gloom. I palmed the wall for a light switch, hit it and recoiled.

'What the fuck...?'

Back down in the sitting room, a red light flashed on the new-fangled home phone and I wondered if that might offer up a clue. I dialled into the answer machine, but heard only my missed calls from earlier.

I then saw a redial button so gave that a whirl.

'Hello, Dr Harnett's surgery,' came a nasal female voice.

'Hi, it's Donal Lynch here, son of Michael and Dolores. I'm at home now and there's no sign of Mam. I just wonder if you know anything.'

'Hi, Donal. Hang on there for a second, I'll check with Dr Harnett.'

This is the same Dr Harnett who golfed with Da and took a three wood to his Hippocratic Oath a few years' back by letting him know I'd joined the Met Police.

'Donal, how are you?' gushed Harnett, the oily snake.

No doctor in Ireland set such store in being called doctor, so I said: 'Fine, Pat. Where's Mam?'

He cleared his throat, I sensed to summon his most comforting bedside manner: 'She's above in Mullingar, Donal.'

'Above in Mullingar?'

'At the hospital. St Loman's. It's what she wanted, Donal.'

'What do you mean, it's what she wanted?'

'She's been in a really bad way, Donal. Some of the things she was saying ... it's for her own safety.'

I felt my temple throbbing against the phone.

'Let me guess, Pat: Michael wanted her out of the way, and you signed the necessary papers. I dare say you'll have a good laugh about it soon,

274

over your cosy game of golf. What I want to know is why he wanted her out of the way?'

I didn't know at which point Harnett had hung up. They really should add a tone, like they do in the movies.

Chapter 25

Mullingar, Co. Westmeath
Thursday, April 08, 1993; 15.30

I bombed it to Mullingar where the notorious St Loman's psychiatric hospital loomed ominous, Gothic and grey against the storm-ripe afternoon sky. As I turned into the drive, only a bolt of lightning and the sound of Norman Bates' raving mother could've added to the sense of foreboding.

I knew that, historically, Ireland locked away more people in mental institutions than any other nation in the world, boasting multiples of even the old Soviet Union. At its peak, we confined 20,000 of our own behind fortified walls like these, almost one per cent of the population. Of course, it had little to do with mental illness. These institutions were yet another way for the State and families to discard their 'undesirables', becoming lifelong prisons to perfectly sane disabled, deaf, blind, dumb, epileptic and even gay people.

As I killed the car engine, I vowed that Mam would not be contributing to this shameful statistic. Not so long as I was alive.

Within minutes, I had an audience with one of those rakish middle-aged men who can carry off shoulder-length white hair. Dr 'just call me Lorcan' Kavanagh seemed almost disturbingly well-prepared for my questions, as if visitors coming in search of snatched relatives was a daily occurrence.

Lorcan explained that Mam had been admitted under an Initial Section Order, which had to be signed by a patient's GP and a member of the family. My eyes shot down to the bottom of the sheet where, sure enough, Dr P.J. Harnett and Michael Lynch had scrawled their signatures. The grounds for Harnett's concerns had been listed in the body of the Order, which Lorcan happily translated into layman's terms.

'She seems to have stopped taking her anti-anxiety medication, so our first job here is to get her back on an even keel,' he said cheerfully.

'She'd never skip her medication, doctor. She might forget for a day or two but...'

'We took a blood sample. She hasn't been taking it for a lot longer than that, I'm afraid. She wasn't able to give a reason. In fact, she flatly denied not taking it, which really doesn't help. The blood doesn't lie.'

'Okay, so her anxiety levels are up. How quickly can you get them back down again so we can bring her home?'

'I'm afraid there's a bit more to it than that.' He sighed. 'She's showing signs of paranoia. She talks about men watching your home, following your father, making threatening phone calls and

276

breaking in.'

He tilted his head and rubbed his chin sagely. I could imagine him rehearsing such learned moves in the mirror.

'The most worrying aspect of her behaviour is that she has these visions of your father being shot on the doorstep. She dreams this scenario frequently and fully expects it to happen at any moment during the day, which has led to some unusual actions on her behalf, as you may appreciate.'

'Such as...'

He allowed himself a little smile. 'Let's just say the postman won't be calling again for a while.'

'But surely this is just an extension of her anxiety, which her medication was treating really well.'

'I'm sure you're right, Donal, but when a patient visualises death, we must consider them a potential suicide risk. We've got to play it completely safe.'

Suicide risk? Mam?

'Which means?'

'She's going to be here for at least a couple of weeks. We've got a lot to sort out. She's currently on Diazepam and Citalopram for her anxiety and Zopiclone for her insomnia. These are powerful drugs and they need time to settle in her system so that we can get her back on the level.'

'Are powerful chemicals really the only way to sort this?'

'If you want her home sooner rather than later, then yes.'

I sighed. 'My brother and I live in London.

277

Dad's away. I worry that no one's here for her.'

'Dr Harnett says he'll pop in regularly.'

That's what worries me, I thought.

'You're free to go see her now. Then you should call her closest friends. It is important that she gets regular visitors. You've got to get her fighting, then we can keep her fighting, okay?'

'Dr Kavanagh ... Lorcan, you've got to trust me on this, what you're seeing is not my mam. She's the toughest person I know. She'll pull through this.'

'I look forward to meeting the real Dolores,' he said, pointing to a seat. 'I'll get one of the nurses to take you through.'

I expected a nurse to come for me after five, maybe ten minutes. Big mistake. Welcome to the alternative GMT – 'God only knows when' Medical Time. I sat there for half an hour watching nurse after nurse pad past at a universal pace that barely topped stationary. Some emphasised their torpor by dragging flip-flops along the hard floor, giving me an overwhelming urge to boot them up the arse.

I checked the time and winced: work had paid for my return flight. I'd struggle to justify missing the second leg.

Finally, a lumpen male nurse came to the door and grunted: 'Donal Lynch?' I almost leapt into his arms.

He punched in a door code, pushed it open and led me through to the life-sucking fluorescent glare of the main ward. Behind me, the door self-kicked and I almost self-combusted from the airless heat. No wonder nurses shuffled about like

278

zombies ... I couldn't help wondering why every hospital I'd ever set foot in had been roasting hot. Surely germs and madness only thrived in such overbearing conditions?

The walls were dotted with curious brown smears and gouges where hunks of paint had dropped off like scabs.

Patients roamed about at will. Some looked empty, others hummed with agitation, bad energy and woeful hygiene. The Starers and the Swearers. I hadn't expected this, and couldn't imagine Mam ever braving a communal area where the clearly unhinged prowl free. The thought of her cowering in some side room angered me. Why the fuck should the law of the jungle apply here, in what is supposedly a place of care?

'Why are most people in here?' I asked my escort.

'The whole range,' he said, 'from the mildly depressed right through to paranoid schizophrenic.'

'And they just get thrown in together?'

He stopped and turned in bored annoyance.

'I get asked that a lot,' he said, 'especially from people who think their relatives are too grand to be here.'

'I'm not saying that. It's just that I find some of the more extreme cases here pretty intimidating.'

'Schizophrenics are people too,' he stated.

'Try telling that to someone who's had a loved one murdered by a schizophrenic,' I snapped.

He looked at me in disgust.

'I'm a cop in London. You've heard about Care in the Community?'

He nodded.

'Well, trust me, it doesn't fucking work.'

He fixed me with a stare. 'Mental illness doesn't discriminate, and neither do we. What were you expecting? Butlins? If it's not to your taste, maybe you should consider going private.'

Off he flounced into an office, fortified floor-to-ceiling by Perspex, as if to prove my point.

I planted my back firmly against a wall and watched intently. I realised that the only decoration in the entire place was a hand-written poster listing banned items: nail clippers, razors, tweezers, lighters, belts, shoelaces, spiral-bound notebooks, medicine, jewellery and underwired bras. Below it, typed for clarity, a legal note stated: *Full body searches will be carried out on all patients on admission. Subsequent body and property searches at the discretion of the on-duty Matron.*

I couldn't block out the indignity Mam must have felt being spread-eagled naked against a wall and failed to quell another surge of guilt-fuelled rage. Yes, I did think she was too grand for this shithole and its prison-like dehumanising brutality. You got a problem with that, nursey?

He'd clearly tired of my schizo-baiting prejudice and sent out an older female colleague.

'How has she been?'

She looked at me out of the corner of her eye, a little guarded.

'She's not eating and she's not associating, so we're a little worried about her.'

I didn't blame her on either front, but decided not to say that out loud. I'd antagonised enough mental health professionals for one day.

She knocked on a door, opened it without waiting for a response and called, 'Visitor for you, Dolores.'

The nurse took a step back, turned to me and nodded. I looked at the door then back to her. I didn't feel like I should just barge in on Mam's private torment, demanding explanations and answers.

'Go on,' urged the nurse gently.

My reluctant feet made meek baby steps into that harsh and Spartan room. I had a sudden flashback to my granny's parlour, being ushered in to see her laid out in a coffin, death draped upon the air like morning dew on a cobweb.

Mam lay sideways on the narrow bed, facing away from me towards the plain cream wall, her head wobbling slightly on a crooked arm. Her white pyjamas clung to her emaciated body. The side of her face looked yellow, her wrinkles deep, entrenched and intersecting, like endless fork marks in butter. Her eyes seemed unfocussed, glazed.

'Mam,' I said gently.

'Mam?' I repeated, a little too sternly.

'What are you doing here?' she said, finally.

'I was gonna ask you the same question.'

I reached down and squeezed the top of her arm. It felt bony and cold.

'How are you feeling?'

'I'm not feeling anything. Sure isn't that the whole point of pharmaceuticals?'

I sighed.

'Don't do that sigh, Donal, like you're disappointed in me. I can't stand it.'

'That was one of my other sighs actually,

281

Mother, from my vast repertoire of non-verbal disapprovals. It was the confused one. The one that's wondering why you stopped taking your medication.'

She shrugged. 'I must have got mixed up. I always take my pills. You know that.'

'They say you're not eating or talking to anyone. Mind you, when I see who's on the loose out there, I can't say I blame you.'

'They stole my cigarettes.'

'What?'

'Some of the scruffy ones. They cornered me in the TV room and started pawing at me. I had to give them my cigarettes and make a run for it.'

'You don't smoke, Mam.'

'What's that got to do with it? Still doesn't make it okay for them to steal off me.'

Christ, I thought, she's in a bad way. I remembered the doc's words – *get her fighting and we'll keep her fighting.*

'Mam, you can't just lie here all day. They'll never let you out.'

'I've made a friend. They call him Flash Lamp.'

'And why do they call him that?'

'Him and his brother used to take turns on Mary Curley while the other held the flash lamp. One day his brother wouldn't let him have his go, so he shot both of them. And now they call him Flash Lamp.'

A harsh alien laugh spewed out of her. I couldn't work out if this was her old piss-taking self, or a glimpse of a new and burgeoning madness.

'I spoke to your doctor,' I said brightly, ever the chipper corner man. 'He sounds confident that once they get your levels right, you'll be out of here in no time and back to normal...'

'Why won't any of you listen to me?'

'What do you mean, Mam?'

'I keep telling your dad, I keep telling Dr Harnett, I told the guards and now I'm telling them here ... there are men watching the house. Busy little men in suits. They do a rota in three different cars. I've made a note of the registration plates.'

She pushed herself up with her arms and spun around on the bed, her eyes re-ignited and focussed.

'I know they've been in the house, Donal. I left little traps, like Sellotape on the doors. They're after your father. I haven't been able to figure out why, but he's in danger, I know it.'

'Did you tell Da?'

'Of course. He just laughed at me. But when I called the Guards he was raging. He told me to keep my nose out. I'm only trying to look out for him.'

'What the hell is going on, Ma?'

She indicated that I should shut the door, so I did.

'Your father has been very uptight these last couple of months. And even more secretive than usual. He has a new mobile phone which he keeps getting messages on, by text, but he never uses it. He's always leaving the house at strange times, day and night. I don't know where he's going but there's something very serious up. Those men watching the house either know about it or they want to know about it.'

'Who are they?'

'Police or government agents of some sort, I'm sure of it.'

'This is not the place to spout off about this, Mam.'

'You believe me though, don't you, Donal?'

'Had I come here first today, Mam, frankly I wouldn't have believed a word. But now, yes I do.'

She frowned at me, confused.

'Does the name Bob Conlon mean anything to you, Mam?'

She froze.

'No,' she said, flatly.

'I can tell it does. You're a worse liar than me.'

She looked at the floor.

'I remember him in the house, Ma, when I was younger. They had an in-joke, about being away visiting some relations. What did they mean by that?'

'He was such a creep. I didn't want to know. I barred him from the house in the end. I said to your father it's Bob or me. You should ask Fintan what's going on.'

'What would he know?'

'Your father won't leave the house these days without calling Fintan. Every single time. He must be telling him where he's going and who he's meeting. That's all I can tell you.'

'As a sort of security maybe, as if, one day, he's expecting not to come back.'

I immediately regretted saying it. Her watery eyes blinked into mine as she grasped my hand hard.

'Help him, Donal, please. I know he's been hard on you, but he is your father. Will you promise me that you'll help him any way you can?'

'Mam, I can't make a promise like that until I know what he's up to. He could be planning to shoot Princess Di for all I know.'

'For me, Donal, please.'

'Of course, Mam, of course I'll help him.'

I drove fast and thought hard all the way to Dublin airport. But each streetlight cast a fresh shadow of doubt across my overloaded brain.

Clearly Valerie Gillespie had been murdered by Robert Conlon. For some reason, after years grooming vulnerable young women for abuse, he'd reverted to a lightning attack on a cracked-out street hooker. Maybe he'd been knocking off the odd prostitute all along, but no one had bothered to properly investigate those killings.

Now we needed to find him before he struck again.

I had to face up to the selfish reasons I hadn't acted immediately on that print Frank sent through yesterday. I figured it'd be far more beneficial for my career to play it safe, check out the source, make sure it's all 'above board'. Since my suspension, I'd grown paranoid about decisions rebounding on me, damaging my precious career prospects.

What an arsehole.

Putting my professional reputation ahead of the lives of vulnerable women made me every bit as culpable as those bent Irish officials who'd been protecting Conlon all these years.

Fintan's words rang in my ears ... *you didn't choose this job to act like a fucking politician. You need to take risks.*

Now I had no choice. I'd been flung headlong into something of grave consequence that I didn't remotely understand.

My mind turned to the other high-profile 'victim' of Conlon's sex party blackmail ruse – the one so dangerous that Frank wouldn't even utter his name aloud. The piece of paper he secreted into my hand had read; 'Sean Scanlon, brother of Conor Scanlon, ex IRA commander.' I now had to confront the unthinkable. Was that what had brought Conlon to London?

Surely Conlon couldn't expect top-level protection in the UK such as he enjoyed in the Irish Midlands for the past decade? Unless ... unless...

The government's secret talks with the IRA had been this year's worst-kept political secret. Irish and English, Protestant and Catholic alike learned about these covert developments with disbelief and suspicion. The same question had swirled around all of our minds:

How did the Brits get the IRA to the table?

No, surely this can't be connected? Surely Conlon wouldn't be deluded enough to believe he could blackmail the British Government or the IRA with his sordid footage of Conor Scanlon's brother engaged in unspecified shenanigans with a minor? The former could have him locked away without trial, the latter whacked and buried in a bog.

The very idea of it simply felt too far-fetched. Insane.

Then Da showed up.

Michael Lynch: IRA sympathiser, fundraiser

and facilitator; new best friend to leader Conor Scanlon. Michael Lynch, of such fervent interest to 'the busy little men in suits' that they camped outside his home, possibly broke in, possibly emptied his study of every single content.

Did he come over to the UK to find Conlon ... negotiate with Conlon ... to set Conlon up to get whacked by the IRA? How did Fintan fit into all this? Da's daily phone pal ... with links to MI5 spooks ... and to someone directly involved in the hunt for Valerie Gillespie's killer, me. Had Fintan any idea about our dad's real motive for coming to the UK?

Was Da using his own sons to help him get to Conlon – holder of a secret so damning that it could make or break the peace talks? After all, Conor Scanlon couldn't afford to have the sordid truth about his brother coming out. It could destroy all of them.

'No, no, no...' I laughed, my twitching hands ticklish and slippery on the steering wheel.

'That's plain ridiculous,' I said out loud.

As for Liz Little, I now had to get my head around the fact she was most likely killed by Conlon too. The anal battery insertion was clearly one of his trademark 'signatures'. And how else would she have wound up clutching Valerie Gillespie's hair in her hand?

These were the hard facts. Evidence.

Wafting about in the back of my mind, that visit Liz made to me last Saturday night. I couldn't just discount what she'd come to tell me. She'd clearly identified the Florentine Gardens Club. Remember?

Dirty cash, blood, skull wounds, a red floor...

There must've been some connection between Conlon and the club, or Conlon and Reilly. Maybe it all centred on the 'racket' Reilly ran using his team of hand-picked IT girls.

At least Spence could now focus on the five names listed by Tammy. Surely some kink in their financial or travel records would throw up a clue. Once we figured out what they'd been up to, we could haul them in for questioning. That should crack the case wide open.

The airport signs loomed. Everyone had been right – the journey's much quicker now than it used to be. I didn't even know what towns I'd bypassed on the way. All I'd seen were those EU signs, reminding us that they owned our asses now. Where Britain had failed over 800 years, Europe succeeded in twenty.

'You'll never beat the Irish,' we sing at the football. We should add a new line: 'But you might soften us up with a few bypasses, grants and tax breaks.'

We'd taken the Federal shilling and were showing the Brits the door. There'd be hell to pay...

I made it to the gate in time to give Zoe a quick call.

'Hi,' she said glumly and I apologised for not calling earlier.

I breezily ran her through my day, as if I'd expected nothing less than a politically explosive revelation from a complete stranger, a burgled home and my mother locked away in a loony bin. When all that failed to elicit any kind of emotional response, I hit her with what my ex Eve coined 'the

288

universal man question': 'Are you okay?'

She sighed. 'I spent most of the day at a really horrible crime scene. It just gets me down sometimes.'

'Forget, Zoe, it was a grisly murder scene that ignited the flames of our passion,' I smiled, then wondered why I always felt emotionally incapable of just allowing someone to be a bit down.

'I think you'd better check it out tomorrow. It's another one close to Finsbury Park.'

My heart fell through my arse. Frank's words from earlier performed a gleeful cancan across my brain.

Jesus, I hope for your sake he hasn't struck again since yesterday.

'Please tell me she wasn't killed in the last thirty-six hours?'

'I doubt if we'll ever know. There was hardly any of her left.'

'Jesus,' I said, a sinkhole of dread swallowing me whole.

Chapter 26

Tottenham Hale, North London
Thursday, April 8, 1993; 23.00

I'd been back in Ireland for less than one day, yet London once again felt like an alien dystopia. Or maybe that was just Tottenham Hale after 11pm.

The Stansted Express proved anything but,

taking almost an hour to trundle the twenty odd miles to this North London outpost.

The station forecourt felt underlit and desolate, a murky grey no-man's-land where – perhaps fittingly – large concrete spheres served as the sole decorative folly. Welcome to London's ball sac...

Stark high-rise blocks and lurid retail signs dominated the night sky. I needed to catch a bus to Finsbury Park out on the main road, which required walking past a menace of hoodies. I felt certain that, two days ago, this wouldn't have fazed me. But now I felt nervous. They'd smell it, of course, then see my little travel bag and think 'tourist, easy prey'. Maybe that's why they hung around there.

I suddenly felt alone and trapped, small and daunted, spinning helplessly through space like your man in *2001*. I needed gravity, perspective, *terra firma*. I needed to share with Fintan, right away.

He was a political animal with a flint-black heart. I didn't possess one fibre of his Machiavellian ability to see angles, perceive motivations and weigh risk. He'd be able to grasp what's really going on here. He probably knew already.

A black taxi suddenly heaved into view, prompting me to adopt the deranged flapping motion of a man on fire. His indicator winked back. He'd be crossing enemy lines to rescue me.

By the time he pulled up outside our house in Arsenal, I couldn't wait to share my spectacular news. But I also had a bone to pick with him about Mam. How could he not tell me?

I walked in to the soundtrack of Fatima

Mansions blaring out of the hi-fi; Fintan only 'did' angry music. I parked my travel bag at the door and flopped into an armchair.

'Where've you been?'

'St Loman's in Mullingar.'

'How is she?'

'Why the fuck didn't you tell me?'

'We didn't want to worry you, Donal.'

'Jesus, have you any idea how patronising that sounds?'

'Well, you are a little prone to hysteria.'

'I'm not prone to hysteria. Jesus.'

'It's not like she's in a straitjacket, attached to electrodes, is it? She got a little mixed up with her medication. They just need to get her back on track. Da said the rest would do her good.'

'If someone needs a rest you send them to a spa, not a nut house.'

'See, you're getting hysterical now.'

'I'm not getting hysterical,' I shouted, a little hysterically.

I forced myself to calm down. I still had my knockout punch to unleash; we'd see who's hysterical then.

'She tells me he calls you every day,' I said.

'Well, you've always been closer to Mam. I suppose I'm closer to the auld fella.'

'He's been very tense, acting strangely, up to something. Every time he goes to meet someone, he tells you who and where.'

'Ah, now that's not true. Talk to her again when she's better.'

'She says he has a mobile phone, for fuck's sake. This is Da we're talking about here, a man who can't use a washing machine. He's getting texts at all hours and suddenly leaving the house. Meds or no meds, she's seen this. And men in suits, watching the house.'

'Tell me, Donal, professionally speaking, would you take this seriously if it came from anyone else currently residing in a mental institution?'

'What's going on, Fintan? I know you know why he's come over here.'

'Honestly, Donal, I don't. He won't tell me a thing. He says it's safer that we don't know and I'm inclined to agree with him.'

'Mam's not who I actually went to see.'

He looked at me, sensing a revelation.

'I've got a contact over there, very high up in intelligence. The thing is, Fintan, I know why Da is here. He's trying to find Robert Conlon. And he needs to get to him before the British authorities do.'

'I fucking knew it. I knew he was up to something.'

He sat forward. It may have been the first time ever that I had him hanging on my every word.

'What the hell's going on?' he asked, his eyes scouring me like searchlights.

'Let me kick off with the revelation that a leading Republican's brother is a kiddie fiddler. Now, go fetch a bottle of Shiraz and two glasses. This could take a while.'

I'd never seen Fintan run before.

Chapter 27

Hornsey Mortuary, Hornsey, North London
Friday, April 9, 1993; 09.30

Someone had taken a lot of trouble to illicitly scrub out the letters 's' and 'e' from the sign that should have read Hornsey Mortuary, and I couldn't help but marvel at such a painstakingly executed act of utter puerility.

It cast my mind back to our police training at Hendon College, and that deadpan briefing about the tragi-comic phenomenon known as Death Erection.

A prim, middle-aged female pathologist had been roped in to warn us about what to expect at crime scenes. She'd let her grisly slide show do most of the talking, which had left the more squeamish of us clutching our blood-light skulls for dear life.

Amid these freeze-framed slasher episodes, our sullen conductress had suddenly poked her pointer at a dead man's clearly erect cock and uttered the unforgettable words 'ah, angel lust'.

I'd surfaced from my self-imposed, anti-fainting headlock to learn that when a man dies suddenly and violently, his final act is to produce one last stonking great hard-on. Her purse-lipped, accusatory expression had seemed to add: 'What else could we expect from you cock-wielding baboons?'

It's known in the trade as post-mortem priapism, terminal erection or, to the more romantically inclined, angel lust. She'd cited death by shooting, aggressive poisoning, hanging or damage to a major artery as the most likely events to bring about this most unhappy of endings.

She had been busy explaining how it's all connected to a part of the brain known as the cellebrum, when a tune from my childhood suddenly floated into my head. I recognised it as the well-known song 'Dem Bones', leaned into the ear of the trainee beside me and sang: 'The cellebrum is connected to the ... bellend.'

A rip tide of uncontrollable laughter swept us both away. If I learned nothing else during that lesson, it was that somewhere deep in my subconscious, death and hilarity are ill-matched but very eager bedfellows.

Now, as I strode into the mortuary reception, I wondered if their cocks remained hard for all eternity. Now that would be a version of hell only a female God could dream up.

I asked for Dr Milne, dearly hoping not to get her glacial assistant, Erika the Viking. Erika seemed typical of every cover-girl beauty I'd ever encountered: so celebrated for her looks that she hadn't bothered developing a personality. Terrified of sending out any kind of signal that might be interpreted by the rabid male masses as a 'come on', Erika had elected instead to shut down transmission altogether. Now, to me at least, she existed like a hollowed-out tree, a hologram, a pretty ghost at home here with all the other soulless stiffs.

'Dedwina' may have been the kind of no-nonsense Tory wife who'd snap the neck of a baby pheasant while listening to Wagner, but she thought like a detective and had a flair for interpreting the tinier, gorier details. What's more, I sensed that she'd taken some sort of maternal shine to me and would help in any way she could.

'Donal,' Edwina hissed from an open side door, making me jump, 'you've got precisely eight minutes of my time so chop-chop.'

I semi-jogged behind her bustling scrubs along the now-familiar corridor, catching her up at the door to the post-mortem room.

She bowed her head conspiratorially.

'I'm taking you through this one myself because, well, it's unlike anything I've encountered before.'

'Wow,' I said, 'that's saying something.'

She frowned. 'I'm not that bloody ancient.'

'I didn't mean it like that, Edwina. Erika said you sometimes perform seven autopsies in a day. You've surely seen it all.'

'That's what I thought,' she said, arching an eyebrow then turning to lead me through the door.

I followed her past a pair of empty chrome autopsy tables to a third at the top of the room. Upon it sat a fleshless partial skull stripped clean of brain, eyes, most teeth, tissue and blood. Below it, a scatter of dry, sharp bones looked like some Stone Age tool kit.

The cogs in my brain spun fast, trying to make sense of this formless, fleshless skeleton. But the harder I revved, the further I sank.

'Is this all of her?' I asked quietly.

'Not exactly,' she said, 'but we'll come to that later.'

'What happened here?'

'Haven't you been told anything at all?'

I shook my head.

'What you're looking at is the remains of a human body after two German Shepherds have lived off it for several days, possibly weeks.'

I closed my eyes for a couple of seconds as my conscience climbed off its cross. My flagging up Conlon two days ago wouldn't have saved her.

'Where are her ... bones?'

'Either devoured or crunched into splinters and dust. We've bagged everything else found at the scene. Like I said, we'll get to that later. The main material I have to work with is here, right in front of you.'

As I examined the freshly chewed skull, it felt as if someone had cracked off the top of my own, as you might a boiled egg. I could feel focus and consciousness leak out, and fought an overwhelming urge to clutch my scalp. That tuning fork buzz grew louder in my ears and my vision dimmed. *Shit,* I thought to myself, *I'm starting to go.*

I realised I hadn't taken a proper breath for several minutes and badly needed to recycle. When I went to inhale, I couldn't – it felt too much like sucking in death.

'Are you okay?' she asked.

'I think so,' I muttered, willing the swoon to pass.

I forced my eyes back to where the dead woman's should have been. In the topside of her skull, matted hair marked out two almost perfectly round holes, similar to those suffered by Liz Little. My mind flashed back to her visit ... the blood that raced down her neck and shoulders had come from those two wounds.

Edwina clocked my recognition. 'Someone in N4 getting handy with a ball-peen hammer again,' she said.

'Any red matter inside those wounds?'

'Not this time.'

'What else can you figure out, from this?'

'It's a small skull without a pronounced temporal ridge and a sharp lower eye socket, so I'm ninety per cent certain it's female. Her third molar isn't fully grown, which suggests she's aged between seventeen and twenty-five. Are you aware of sutures in the skull?'

'Yes, they're the joins where the skull bones meet.'

'Correct. The one at the base of the skull, the basilar suture, should fully close between the ages of eighteen and twenty-four. Hers hasn't, so we can put her age at anything between sixteen and twenty-five. Also, the hammer blows to her head didn't kill her. There isn't enough for me to establish cause or time of death, I'm afraid. The dogs have seen to that.'

'I thought they're supposed to be man's best friend?'

'The dogs didn't kill her, Donal. They just did what they're genetically programmed to do, which is to eat the best form of nourishment available. It's their ability to consume human remains that made them our best friends in the first place.'

I looked at her quizzically.

'Thousands of years ago, wild dogs scavenged around the outskirts of human settlements, eating human waste. We realised how useful these garbage compactors could be and began to let the less aggressive pups get closer. There's evidence in the Bible, the Koran and the Iliad that dogs ate corpses like any other waste product. I trust you're a good Catholic boy, Donal?'

I smiled. 'Of course.'

'You know about crucifixion then. The Romans considered the lower hanging cross a crueller form because it enabled wild dogs to rip the body apart. Some secular historians believe that Jesus Christ was eaten by dogs and that his followers invented the whole tomb and resurrection story as a coping mechanism.'

'I can't wait to tell my mother.'

'Dogs have been eating human remains for thousands of years. That's why post-mortem animal depredation isn't uncommon in forensic autopsy.'

'You've come across this before?'

'Yes, quite often, though not on this scale. A colleague of mine had a case where a dog chewed three toes clean off the right foot of its unconscious owner. Turned out the toes were gangrenous. The dog could smell something was wrong and ultimately saved the man's life.'

'You make it sound like this woman's dogs did her a favour. I'm not sure she'd see it that way right now.'

'These dogs weren't waiting for her to drop so that they could pounce on her and gobble her up! They would've been starving, right at breaking point. They licked and pawed at the woman's face to try to wake her up. Eventually, they'd draw blood and that's when the primeval instinct kicks in. They go for the softest bits on show first, the nose, lips and ears, then the rest of the face, the neck, moving down to the arms.'

'I don't know, to me, it feels like doggie cannibalism.'

'When they get no response, they recognise only a large piece of meat. What does surprise me here is how thorough they've been. There literally wasn't a drop of blood left. I've only heard of that before in cases where the human had been a Class-A drug user. Dogs can become addicted to the drugs still in the corpse's system, and they keep eating in search of their next hit.'

'So she might have been a drug user?'

'I won't be saying that. I can't. I've got no decent uncontaminated blood to work with and not enough hair. They didn't find drugs paraphernalia at the scene. In fact they didn't find anything at the scene to say who she was or how long she'd been living there.'

'So we've got no means of identifying her?'

'Not quite.'

I followed her to a wall of lockers. She opened a door and stood back. Two shelves heaved with large freezer bags full of what looked like shit.

'Some hardy scene-of-crime officers went through all of the dog faeces and vomit at the scene. They managed to dig out a couple of adult teeth. We made an impression and put it out there, but we haven't had a positive ID yet.'

I stared at the bags in utter disbelief. No wonder Zoe had felt down. Fingering through the rancid waste of a pair of man-eating Alsatians would leave me suicidal.

'You're keeping this?'

'We have to keep everything until the death certificate is signed.'

She reached in and pulled out a bag.

'Look what's in here,' she said and my eyes immediately seized upon it.

'Another A3 battery, this one vomited by one of the dogs. There's no way of telling where it had been, but my guess is inside the victim's anus. Now whether the insertion caused perimortem injuries, as it had to Liz Little, we shall never know.'

'Sorry, what injuries, Edwina?'

'It's in my pathology report. Liz Little suffered perimortem injuries to her coccyx, caused by the violent insertion of the battery into her anus.'

She read my confusion.

'Perimortem injuries are caused at or close to the time of death because the bone shows no sign of repair. I included this in my brief. The one I prepared especially for you.'

'It's the first I've heard of it, Edwina. So the battery was inserted as an afterthought, almost, to make sure we connected it to Valerie.'

'Who can possibly say, except the person who put it there? But it was definitely inserted close to when she expired.'

'Whereas with Valerie?'

'The battery caused no bone injuries. We don't know when it was inserted. Are you quite certain Erika didn't mention this?'

'I was a little blinded by all the science to be honest, Edwina,' I smiled, 'I may well have missed it.'

I could sense she'd saved the best for last. 'Then there's this,' she said, pulling out a smaller forensic bag. 'Erika is specialising in hair identification. Well, her expertise has struck again. She managed to extract human hair from the dog waste and found that it's a direct match to Valerie Gillespie. Whoever killed this woman planted strands of Valerie's hair at the scene, just as he did at the Liz Little murder scene.'

'Wow. You say Erika struck again…'

'She was the one who recognised Valerie's hair last time round. She'd studied it a few months earlier when we were struggling to identify Valerie's body. That's not *how* we identified her body. We actually sourced her breast implants through their serial number. But Erika remembered Valerie's hair because it has a very distinctive medulla and pigment dispersal.'

'Wow, that's impressive.'

'That's what I said. But she remained stoically Teutonic about it all, insisting that it had all been the happiest of academic accidents. She's a solid girl, but a bit of a cold fish. I can't imagine her in any other line of work to be honest.'

I figured Zoe would be at the murder scene so headed there. I wanted to find out if anything else of evidential value had popped out of those case-cracking German Shepherd sphincters.

The flat was just north of Finsbury Park, on the Woodberry Down estate, which began where a notorious section of Green Lanes ended. As I inched through its eye-watering 24/7 congestion, my mind wound back to that intelligence lecture about organised crime in London. They'd described Green Lanes as an enclave ... the Republic of Heroin. Everything east and directly south of here – Finsbury Park, Arsenal, Islington – was controlled by the Evans brothers from Islington. Everything east of that belonged to Jimmy Reilly.

I drove into Woodberry, past brutalist blocks and fruitless knots of slouching youth, all watching. This vast 42-acre estate had recently been officially recognised as cinematically grim. Steven Spielberg filmed here for his upcoming movie *Schindler's List* – using it to double for the war-ravaged Warsaw Ghettos. Locals agreed that seemed a little harsh. On war-ravaged Warsaw.

I pulled up outside Ennerdale House, a classic five-storey brick and balconied council block freckled with white satellite dishes, bad graffiti and, on a top-floor balcony, a bustle of busy white forensic suits.

As I walked across the quadrangle, I became aware of countless windows watching my progress. I remembered a line from that Yeats' poem ... great hatred, little room.

The main door hung open apologetically, having long-since been stripped of its purpose. A flickering piss-green light buzzed on and off irritably. The door to the lift looked scorched and bruised, as if some thwarted pyromaniac had set about it with a sledgehammer. On closer inspection, every pore of that door's thick metal armour had been scratched and scraped so that it resembled a skating rink. The whole place screamed simmering, tinder-box rage.

Some unidentified purple substance covered the call button. I looked around for a fake finger and spied burnt coke cans and improvised crack pipes in the corner. That shit must be good, I thought, for someone to sit and smoke it right there, in a perma-puddle of piss.

I found an empty box of Superkings, scrunched the cardboard into a point and jabbed it against the call button. A clattering shudder echoed somewhere above, as if I'd just delivered an electric prod to an enormous metal monster.

The lift's wake-up cough was followed by an ominous hum and convulsive splutter.

'It hasn't worked for months,' rasped an elderly lady's voice. I turned to see her gingerly descending the concrete steps, shopping cart bouncing in her wake.

'Thanks. Can I help?'

'I don't need help,' she wheezed, refusing to look at me. I wondered if she'd look anyone in the eye today.

I couldn't help thinking ... what a place to end your days. Then I thought about Mam in that Gothic horror house. Tonight, I'd call her sisters again, make sure they've sprung into action. I wanted Mam back in the garden, medicated to the gills, pulling weeds and tutting at the talk-in show on her little transistor radio. As I tackled endless steps, breathless and slightly dizzy, I batted away those worries about how she'd cope after Da goes.

Or when he's away *visiting some relations...*

Zoe stood smiling at the summit, my Sherpa. She must've spotted me parking up. A tiny part of me dared to hope she'd been keeping an eye out. I wished she hadn't now. Sweaty palpitations were never my best look.

'Hey,' she called, coming in for an embrace which I skilfully fended off, a snub she took alarmingly well.

'Count yourself lucky you're a day late.'

'I trust Matthew won't be getting a puppy for Christmas.'

'I'll never turn my back on a German Shepherd again.'

That's what German sheep have been saying for years. But no one listens.'

Her eyes drifted to a middle-distance stare. She wouldn't be forgetting yesterday's dog's dinner in a hurry.

'They dismembered her and dragged the bits all over the flat,' she said quietly, transfixed by the memory. 'They must've been desperate by the end, because they kept trying to eat bits that they couldn't digest, like some of the larger bones, the very bilious parts of her intestine, her hair. There were pools of vomit and diarrhoea everywhere.'

'And you had to go through that?'

She nodded sadly. 'We were told to extract anything that appeared inconsistent with typical stomach contents. It's bad enough dealing with human waste, and I've had it all, faeces, semen, urine, even earwax. But dog shit and vomit is a new low. I would've quit yesterday, if I didn't need the money so bloody badly.'

'You poor thing. Honestly, I couldn't do it. What happened to the dogs?'

'No one knows.'

'I've heard that once they taste human blood,

because it's saltier, they're more likely to go for it again, if they get the chance.'

She laughed. 'Do you reckon they'll start snatching kids off the street and out of playgrounds now, like man-eating lions? Who told you that?'

'My dad. He kept dogs all his life.'

'Oh. And did your dad have your dog put down, by any chance, for this very reason?'

'Yes, actually he did. He took him out the back and...'

'What? He shot your dog?'

'What can I say, country life. He did bite the postman!'

'That's awful. I mean about the dog.'

'I was devastated,' I said, the buried sense of injustice erupting, swiftly followed by the sinking realisation he'd conned me. 'So you're saying that's not true?'

'Of course it's not true, Donal.'

'What about that Nazi guard, you know, the Hyena of Auschwitz, Irma Grese. She used to set her dogs on prisoners.'

'She kept them half-starved. That's the only way a dog will eat a human, if they're starving and if the human is dead. Even then they don't usually. We've come across dogs who starved to death rather than eat their owners. German Shepherds are the exception.'

'Well, I have to say I'm relieved to hear that, even if it has come eleven years too late for poor old Mandela.'

'You called your dog Mandela?'

'Yeah, well he was black, and mostly locked up.'

She looked around conspiratorially. 'On the

plus side, I did find this.'

She opened her hand to reveal a tiny vial.

'What is it?' I asked.

She slid it back into her pocket and nodded to the stairs.

Up clomped Fintan, totally unruffled by the climb, and I wondered why nature always seems to favour the evil. A chubby snapper laboured in his wake, nodding like a knackered old beach donkey.

'You can't take photos,' announced Zoe.

Fintan shrugged. 'Don't worry. He follows me round because I feed him biscuits. This is purely social. Your boyfriend invited me.'

She turned her frown to me.

'I thought he might be useful.'

'Okay, well, there's nothing left to see so you may as well come in. Except him,' she said, pointing to the lens man swaying up the final step. He stopped, open mouthed and sagged.

She led us through the front door. 'No one actually lived here. Not properly.'

Sure enough, a single wooden chair proved the sitting room's solitary feature. The kitchen had cupboards and an oven, but no crockery, cutlery or utensils. The bathroom featured a water-free toilet. 'The dogs drank it,' she explained.

Naked light bulbs blazed in every room, and each window had been blacked out with opaque sheets.

'Someone must have been paying bills here, gas, electricity,' I said.

'All metered,' said Zoe, pointing to a pair of archaic metal boxes skew whiff on the hallway wall.

'Who owns this place?' I asked.

Fintan chirped up. 'An elderly couple. They bought it under the right-to-buy scheme three years ago and relocated up north. They let it through a management agency, Osmond and Co on Blackstock Road. They must have some details about the current tenant. And I, personally, never miss an opportunity to persecute an estate agent.'

I turned to Zoe and spoke quietly. 'Do you need to talk to me now, you know, about what you found?'

'No need.' She smiled. 'The wheels are in motion. Let's just say this could be your red-letter day.'

A quick scan of the properties emblazoned across the front window of Osmond's confirmed they specialised in the Warsaw Ghetto end of the market. Inside, a pair of Burton-suited spivs in their twenties sat jabbering on their phones. Fintan and I peered in and resumed our ongoing wager: 'Guess their Christian names'.

'Jason and Dazza,' I ventured.

'I'm going more aspirational. Dale and Kenny.'

They blanked us as we walked in. Fintan turned to me, pointed to his left nipple and nodded smugly towards the guy on the right. His name tag said Kenny. The fucker was good. Or he'd checked earlier. I wouldn't have put it past him.

Gaz, the older one to the left, was busy telling someone they needed to commit right now or the property would be snapped up by someone else offering more.

'Gaz ... ump by name...' smiled Fintan.

Meanwhile, Kenny was telling the woman on the other end why she wouldn't be getting her deposit back, despite having had her former rental property professionally deep-cleaned.

'Kenny ... Rogers tenants,' I said.

'Nice,' said Fintan.

Gaz hung up first, writing a series of notes in a diary without even looking up. Welcome to the fag end of the rental market – no manners required. I looked forward to giving this property pimp a right good jolt.

'Yeah?' he said finally, briefly glancing up from his diary.

'DC Donal Lynch,' I said, producing my warrant card.

He looked up now alright.

'How can I help you, officer?' he said urgently.

I gave it a few seconds, cranking his ulcer to bursting.

'Number 42 Ennerdale House. I need to know who was renting the property.'

'May I ask why?'

'Let's just say you'll be putting it back on the market again soon, once they finish scraping up the current tenant's body.'

His mouth fell open. 'What?' he squeaked.

'A woman's been murdered at that property. We've spoken to the owners. They say you'll have the records of the current tenant.'

Gaz was on his feet before I'd finished the sentence. As he rifled through a filing cabinet, colleague Kenny suddenly folded on the disputed deposit and hung up. Fintan gave me the eye, the scent of fresh prey tickling his nostrils.

308

Gaz returned with a file.

'That property hasn't been rented for five months,' he said, without looking up.

'Let me see,' I said.

He placed the file on the desk and spun it round to my favour. The bank record showed a series of monthly direct debit transfers into Osmond's account, ending last November.

'It's been on the market since then?'

'It's not a very sought-after area,' said Gaz with a dismissive sniff.

'That's strange,' I said, 'I keep reading about this housing crisis, how there's not enough rental properties now that all the council homes have been sold off. How many empty properties do you have on your books?'

'Not many–' he laughed a little nervously '–but some people won't move into an estate like Woodberry, no matter what.'

Fintan turned to me. 'Do you remember your old friends in South London, the Dentons?'

I nodded.

'I never thought I'd be thanking them for inspiration.'

He turned back to Gaz. 'Can you give me the addresses of these empty properties on your books?'

'We're not at liberty to give out that information, Data Protection and all that.'

'Oh, fuck off Gaz.' He laughed, waving his mobile. 'I can dial up a warrant right now.'

Fintan shot to his feet suddenly and walked out. I turned to see him scanning the window. He came back in sporting a knowing grimace.

'I don't see 42 Ennerdale House on that window. And I'd bet the other empty properties on your books aren't up there either.'

Gaz glanced over at Kenny. I sensed some sort of 'checkmate' moment.

Fintan smelt the kill. 'Tell me about these empty properties, Gaz. I bet they all have absentee landlords, based far away, in places like Yorkshire and Glasgow. Elderly people, so not likely to come down and check. In fact they probably feel a little guilty about this sudden windfall in their lives, so not the types to be greedy and push too hard.'

I sat there marvelling at Fintan, his instinct for sniffing out the venal in others so clearly rooted in his own aptitude for corruption.

He had it all figured out. 'So when someone comes in with cash, looking for a short let ... say three months ... you and your chinless little pal there pocket the dough and tell the landlord the property's not shifting. I've a good mind to arrest you here and now on suspicion of fraud.'

His words vacuumed the blood out of Gaz, who'd slipped into open-mouthed paralysis.

'You're not stupid though, are you, Gaz?' he went on. 'You don't know these cash renters. They might change the locks and refuse to leave once their let is up, or sell the key. Or use the property for illegal purposes, drugs, hookers, stolen goods. You can't risk that, so you have to know something about them, otherwise you're basically handing over someone else's property, to a complete stranger.

'You've got a special file for these cash lets, haven't you, Gaz? I bet you and young Kenny there have even dreamed up a whacky name for this top-secret folder. Come on, boys; let us in on the laugh. What do you call it? The Fun Fund? The Cash Stash? The Whore Chest?'

I suddenly suspected his familiarity with this con may be connected to how he ran his newspaper expenses.

'Now here's the deal,' said Fintan, 'you show us your secret file on 42 Ennerdale House, and we won't blow the whistle on this or your other little rackets. Got it? Oh, but you need to commit right now, Gaz, otherwise this deal will be snapped up by someone offering more.'

Gaz's loud exhalation announced immediate surrender.

'It's in my car,' he said.

'Chop chop,' said Fintan.

They both got up.

'Ah ah, you stay right where you are, Kenny Rogers.'

Gaz returned with a concertina file tucked under his arm. He sat at his desk, pawed his way to 'E' and pulled out a transparent plastic file containing a utility bill and a document on headed notepaper.

'You better start talking, Gaz,' I said. 'You're not out of the woods yet.'

'A big fella came in, shaved head, stocky, said he needed a place for two months. I told him the minimum we did was three. He took out this massive roll of cash and said "I'll give you a grand, you give me a set of keys and I'll be out of there in eight weeks." He placed the money on the desk and said "Well?"

'I said you have to fill in a form and provide

some identification. He said it wasn't for him, it was for his girlfriend and produced a gas bill from her previous address.'

He slid it over. Fintan took one look. 'Ding dong,' he said, pushing it over to me.

The name immediately clicked; Georgina Bell had been one of the six on Tammy's IT girl list. A shiver made my shoulders perform an involuntary roll.

'He also filled in this form,' said Gaz, sliding the headed paper over next.

Fintan devoured the contents.

'He's not given his own address,' snapped Fintan. 'He's just given hers again. And who the fuck has a name like that? It's clearly made up.'

Gaz feigned surprise.

I grabbed the document. It listed a series of conditions next to pen-ticked boxes, signed Dean S. Sombrero.

'Have you got a loo?' asked Fintan, suddenly.

'Just through there,' said Gaz.

'Excellent, because when I come back, I'd like to talk to you about a short-term let. For cash, of course.'

Minutes later, Fintan handed over 500 pounds in return for a piece of paper and a set of keys to another flat on the estate. My face had to work overtime not to betray my confusion and anxiety. Not for the first time, teaming up with Fintan had quickly escalated into Joint Criminal Enterprise. I wished he'd consult me before embarking on these hair-brained schemes.

As we walked out, Fintan turned to Gaz.

'This Dean S. Sombrero guy, did he have a

Brummie accent, by any chance?'

Gaz nodded.

'A chunk missing from his left ear?'

Gaz looked over at Kenny.

'Come on, fellas, no one forgets something like that.'

Kenny did the nodding this time.

'We'll be seeing you both again soon,' he smiled. 'And so much sooner than either of you would like.'

'What was all that about?' I asked, once we were outside.

'Well, we need somewhere to put Da up,' he said, 'and I felt an overwhelming urge to turn those fuckers over.'

He reached into his inside jacket pocket and pulled out a Dictaphone.

'Popped it on in the bog ... now I have a nice little scoop, we can move Da into Woodberry and the paper will cover the five-hundred quid as legitimate expenses. Oh, and because I guessed Kenny's name, you owe me lunch.'

'And who's Dean S. Sombrero?'

'It's an anagram, you halfwit. Dean S. Sombrero, meet Bernard Moss.'

As we walked into the Star café, I realised that the 'specials' on the window had been 'special' now for the entire six months I'd lived here.

'I mean what's so special about them?' I asked.

'Microwaved, not fried, so less chance of human contamination during the cooking process. I'd say that's pretty special.'

Human contamination. I tried to remember

313

where I'd heard that term before.

I settled for a tea, Fintan a can of 7 Up, his wipes at the ready.

'I don't understand why Bernie would risk using an anagram,' I began. 'He must've known someone might crack it. We've still got his *Times* crossword. We can get a handwriting expert in now to confirm it's his scrawl.'

'He thinks he's a bit clever though, doesn't he?' said Fintan, 'what with his literary quotes and knowledge of Viennese flooring. He'll probably find it poetic if we nail him for this, you know, the bittersweet hubris of his own pedantry. God, is there anyone more boorish than an ex-con with a few O levels from prison? They all think they're Charles Bukowski.'

'If we can find Bernie's print anywhere at Ennerdale House, then he's implicated in Georgie Bell's murder. She's on Tammy's list so that drags Jimmy Reilly into it too, right?'

Fintan leaned back and lit a cigarette.

'Any senior cop will say you need more. You'd have to get Tammy on board, and the only way you can make that happen is to place her in the witness protection programme. Even then, you'd need to trail the other IT girls before, during and after a trip abroad, find out what they're doing for Jimmy. Then you'd need at least one of them to break rank.

'You're talking about a major international investigation here, Donal. It's another league. We need to get the Regional Crime Squad involved. They've got a unit that targets major organised criminals. Guess who's heading up that unit? Our old friend Shep.'

The mere mention of his name re-activated a long dormant geyser of resentment. Two years ago, Detective Superintendent Dan 'Shep' Shepard gave me my first big break onto a murder squad. He then tried to break me. Shep openly accused me of leaking intelligence to Fintan, when he'd been the source all along.

'Your old friend, more like,' I snapped. 'I don't think Spence would be very happy about that. He's been on a personal mission to bring down Reilly for years.'

'Who cares about Spence's personal mission? We're talking about taking down a major criminal here, possibly saving the lives of the four other women on that list.'

He could tell I wasn't budging.

'Oh, I see. You're on a promise of some sort. Come on then, Donal, you can tell me. What's your little arrangement with Spence?'

I reddened. 'He's asked me to brief him personally about any developments in the Liz Little case. He says we have to keep it tight because Reilly has so many bent cops on his payroll. Sounds fair enough to me.'

'And what has he promised you, Donal, in return for these personal services?'

'You don't have to make it sound so squalid. If I deliver Tammy, he'll bring me onto his squad. I've already delivered Tammy's list. Georgie Bell's murder shows that this list is right on the money. Jimmy Reilly must be knocking off his IT girls, one by one.'

Fintan put out his cigarette. 'What about Robert

315

Conlon? Last night you seemed convinced he was your prime suspect.'

'That was before we knew that a second girl on Tammy's list has been murdered.'

'Please tell me you've kept the original copy of that list?'

'I'm not stupid, Fintan.'

'Where is it?'

'I'm not telling you that.'

'Okay, well, just don't keep it in your jacket pocket or in a drawer at work. I've got a personal safe deposit box. That's the kind of place you need to keep stuff like that.'

I sighed, pulled it out of my pocket and handed it over.

'Why is it so important where I keep it?'

'Because if both copies go missing, then it never existed, especially if Tammy disappears. This perfectly illustrates my point. You and Spence are way out of your depth here. What's he playing at, thinking he can take down Reilly on his own? Especially with his piss-poor track record in major cases.'

'Piss poor?'

'I told you about that major villain who got out on appeal because one of his officers illegally bugged a hotel room. Then there's the Helen Oldroyd murder, when they fucked up the crime scene.'

My mind flashed back to the Oldroyd case, which I'd looked into only a week ago. She'd been co-owner of a Bureau de Change in Paddington. They'd found her stabbed to death at the wheel of her racing green Jag in a leisure centre car park in Brentford, West London. I'd requested a forensic

316

sweep of the Jag only to discover that undertakers had contaminated the scene. Of course ... *human contamination;* that's where I'd heard that phrase.

'He was in charge of that?'

He nodded. 'I mean to lose one major case may be regarded as a misfortune, but to lose both...'

My mobile rang. Zoe.

'As usual, I bring news both good and bad,' she said as soon as I answered. 'Shall I hit you with the bad first?'

'If you must.'

'Forty-two Ennerdale House is clean. We didn't find anything non-canine.'

'And the good news?'

'A fingerprint at the Melinda Marshall murder scene matches Robert Conlon's. They found it on her balcony rail, of all places.'

I rewound that case through my bewildered mind. Melinda from Bristol had been on the books of a 'high-class' escort agency. Her client failed to show on New Year's Eve. The Waldorf turned her away at 11pm. Her flatmate found her stabbed and battered to death next morning at their flat-share in Chelsea. Happy New Year. The prime suspect had been an untraced minicab driver.

'Thanks, Zoe,' I said.

'I've been very good to you, mister. I expect a full refund this evening.'

'How could I possibly repay you?'

'I'm sure you'll think of something.'

'I'm sure I will,' I said, unable to prevent my laugh escalating into a dirty cackle. 'See you later.'

'Glad I haven't eaten. Jesus,' he said.

'You always were a romantic, Fintan.'

'Just try not to fall head over heels every time, bro. Otherwise she'll walk all over you. The way Eve did.'

Nothing he said could twist off my happy tap.

'They found Conlon's prints at the Melinda Marshall scene.'

'Yeah, I heard. You need to work out how to control the volume on that thing.'

'What was he doing in the West End at eleven o'clock on New Year's Eve?'

'Maybe it's like that hooker Jo said, we never hear about the girls who fight back.'

My face told him I didn't follow.

'What if Conlon picked up a prossie that evening and failed to overpower her. In a rage, he drove to the West End to find a lone woman pissed out of her head. You know how hard it is to get a cab of any sort on New Year's Eve.'

I visualised the scene. 'He spotted her. She looked upset and hammered. He claimed to be a minicab driver. Jesus, it's only a matter of time before he kills again, if he hasn't already.'

'You need to forget about Reilly,' said Fintan. 'I think you've been seduced by the size of the collar. It's blinding you to the facts. You've got nothing on him. At the same time, you've got fingerprints connecting Conlon to the murders of Valerie Gillespie and Melinda Marshall. You've got MO and Valerie's hair linking him to Liz Little. You could charge him right now for all three and win Cop of the Year. All you need to do now is find the fucker.'

We both knew what had to be dealt with next.

'So, have you spoken to Da today then?' I asked.

He shook his head. 'Not properly. I'm a bit pissed off to be honest that he came over here thinking he could piggyback us to get to Conlon.'

'What do we do now?'

He leaned forward, a man with a proposal to sell.

'I've been thinking, the three of us want the same thing, Donal, and that's to find Robert Conlon, correct?'

I nodded.

'If I thought for one minute he was setting Conlon up to get whacked by the boyos, then I wouldn't be suggesting this. But he swears on his mam's grave that all he wants to do is talk to Conlon, face to face. In other words, he needs Conlon alive even more than we do. I think we should offer to help him. He's flesh and blood after all. But he's got to help us first.'

'How?'

'I'm gonna call him, meet him somewhere quiet like the Manor House pub up near Woodberry for a pint and suggest he tells me everything he knows. He must have a way of contacting Conlon, otherwise he wouldn't have come here. If that's the case, he can help us set a trap. We catch Conlon, he gets his few minutes to say whatever it is he needs to say to him, I get the story, you get the collar.'

'What if he says no?'

'Then he's on his own. He won't be staying at ours and I won't be giving him the key to the place on Woodberry.'

'But if he's in touch with Conlon...'

He smiled. 'The first thing he asked me to get him when he arrived was a pay-as-you-go mobile phone. I've already got my helpful ex-copper pulling the records of every number he's called since he got here. We'll soon have Conlon's number, one way or another.'

Chapter 28

**Crouch End, North London
Friday, April 9, 1993; 19.15**

I ignored the bell, tapping Zoe's front door instead so as not to wake Matthew.

I tapped a second time, a little louder, and congratulated myself on such paternal forethought. Step-fatherhood? Piece of cake.

The door opened six inches to her deranged eyes, askew make-up and Jackson Pollocked clothes, bringing to mind one of those tranny junkies from Andy Warhol's factory. Matthew's caterwauling completed the desperate scene.

'Can you come back in an hour?' She didn't so much suggest as insist.

'Of course,' I said, backing away slowly from her Gary Busey stare.

I slipped into a reassuringly dreary local pub, ordered a pint and smiled to myself: *well, she did warn me*. Matthew would always come first. I'd forever be the supporting actor, the assistant coach, the man at the front of the toboggan, Jim from the Corrs. In the race for her affection and love, the best I could ever hope for was silver, or a non-fatal head-on into a frozen snowdrift.

For a man with a healthy ego, this might present a challenge. Not to me. I could be her fun diversion, her occasional escape, something she can reach out for when it all gets too much. Her bottle of Shiraz.

Thinking about it practically, Matthew kept her busy and out of the way of more desirable men. Sure if it wasn't for Matthew, she probably wouldn't have looked at me twice.

I felt a sudden twinge of agitation. So that's all you are to her then, I taunted myself, *the most she could hope for, given the circumstances?* Someone to 'settle' for; to provide stability for blameless Matthew and comfort to critical parents. She'd said as much herself.

They're desperate for me to meet a man, of course, so that they can offload us.

I ordered a pint and a Scotch, hoping the chaser would scatter these uncertainties. I sank it in one and toasted the Dutch for their celebrated cowardice.

The hour spread to another two pints and chasers so that I strutted back to Zoe's a cocky gunslinger, primed to gun this lady down.

'Wow,' I said to the smoking hot lady who answered the door.

She smiled. 'A lot of slap and Chardonnay.'

'You look stunning,' I said, all matter of fact so that it wouldn't sound creepy.

'You'd better come in.'

The little black dress led me into a sitting room with closed blinds and a candlelit table set for two. As if to offset any romantic presumptions, a corner lamp blazed a couple of notches above 'intimate' and toys littered the floor.

'Sorry about the mess,' she said, niftily side-footing a miniature building site out of her path.

'He went down okay?'

'Eventually. People keep telling me he needs routine. Try telling that to him! He's different every evening. Anyway, I promise not to talk about Matthew all night!'

'Talk about whatever you want to talk about; Zoe,' commanded the triple whiskey. 'Don't even think about it.'

She made a face that I think meant 'thanks', then nodded towards a battalion of bottles on the sideboard.

'I bought the most expensive Shiraz Budgens could offer.'

'Thank you.' I beamed, pretending I hadn't already clocked it, for I'd scoured the room on entry, certain that only the crutch of good liquor could control my crippling nerves tonight.

'Help yourself.' She smiled. 'I'm just knocking up some chilli and rice.'

I poured a large one and was busily launching into an aquarium-scaled guzzle when she walked back in.

'Better get the work stuff out of the way,' she gabbled, 'you know, before we eat.'

I nodded, discreetly allowing a quarter pint of red to slosh back into the glass.

'In the dog vomit, I found a chunk of hair with a little red stain. That's what I was trying to show you this morning when Fintan turned up. It looks the same as the paint we found in Liz

322

Little's scalp wounds, so I sent it down to those specialists in Teddington. They rang back this evening confirming that it's paint and a large enough sample to identify.'

Freeze-frame images of Liz flashed before my eyes like lightning strikes: sashaying towards me in our sitting room, smiling coyly, blood pouring from those perfectly round holes in her skull. We're doing all we can for you, Liz, my brain told her, I promise.

'I probably should have left it for the pathologist,' she said, 'but I wanted to save time and get it down to them right away.'

'Zoe, this is brilliant news. I'm so touched that you did that for me. I know it feels like a long shot.'

'Well, they're lovely, these paint people – real geeks and ridiculously excited about it all. They're going to analyse it first thing and get back to me. Ooh, that sounds like the rice boiling over.'

She returned with two heaped plates to just one appetite. I picked at mine absently, chewing through the motions. She tore into hers ravenously, shovelling spooned piles into her chatting gob in a refreshingly unladylike fashion.

She talked and talked, the headlines going something like this:

* Became a forensics officer through a combined passion for Nancy Drew, her chemistry teacher and Quincy.

'Jack Klugman was my first crush, weird or what?'

Not nearly weird enough to tell her mine...

* Had specialised in ear identification at college

323

... 'better than fingerprints ... no two ear lobes are the same...'

* Finds her job emotionally difficult since having Matthew. She now 'feels' too much.

* Has to constantly remind her mum not to interfere with how she raises Matthew.

* Dad's a workaholic who doesn't take a lot of interest in any of them.

* One sibling, older brother Richard, something in the City but very nice.

* Loves the theatre. Set design is what she'd really like to do. Hasn't been since Matthew's birth.

* Reads the *Guardian,* votes Labour and considers herself a socialist.

* Hopes to make enough money to buy her own place somewhere with good schools.

By midnight, we surrendered to a glorious couch-based haze of wine, 80s indie and stale cigarettes. She'd given up while pregnant but stashed a box of twenty in case of emergency. Our mutual unspoken fear of disastrous first sex was that emergency.

In the absence of a lighter or matches, we had to ignite them directly off the gas oven ring, a tricky undertaking that inexplicably reduced us to hysterics on several occasions. At one point, I genuinely feared we were high on North Sea Gas.

We barely touched on my life story at all, which suited me fine.

Me, oh well, let's see now, Da's in the RA, Ma's in the mental, Fintan's going to hell and I see dead people. Oh yeah, and my ex-girlfriend is a convicted murderer.

It seemed a shame to spoil things so early.

'Oh my God, it's twenty past one,' she gasped, then groaned. 'He'll be up in five hours.'

I got to my feet and offered her a hand. As I did, I noticed strange green goo literally wrapped around her feet and ankles.

'Oh dear,' I said, 'it looks like you've been knitted in Hulk shit.'

She leaned forward and looked down.

'Oh Matthew!' she moaned, 'it's his bloody glow in the dark Gak. It must be under the sofa. These are my best shoes.'

'You cross and uncross your legs a lot.'

'I never realised I did that.'

'I like uncrossed better. Don't move,' I said, dropping to my knees in front of her.

I set about unpicking the rubbery luminous gloop and unwinding it from around her shoes, nyloned ankles and calves.

'This is very kind of you,' she said.

'That's quite okay, I have a bit of a fetish for tights anyway.'

'These are stockings actually.'

I swallowed hard and kept my focus on her ankles.

'I hope you approve.'

'I think there's a good chance I might actually die of desire.'

When our lips met it earthed every volt in the universe right through me, causing the house lights to literally flicker off and on. That has to be a good sign, I thought, as her warm soft lips explored mine. I let my hands do the same. Then everything went black.

'Shit,' said Zoe, leaping to her feet, knocking

325

me backwards off my knees.

The side of my head hit something hard. Fireworks exploded. My mind flailed.

'Georgina?' I shouted. Had she come to me, right now?

A banshee wail suddenly pierced the blackout.

'Oh, well done,' snapped Zoe, 'now you've woken him and he's terrified of the dark. That's my hopes of sleep gone for tonight.'

I lay there, paralysed, woozy, shocked at the violent certainty of her rejection.

'Sorry,' I gasped, 'what the hell's happening?'

'The bloody electric key has run out. Mum was supposed to get it charged today. I'd better get up there. Oh Christ.'

I shook the stars out of my head and hauled myself up.

'Have you got a torch or candles?' I croaked.

'There's a box of candles in the kitchen drawer.'

'Right, I'm going to open the curtains to let some street light in. Then we'll head to the kitchen, find those candles and light them. If we put enough of them in his room, he'll be okay, at least until I get the key charged.'

Streetlight peered in reluctantly, eventually moulding shapes out of the black. I followed Zoe into the kitchen.

'We'll laugh about this in a few weeks,' I said.

'I've only just got him into his own room. With his dad not being here ... it's all been a bit, well, you know...'

She palmed the kitchen units, pulled a drawer and tipped candles out on the top.

I turned a dial and pressed the igniter as the

howling upstairs grew hysterical.

'Oh God,' said Zoe.

'Here,' I said, lighting four at the same time, 'take these, go to him. Just tell me where the electric key is.'

'White box above the front door. The charging station is next to Our Price on the High Street. Have you got change?'

'That's the great thing about boozers, we always have change. I'll be as quick as I can,' I said, but she'd already gone to him.

Thirty minutes later I slotted in the charged key, recharged my wine glass and took to the sofa.

Matthew settled eventually and Zoe appeared, looking every bit as burned out and melted as the candles in her hand. It wasn't just the power that zapped off half an hour ago...

'I'll head out and grab a taxi,' I said, standing.

'This is the suburbs, Donal, taxis don't come here.'

'I'm sure I can track down some dodgy minicab...'

'I think you've done enough wandering about on our behalf for one night. Take the couch. Matthew will come in with me in the morning, so as long as you're out by 7...'

'Well, it is a bit of a trek back...'

From nowhere she produced a duvet that smelled of flowers, a crisp pillow and a natty little toiletry travel bag. 'A coat and a couch is the best you'd get at ours.'

'Maybe next time I'll get Mum round and we can meet somewhere out, like the theatre,' she said, shaking the folds out of the duvet.

What did that mean ... that tonight had been a disaster?

'Goodnight,' she said and the light clicked off once more to taunt me. I'd been that close. Someone up there was determined that I die a virgin.

I checked the time ... 02.50. I sensed that sleep might not take me at all tonight, so decided to treat myself to a nightcap. Anything to stop me thinking about Zoe peeling off those black stockings...

As I tiptoed towards where I thought I'd left the bottle, I stepped on something soft and furry, which set off a tinkling, high-pitched nursery rhyme.

I froze. Should I pick up and muffle this creepy little jingle, or just let it play out? Instead, I found myself humming along to that tune from my childhood.

How much is that doggie in the window?
The one with the waggly tail.
How much is that doggie in the window?
I do hope that doggie's for sale.

The tinny little tune died. As, nearly, did I when a soft woman's voice carried on singing.

I must take a trip to California.
And leave my sweetheart alone.
If he has a dog, he won't be lonesome.
And the dog will have a good home.

I inched around slowly towards the sweet voice.

Georgina Bell swayed from side to side a foot or so above me, her eyes all white, like a pair of table-tennis balls, clutching a small knife to her own throat. Suddenly her top lip curled in malignant hate.

I read in the papers there are robbers.
With flashlights that shine in the dark.
My love needs a dog to protect him.
And scare them away with one bark.

She plunged the knife into her lower stomach, dragging it across until blood poured. She dropped the knife and pulled the wound open. Blood spilled out, followed by guts linked like pink sausages. A cascade of loose change bounced deafeningly off the hardwood floor. A whole choir of women's voices now sang, hideously off-key...

I don't want a bunny or a kitten.
I don't want a parrot who talks.
I don't want a bowl of little fishes.
He can't take a goldfish for a walk.

Georgina dropped suddenly so that she was an inch from my face, swinging from side to side by the neck, her wet lips quivering grotesquely. The banshee choir howled:

How much is that doggie in the window?
The one with the waggly tail.

I spun around in horror. Another body fell down fast in front of me, so that we were nose-to-nose.

Liz Little's Glasgow Smile sang along to the tune, like some grotesquely gurning carp whose lipstick had been applied by a toddler.

How much is that doggie in the window?
I do hope that doggie's for sale.

I screamed and felt the corners of my mouth split. The rip continued all the way to my ears so that I could actually hear the flesh wrenching apart and flapping. I braced myself for pain but felt none until the fault line reached my lobes. Both ears suddenly raged as if on fire.

I screamed and spun again, lost my footing and crash-landed face-first into a world of jagged pain. A white flash convulsed me into the foetal position. My right eye flickered open to a Mutant Ninja Turtle. Donal, meet Donatello.

'Cowabunga,' I groaned.

'Donal?' hissed Zoe.

I couldn't face her, not yet, so I propped myself up and winced at the wreckage. It looked as if I'd spent several minutes pogoing on poor Matthew's toys.

'I didn't think you were this pissed,' she spat, witheringly.

I turned to see her standing at the half-open door, Matthew whimpering in her arms, his big old watery eyes molesting mine. No Irishman will ever accept that he's drunk. A bit worse for wear, perhaps. And I wasn't about to buck that proud tradition. Far better, my male pride reasoned, to hold up my hands to a quasi-psychotic dream episode than some emasculating squiffy tumble.

'I'm sorry, Zoe, I had this terrible dream. God, I hope I haven't broken too much.'

'You've scared him half to death.'

'Sorry, Matthew,' I patronised, as you do with kids. 'I fell off the couch.'

He froze briefly, then glowered at me from beneath his David Cassidy fringe, like that creepy little boy out of *The Shining*. Zoe wore that look of betrayal I knew so well from previous romantic car wrecks.

'I'll tidy up and leave you in peace,' I said, 'and I'll replace any damage. I'm really sorry, Zoe. Sometimes I get these horrendous dreams, you know, when I've had a shock.'

'I think you need help,' she said blankly, making me wish I'd just accepted her original prognosis of blind drunkenness.

'How can I ever trust you to take care of us?' she added, choking on indignity, 'or to take care of Matthew, when you can't even take care of yourself?'

Chapter 29

Arsenal, North London
Saturday, April 10, 1993; 08.30

'As you were the one so keen to get rid of Da,' said Fintan, crunching on his Shreddies, 'you can help me move him into the flat in Woodberry this morning.'

'What did he say last night, about helping us set a trap for Conlon?'

'He's up for it. The only problem is he hasn't heard from him in days. I sense he'd do anything to get to him. Conor The Beard's clearly entrusted him with getting hold of this damning footage. They're all desperate.'

'What is he going to offer Conlon, on Conor's behalf?'

'A pot of cash and a personal guarantee that he won't be whacked or prosecuted.'

'Why isn't Conlon answering his phone? Maybe he's already handed it over to the Brits?'

'Jesus, don't say that in front of Da.'

'Have you managed to get hold of Conlon's mobile number?'

'Not yet. But when I do, my ex-copper pal Dennis reckons he can get someone to trace the signals for us. We find him, Da has a word, you take him away. Everyone's happy.'

'Yer certain Da's not gonna do something to him?'

'As certain as anyone can be. Da reckons Conlon's entrusted the footage to someone else who'll release it to the media if any harm comes to him.'

'Fucking hell, he's got some balls on him, that boy.'

Fintan drove me over in the Mondeo, still wittering on about its unique state-of-the-art features. We picked up Da outside the Manor House pub. I hadn't seen him since our 'chat' Tuesday night.

'Thanks for telling me you know Conlon,' I said, as soon as he slammed the back door, 'and for trying to use us to get to him. Jesus, how can you expect us to trust you ever again?'

He shook his head. 'I don't know if you've noticed, Donal, but there's a fucking war going on. We've had three thousand people killed over the last twenty-five years. Sorry if I didn't level with you about everything. Sorry for putting the chances of peace ahead of your murder hunt.'

Rage gripped my entire frame. 'Oh, forgive me, Da, I'd no idea you and your Provo pals had been mongering peace all this time. And now you're trying to cover up the fact Conor's brother is a paedo. How fucking honourable you all are.'

'Why should something like that fuck up the first chance of peace we've had for a quarter of a century? Do you ever stop to think about anything above your own immediate needs?'

We sat in silence the rest of the way.

As we parked up outside the eight-storey Nicholl House, I imagined being the person who brought Georgie Bell's dead body here. Maybe going 'method' would offer up a fresh clue.

'Where is this flat?' I asked Fintan.

'Third floor.'

'Shouldn't we check it out first?'

'God, yeah.'

We took the lift. The windows to number 36 had been completely blacked out.

'How do we know there aren't squatters in there?' I said.

Fintan gestured at me to stay quiet and planted an ear to the front door.

'All clear, I think,' he said.

He unlocked the door and pushed it in. Pitch black. He tried the light switch. No response.

'Have you got a torch?' he asked.

'No.'

'There could be anything in here. Have you got fifty pence?'

I rummaged.

'Yes,' I said, offering it to him.

'Well, stick it in the meter then.'

'You stick it in the meter.'

'I've just unlocked the door.'

I grumbled and crept reluctantly into shadow. I found a meter and groped it until the slot found my right hand. It took several attempts to angle the coin's edges into the tiny slot. The handle resisted my twist. Finally, the flat zapped familiar yellow, soothing our nerves.

'My God,' I said, as I dialled Zoe's number, 'this has just given me an idea.'

I gave the outside of number 42 Ennerdale House a ferocious pacing, but it failed to banish last night's Rolodex of horrors flipping through my mind.

For starters, I got way too pissed. Then she practically drop-kicked me across her sitting room; an instinctive violent reaction to the black-out or to my straying hands, only she knew for certain.

I'd woken Matthew twice and crushed 30 per cent of his toys. To top it all, she found me foetal on her sitting room floor, howling at some canine-themed cabaret performed by the ghosts of two recently slain women.

Yeah, sure Zoe, let's book tickets to the theatre... I haven't got half enough piss-poor, shouty drama going on here in my own cursed head.

334

Only a cameo appearance by Robert Conlon, Matthew's errant dad or a pair of puking German Shepherds could have zapped her ardour more effectively.

Any second now, she'd get to the top of those rancid stairs and seal our fate with just one glance. Brisk, business-like and efficient, and we're through. A smile, then I'm still in there with a shot. Never had I craved facial acquiescence so desperately. Pontius Pilate's thumb had nothing on it.

A set of tired feet clomped the concrete and I held my breath. She clocked me with one of those inscrutably flat, closed-mouth grimaces and a nod. I beamed like leaking radiation.

'I've got literally five minutes,' she panted.

'Thanks, Zoe, I really appreciate this.'

'Just so we're clear, intrigue alone brought me here. What's got you so worked up?'

My chin soaked up her first jab and I danced on.

'Funnily enough, the idea came from helping someone move this morning, and our un-scheduled blackout last night.'

'Ah yes, that,' she said, avoiding my eyes while fishing around for a key to the front door.

'So, let's suppose Georgie's killer brought her here either dead or unconscious. Locals say the lift hasn't worked for months. That makes me think Bernard Moss paid for the flat without checking it out first. You wouldn't elect to carry a lifeless body up four flights of stairs.'

'And they wouldn't have risked it in daylight, surely,' said Zoe, producing the key and slotting it into the hole.

'Wait a sec, Zoe. Don't open just yet. I've been thinking, if I turned up here in the middle of the night with a body in the boot of my car, I'd want to recce where I was taking it first, just in case.'

She nodded. 'There could be a gang of kids on the stairs say, or a party in the flat next door.'

'So Bernie or Robert Conlon ... the suspect ... walks into the communal hallway downstairs, realises the lift is out of order, but it's too late to turn back now. He wants to get that body out of the car as soon as possible. He decides to take the walk alone first, so he climbs the stairs and walks up to this door. What would you do next?'

She frowned and took a look around.

'I'd make sure the coast was clear,' she said, 'and I'd probably take a look through the window, to make sure no one was inside.'

'The windows are blacked out.'

'I'd listen at the door,' she said.

'With your good ear, you know, the one with the hole in the lobe, or with the one that'd been badly damaged by shooting?'

A celestial shadow drifted across her wide-eyed face.

'Oh my God. If Bernie brought the body here ... he's so tall that his ear print might still be there. That's ... how did you think of that?'

'What you told me last night, about ear lobes. And a little dramatic reconstruction,' I said.

She tilted her head sceptically.

'I used to laugh at those hammy segments on Crimewatch, but I actually tried to walk in the killer's shoes this morning. I went method on it too. Which is why, if you'd like to step inside, I've had another thought.'

She smiled, albeit wanly, but it felt like a blow-torch to my frozen hopes.

I led her into the hallway and pointed to the electric meter.

'That meter takes fifty-pence pieces. I had one in a house share in Harlesden a couple of years back. I'm sure they were a great idea in the '60s when fifty-pence worth of power lasted a few days but now, well ... it used to run out every time someone took a hot shower. Anyway, I've been thinking, whoever last legally rented this flat five months ago probably left a light on, or the fridge plugged in, before they left. Over a few weeks, that would've run the power down. So when the suspect gets here in the middle of the night, he has to feed the meter. Here, have a go,' I said, handing her a coin.

'You slot it into that tiny little groove thing, then twist the handle...'

'Oh, thank God you're here,' she said, 'my female brain would never have worked that out.'

Ouch.

'Sorry,' she added quickly, fumbling with the slot, 'I'm feeling so ropey today. I haven't drunk like that since ... well, our last date, in fact.'

Even with her dainty hand, it took quite a few attempts to slot the coin into position.

'You reckon you could do it with gloves on, in the dark?'

'Maybe with a torch.'

'Think about Bernie's big meaty hands.'

'I'd rather not.'

'Look,' I said, pointing out the glass section

337

above the front door, 'anyone passing sees torch-light, they might think burglary and call the cops. He'd want to get the house lights on ASAP. So he rummages around for fifty pence. He probably has to take his gloves off just to get his giant hand into his pocket.'

'The thing is we dusted the meter, Donal. It's clean.'

'What if he slotted a 50p coin into the meter with his bare hand, then put his glove back on? I know it's a long shot but it's not beyond the bounds of reason, is it? All we need to find is a single print to place him here. There's a phone number for the electricity people on the box. I'm sure they can come out and unlock it.'

She nodded. 'Okay, I'll call the office right away. If this works ... well, I'll be almost suspicious...'

'Like I said, the blackout at yours got me think-ing. Then I had that nightmare when my ears felt on fire. It happens sometimes when I'm focussed on a case. I have weird dreams about it.'

I stopped right there, on the threshold to my secret Twilight Zone. I'd treated her to enough of my inner turmoil for one twenty-four-hour spell. I reminded myself: what goes on inside my head concerns only me. Look at all the trouble blabbing about it caused last time round. Time to change tack...

'So at least our unscheduled blackout wasn't a complete disaster then!'

She exhaled pointedly. 'Look, Donal, it wasn't you, honestly. I got such a shock when the lights went off, I thought immediately of Matthew. I knew he'd freak out. Then your hands suddenly ...

they were so cold. It was all just a bit of a shock.'

'I'm sorry, Zoe, I...'

She raised her palm, indicating that I should shut up.

'I used to go all in, you know, Donal, holding nothing back. But I've been burned badly, twice actually. Now I've got to make sure I'm doing what's right by Matthew too. But I want things to work out between us. I really do.'

'I must take you to more murder scenes.' I smiled. 'It seems to bring out the romantic in you.'

'Is it some sort of a tic of yours–' she mock-frowned '–having to ruin any moment that even threatens to get deep or meaningful?'

'I really want things to work out between us too, Zoe, which is why I'm going to leave now. It's called getting out on top.'

'And I can't believe you're not hungover,' she called after me. 'What the hell is wrong with you?'

Chapter 30

Woodberry Down Estate, North London
Saturday, April 10, 1993; 13.30

I skipped down Ennerdale House's makeshift concrete urinal in record time, feeling giddy, light and unstoppable. Zoe had seen me at my very worst and not dumped me.

My God, maybe I can tell her everything! Maybe she'll understand!

The estate's basketball courts heaved, the thudding of balls and squealing of trainers sounding like a massacre at a school for mice. A car alarm's shrill whistle pinged about the tired old tower blocks, like the yelps of a seagull strapped to a high-speed propeller. A souped-up, blacked-out Ford escort growled past, its drum 'n' bass heart spreading Kiss FM and fresh defiance.

As I got close to my car, two large men in dark clothes appeared. One leaned against my driver's door while the other walked towards me.

'Donal Lynch?'

'Not me,' I said, veering sharply to my left and taking a route between two rows of parked cars.

The car leaner read it well, heading me off where the final two vehicles stood off, face to face, like duelling cowboys.

So did we...

Behind him, a large, blacked-out jeep pulled up. The back door ghosted open.

'Get in,' his strong Dublin accent insisted, and I found myself hoping to God this was the IRA. At least I had some leverage with the boyos.

But the acid sizzling my gut told me these were Jimmy Reilly's grunts, and that he'd dreamed up something diabolical for them to do to me today.

'Shove up,' said the Dubliner, forcing me to arse-shuffle towards a dead-eyed Eastern European.

Dubliner slammed the door shut behind him, but it made no sound. The jeep sped off in total silence.

The first emotion to penetrate my numb shock was sheer disbelief. I had been abducted, in broad daylight. What the fuck were these men going to do to me?

Real terror kicked in now, sending blood gushing to my temples so that they throbbed hard. My heart felt like a midget on a pogo stick. My icy back cried hot tears.

We raced through Camden, down the warehouse wasteland of York Way towards King's Cross. I recognised the desolate spot where Valerie Gillespie got a hammering from those crack-crazed street cats.

My vision flashes white. I see a bath full of blood. Valerie's left leg surfaces, on its own. Then her right leg. Then her arms and those ridiculous fake tits. The arms and legs all bob off in different directions. Then a face emerges from the brown red water.

My dead face...

My head reeled and span, no longer connected to my nervous system. Every bone in my body turned to liquid so that I flopped in the seat like a corpse, but fully alert. Lucid.

'Stop fucking messing,' said the Dubliner, unwinding his window.

'I think he's having some sort of seizure,' he told the car.

'Maybe he's an epi,' said the driver.

'Epis shake, don't they? This fucker looks like he's passed out, except his eyes are open.'

'Sounds like one of your sexual conquests, Sean, you know, after you've slipped her a roofie,' quipped the driver.

They all laughed.

'You'd better fuck him while he's still quivering.'

They all laughed harder.

'We'd better not spoil Jimmy's fun,' said Bernie.

'Give him a slap.'

Mulletski didn't need to be told twice. Bang. Helplessly, I keeled over face first into the Dubliner's lap.

'Get off me, ye fuckin' freak,' he roared, hauling me back upright. I felt myself loll then face-plant forward, my forehead bouncing spectacularly off the leather console between the front seats.

'Jesus,' yelped Bernie, triggering another round of callous laughter.

'Fuck it, leave him there,' he said.

After a minute or so, my feet tingled. Feeling rose slowly up through me like life-affirming sap. Once it passes, a cataplectic attack has the curious effect of rendering me totally relaxed, an eerie calm after the neurological storm.

I looked up to see us crawling along Regent Street. They were taking me to the Florentine. *Shit.*

The jeep turned right into the fringes of Mayfair, zigzagged through a series of impossibly twee narrow streets before pulling up at a fearsome and opaque security gate. The driver tapped in a number and the metal wall retreated ceremonially, in total silence. The jeep pulled up again in a yard the size of two tennis courts. The Dubliner helped me out. The first thing I spotted was a red Bentley with the plate JDR 14. His fourteenth car? His fourteenth murder victim? Whatever it meant, Jimmy Reilly was waiting inside. For me.

Bernie invited me to walk ahead of him towards an ominously plain black door. My footsteps echoed around the high brick walls that surrounded us on all sides, bringing to mind a prison yard. The only difference being I couldn't see a single window or door other than the one directly ahead of us. The only hint of outside world came courtesy of a three-foot-wide section of mesh fence between the yard and an alleyway to the side of the club. Had it really been just a week since I'd clobbered Slob and fled into that rat run?

Bernie tapped a six-digit number into a metal box, pushed the black door open and nodded me in.

'Where are the dogs?' I asked, remembering the German Shepherds he'd been comforting during the evacuation.

His eyebrows shot up. 'Somewhere they'll get treated right.'

I walked in as he hit a switch. Piss-green fluorescents blinked on sleepily, revealing a long, ominous hallway.

'What's going to happen to me?' I asked flatly, neither feeling nor showing fear.

'I don't know,' said Bernie.

'Do you enjoy working for a psychopath, Bernie? You seem too civilised to me.'

He looked at me like a wounded bear.

'I used to have to crack heads in Basildon, Donal. Trust me, I feel like the Fresh Prince of fucking Bel Air.'

He led me past a row of dressing rooms.

'You're not happy about what he did to Liz though, are you, Bernie?'

He stopped at another security door.

'Take your clothes off.'

'What?'

'You heard me. Down to your kecks. He's des-

343

perate to fuck an Irish boy.'

'He'd have to kill me first.'

'I'm kidding. He's paranoid about bugs. Get on with it. He's waiting.'

'Fuck's sake.'

As each item hit the floor, he picked it up and patted it down.

'I don't walk around permanently wired, Bernie. How did you know where to find me today?'

As if to answer my question, he whipped my mobile phone out of my jacket pocket, checked who I'd called and slid off the battery.

'You can't trace a mobile phone when it has no power,' he said.

He tapped six digits into the security pad and the door clicked.

'You're on your own from here,' he said. 'Good luck.'

I walked into the pitch-black nightclub. What now? Where was he? My eyes slowly adjusted to the gloom. The space seemed smaller with no one in it. I walked past the spot where Fintan and I had sat, then down those two steps to the blood-red terrazzo floor and the glass stage.

'So glad you could make it,' came a hoarse cockney voice to my right. I turned and peered into the shadows. I couldn't see anyone.

A sudden thud overhead made me jump. I looked up as a spotlight pinged on. More dull thuds followed as, one by one, the house lights flickered on, scoring my sight. I squinted, but not enough to defend my eyes from a swirling disco searchlight's direct hit, forcing me to briefly scrunch my eyes shut.

Bobby Darin's 'Mack the Knife' kicked in, that upbeat tribute to a violent, serial-killing pimp. Good God, was Reilly modelling himself on a mythical villain?

I turned back to where the voice came from. No one there. Something pressed against my back, making me jump fully six inches in the air.

'Which version do you like best?' rasped the cockney voice in my ear, 'Bobby Darin or Sinatra?'

'Bobby Darin, every time,' I said, my voice high and dry.

'Good boy. I love Sinatra but he fackin' murdered some songs, didn't he? Like "Fly Me To The Moon". Julie London does a lovely job on that, doesn't she? Sinatra's is awful. "Mrs Robinson", "Downtown", "The Impossible Dream" ... he facked 'em all up, didn't he?'

I clenched everything in preparation for the song's ending. I dreaded to think what he had planned for me. A beating? Worse?

Surely he can't... I'm a serving policeman.

The song ended. Silence never sounded so sinister, or deafening.

'Of course, the German original is so much darker,' he said. 'You've got the arson deaths of seven kids and the rape of a widow. But here in dear old England, popular culture has to be a watered down version of middle-class culture, doesn't it? We water everything down, don't we? From our beer to our fackin' nursery rhymes.' Suddenly he bellowed, 'To the bridge,' making me jump again.

I followed him out to the foyer, up that spiral metal staircase, to the right and through a heavy

345

oak door. He moved swiftly, light on his feet, Jimmy the cat.

'Take a seat,' he commanded. 'Have a drink.'

'No, thanks.'

'Suit yourself.'

He walked over to a drinks cabinet, grabbed a tumbler and buried it noisily into a bucket of ice. As he selected a Scotch, I took a quick scan of his bird's nest. To my right, a glass wall overlooked the dance floor. In front of me, his antique, leather-bound desk fronted that ornate drinks cabinet and an enormous steel safe. Behind me, a bank of CCTV screens flickered behind a microphone and a joystick. To my left, a life-size portrait of the Marquis de Sade had been painted directly onto the wall. Beside it, a fish tank built into the wall appeared to stretch back forever. Next to that, a cabinet heaved with boxing trophies and memorabilia. Fine liquor, voyeurism, sadism and the sweet science were clearly the mainstays of his existence. Here in his own fiefdom of decadence, I guessed he could engage in all four at the same time.

With his slicked-back, shoulder-length grey hair, bolt upright posture and fine features, Jimmy had the raffish look of an aristocratic pervert like de Sade, or a leading barrister. Everything about him seemed coiffed, controlled and precise which, in my experience, masks a chaotic and chronically unfulfilled inner life. Of one thing I felt instantly certain: Jimmy couldn't get no satisfaction. Ever.

Only his voice undermined his otherwise studiously upmarket image. He wheezed like a toothless old Billingsgate fishmonger.

346

He turned to find me inspecting the de Sade portrait.

'Educated by Jesuits,' he said.

'No wonder he was a pervert.'

'First person I ever gave a hiding to was a Christian Brother.' He cackled. 'Lord have mercy on the dirty old bastard.'

'Well, at least they gave you a good education,' I said.

He glowered.

'What do you mean by that?'

'I bet you could've gone to university, had you chosen that path?'

'Had I chosen that path?' he repeated, his voice cutting now, drenched in menace. 'Had I chosen that path? That's the trouble with your generation. You don't know what real fackin' poverty is. Chosen that path? My mum had to perform abortions in our fackin' shed so we didn't starve, so don't talk to me about fackin' paths, you middle-class cant.'

I needed to calm him down, and decided that the best way would be to remind him of the grave folly of abducting a cop.

'I'm on duty right now,' I stated. 'My boss, a detective super, will be trying to contact me.'

'No one forced you into that motor, did they? I invited you here and you agreed to come. End of.'

'So you won't object if I get up and walk back out again.'

'There are some things I think you should see,' he said. He walked over to his safe, dropped to his haunches and twisted the dial. He heaved open the door, plucked something out, closed it again with a decisive thud and re-spun. He walked over briskly and showed me a piece of paper.

I recognised Tammy's list right away.

'Who gave this to ya?'

'I'm formally telling you, Mr Reilly, that I want to leave. Right now. If you stop me, you're breaking the law.'

'Oh, you can go, Lynch. Just tell me one thing. How many of our girls did you talk to last Saturday night?'

'Lots.'

'That's a shame,' he said, grimacing, 'because if you don't tell me which girl gave you this list, I'll have to go back through the CCTV and get rid of 'em all.'

I stood. He glared.

'I can't have a fackin' grass here,' he roared, eyes ablaze, head wobbling in wild fury.

'Is that why you killed Liz and Georgie?' I said.

'We don't play fackin' detectives. But right is right. I got a grass. On my daughter's life I'll fackin' kill 'em all. It's right, Lynch. It's right. Right is right. On my daughter's life. I know what I'm gonna do. On my baby's life, I'm gonna cut 'em 'til they talk. One by one. I'm gonna go to them "I'm the cant. I'm the cant" and fackin' carve 'em up. Do you understand? On my baby's life. I'm gonna fackin' do it.'

He spun around, decimating his desktop with a flailing forearm.

'Their blood will be on your fackin' hands,' he screamed as I bolted through that oak door.

Bernie stood in the foyer. My clothes lay on the reception desk.

'He's out of fucking control, Bernie, and you know it. Don't let him hurt any more of the girls.'

'Who says he hurt any girls?' he said.

I grabbed my trousers first.

Bernie spoke quietly: 'That list he just showed you is a photocopy. I could see where the original sheet had a piece ripped off the bottom.'

I got into my shirt next, then my socks.

'This piece,' he said, and I froze. He'd found Tammy's phone number jotted on that ripped-off piece of paper in one of my pockets.

'Bernie, please, I don't want any more blood-shed. I'll walk away from this whole thing now.'

'I'm not sure I can let you do that.'

'Bernie, I'm begging you. Please. I'll burn the fucking list and never bother any of you again.'

'Like I said, I'm not sure I can let you do that,' he said, holding the slip of paper out for me between thumb and forefinger.

'Thanks,' I said.

'You need to be more careful, copper.'

Chapter 31

Regent Street, London
Saturday, April 10, 1993; 16.20

I walked down Regent's Street reeling and raging.

Jimmy must have killed Liz and Georgie. Where the hell did that leave Valerie Gillespie ... Robert Conlon? I'd have to figure it all out later. Right now, I had a woman's life to save.

I found a phone box, called Tammy's number and made it clear to the man who answered that it was an emergency. He assured me she'd call back in five, so I stayed put.

Somehow, I had to stop Reilly hurting her. How could I save the other girls who spoke to me Saturday night? Could Tammy warn off Lenka and Kate? What about the girls who spoke to Fintan? Were they in danger? What about the other four IT girls on Tammy's list?

'Fuck,' I cried.

Fintan had been right. We should have taken it all to Shep. Because now it had spiralled out of anyone's control.

The phone rang. Tammy sounded cagey. I told her what just happened. She didn't speak for several seconds.

'You fucking asshole,' she said, finally. 'You've just gone and completely fucked my life. Asshole!'

'You can't go back there Tammy,' I said.

'What do you mean, I can't go back there? If I don't show up, they'll know it was me. Jimmy will find me and kill me, for sure. Look what happened to Liz and Georgie.'

'Listen to me, Tammy, he's probably looking at us on the CCTV tapes right now. If you go in tonight, I don't think you'll come out again alive. Can't you call in sick? Get Lenka and Kate to do the same?'

'What sort of fucking detective are you? I mean how obvious is that gonna look?'

'I've got an idea. Can you meet me this evening, before you go to work? There's a pub on Greek Street called the Coach and Horses. Say six o'clock?'

'I guess I've got no choice. Asshole.'

Next I called Fintan and told him the news.

'I've just had an audience with Jimmy fucking Reilly and he showed me a copy of Tammy's list.'

'Jesus.'

'You were right. We need to get the big guns involved here. If that means Shep then...'

'Already done,' he said.

'What?'

'I saw Shep Thursday. The four girls on Tammy's list are under surveillance. He tells me they're flying out to Malaga tomorrow. He's got a customs squad ready to swoop when they fly back in Monday night.'

'Jesus. You can't just steal my investigation and give it to someone else.'

'You said I was right Donal. What just happened to you proves it. Feel free to thank me later, once your male pride recovers.'

'I've arranged to meet Tammy in the Coach at six, before she goes into work. I really don't know how I can protect her, or the others. The way Reilly was behaving ... he's ready to kill.'

'I'll get Shep along too. I'm sure he'll think of something,' he said, before ending the call.

I'd missed several calls from Zoe, and as I dialled her number, decided against telling her today's news. She worried too much already.

'Has anyone ever told you you're a genius,' she gushed.

'Er, no, I can safely say that has never happened.'

'Well, I think you are. We found Bernie's finger-print on a fifty-pence piece in the electricity meter. The expert here reckons it's a couple of weeks old. We also recovered an ear print from the front door with a distinctive gap in the upper lobe. I think I can say with complete certainty that Bernard Moss has been outside and inside 42 Ennerdale House in the past three weeks.'

'You're the genius, Zoe. Believe me, you've delivered this in the nick of time. Any news from the paint people?'

'That's less clear-cut, unfortunately. How's your chemistry?'

'You know the term non-existent? Well, it's a couple of notches below that.'

'Okay, well, they can't tell us what the paint is, but they can tell us what holds it together. It contains an unusual binding agent called Epoxyester D4. Also the zinc in the paint isn't new. It's been reconstituted. The good news is there's only one plant that distributes this binding agent. The bad news is it's in Dortmund. However, undeterred, our paint geeks are getting a list of all their British clients by fax as we speak.'

'Epoxyester ... any idea what it's used for?'

'The hulls of yachts, they said. What are you doing tomorrow night?'

'Why do you ask?'

'An old friend from my drama days is in a play at the Hen and Chickens in Islington. I've just bought two tickets. Fancy it?'

'You're on. So long as it's not Guys and Dolls. I've had enough gangsters and molls for one week.'

Chapter 32

Soho, London
Saturday, April 10, 1993; 18.00

I arrived to find Shep in full flow, his neat double Scotch screaming for a refill.

'It all stems from intelligence-led policing, Lynch,' he lectured Fintan. 'We had it back in the seventies with all those supergrass scandals. When the cop and the criminal want the same thing, it creates an environment in which corruption flourishes. It's the policing equivalent to insider trading.'

Fintan editorialised to catch me up. 'Shep reckons Reilly is a registered informant, handled by Spence.'

353

I laughed. 'No way can Reilly be a grass. Not after what he said about grasses today.'

Shep shook his head in disbelief. 'You don't believe any of that "honour amongst thieves" nonsense, do you, Lynch? All major criminals are informants. They have to be. It's the only way they can flourish. They just hate the fact that others are playing the same game.'

'They can't all be...'

Shep talked right over me. 'Earlier this month, one of my team had a tip from a Turkish heroin dealer he handles about a load coming through Folkestone. This tip directed all of customs' resources towards one particular lorry, which was seized with forty kilos of heroin on board. Great result. Customs look good. The handler looks good. The Turk gets a hefty reward. Of course, the Turk had his own lorry load of heroin on that same ship, which sailed through unscathed.

'So with one tip off, he guaranteed the safety of his monster load of smack and brought down a competitor. So you can bet Reilly is at it too. These days, a criminal can't afford not to be. Reilly's intelligence has probably made Spence's career.'

'There's got to be more to it,' I argued, 'for Spence to hand over Tammy's list like that ... Reilly must have him by the balls.'

'I had a little look at Spence today,' said Fintan. 'Get this, he attends Gamblers' Anonymous and still has accounts with three bookies, owing several thousand to each. He's also paying out a monthly sum to one credit company. I won't be able to check it out until Monday but, if I were a betting man...'

Shep grimaced impatiently. 'Reilly's name won't be on any of that credit company's paperwork.'

Fintan smiled. 'Of course not, but I've got a list of the directors and secretaries who front all his other legit companies. If any of their names turn up, then we know what's happened. Reilly found out about Spence's gambling problem, bought his debts and used it to break his balls.'

'I saw him coming out of a bookies' with half a dozen betting slips the other day,' I said. 'When did he start making these monthly payments to the credit company?'

'Almost two years ago,' said Fintan.

'My God, so Spence has been in Jimmy's pocket for two years. We should trawl through all the cases he's headed up during that time, see if we can identify any other favours he might have done for Reilly.'

Shep gave me the Clint squint. 'Lynch, you didn't tell Spence who gave you that list, did you?'

'No, thank God. He has no idea.'

'Good man. Okay, so we don't have anything solid linking Jimmy to any of these murders,' said Shep.

'Not so fast,' I said, relishing the moment. 'Today we found Bernard Moss's prints inside and outside 42 Ennerdale House. Both had been left in the last month.'

Fintan's eyes widened. 'With Bernie's signature on the lease document, surely you've got enough to at least question him,' he said. 'That'd put the wind up Jimmy.'

Shep scoffed. 'You know what Bernie will say. He rented the flat for an old friend and has no idea what we're talking about. We need more.'

He registered our disappointment.

'We're still in the box seat,' he said. 'Monday night, we'll find out what those girls have been doing for Jimmy. The four of them are booked on the same flight in and out of Malaga and they're staying in the same hotel. Today they all picked up cash at a Bureau de Change in Paddington. Monday evening, customs are primed to stop all four, separate them and conduct a search. Whatever they're bringing in for Jimmy, we'll find it either on their person or in their luggage. We arrest them, break them and then we take down Jimmy Reilly. If we're lucky, we'll also find out why Liz and Georgie were murdered, and who did it.'

'Whatever these girls are up to,' said Fintan, 'they've been getting away with it for years. Why haven't they been stopped by customs before now?'

'They're all registered employees of some obscure Angolan airline called Ibis, owned by one of Reilly's dodgy pals,' said Shep. 'We suspect they wear the Ibis air stewardess uniforms on these trips and just waltz through unchecked. Now, more pressingly, I'm supposed to be taking the missus to the pictures tonight. Where's this Tammy girl?'

'She'll be here,' I said, but a large part of me feared otherwise. She sounded fatalistic, almost reckless on the phone.

'Tell me about her,' said Shep. 'Everything she told you.'

I ran him through our encounter, then asked how we could protect her, Lenka and Kate from the homicidally vengeful Jimmy Reilly, first tonight, then forever.

He said yes to a Scotch from Fintan and cradled his jaw in thought.

'The club doesn't open Sunday or Monday nights, correct?'

I nodded.

'So if we can sort out tonight, that buys us three days to make this stick?'

I kept nodding.

He accepted the neat whiskey from Fintan, downed it in one and produced a mobile phone from his inside jacket pocket.

'DS Shepard,' he barked into it. 'A serious allegation has been made against the Florentine Gardens Club in the West End. A serving police officer claims he was abducted, held there against his will and threatened. We need to seal it off for forensics.'

He nodded. 'Yes, right now.'

A pause. 'They'll just have to shut for the night then, won't they?'

Right on cue, Tammy appeared, looking older, meeker, no longer owning the room.

She stopped several feet from our table and threw me a bitter smile. I jumped up, escorted her over, made the introductions.

Shep stood, eyes glistening, clearly enraptured.

'Charmed to meet you,' he gushed, 'I've always liked Americans. So polite.'

'Gee, thanks,' she said, looking slightly alarmed.

'Now I don't know what your full name is, Tammy,' he said, 'but I'm arresting you on suspicion of soliciting and living off immoral earnings.

You have the right to remain silent...

'What the fuck?' screamed Tammy as Shep spun her round and slapped on a pair of handcuffs.

'Jesus, what's he doing?' I roared.

Fintan smiled. 'I think he might be persuading her to go into the witness protection scheme.'

Tammy turned and glared at me. 'You set me up, you fucking asshole.'

Chapter 33

Arsenal, North London
Sunday, April 11, 1993; 08.05

The mobile phone's shrill ring levitated me fully a foot off the mattress.

'I've got to figure out that volume control,' I muttered, leaning over and picking up.

'Donal?' jabbered Fintan.

'What?' I groaned.

'Listen carefully. Robert Conlon's at the Pembroke Hotel, opposite Finsbury Park. You're less than a mile away. Go get the fucker.'

'How do you know this?'

'Someone just called in. He was right under our fucking noses all along.'

'How ... what?'

'Pick up Da on the way. He's waiting for you outside the Manor House pub.'

'And where are you?'

'The wrong end of London. For the love of

God, will you just go?'

'I need to borrow your car.'

'What?'

'Mine's still outside Ennerdale House.'

'Take it, this is your career-defining opportunity, Donal, but you have to fucking move. Fast.'

Before my brain mustered up enough revs to reason, Da was hopping into the passenger seat asking me if I knew the way.'

'Of course I know the way,' I hissed. 'I can see it from here. What I'd really like to know is what you know. What the hell is going on?'

He turned the *Sunday News* page seven lead story my way.

'The Paedo Next Door' screamed the headline.

'Help Us Find Sick Kiddie Rapist' thundered the subheading, next to a photo of Conlon inside a set of graphic cross hairs.

I sighed. 'Oh, for fuck's sake.'

'Today the Sunday News *is offering a £10,000 cash reward to anyone with information about the whereabouts of a twisted child rapist and killer.*

'Robert Conlon, 45, dubbed the Beast of Browns-wood by cops, is believed to be holed up in North London, plotting his next vicious attack.'

'Oh, this is just great,' I said. 'Let's hope we get to him before some vigilante mob. What was he thinking?'

'Conlon stopped answering his phone days ago,' said Da. 'We needed to flush him out. Now drive for fuck's sake.'

I floored it.

'Remind me what your plan is again, Da? Please tell me you're not packing a pistol.'

'I'm just going to talk to him, Donal. If he hands that footage to the Brits, the IRA will kill him. He's got to destroy it, before it destroys the best chance we've ever had of peace. If he tells me where it is, I can ensure that it never sees the light of day, and Conor will make sure no harm comes to him.'

'And if he refuses.'

'Then I did my best. That's all they're asking me to do. Try to make him see reason.'

'Yeah, right. See reason or we'll shoot you. For fuck's sake. How you can morally support their carry-on, I'll never know.'

Da didn't even wait for the car to stop outside the Pembroke. I caught up with him at the reception desk, against which he'd planted a despairing forehead.

'He checked out very early this morning,' he muttered darkly. 'They don't know where he's gone or what he's driving.'

He turned to me, his face ashen. 'He was in the company of a young woman.'

'Top work, Fintan,' I barked down the phone. 'Conlon's gone to ground with some woman that no one can describe, probably a desperate skank he picked up at Brownswood last night who he's chopping into pieces as we speak?'

'Oh, come on Donal, if you caught him, you'd be thanking me now for saving your career.'

'Well, I didn't fucking catch him, did I? And we're definitely not going to catch him now, are we?'

'You lot were never going to catch him,' he snapped. 'The will just wasn't there, was it? You

360

were doing what you always do, waiting for him to strike again, hoping he'd make a mistake. If you'd launched a proper manhunt, it'd be different. I had to do this. How else could we flush him out?'

'It's not your job to flush anyone out. There's a good chance he'll get beaten to death as a result of your article, and you'll get charged with incitement.'

'God, the editor would love that,' he gushed. 'He wants to start a campaign, outing paedophiles. They're like the ultimate tabloid bogeymen. Would you really give a shit if he got beaten to death?'

'It's not the ideal way to conduct justice, is it, Fintan?'

'Well, Lynch by name... Look, Da was desperate. Conlon stopped answering his phone days ago. He practically begged me to do it.'

'I've got to call this in now,' I said. 'Give me Conlon's mobile number and let me know if anyone else contacts you with any information.'

'No problem,' he said. 'Hey, you know how we went down to Brownswood the other night with a photo of Valerie Gillespie?' he said. 'We should really go down there with a photo of Conlon. He's been around that area all along. Some of the other girls must know him.'

'Why don't you do that now?' I said. 'Even a vague description of his car would help. We've got nothing.'

'What are you gonna do?'

'As soon as I make this call, they'll want me straight in to brief them. We're now looking at a live incident, possibly an abduction.'

'You should take Da with you.'

'What? Why?'

'Conlon will be starting to feel pretty desperate and hunted by now. If he's going to call anyone in this situation, it'll be Michael Lynch. And we don't want him going to see Conlon alone, do we?'

Chapter 34

Central London
Sunday, April 11, 1993; 09.40

'I wonder has anyone ever driven to New Scotland Yard before with a rabid IRA man in their passenger seat?'

Even Da had to smile.

'Hey,' I said as we drove past the Tower of London on the edge of the City, 'this is like a whistle-stop tour of all the places you'd like to blow up.'

As the Houses of Parliament loomed, he finally spoke. 'Don't even start.'

I knew the streets round the Yard inside out, including where to park free on a Sunday.

'You know I'm going to have to leave you here in the car?' I said, 'but don't worry, I'll unwind the window an inch so you don't suffocate.'

As I walked past the Yard's iconic rotating sign into the soulless reception area, I couldn't resist a smirk. Last time I'd been here, two men toting machine guns had to escort me out.

Post bag search, frisk and airport-style metal

detector, I headed to the third floor where a detective sergeant took my statement. I told him everything, except the fact that my dad, suspected IRA member Michael Lynch, had accompanied me throughout the entire escapade. Where could I even start with that?

As a parting shot, I shamelessly mentioned how much I'd love to assist in the hunt for Conlon. 'I feel like I've developed a good insight into his character and habits that might prove useful,' I smarmed.

'Well, we're desperately short of manpower. Why don't you head into the briefing across the corridor, I'll have a word with human resources.'

Some thirty officers already sat before an empty top table.

Unsure of the etiquette, I took a chair near the back and waited.

Finally, two uniformed heavyweights lumbered in.

The slimmer, younger of the two spoke. 'As some of you already know, I'm Superintendent John Knox from Special Branch.'

That sent sparks through the room. Special Branch meant National Security.

'This is Commander Neil Crossley from the Kidnap and Extortion Unit. He'll talk you through the operational side of things shortly. Firstly, I'd like to give you a heads up as to where we are with this investigation.

'Having been bounced into it as a result of some highly irresponsible journalism, we've just had a reporting ban invoked at the High Court covering all aspects of this case. So we'll have no

363

more trouble from that lot.

'As most of you know, Robert Conlon, age 45, is wanted in connection with the murder of three women, Melinda Marshall, Valerie Gillespie and Liz Little. He was last seen at about seven o'clock this morning checking out of the Pembroke Hotel in Finsbury Park in the company of a female. Staff members were unable to offer a description of the woman or any information about Conlon's vehicle.

'Conlon has since got in touch, first by dialling 999 from his mobile. Now he's calling us on a specially assigned direct-dial number, also from his mobile. He's with a woman called Karen Hartley, age 20, who works as a prostitute in the Brownswood Road red-light area. She sounds in a bad way, very stressed, very scared.

'Conlon is making demands, and threatening to harm this woman if his demands aren't met. That's why we've drafted in Commander Crossley. We are now treating this as a kidnap situation. Commander?'

Crossley stood and surveyed the room, seemingly taking command of the very air we breathed.

'You're mostly murder detectives,' he almost whispered in working-class cockney. 'When you investigate a murder, you can't bring the victim back. Kidnap is different. It's a crime in action. Every decision you make can be the difference between a kidnap victim living or dying. I want you to keep that at the forefront of your minds at all times. Kidnap investigations require patience and caution. Guile. Do not be gung-ho. Always consider the consequences. The most successful kidnap investigations don't have heroes.

'Now, let me explain the priorities in a kidnap case. Priority number one is getting the kidnapped person back safe and well. Priority number two is catching the culprit. So the victim's welfare stands alone as our principle goal, and comes before anything else. Understood? In a straight choice between releasing the victim and apprehending the kidnapper, you always free the victim.

'We've already achieved our first priority today, which is proof of life. Karen spoke to us briefly on Conlon's mobile phone. She's not coping very well. But we can use that to keep him on the phone, and that's a good thing as I'll explain in a while.

'Our mission now is twofold. We must keep Karen alive and safe, but we must also buy time for you to investigate. We, the negotiators, do this by finding plausible logistical reasons to delay meeting the kidnapper's demands. To give you an example, we've explained to him how cash is difficult to raise on a Sunday. Some major decision makers are away with their families and uncontactable. We're buying time so that you guys can get out there and rescue her. Apprehending him, don't forget, is just a bonus.

'Often, our only chance of arresting a kidnapper or extortionist is when they break cover to collect the money. But there's always a risk he's working with a partner. If we swoop in and arrest him, the partner might kill Karen. I'd rather he walk away with the ransom than risk Karen's life.

'So, where is he?

'We've had audio experts in. They're convinced

that he's calling from a vehicle while driving around London, and that Karen's in the same vehicle. We don't have a lot else right now. So the only thing we can usefully do is get boots, eyes and ears out there on the ground.'

He walked over to a map of London.

'Thankfully, we've got a virtual open line to his mobile. We've been tracking his phone signals and we're establishing a general pattern of where he's driving, broadly between Maida Vale in West London and Battersea in South London. We can only speculate as to why he's sticking to these locations. But it means he's crossing the Thames, over and back, several times. We've got five bridges that he's most likely driving across on these routes, Wandsworth, Battersea, Albert, Chelsea and Vauxhall.

'We're going to deploy you in teams on both sides of these bridges. What are you looking for? Any vehicle that looks like it's been modified for kidnap. Erratic driving. Counter surveillance techniques. Someone clearly disguising their appearance. Listen in on your police radios; we'll isolate a frequency so that you'll at least know in which direction he's driving. Our tracking system is a couple of minutes behind but it's the best we've got.

'The rest of you will be tasked with checking out hotels, B and Bs, car-hire companies. Remember the aliases he frequently uses, Lesley Cahill and Thomas Koschei. Now any questions?'

'What are Conlon's demands?' came one.

Crossley looked to Knox. 'Money and a deal, basically; the details aren't important.'

'Why is it a matter of National Security?'

'I can't possibly comment,' snapped Knox, 'but trust me when I tell you that it is. And we're probably not the only ones looking for him.'

'Who else is looking for Conlon?'

'Strictly off the record, the Provisional IRA is believed to be looking for Conlon, so let's make sure we get to him first.'

Chapter 35

Albert Bridge, London
Sunday, April 11, 1993; 14.30

'This is ridiculous,' Da grumbled, 'I'm going cross-eyed looking at fucking traffic.'

I'd volunteered to take the south side of Albert Bridge, but the relentless stream of vehicles suggested lost cause. Even when the police radio announced his approach from the north, we failed to see anything suspicious.

'Unless he's wearing a balaclava,' moaned Da, 'and her legs are sticking out of the boot, we'll never spot them.'

I reached into the glove compartment and threw him a London A to Z. 'You got any better ideas?'

He fingered the pages exhaustively, as if checking for nits.

'He's not a city boy,' he said finally.

'What a shame they don't have hookers for him to savage in the countryside.'

'We shouldn't be looking at where he's driving.

We should be looking at where he's stopping.'

He turned the open pages towards me and jabbed at a lump of green. 'Battersea Park,' he said.

'You think?'

'He can't leave the car if she's in it. And that's the only place you can stop south of the river that isn't a street. He'll be making these calls to the cops somewhere quiet like that.'

'It's a big park.'

'Tell me, detective,' he smiled, 'where's a better place to hide a needle than in a haystack?'

I smiled back. 'What a family of riddlers we are.'

'With other needles,' he said. 'Let's go check out all the parking areas in Battersea Park.'

We cruised the park, hungrily hunting out opportunity like some father and son dogging combo, when Fintan called.

'You'll never guess who I'm sitting with outside the Finsbury Park Tavern?' he said.

'As much fun as guessing would be Fintan,' I said, 'we are a tad pressed for time, you know, what with hunting down a homicidal maniac and the woman he's about to kill.'

'Jo from Middlesbrough!'

'Ah, yes, Jo the frosty hooker. How is she?'

'You know how she takes the registration plates of cars she doesn't recognise? Well, I'm currently looking at a line on her list from last night that ends KH, for Karen Hartley.'

'Oh my God.'

'Now pass the phone over to Da.'

'What?'

'I'm not telling you because you'll do the right thing and tell your boss. Da needs this more than anyone.'

'Ah, come on,' I protested, 'we're all in this together.'

'We made a deal. Dad, now.'

Da's enthusiastic 'yeahs' felt like slash wounds to my chest; his 'brilliant' and giggled 'genius' daggers to my heart. He'd never said anything like that to me, ever. Yet here I was, upfront with him on the actual hunt, breaking every rule in the handbook.

'Right so,' he said, hanging up, 'we're looking for a Volvo 940 estate. Fittingly enough, they look like hearses, except this one is racing green. I've memorised the registration. Do another lap.'

We drew a blank.

'Again,' he said.

'I'm a bit worried that we've abandoned our post.'

'You've a choice in life, Donal, either follow orders or think for yourself. Why don't you trust your own instincts, for once?'

I laughed. 'What's this got to do with instincts? I'm just following your orders instead of theirs.'

'Well, just do it so.'

As I drove out of the park's east side, onto Queenstown Road, Michael shouted, 'Stop!'

'Turn around and drive past that row of cars, nearest the river.'

'I can't turn here. It's illegal.'

'You're a cop for Christ's sake! Turn.'

My gear-crunching, six-pointer felt less *Bullitt,*

more *Driving Miss Daisy.*

'You must be the most useless fucker God ever put on four wheels,' Da observed, as the Volvo passed us on its way out.

'Get after it, but not too close.'

'Yeah, I've seen the films, Da. Jesus.'

Halfway across the bridge, we were just three cars behind. I couldn't make out anyone through the Volvo's rear-window reflections.

'I should radio for back-up.'

'No, you shouldn't,' said Da. 'He's probably listening in.'

I remembered the forensic psychologist's warning that serial offenders often use police scanners. How did Da know this? It would have to be my excuse later for not letting HQ in on our pursuit…

The Volvo continued up through Sloane Square towards Knightsbridge, then turned right towards Hyde Park Corner.

'Shit, we'll never stay with him through there. It's a mess.'

'Get right behind him,' hissed Da.

'We don't want him clocking us,' I protested. 'He might kill Karen.'

'You can't fucking lose him now, Donal. She must be in the boot, anyway, look. I can only see his head. If she's in the boot, he can't hurt her. Not if we're right behind him.'

'She might be lying on the back seat.'

'Then the closer we are to him the better.'

'Fuck it,' I said, cutting someone up to make the outside lane, then veering back in right behind the Volvo. Incredibly, he didn't appear to react.

'Sure isn't that how everyone drives over here?'

said Da.

The Volvo continued left up Park Lane, then onto the Edgware Road.

'He must've seen us by now.'

'I'm not sure how much more of this I can stand,' said Da.

The Volvo sped up and made a sudden left into Sussex Gardens, then slowed right down.

'Shit, he's onto us,' he said as I braked hard to tuck in behind him.

'Fintan loves this car, you know,' I said.

'Jesus, don't talk to me. The Ford fucking Mundano I call it. Lord help us.'

We turned to each other and smiled. *My God*, I thought, *we've bonded at last. And all it'll cost is one brand new Mondeo.*

I gunned the engine and overtook the Volvo, then swung the steering wheel left with all my might. My arse seemed to take off as the world spun wildly around us. Suddenly, we were face to face. As the Volvo braked, I sped up.

Deafening bang. White flash. That terrible silence when even the birds stop singing.

I battled the squelching airbag to get out. Da was already opening the green driver's door. The man who slumped out wasn't Robert Conlon. Da looked at me, mouth open.

Remembering Crossley's 'victim first' declaration, I went straight to the back door and opened it. No Karen.

'Grab the keys,' I said to Da, 'she must be in the boot.'

I twisted the lock and lifted. Empty. *What the fuck?*

Crossley's flat voice from earlier purred in both ears: *Every decision you make can be the difference between a kidnap victim living or dying.*

Suddenly, I spotted Da at the front passenger door, shouting.

'Bob, you have to tell me or they'll kill you,' he roared.

I ran up to him. 'Bob, Bob,' he screamed.

He looked at me and lowered his right hand from his ear. His shaking palm opened to show two mobile phones, crudely taped together. 'He's hung up,' he said.

'Fuck,' I said, 'I think we've just killed Karen Hartley.'

As soon as I flashed my warrant card, Taz from Tottenham couldn't stop talking.

He'd got to know 'Mr Bob' in the Manor House pub in recent months.

Hang on, I thought, wasn't that where Fintan met Da the other night? Too much of a coincidence, surely? What did that fucker really know?

Taz stopped off most nights for a pint on his way home from work. He drove a minicab for a company based near King's Cross. This morning, Mr Bob called him at work, offering £300 for an all-day job. How could he say no?

Mr Bob came to the office, handed him two mobile phones, a roll of gaffer tape and the keys to his Volvo. His instructions had been simple. One: drive around London all day on a pre-appointed route between Paddington and Clapham. Two: whenever a mobile phone rings in the car – either Taz's or the two he'd just acquired from Bob –

answer it without speaking. Three: follow my instructions, which may involve dialling numbers and taping the two acquired mobile phones together, head to toe, so that the people on the other end of both phones could talk.

In classic petty-criminal fashion, Taz had neither asked nor considered what might've been going on here.

When quizzed as to why he sped away from us on Edgware Road, Taz explained: 'I thought it was like a racist road-rage thing. I get it all the time. People shouting Paki bastard, trying to run me off the road. I wouldn't mind but I'm Turkish!'

Of course he had no idea where Mr Bob might currently be. However, his last request had been that Taz drop off the racing-green Volvo behind the Manor House pub some time tonight.

The tank-like Volvo looked like it had suffered no more than a prang.

'Make yourself scarce, Da, until I deal with all this shit,' I said. 'Come back in an hour. Taz here can then you drop you back to Manor House in the Volvo.'

The same question preyed upon my addled mind. *What if he kills Karen now?* How was I supposed to live with that?

I'd blown our covert operation wide open. I couldn't stop imagining her, tied up in some ghastly space, listening in dread as her captor's sick mobile phone ruse came unstuck. What must have gone through her mind? Conlon would have responded in a blind, murderous rage.

He probably killed her, there and then.

'We all would've believed she was in that vehicle,' said Commander Crossley. 'We would have instructed you to do exactly what you did, except perhaps for deliberately shunting into it.'

'You can't blame yourself,' said Zoe over the phone. 'You risked your life trying to save her. What else could you do?'

'You did what to my car?' cried Fintan.

They sent me home and insisted I stay there until morning. As soon as I got in, Zoe called.

'You can't sit there drinking all night and dwelling on it,' she instructed. 'You're coming to the theatre with me, as planned.'

'I'd really rather just be on my own tonight,' I wanted to say, but couldn't summon the courage.

I showered and, changed in a state of mild dread. Nothing reminded me I didn't belong in England more than a trip to the theatre. To me, it felt like a place where Middle Englanders gathered for a good old sneer at the pompous upper classes and the ignorant working classes. Every British play I'd ever suffered through featured at least one of those elements. Theatre was a club to which I didn't belong. I made a mental list of what I hated most: the people; the heat; the actorish shouting; at number one, having to 'jostle violently for your one £3 bottle of pre-paid Becks during the interval.

However, I sensed that for Zoe, being able to tell family, friends, colleagues about our shared night of culture would somehow legitimise our relationship. I hoped she still liked me dry.

At least it was upstairs to a pub. I managed to cram down three pints in advance, and smuggle in two bottles of wine. Not nearly enough, as it turned out. *Bang to (Women's) Rights* the play was called, and it turned out to be every bit as preachy, bunkered and anti-male as the title had promised.

Mercifully, the second half barely registered at all; some daft caper in which a hitman and his supposed target plot together to frame her philandering husband. At one stage, I kicked over one of my empty wine bottles and got hissed at. I may have told the hissers to 'fuck off'.

Next thing I remember, we were making love in my bedroom. Then she got up and left, motivated by maternal duty or crushing disappointment, I couldn't tell. But she'd piled a shitload of fax paperwork on our sofa, detailing the British clients of that chemical company in Dortmund.

As soon as I woke, I texted Zoe to make sure she got home okay, then tore into the list. I rang each company and asked the same two questions: do you produce a paint with the binding agent Epoxyester D4? Does it also contain reconstituted zinc?

Just one plant manufactured a paint matching these criteria. The man on the phone explained that it's a highly specialised, super-strong substance used mostly on yachts heading into especially wild seas.

'Anything else?'

'Not that I know of. You might be best speaking to the people who sell it. We've only got a handful.'

London-based outlets for this torpedo-proof paint numbered just three. The manager of one shop explained just how exclusive this product's devotees were: 'People who yacht in extreme conditions and people who own terrazzo floors.'

My whole body shook. My vision of Liz that first night had set me on the trail of this substance. Her non-appearance on the second night, after I'd attended Brownswood Road, seemed to suggest she'd been murdered inside the Florentine Gardens Club. This paint – which an eagle-eyed pathologist had scraped out of her head wounds – might just prove it.

If Jimmy Reilly used this particular brand of paint to repair his terrazzo floor, then that links her body directly to his club. The ball-peen hammer that inflicted these injuries must have come from that building. Could it be buried under that frequently repaired and re-sealed terrazzo floor?

All three stores selling it in London agreed to let me scan their credit-card transactions from the previous six months. In Laidlaws of Bloomsbury, my eyes fell upon the smoking-gun evidence I needed.

I called Shep right away.

'Guy, I've just found what we need to arrest Bernard Moss.'

Chapter 36

Arsenal, North London
Monday, April 12, 1993; 07.20

When I heard Commander Crossley's earnest voice on the other end of the phone, every fibre of my being clenched and tensed, braced for the news that would haunt me until my dying day.

'They've found Karen,' he said. The world, stopped spinning, hurling me headlong through space.

'She was staggering around Finsbury Park in a right old state.'

'She's alive?' I squeaked.

'She's alive,' he said, his voice cracking with emotion. Tears rained down my face as I tried but failed to swallow a sob.

'Thank fucking God,' I managed.

'She's at the Whittington Hospital,' he said, 'recovering from her injuries. She'd been blind-folded during the whole thing, and raped repeat-edly. Sometime early this morning, he forced her into a car and threw her out on the street, still blindfolded.'

As blissful, dreamy relief anaesthetised my agon-ised soul, his words turned into a jabbering blur.

'We're still negotiating with Conlon ... it's no longer a manhunt ... Karen's safety was always our priority... Best left to Special Branch.'

Chapter 37

Archway, North London
Monday, April 12, 1993; 12.00

It was Zoe's idea that we pay Karen Hartley a visit, delivered via a blunt text message.

I just wanted to see Zoe, find out how badly I'd fucked things last night. Quite literally.

As soon as she emerged from Archway tube station, my guilt and paranoia accosted her.

'About last night,' I started, but she cut me dead.

'Don't feel bad. You'd had a lot to drink.'

'But we did, didn't we?'

'Sort of.' She smiled. 'I think you need to cut down on booze.'

'Sorry.'

'Don't be. It's the first time I've ever laughed myself to sleep.'

'Wow, as first-night reviews go, that's pretty damning.'

'I'd no idea you were a virgin, or that you loathe theatre so much. It was hard to tell which you felt more passionately about.'

'You're right. I need to cut down.'

'About bloody time,' said Karen Hartley, sitting up in bed, stopping us both dead in our tracks.

'Yer coppers, right?'

'Well, yes,' I blustered, 'but we've just come to

see how you're doing.'

'Never mind about that,' she said in a broad Mancunian accent, 'you need to catch the bastard.'

'We'd love to,' said Zoe, 'but we were led to believe you couldn't tell us much.'

'You didn't fuckin' ask. I kept saying I could help but you lot don't want to know.'

'Please, shoot,' I said.

'I know roughly where he kept me. I could hear train announcements ... not specific words, but like the buzz. I could hear underground trains and ambulances. And traffic overhead on the Westway. I was close to Paddington station.'

'How certain are you of that, Karen?'

'One hundred per cent certain. I used to work down at Sussex Gardens. I know what Paddington sounds like.'

'Lots of places in London have overground and underground stations and flyovers,' I said, as gently as I could.

'Yeah, but what about the singing?' she argued, as if we'd conducted this debate before. 'I thought I was fucking dying or something when I heard this beautiful singing, like angels. Then I realised it must've been about six on Sunday. It was coming from St James' Church. They always have evensong at six on a Sunday. I used to sneak into the back and listen to 'em. I recognised the songs and the organ.'

'Is there any way you could identify the actual house where he kept you?'

'That's what I've been trying to tell you. He put a motorcycle helmet over my head when he led

379

me in, but I could see the paving stones. I'd recognise them if I saw them again.'

'You've got to recover first,' said Zoe. 'You've been through a terrible ordeal.'

'I wanna go now. I want that bastard caught. I was gonna discharge meself anyway. I was just waiting for you lot to turn up and question me. Are you trying to let him get away with it or what?'

Chapter 38

Paddington, West London
Monday, April 12, 1993; 14.30

We parked up at St James' Church in Sussex Gardens. A sign outside confirmed Sunday evensong at 6pm.

'Could you tell where the singing was coming from, even roughly?' I asked.

'Yeah,' she said, pointing to Westbourne Crescent, 'I was somewhere over there.'

We walked along a row of elegant six-storey Georgian townhouses, inspecting each basement flat for clues.

Then I saw it. The racing-green Volvo, sat outside number 39.

Bloody hell, he had the brass neck to go pick it up at Manor House last night or this morning and drive it back here. I should've had it staked out.

I said nothing.

As she drifted past 37, she stopped suddenly.

'This one,' she said.

We peered down at the black and white tiled steps.

'It looks just like the others,' I said.

'I remember the drain cover,' she said, 'Stanton and Staveley Trojan. And the door handle. I'm certain that's where he kept me.'

I turned to Zoe. 'We'd better call in backup.'

A bang made me jump.

I turned. *Where the fuck is Karen?* More banging. She was shouting now. I looked down to see her bashing that basement flat door, screaming her head off.

'Shit,' I said.

'Karen,' I called, 'stop it.'

She kept punching the door.

'We've got to go in now, Zoe, like right now,' I said, and I piled down those steps.

'You're too fucking chicken to face me,' screamed Karen through the door.

'For Christ's sake, Karen,' I barked, grabbing both her arms, 'you're giving him a chance to get out the back.'

I let my fingers sink into her flesh until she stopped flailing. 'Karen, listen to me. Let me boot this door in. Then let me go in first, okay?'

She nodded.

I kicked at the handle with all my might. It took three more to drive the lock through the wooden frame.

'Police. Don't move,' I shouted, as everything turned woozy and slo-mo.

I crept through the sitting room and kitchen. Clear.

'Police,' I shouted. 'Come out into the hallway now and I won't shoot.'

No response.

'Is this the place, Karen?'

'I'll know in a sec,' she said.

She walked slowly to a cupboard door and opened it. She got down on her knees and ran her fingers along the edge of the carpet.

'What are you doing?' I whispered.

She turned to me and opened her hand. 'They're bits of my fingernails,' she said, 'I peeled 'em off and tucked them in between the carpet and the skirting board, just in case.'

'You're one smart lady,' I said. 'You should've been a cop.'

'I thought you said I were smart?' she muttered.

I moved slowly down the hallway. The first two of three doors hung open. I peered into one. A bathroom. Empty. Silently opened the second. Empty. As I approached the third, closed door, I said a little prayer: *Please God, don't let him be inside waiting to shoot me.*

I took three deep silent breaths. My brain started humming that song again... *How much is that doggie in the window...*

I pulled down slowly on the handle. When it hit the bottom, I hit the door, hard.

A man lay on the bare, stained mattress, on his front, naked save for a hood over his head. Blood had dried brown on his neck and right shoulder.

'Why won't you help me,' Da's voice pleads in my head, over and over.

'Oh Christ. Da,' I cry. I need to take off that hood.

382

To hold his face. But I know it's packed with brain maggots...

'Brain matter looks like puked up shepherd's pie,' the crime scene expert had warned us. I rolled the body over with considerable difficulty.

The cellebrum is connected to the ... bellend. The angel lust confirmed a swift and brutal end. I pulled up the hood an inch.

It wasn't Da.

That dream hadn't been about him. It had been about the man lying here with a single, expertly dispatched bullet wound below his cold dead ear.

Robert Christopher Conlon.

Or had it? Dad had been driven back to Manor House in the Volvo last night. Did he stay with it to keep watch, to trail it here ... to finish him off...?

Crossley's words from earlier drifted in. *'We're still negotiating with Conlon ... it's no longer a manhunt... Karen's safety was always our priority... Best left to Special Branch.'*

Negotiating what, exactly?

I took a look around the room as my brain careered around the case.

There are always bigger plays, Lynch. Always. Remember that.

Da had found those mobile phones strapped together in the footwell of the Volvo's passenger seat. That breathtakingly simple ruse had convinced us that Conlon had been driving around London with Karen in the car. All that time, he'd been holding her here.

I stalked out to the hallway and heard sirens approaching. 'He's dead,' I told Karen. 'Shot once

383

in the head. Feel free to leave now.'

She just stared.

'Go in and see for yourself,' I told her, 'if it'll help.'

She strode to the door. 'Good fucking riddance,' she said, finally.

'Where would they have put his clothes?' I asked her. She turned with a frown on, walking past me towards the kitchen. I followed.

She opened the washing machine's circular-door just as those wailing sirens hit Westbourne Crescent. A red light flashed in the top corner of the Toshiba.

'They switched on the power and set it,' she said, 'but they didn't press the start button.'

My mind flashed back to our kitchen, Tuesday night, Da's well-intentioned but ultimately doomed tilt at domestication.

I leaned in and patted Conlon's clothes, in search of those keys to the Volvo. Their presence would confirm he'd driven it here himself from Manor House. Not Da.

I didn't find the keys. But I did pull out something else, a device that I'd seen in action a few days earlier.

Fuck me, I thought, this might reveal everything.

'Place your hands where I can see them, both of you,' commanded a voice behind me as I slipped it into my jacket pocket. 'Don't turn around or we'll shoot.'

'What the fuck were you thinking, Lynch?' barked Superintendent John Knox from Special Branch.

'You can't just spirit people out of hospital and

go charging into properties. Not when it's clearly a matter of national security. Did you not think for one second about the potential consequences?'

'Sir, my friend over their called in back up as soon as Karen identified the property. Believe me, I didn't want to go in. Had she not attacked the door and made a scene, I wouldn't have. I didn't want him to get away. Not again.'

'I've a good mind to demand your warrant card, here and now.'

'I'd like to refer this to the Police Federation, sir.'

Indignation wobbled his entire frame for twenty seconds before he flounced off.

There are always bigger plays, Lynch. Always. Remember that.

What had been the bigger play here? I felt certain that it'd catch up with me very soon.

'I need to take a walk, Zoe,' I said, 'clear my head.'

'I can't believe what you just did, for her,' she said, gripping my right shoulder. 'It was so brave. I could never have done that.'

I smiled. 'I didn't have time to get scared.'

'Thank God you're okay, Donal,' she whispered, her eyes welling up, 'because in case you hadn't noticed, I'm falling in love with you.'

She came in for a hug as I ordered myself not to crack. Not now.

After what seemed like several minutes, she broke off.

'I need to get back to work,' she sniffed and smiled. 'They'll never believe what happened here.'

'I've a feeling we haven't heard the last of it.'

I marched down to Praed Street tormented by questions. Conlon's killing bore all the hallmarks of an IRA execution. How the hell had they found him? Did Da set him up after all? And where was this damning footage that could make or break the peace process?

None of it made any sense.

I stood at a set of lights, waiting to cross when a shop sign snagged on my brain.

'Money Transfer', 222 Praed Street. Then I remembered; this had been the Bureau de Change co-owned by Helen Oldroyd, the Jaguar driver stabbed to death in the car park of that West London leisure centre eighteen months ago.

'How strange,' I thought, as I pulled my phone out to call Fintan.

'Where's Da? He's not picking up.'

'Why do you want him?'

'We've just found Robert Conlon at an address near Paddington. Classic IRA-style execution of an informant. Naked except for a hood, one-behind-the-ear.'

'He's gone home.'

'What, to the Woodberry estate?'

'No, home, home. He should be on the plane right now.'

'What a coincidence.'

'He said it was out of his hands. He's done all he can.'

'He's clearly done exactly what we feared he'd do. He set Conlon up to get whacked by the IRA. Then he scarpered. I want you to book two plane tickets to Dublin this Sunday, Fintan. We're going to have a long overdue family showdown.'

'You sure?'

'I can do this alone...'

'Okay, okay.'

'Shame the fucker's not here,' I told him. 'Arresting my own dad for murder ... now that'd get me noticed by a murder squad.'

'You wouldn't.'

'For this Fintan, one day I will.'

Chapter 39

East Dulwich, South London
Monday, April 12, 1993; 17.00

'Showtime.' Shep smiled, rubbing his hands, as I joined him spy-side of a two-way mirror.

He introduced me to the interrogators limbering up behind him, Detective Sergeants Price and White. On the other side of the glass, Bernie Moss sat alone, staring into the tabletop.

'He arrived without a brief, Lynch,' said Shep. 'What do you make of that?'

'Well, he thinks he's pretty smart. He likes to show off how well-read he is.'

'Maybe he doesn't want Jimmy Reilly to find out he's here. Everyone knows how much he hates rats.'

They all had a chuckle about that.

'You've met Bernie, haven't you, Lynch. Any tender spots?'

'He seemed genuinely shocked when I told him

about Liz Little's murder. I don't think he was involved. He might even have had feelings for her.'

Shep squinted at the glass. 'Or he was in on her shakedown, whatever that was. Either way, he'll be thinking only of self-preservation now. We've got our knock-out punch worked out though, Lynch, so sit back, look and learn.'

Price and White walked in, switched on the tape recorder and set to work.

'Bernard Moss, is it okay if we call you Bernie?'

'Everyone else does.'

'Tell us where you work and your position there.'

'I'm head of security at the Florentine Gardens Club, on Conduit Street, W1.'

'Have you ever been to 42 Ennerdale House on the Woodberry Estate in North London?'

'Yes.'

'Can I ask you when and what you were doing there?'

'About three weeks ago, one of the girls who works at the club asked me to sort out a flat for her. She was having domestic trouble with an ex-boyfriend. So I arranged a short term let at that address.'

'Which girl asked you to do this?'

'Georgie. Georgina Bell.'

'You are aware that Georgie is now dead?'

'Yes, terrible business that. Terrible.'

'Why would a girl earning all that money go and live in a rough old estate like the Woodberry?'

'I got the impression most of her money went up her nose. She had a bad coke problem.'

'The pathologist didn't find any evidence of cocaine in her system or at the scene.'

'That's because there wasn't any of her left,' he sneered. 'At least that's what I heard.'

'Who killed her Bernie?'

'I don't know that she was killed. I assumed she'd had some sort of coke seizure, collapsed and died, then the dogs had her for dinner.'

'We've found your prints at the scene, Bernie. You brought her dead body there, didn't you?'

'No.'

'And you then brought the dogs, didn't you?'

'No. I went to that flat once, and that was to make sure it was safe for her to move into. That's the only time I set foot in it.'

'What can you tell us about Liz Little, Bernie?'

'I didn't know her that well. She seemed a bright girl. Popular.'

'Did she have any enemies?'

'None that I know of.'

'When did you last see Liz Little?'

'I saw her at the club on the night before she died, the Friday.'

'Did you speak to her that night?'

'No. She was flitting about, talking to different people, then she was gone. I didn't see her leave.'

'DS Price is producing a piece of paper with a typed list of six names,' White told the tape recorder.

'Take a look at this, Bernie,' said Price, handing it over.

'Tell me about the girls on this list.'

'They all work as hostesses at the club.'

'They're a select group, known as the IT girls. Tell us what IT stands for and what these girls do for Jimmy Reilly.'

'I don't know what you're talking about.'

'We've got their travel records, their bank accounts. You might as well tell us.'

'Tell you what? I don't know what you're talking about.'

'DS Price is now producing a can of specialist paint. Do you recognise this paint, Bernie?'

He nodded, slowly.

'You have to speak for the benefit of the tape, Bernie.'

'Yes.'

Shep leaned forward. 'His brain's doing fucking cartwheels now.'

'How are you familiar with this paint?'

'Jimmy uses it at the club, to repair cigarette burns to the terrazzo floor.'

'We found traces of this material at both the Liz Little and Georgie Bell murder scenes, Bernie. Do you know how it would have got there?'

'No.'

'Someone employed at the Florentine Gardens Club killed both women. And this proves it.'

'I don't know anything about that.'

'In fact, we feel pretty certain that both Liz and Georgie were murdered inside the club. The traces of paint inside their wounds prove that. As Jimmy's head of security, you must have known about it.'

'No.'

Shep shuffled in his seat. 'Missile one, incoming.'

'How important is that terrazzo floor to Jimmy?'

'He loves it. It's his baby.'

'How do you think he'll feel when we turn up

later today with a forensic team in tow to dig it up?'

He laughed. 'You can't do that. It's protected by a preservation order.'

'Oh, but we can,' said Price, 'and we're at the High Court securing that order right now.'

Bernie's face fell.

'Imagine,' said White, 'his head of security's in custody and suddenly we turn up and start smashing up the terrazzo? That's gonna put him in a great mood.'

The officers had a good laugh at that.

White continued. 'Do you know a senior police officer called Alex Spence?'

'Missile two,' said Shep.

'I don't think so.'

'Oh, come now, Bernie, have a think.'

'No, I can't say that I do.'

'DS Price is passing a photo of Superintendent Alex Spence to the suspect. Recognise him, Bernie?'

'No.'

'Interview terminated at sixteen-o-seven hours,' White told the tape.

Both men got up and walked out.

Shep stood. 'There may be trouble ahead,' he sang as he strode out to the hallway, then into the interrogation room.

'But while there's music, and love and romance,' he sang, doing a little Sammy Davis shoe shuffle, 'let's face the music, and dance.' Bernie didn't even blink.

Shep raised an apple to his mouth and took a noisy bite.

'Bernie, Bernie, Bernie,' he said, chomping and pacing about at the top of the room.

'You might not know Superintendent Alex Spence, but Superintendent Alex Spence certainly knows you.'

Bernie pulled a contemptuous face as Shep took another crunching mouthful.

'And he's very close to Jimmy Reilly. In fact, it was Spence who provided him with that list of IT girls we just showed you, you know, the one with the two murder victims on it.'

He stopped pacing to inspect the apple and take another bite. He leaned down against the tabletop on both hands, peering intently into Bernie's bored face.

'Spence is what we call a bad apple, Bernie. Now your boss Jimmy is very keen to know where we got that list of names from. We all know how excitable he gets about grasses, don't we? I've got an officer sitting behind that glass willing to make a statement that he got this list from you. I've got a handwriting expert poring over your *Times* crossword that we lifted from your club last Saturday, willing to confirm that some handwriting on the original list is yours. And then I'm going to make sure Spence accidentally gets wind of this shocking little development.'

'That's not my writing, and you know it.'

'Yeah, but dear old Alex Spence doesn't, does he? Or Jimmy Reilly? And who are they to over-rule a venerable handwriting expert?'

'Jimmy won't fall for any of that shit.'

'Jimmy will also be somewhat alarmed tonight when his four IT girls get lifted on their way back from Malaga. You won't be able to do anything about it because you'll be here, in custody. And you've already made your phone call, haven't you, Bernie? I wonder what will Jimmy make of that? His smuggling team gets busted six hours after his head of security gets arrested! All while we're digging up his precious floor. Dear oh dear.

'And we'll get those girls talking tonight, Bernie, you can count on that. Because if they don't, their mums and dads will be reading about how they really earn their livings in this weekend's *Sunday News*.'

Bernie crossed his arms and shook his head, seemingly in mild amusement.

'The wheels are starting to come off, Bernie. And there's going to be one hell of a crash. You're a smart man, I'm told. The smart thing to do right now would be to switch horses. We could provide you with a very attractive package. And that sounds a lot more pleasant to me than propping up Jimmy's terrazzo. You've got eighteen hours now to think about it in the comfort of your cell.'

Shep strode to the door, humming merrily. He opened it and turned: 'You can't have Jimmy finding out that you were helping Liz – or was it Georgie – shake him down either, can you, Bernie? Imagine, while we're interrogating those four girls tonight, if that rumour were to reach our old friend Spence?'

He took one final bite and tossed the apple. Bernie swerved it, just.

'They have their uses, you know Bernie, these bad apples. And you might not be able to dodge it next time...'

Chapter 40

East Dulwich, South London
Monday, April 12, 1993; 20.00

Fintan joined us in East Dulwich for tonight's radio feature, 'The Heathrow Hustle'.

He sat with Shep and me at the helpless end of a customs radio link, eavesdropping on the shakedown of Jimmy's four remaining IT girls as they flew in from Malaga.

To pass time, we speculated on the nature of the racket.

'Chemicals,' said Fintan. 'Raw materials for these designer drugs he's developing, so not technically illegal.'

'Too tacky,' said Shep. 'I'm plumping for gems. Easiest thing in the world to smuggle. You just have to set it in jewellery and wear it. A massive stone wouldn't look out of place on any of those girls.'

'Gold,' I said, 'a classic VAT fraud. Each girl carries in one twelve and a half kilo bar on each trip. Reilly passes it on to a dealer and they split the VAT on the sale. That gives them a fifteen grand cut each per bar.'

Shep dialled in all three scenarios to our customs' foot soldiers. They didn't bother disguising their resentment.

'I don't care what their racket is, so long as you

bust them with something,' demanded Shep. He turned to us: 'That'll give us the ammo we need to bust Bernie's balls.'

After an agonising wait, our airside contact finally buzzed in.

'All four girls clean, all their belongings clean,' he stated flatly.

'What about the dogs?' said Shep. 'All we need is one growl to arrest.'

'No reaction. None of the four has been in contact with drugs in the past couple of days.'

'Are any of them talking?'

'All no comment. We can't hold them for much longer.'

'What the hell are they up to?' boomed Shep. 'If they're not bringing something in, what are they taking out?'

'Dirty money, perhaps,' said the man from customs, 'We'll never know now.'

Liz's visit all those nights ago flickered in my vision, those bundles of filthy banknotes tumbling out of her puppet-like figure. *Of course,* I thought, *this is what she'd been trying to tell me.* I needed to have faith in these visions, invest more time into deciphering their meaning.

'Okay, let them go,' Shep said with a sigh.

'Why would they take cash abroad for Reilly?' asked Fintan.

'To pay criminals or drug suppliers? Who knows?' said Shep. 'Whatever it is, that's our chance to find out gone.'

My mind snagged on a minor detail and wouldn't let go. 'You said the girls all went to the same Bureau de Change before the trip,' I said.

'Which one?'

'It's in the paperwork somewhere,' said Shep. 'Is it important?'

'Could be.'

He rifled through his briefcase, finally pulling out a report.

'Money Transfer, 222 Praed Street, London W2,' he said. 'Ring a bell?'

'Every bell in London, guv. I think we've cracked it.'

They hauled Bernie back to an interview suite as I tried to stop his excited visitors pissing the floor.

The mention of those sniffer dogs at Heathrow first set my nose twitching.

At the Florentine Gardens Club that first night, Bernie had stated his pet hates to me: rudeness to service staff and cruelty to animals. I'd seen him run to check on those dogs after Tammy's pepper-spray assault on the club's air-con vents. Slob claimed he preferred animals to people. He'd been an animal rights' extremist and a hunt saboteur.

No one else's prints had been found at 42 Ennerdale House. I allowed myself to draw three conclusions. One: he brought Georgie Bell's dead body to the flat. Two: he brought the dogs that devoured her dead body to the flat, unwittingly. Three: he took those dogs away again. *'There wasn't any of her left … at least that's what I heard.'*

Of course Georgie Bell's wham-bam am-dram performance the other night had sowed the seeds for this narrative leap. *How much is that doggie in the window...* Now I was counting on a pair of

396

whining mutts to prove my theory.

Jimmy Reilly would've told Bernie, in no uncertain terms, to destroy these dogs as soon as they'd devoured Georgie. After all, their doggie DNA could connect Bernie to the crime scene. It should've been the final, straightforward act in a painstakingly planned and executed 'perfect murder'.

But animal-loving Bernie couldn't bring himself to do it. The dogs had suffered enough. Surely better that he find them a loving owner.

Where are the dogs?

Somewhere they'll get treated right.

Where's a better place to hide a needle than in a haystack? With other needles...

An hour or so ago, I drove down to Battersea Dogs' Home to ask if one Dean S Sombrero may have donated a pair of emaciated German Shepherds. They hadn't heard of Senor Sombrero but, three mornings ago, they'd found two maltreated hounds of that breed tied to an external gate.

Now Shep couldn't wait to cry havoc and release these dogs into suite three.

Their frantic yowling gave them away before Shep managed to get the door open.

Bernie's face shot up at the canine clamour, wide-eyed with joyful surprise, then dawning horror as they raced in and mobbed him.

'Dog hair, the bane of my old lady's life,' declared Shep solemnly. 'Devil's dandruff she calls it, Bernie. She spends half her life vacuuming it up, the other half beating rugs and throws out in the back garden.'

Bernie now bore the look of a beaten man.

'But it has its uses too,' said Shep. 'Even minus a root, we can extract a dog's DNA profile, which is something we can't do with human hair. And dog hair is tough. You can clean it, burn it, bury it or leave it out in the open for months, and we can still extract what they call mitochondrial DNA, which is very stable.

'But here's my favourite part, Bernie. Because they self-groom, each hair usually comes with a bonus, a lovely coat of thick doggie saliva.

'As we speak, forensics officers are searching your home and car for stray dog hair. And we're currently awaiting a warrant to search the Florentine Gardens. But here's the best bit. I'm sure you know all about the murder of Helen Oldroyd? She was found stabbed to death in her Jaguar car, outside a leisure centre in Brentford. Well, it turns out that the Bureau de Change she co-owned in Paddington – Money Transfer on Praed Street – is the very place Jimmy's IT girls have been laundering his dirty money to smuggle abroad.

'Now we know that our resident bad apple, Detective Superintendent Alex Spence, made sure that Oldroyd's car suffered human contamination at the scene, to take the heat off his new pal and significant creditor, Jimmy Reilly.

'Guess what. Her car is still in our pound. And even though it was contaminated by humans, so to speak, it hasn't been contaminated by dogs. So we're searching that car for doggie hair too. All we need is a single strand to match either of these dogs, and we've got you. So this Bernie has turned into your very own Dog Day afternoon.'

Chapter 41

East Dulwich, South London
Tuesday, April 13, 1993; 09.10

Bernie sought a deal.

Shep spelled out the terms and conditions.

'You cough, Bernie, about everything, and I'll think about whether or not you merit a berth on our much-coveted Witness Protection Programme. Trust me when I tell you it'd be easier to get a seat at the Last Supper.

'You see Bernie, I've got to ensure that the hard-pressed British tax payer will be getting value for money supporting you for the rest of your life. And value for money represents nothing short of the taking down of Jimmy Reilly. Understand?'

Bernie understood only too well, launching into a confessional free-fall like a pregnant nun shot out of a cannon.

He started with Helen Oldroyd's murder.

'She'd been helping Jimmy launder money for years, transferring his dirty cash into massive foreign notes, thousand-dollar Canadian bills and thousand Swiss franc bills, to make it easy to smuggle out.

'So whereas one million pounds required ten thousand one-hundred-pound notes, weighing ten kilos, you only needed one kilo of these larger notes. You could stuff a million into a cereal box.

The girls were usually too thick to realise they were breaking the law. They just saw themselves as money couriers.'

'Who gets this money?'

'All sorts of people. Drug suppliers, money launderers. He buys dodgy booze for his clubs and restaurants. He's got investment brokers buying foreign property, art, wine for him. He can't clean it quickly enough.

'Of course, she got greedy. It's always the same, isn't it? She wanted a bigger slice. He told me and Slob to make her see sense. So we came up with a plan.

'Jimmy told Helen to pick up Slob at Kew train station because he had a delivery for her. That usually meant a sports bag full of cash. She always picked up the courier outside that station as there's no CCTV, then drove onto the leisure centre car park to put the bag in the boot while the courier makes himself scarce, 'cos there's no CCTV there either.

'The thing is, she loved cash. Loved it. She'd always open the bag in the boot at the leisure centre and stare at it. Every time. It's like she couldn't help herself. Except today, we had something else in the bag for her.

'All Slob had to do that day was get into her Jag with his sports bag and accompany her to the car park. She obviously said something to upset him. She could be a right snarky cow. So Slob opens the bag up and shows it to her as she's driving. It freaks her right out.'

'What was in the bag, Bernie?'

'A load of stuff we'd nicked from her 9-year-old

daughter's bedroom during the night. You know, dolls, photos, shit like that. Like I said, the plan was to shake her up, not hurt her. But according to Slob, she produces a knife from the door pocket on her side and lashes out. Slob grabs the knife, and then they're wrestling. He manages to jab the blade into her a few times. He finally takes control and gets her to drive into the leisure centre car park.'

'Where were you during all this?'

'I'm parked there already, waiting to pick Slob up. I see her car driving in, weaving all over the place. When it stops, I drive over and park next to her. She's freaking out, screaming at me to help her. It's a bad situation. If people start gawping, we're fucked. I have to make a snap decision. I tell Slob to finish her off. He starts jabbing the knife into her, doing it all wrong. I felt sorry for the cow, I really did. So I get the knife off him and finish her off, proper like. We then get into my car, drive off and call Jimmy.'

'What can you tell us about Liz Little's murder?'

Bernie sighed. 'On a couple of these trips abroad, some suppliers complained that their cereal boxes were a little light. At least one of the girls had been helping themselves to the occasional thousand-dollar or thousand-franc note. Jimmy asked me to find out which one. I already knew Liz was struggling with money on account of this flop of a play she'd invested in. Then I discovered that bank notes had gone missing from all of the girls' packages, except hers. That's how she'd unwittingly exposed herself. At least that's what I thought.

'Jimmy told me to have a word with her. Liz denied taking any money and insisted that the other five girls were in cahoots, ripping Jimmy off. According to Liz, they had openly discussed blackmailing him on several occasions. When I asked her who the ringleader had been in all this, she said Georgie Bell. She also said she'd warned a police officer friend of hers that she was doing something illegal for Jimmy Reilly. If anything ever happened to her, he'd come looking for answers.

'I reported back to Jimmy, stressing that it was all hearsay. Jimmy said that the missing money was proof enough for him that he had to teach the girls a lesson. I thought he'd use Spence to set them up somehow. I'd no idea he'd kill them.'

'So you're accusing Jimmy Reilly of murdering both Liz Little and Georgie Bell.'

'Yes. He believed that Liz and Georgie were either ripping him off or plotting against him. He wanted to make an example to the other girls. I don't know how you prove it, but that's what happened. It's obvious, isn't it?'

'And what lay behind the barbaric torture of Liz Little?'

'Two things. He didn't like the fact she'd grassed the other girls up. He's funny that way, Jimmy. He has this psychotic hatred for anyone who rats out anyone else, even if it's to his bene-fit. Then when she said she'd told a cop about the racket, well, that signed her death warrant.'

'What about all the signatures at the scene ... cutting her in half, her slashed face...?'

'One of his great passions is the Black Dahlia murder. He has all the books, the documentaries, the FBI files. That's why he named the club the Florentine Gardens.'

'I don't understand,' said White.

Bernie made a 'don't tell me this guy's for real' face. 'That was the name of the club in Hollywood that the original Black Dahlia worked in.'

'Why did Jimmy have her body dumped at the Brownswood red-light zone?'

'I don't know.'

'How did she come to have Valerie Gillespie's hair in her hands?'

'I don't know.'

White again: 'They found a battery inserted into her anus. Any theories as to what the significance of that might be?'

'I have to say that's not Jimmy's style.'

'Oh, I see, he has strict standards does he, about how he tortures and murders people?'

'In his own weird way, yes. He'd never rape a woman. Never.'

'Liz Little had been cut, slashed, beaten with hammers. Is that more Jimmy's style.'

'He would've kept going until she told him the truth, you know, about skimming from his cereal boxes,' said Bernie. He winced suddenly, the weight too much. 'My worry now is that she'd been telling the truth all along. He just couldn't accept it.'

'Fucking hell,' said Shep, turning away with a grimace. 'That poor girl.'

'Where would we find the weapons used to torture and kill Liz Little?' said Price.

'Under the terrazzo floor. Jimmy always boasts that it can't be dug up because of a preservation order. God knows what's under there.'

'Where was Liz Little tortured and killed?'

'I'd say look in the club. Same as Georgie Bell. But neither happened on my watch.'

'Tell me about your connection to 42 Ennerdale House, the flat where dogs ate Georgie Bell's body.'

'Jimmy asked me to rent a flat for six to eight weeks, somewhere neighbours don't ask questions. A mate told me about a dodgy lettings agent in Finsbury Park. I paid 'em a grand and they gave me the keys. I went to check it was kosher and gave Jimmy the keys. That's the sum total of my involvement.'

'So you never returned to that flat again?'

'No.'

'So who took her there?'

'I don't know. He wouldn't ask me because he knew I didn't agree with what he was doing. Not without proper proof.'

'Who took the dogs there? I thought you took care of them?'

'I wouldn't do what they did to those dogs,' he snarled, flushing. 'Anyone who knows me will tell you that. I loved them fucking dogs.'

White changed tack. 'Two Saturdays ago, you asked a police officer on a private visit to the Florentine Gardens to see you up in the club's VIP area. Why?'

'I wanted to know what he was doing in our club.'

'Had you discussed this with Jimmy Reilly?'

'I pretended Jimmy was on his way, just to shake him up. But he wasn't. I wanted to talk to him myself. That's my job, or at least it was.'

'When did you next see this police officer?'

'As he ran out of a fire exit door that night.'

'And after that?'

'Last Saturday, we picked him up outside Ennerdale House. To go see Jimmy.'

'He says you abducted him.'

'No one laid a finger on him. He came of his own free will.'

'Who told you to go get him?'

'Jimmy told us where he was and to bring him to the club.'

'Jimmy threatened to harm all the girls who spoke to this officer the previous Saturday night. Has he identified those girls?'

'No.'

'This is important, Bernie. These girls could be in serious danger.'

'He didn't see any CCTV, I know that much.'

'Explain?'

'I destroyed it.'

'What?'

'There's been too much violence. So I got one of the guys to wipe it. I'm head of fucking security. I'm there to protect everyone.'

'How did Jimmy react to the fact it was gone?'

'How do you think? He told me if I didn't find out which girls Lynch spoke to, he'd fire me. That's one of the reasons I'm talking to you now.'

Price sighed. 'I want to move on to something that's baffled everyone: these spoon-sized gouges of flesh that had been removed from Liz Little's body prior to her death. The pathologist can't identify the cause. Forensics can't identify the cause. Can you enlighten us?'

Bernie shifted in his seat. 'Jimmy has two Holy Grails. Making that terrazzo floor damage-proof, and being able to make a dead body disappear. I mean without having to chop it up, bury it in lime or at sea, feed it to pigs or smuggle it into an incinerator. He's obsessed with it, especially now with DNA profiling. That's got people like Jimmy really shaken up.

'He's always fancied himself as a chemist. Or an alchemist. He owns labs and takes a real interest in that side of things. When he found out I did a chemistry A-level, he started telling me all about it. Literally every day he updates me.

'It turns out that his efforts to protect the terrazzo floor using epoxy products led to his lab technicians discovering something terrifying.'

He shuffled and coughed. 'Look, you're going to find what I'm about to tell you incredible, but I saw it with my own eyes. And he's got to be stopped. He told me that they'd isolated the single chemical component in blood that creates the metallic scent that drives carnivores wild, and that it derives from the epoxy they'd been working with for years. I remember he said it's an organic aldehyde compound called trans epoxy something.

'I didn't believe him. He got the hump and brought it in one day. He spread some on the floor, because it worked as a floor sealant as well. He took an enormous sniff and he said to me "what does that remind you of, Bernie?" He said "come on, breathe it in". He was stoked. So I sucked on it hard and he said "it smells like blood, doesn't it?" And it did, I have to say. It was metallic, like blood. I recognised it as soon as he said so.

'He looked at me with this crazed expression. "Get the dogs in," he said. They can't sniff that stuff, I said, or they'll do themselves harm. He turned and shouted in my face "get them fackin' dogs in here, now".

'I brought them in from the yard and they went nuts, pawing and licking at the floor, yelping and frothing at the mouth. They wanted to eat the fucking floor. Jimmy says something like "if we can get some of that into the veins of a corpse, they'll fucking devour it for us". I told him to try it out on some other fucking dogs. I meant it too. I'd take on Jimmy and all his armies if it came to defending a defenceless animal. That's just the way I am.

'He didn't even hear me. He says "I'll tell you what, Bernie, my piranhas are carnivores. This'll drive 'em fackin' mental. Think about it. They can strip a cow to a fackin' skeleton in two minutes. They'd hoover up a human corpse in thirty fackin' seconds."'

'He owns piranhas?'

'He has a tank full of them, in his office, upstairs at the Florentine.'

Bernie stretched out his arms across the table, as if breaking free from some imaginary shackle.

'I thought he was raving. Then one morning, Slob told me what he'd seen the night before. Jimmy had isolated a piranha into its own tank, injected some of that resin into a body that was still alive, so that it got pumped around her veins. Then he had Slob and some of the boys place her in the tank. The Piranha went wild, taking out lumps. I now realise that the guinea pig must've been Liz Little.

'As soon as I heard about Georgie, I realised he must've injected her with this epoxy stuff too. He then effectively fed her to my fucking dogs. The way they went at that floor. I know they wouldn't have waited 'til she was dead. Jimmy would've loved that, the sick fuck, watching her getting torn asunder like a piece of fucking KFC. He would've laughed his head off too. "Look at those dumb fackin' dogs, eating all the evidence". I'm telling you, he's the fucking animal.'

'I believe Bernie,' said Shep, 'and I want to dig up that terrazzo floor and discover Jimmy's secret vampire formula. But...'

He turned to us all, widow stern...

'...we don't have anything solid on Reilly except money laundering. As we all know, that has to go through the Fraud Squad, taking years. If he lives long enough to get charged, his lawyers will spend three years bamboozling the jury with jargon and he'll walk. If all else fails, he'll get some dodgy prognosis of early on-set Alzheimer's or dementia. So we have to charge Reilly with murder or no dice.

'Even if we find weapons under that terrazzo floor bearing his prints, or bodies bearing his thumb marks, his own cock up a dead woman's arse ... he'll just blame it on his uncouth Eastern European employees. They'll make like they'll take the rap, then vanish. We just don't have that smoking-gun evidence.'

'Bernie must know much more,' argued Price.

'Maybe we can get Reilly on less-serious charges to start with ... assault, kidnap.'

'No,' said Shep decisively. 'We release Bernie back into the wild. Frankly, he hasn't produced an incriminating pot for us to piss in.'

'What about conspiracy?' White argued.

'A term usually followed by "theory", in my experience,' said Shep.

'Guy, you make it sound like unless we actually catch Reilly in the act of killing someone, we can never get a conviction.'

'Bang to rights is what we're after,' said Shep.

Bang to Rights. The words instantly summoned the stilted horror of Sunday night's drama production at the Hen and Chickens.

As I recalled the ludicrous plotline, an outlandish idea took hold.

'Hang on,' I said, 'we know Jimmy's a maniac, Bernie's desperate. We've got Tammy on side. I've just had an idea...'

Chapter 42

Conduit Street, Central London
Wednesday, April 14, 1993; 22.40

'Fucking hell,' I gasped, as that familiar twang of dread strummed my nerve endings, 'I never thought we'd darken this doorway again.'

'Carousing at the taxpayers' expense,' beamed Fintan. 'This might actually be the single greatest night of my life.'

Fintan bristled with confidence as he strode past the dead-eyed meat rack of bouncers into the Florentine Gardens Club. My heart flapped so wildly, I felt certain Shep must be picking it up over my shirt's button bug.

Fintan's peace-hating spooks had been only too willing to showcase their talents to the Regional Crime Squad, replacing one of my single shirt buttons with a listening device boasting a range of 500 yards. A small army of plain-clothes cops surrounded the club. More were inside; Operation Tammy had no shortage of male volunteers.

Now we just had to hope Jimmy would bite.

Fintan insisted on ordering the £750 Dom Perignon, but agreed to draw the line at a £50 bowl of soggy McCain oven chips. 'That's taking the piss,' declared Bob fucking Geldof.

'What I still don't get is how Valerie Gillespie's hair ended up at the other two murder scenes,' he said, lighting a cigarette. 'That makes me think Jimmy Reilly can't be the killer.'

'Please tell me you didn't buy those cigarettes out of your Met Police *per diems?*'

'Of course I did,' he protested. 'It's a crucial component to my undercover persona.'

'But you smoke anyway.'

'Yes, but now I'm smoking on police time. I'm not donating my own cigarettes to the cause. Jesus. So, Valerie's hair? Theories?'

'It must have been planted at both scenes.'

'By who? She was cremated in March!'

'Maybe the girl at the mortuary made a mistake,' I said. 'She is only an assistant. And they say hair isn't an exact science.'

'So many loose ends...' he said and I smiled. He didn't know the half of it.

How did Valerie get into my head that night when I'd never been anywhere near her dead body? The A3-battery connection? Liz Little's 'after thought' perimortem injury to her coccyx, inflicted moments before her death?

The champagne landed, and so did the first girls. Even live broadcast failed to thwart Fintan from giving full vent to his infantile fantasies. Tonight, he elected to play the part of a Harley Street plastic surgeon, specialising in 'breast augmentation' and 'designer vaginas'. I couldn't even bring myself to listen.

Instead I scanned the club. 'Come on, Tammy,' I muttered, fighting the urge to guzzle my £200 glass of fizz. I took a quick look up to the VIP area. A back-lit figure stood there, still and alone. Bernie needed this more than anyone. I wondered how he felt right now, staring down at that blood-red terrazzo floor. His life depended on what lay under it. At best, he'd be relocated to a rent-free house in some Northern town, knowing that one slip or chance encounter could lead to exposure and certain violent death. At worst, Shep will declare 'no deal', abandoning him to a criminal limbo of paranoia and dread, a life spent waiting for that horrible moment when Jimmy Reilly finds out he talked and turns on him.

Still no sign of Tammy. A horrible realisation suddenly seized me. Shep had treated her appallingly. Her 'no show' tonight would be perfect, sweet revenge. What if she'd tipped Jimmy off, to earn a reprieve? She wanted Tammy to 'go out with a bang'; that would plant a bomb under all our careers.

My guts yanked and kinked to breaking. I had to *do* something, so I shot up and went for a walk.

As soon as my feet touched terrazzo, my eyes seized upon the last person I expected to see here. She looked directly down at me from the glass stage, her cold blue eyes blinking once to focus.

'Holy shit,' I said out loud, turning and scampering back to our table.

'Fintan, listen to me, we've got to get out of here, right now. My cover's blown.'

'Behave yourself,' Fintan hissed, jabbing his finger towards my button bug. 'We don't want the cavalry charging in now and blowing the whole operation. Calm down and tell me what's happened?'

'The girl on the stage, the blonde, she knows me.'

'How well?'

'I met her once. But I could tell she just recognised me. She almost stopped dancing.'

'Hang on,' he said, turning to his hired admirers. 'Girls, would you say my friend here has a memorable face? Be honest now or you won't be getting that discount we discussed.'

They both shook their heads and giggled.

'Thanks for your brutal honesty,' he smiled.

'See, Donal? To paraphrase dear old Nat King Cole, you're forgettable, that's what you are. So forgettable, whether near or far.'

'She's the assistant at Hornsey Mortuary. She briefed me about Liz Little's post-mortem.'

'Oh my God. That's Erika the Viking?'

We stared in mutual disbelief as realisations rained in like mortar fire.

'She must've supplied Reilly with Valerie Gillespie's hair,' he said slowly, wide-eyed.

'And tipped them off about the weird battery-insertion MO. They knew that by doing the same to Liz and Georgie, we'd link all three.'

Fintan shook his head. 'I wonder what else she's done for Reilly? Having a mortuary at her disposal ... it's perfect.'

I suddenly remembered Valerie's visit to me that night. Her appearance had proved crucial, leading me to Conlon's fingerprint. I couldn't understood how she'd reached me. I'd never been anywhere near her dead body. She'd been cremated several weeks earlier. Now I understood. That same day, I'd attended Hornsey mortuary; I'd been close to her body after all.

'Oh my God, she must have kept Valerie's head,' I gasped. 'She told me that she signed out Valerie's body herself, in a closed casket. But who would've checked inside? No one.'

Fintan put a hand on my arm. 'We have to assume she didn't recognise you just now, Donal, or can't quite place you. We can't abandon Tammy, or Bernie for that matter. Don't go walkabout again and keep your head down. I'll go and see if I can find Tammy.'

It felt perverse sitting with my back to the stage, cringing at the prospect of a tap on the shoulder from a bouncer, Jimmy Reilly or Erika herself. It began to sink in just how effortlessly she'd been playing us, all along.

She must have recognised the criminal potential of Valerie's distinctive hair right away. The head had already been severed, so she kept it refrigerated in a place where it wouldn't be found. *With other needles...* How difficult can it be to hide a body part in a busy mortuary? Even a head?

She ripped the hair out violently, so we'd assume it had been forcibly removed during her murder.

She tried to credit Edwina with identifying Valerie's hair, to deflect attention.

She deliberately didn't tell me about Liz's perimortem coccyx injury because she knew it made the battery insertion look staged, like an afterthought.

I remembered Edwina's gushing tribute: *Erika has struck again...*

How dogged she'd been to discover Valerie's hair amid the dog waste at Georgie Bell's murder. I scalded myself for not picking up on even one of her suspiciously impressive 'breakthroughs'.

'Hi,' boomed Tammy, acting her little heart out to make it seem like she didn't hate my guts.

'Hi, Tammy. How have you been?'

'You don't have to act sheepish, Donal. It's okay. Tammy's going out with a bang after all, just how I wanted her to.'

'I don't want you bullied into anything...'

'That bastard Shep found out my visa's expired, so I'm heading home. They dropped the charges after I agreed to go through with this first.'

'Are you okay with it?'

'What does it matter? It is what it is. I'll survive. At least you didn't rat me out to Jimmy or one of his bent cops. For that I should be grateful, especially after what he did to Liz and Georgie. Okay, order a bottle of Dom Perignon? I'll point out the four IT girls and then we leave this place for the last time, all captured in glorious technicolour CCTV.'

'Dom Perignon it is,' I smiled, 'you fancy a fifty-quid bowl of soggy oven chips with that?'

'Hell, yeah!'

Chapter 43

Conduit Street, Central London
Thursday, April 15, 1993; 09.00

Fintan, Shep and I scrummed down in headphones for our second live broadcast of the week, this time transmitted to our blacked-out van on Conduit Street, courtesy of Bernard Moss's wire.

Shep had outlined stage two of Operation Tammy to the three of us at dawn. 'Okay, Bernie, you show Jimmy the CCTV footage of Tammy and Donal deep in conversation last night, then you need to achieve just one more thing. Get him to offer you money to either whack Tammy yourself or to get her whacked. Then we can charge him with conspiracy to murder,' he said. 'Don't lead, don't put words into his mouth. He has to say it. As soon as he does and you leave the building, we go in. Any questions?'

Bernie had just one. 'What happens if he smells a rat?'

'The three of us will be listening in as it happens. I've got a radio link to two armed units ready to move in on my order.'

Bernie didn't need any further instruction. He had that raw, instinctive smart that you just can't teach.

He walked in and got straight down to business, cool as a breeze.

'Boss, I need to talk to you. That cop turned up again last night, the one you had a word with on Saturday. DC Lynch.'

'What, that fat little Irish cant? What the fack is he playing at?'

I baulked. 'I'm not fat!'

'Ah now, you have piled on a few pounds recently,' said Fintan.

'Yeah, but I'm not fat.'

'Shut up,' barked Shep.

Bernie didn't rush to fill the silences ... what a pro.

'He turned up with his brother again, the *Sunday News* reporter,' Bernie continued, 'I kept an eye on which girls they spoke to. I think I've finally figured out who gave him that list of names.'

'About fackin' time too.'

'The cop, Donal, spent about twenty minutes talking to one of our girls called Tammy. She's a Yank, she'd been quite chummy with Liz Little.'

'Ah, poor Liz. Brave as a lioness. Remind me, which one is Tammy?'

'Loud. Cocky. Massive mouth.'

'That could be any fackin' American, Bernie.'

'I've pulled the CCTV so you can see them together. Here, I'll set it up.'

Nerves nibbled away at the inside of my skin, like Jimmy's piranhas.

'I was watching them from the VIP lounge,' said Bernie. 'See the way she's pointing. She's picking out the other four girls on the list.'

'You absolutely certain, Bernie?'

'One hundred per cent boss.'

'Look at the state of him!' said Jimmy. 'He's hammered.' His guffaw took hold deep in his chest until he laughed and coughed simultaneously, like a tumble dryer churning a half-load of phlegm.

'Very thorough, Bernie,' he stated, dead serious now. 'What are you gonna do about it?'

'I was gonna ask you boss. How should we play it?'

'What would you do in my shoes, Bernie?'

'I'm not in your shoes, Jimmy.'

'Don't play silly buggers with me, Bernie. I know you got soft on that Liz girl, you silly cant. Did you really think an ape like you stood a chance with a classy piece of bottle like that?'

His phlegmy laugh sounded forced now, as if dredging up some deeply buried rage.

'Now, what's the one thing we can't have in this team?' he rasped, in a pitch I recognised from our terrifying face-to-face. 'A fackin' grass, Bernie. A fackin' rat fackin' everything up. I can't have it. On my daughter's life, I'm fackin' dealing with it myself. I'm the cant. Yeah? I'm the cant. You know what I mean, Bernie.'

A sharp inhalation sounded like a primeval, in-ward scream.

'I know. You fackin' talked. You grasping cant,' chanted Jimmy to Bernie's staccato yelps.

'Better get in there,' I called.

Shep stared straight ahead, the radio clasped tightly to his heart.

'Shep,' roared Fintan, 'Reilly's killing him.'

Dull frenzied thuds. Sickening gargles. A breathless rattle.

'All units, move in,' ordered Shep, finally. 'Arrest everyone on the premises. Lynch, call an ambulance.'

Fintan dialled and jabbered, on autopilot.

'My God, you just let him kill Bernie,' I shouted.

'Well, we've got him bang to rights now, haven't we?'

'You fucking animal.'

Shep's eyes recoiled in a blink, wounded. 'They were never going to put him in witness protection. Not after last year's overspend. Jesus, I had to beg them to pay for Tammy's plane ticket.'

I suddenly recognised what had gone on here.

'My God. You set Bernie up. You made sure Spence found out that Bernie had talked to us, and engineered this whole thing.'

'I don't know what you're talking about,' he huffed.

My face burned. 'You're no different to Spence. You're worse than Spence.'

He sighed. 'I'm going to call forensics now, get that terrazzo floor ripped up. Shame you can't be here to see it.'

He relished my confused reaction, one step ahead as usual.

'Oh, didn't I mention it?' He smiled. 'DS Barrett is expecting you back at your desk at 11. So you'd better fuck off now.'

Chapter 44

Irish Midlands
Sunday, April 18, 1993; 11.00

'What are you planning to spring on him?' demanded Fintan, speeding us west from Dublin airport.

'Let's just say Robert Conlon recorded a lot of what went on. Right up until the end. I want Da to talk us through it, because it doesn't stack up. Someone's telling big fat porkies.'

'And then?'

'Then I've got to do the right thing.'

'So you'll hand these tapes over to the authorities, land your own father in jail, or worse.'

'He used us to get to a man who he then had murdered, or murdered himself. Are you telling me you're comfortable with that?'

'Oh, and what a great loss to society Robert Conlon is.'

'If it wasn't Da, what would you do?'

'That's the whole point though, isn't it, Donal? Blood is thicker and all that... Don't forget about Mam in all this. If he gets put away ... Jesus, it'd kill her.'

'He should've thought about that, shouldn't he?'

But he'd needled my weak spot, of course. Poor Mam.

As we stewed in silence, I let the words of all those who had brought us here ferment in my mind.

Don't worry, in an exercise like this, the truth is merely the starting point...

If you look at anything closely enough, for long enough, you'll find its dirty little secret...

There's always a bigger play, Lynch. Always. Remember that...

We didn't speak again until he pulled up outside our home. Fintan turned and grabbed my upper arm, hard.

'Just make sure you consider Mam in all this,' he said. 'Don't rip this family apart.'

As soon as our feet hit gravel, Da opened the front door. 'Well,' he said, 'shall we get this over with?'

He led us through to the kitchen and sat at the head of the table. He seemed younger, fresher. At peace. Could this relaxed, middle-aged man in achingly cheerful golf-themed leisure wear really be a cold-blooded murderer?

I had a sudden flashback to Bernie earlier this week, spewing like a ruptured dam. Had part of Da secretly yearned for this moment, for total and utter cathartic release? After decades of clamming up, shutting down, treading mine-laden eggshells, did he now relish the prospect of opening up that steaming, sweating valve, and letting it all go.

'Why is Mam above in Mullingar?' I began.

'I had to get her out of the way,' said Da. 'You two can throw anything you like at me but I'll tell you one thing now, I'd never let any harm come to that woman. Ever.'

'We know that,' said Fintan.

Da charged on: 'I couldn't know what Conlon was capable of, and people were harassing the shit out of me, day and night, about this footage. I had spooks following us, watching outside, even breaking into the house when I wasn't here, emptying my office just to freak me out. Of course, she'd cottoned on to it. She knew something was seriously wrong and she wanted to do something about it. Unfortunately, this made her a danger to herself.

'I wanted to guarantee her safety, no matter what happened to me. I didn't know what to do. Then Pat Harnett had the idea of switching her medication for placebos. After about a week, she asked to go into the hospital. I'll tell you now, the moment they took her in, I stopped worrying. I knew no one could get to her there and I cried out of relief. Okay?'

He breathed hard, focussing on one spot on the table, hauling back his composure.

'Look,' he said, strong again, 'I don't give a shit about what happens to me, right? I chose this life. But that woman is a saint. I thought I was going to die and all I wanted was to know she'd be okay. I'd die happily enough then. I don't expect either of you to understand that.'

He surveyed us now, bitterly. 'Sure how could ye? Neither of ye has a clue about anything.'

Fintan's eyes blinked in wounded shock. I'd heard it all before. But this was my rodeo so I reclaimed the chair.

'You never were very domesticated, Da,' I began, rummaging in my bag for Conlon's Dictaphone.

421

'You forgot to press the "start" button on that washing machine in Paddington. I found this in Conlon's jacket pocket. I've edited it down to the most significant parts, otherwise we'd be here for days.'

Michael Lynch's eyes didn't even flicker. Fintan's looked set to topple out onto the table.

I pressed play.

CONLON: Why are you stalling on me, John? I've fulfilled my side of the bargain. I want my package now.

JOHN KNOX, SPECIAL BRANCH: You'll get your package, Bob. It's taking a few days to sort out, that's all. It's not like we have great wads of cash and empty houses sitting abroad waiting for occasions like this. I need to get it signed off, and there are layers of bureaucracy. You know what it's like.'

I turned it off.

'Conlon had already handed over the footage to Special Branch,' I said. 'They'd promised him a house abroad, a pay off.'

Da sniffed.

'I didn't know that,' he said, looking me directly in the eye. 'I swear to you on my mother's grave. Not until the end, anyway. I told ye the truth that night. Conor sent me over to appeal to him personally, to beg.'

I pressed play.

CONLON: You said all that yesterday, John. I've kept a copy, you know? I'll release it to the media if you don't give me my fucking package. That'll fuck you all up.

KNOX: Bob, please. We're so close to sorting it

422

all out. If you release it to the media, you're left with no leverage at all. And you'll fuck everything up. Come on, we've put you in a safe house. We've pulled the cops off, which had to go to ministerial level. That shows how committed we are to you.

CONLON: You're hoping I get shot, aren't you? Then you won't have to pay me a penny.

KNOX: You've got to trust me, Bob, after all we've been through over the years. How long have I had your back now? Twenty fucking years. Does that count for nothing?

Click.

'Jesus Christ,' gasped Da, his gaze seeking out anywhere but here, his brain in spasm, unable to cope.

'Oh my God,' he added as the impact kicked in, first bowing his head then clasping it in both palms.

I decided to editorialise. 'John Knox spent fifteen years in the north, working for the Force Research Unit, a shady military intelligence outfit that actively recruited, or should that be blackmailed IRA members to become spies. Bob had been a snout for the Brits since the early seventies. Is that why you set him up to get shot, Da?'

'I did no such thing. I'd no idea he was working for them. No idea at all. As far as I knew, he was trying to shake down Conor for a deal. And Conor was willing to do a deal. But Conlon went cold.'

I played the next instalment.

CONLON: I've got Michael Lynch calling me every five minutes, wanting to do a deal. My big mistake was trusting ye. What am I supposed to say to him?

KNOX: He doesn't know you've given it to us. We're listening in on all his calls. He has no idea. Talk to him, Bob, string him along. You only need to keep it up for another day or so and then we'll have you on that plane.

Da piped up first. 'You heard the man. I'd no idea he'd handed the footage over to the Brits, or that he was working for them all along. Why would I have bothered chasing him had I known that? It was all about the footage for me. I'd no other agenda.'

'Is that right?' I snapped, challenging his stare. 'What you're about to hear now, Fintan, is Da turning up unexpectedly at Conlon's safe house.'

I thought I'd feel intimidated. I didn't. And so I asked.

'How did you find it, Da?'

He didn't answer.

'I found Conlon's Volvo parked outside,' I said, addressing Fintan. 'At first I thought Da must have trailed him there, you know, after Conlon picked up his car at the Manor House pub on Sunday night. Or he'd put some sort of a tracker on it. Now, I'm not so sure. You'll hear Conlon answering his phone first.'

I set off the recorder.

CONLON: How the fuck did you find me here?

CONLON: Ah, I may as well tell you. Hang on.

MICHAEL: So, you've gone with them then, judging by the look of this place?

CONLON: I did a deal, Michael. I'd nowhere left to turn.

MICHAEL: You've given them the footage?

424

CONLON: What can I say? They can protect me, you can't. New identity, house abroad, the lot. There's a car picking me up any minute. You're not going to make a scene now, are you, Michael?

MICHAEL: It's too late for that.

KNOX: Oh, what a tangled web we weave, gentlemen.

CONLON: What in the name of ... did ye come here together? Are ye...

KNOX: It's all worked out beautifully. Michael, don't you see? You can now go back to Conor, tell him you tracked down Bob, found out he'd handed the footage to the dastardly Brits so you whacked him. They'll see you in a new light then, won't they? Sorry, Bob. Heads you lose. You'd better start taking your clothes off. I'll make sure it's instant.

MICHAEL: Bob, I didn't know he was coming here: I swear to God.

KNOX: Poor Michael. You still haven't got it, have you? We run this war now. In fact, we've run it all along.

'That's the last thing on the tape,' I said, snapping it off. 'Da, you said to Conlon: "It's too late for that". What did you mean by that?'

'I meant that I wasn't going to make a scene. I was letting him go.'

'It sounded like the opposite to me, like you'd already decided to kill him. Did you?'

'No,' he shouted. 'Of course not. I didn't have a gun. Even if I had ... what do you think I am?'

'That's what I'm trying to establish. Tell us, Da, what did Knox mean, about it working out beautifully?'

He took a long, almost ceremonial breath, as if relishing his last as the man we thought we knew.

'They set me up,' he said quietly, staring aghast into the middle distance. 'They made sure I tracked him down so that they could get rid of him, you know, and make it look like I'd done it. It saves them a fortune. They don't have to cough up what they promised him for the footage.'

Fintan's voice thinned into the whine of a disappointed boy. 'But why would they want to make it look like you shot him, Da?'

He dry coughed, rubbed his mouth and looked at us both in shamed resignation.

'Because it boosts my standing within the IRA. I'd no idea I was being played. I fucking hate working for those bastards.'

Fintan recoiled. 'You've been working for British intelligence? You?'

Da found that spot on the table surface again. 'Yes. For the past couple of years. They forced me into it. God knows I didn't want to.'

I watched his sulking, helpless, bullish pride wither and realised I could never hate him. Fuck it. I loved him. All I needed was for him to like me back. To not hate me would do...

'It's the last thing I'll do for them,' he blurted, 'I don't care what they threaten. We're nearly there now with peace anyhow.'

Fintan had caught up. 'So they turned you, Da. How?'

He didn't move. His eyes flicked into defocus as his world caved in.

'Well?' demanded Fintan. 'What the fuck's been going on?'

He tried to clear his throat but failed, so that he sounded like a man crying inside.

'Bob used to have these parties...' he began croakily. I didn't want to hear the sordid details, stood and walked out that front door.

I crushed the cassette tape under the heel of my shoe and lobbed the shattered remains into a ditch. I then drove to Mullingar.

We needed Mam back where she belonged. At home.

Postscript

Ironing out the plots intertwined by the Gillespie and Little murder cases sustained us all the way back to London.

Since the 1970s, Robert Conlon had risen through the ranks of the IRA and grown close to our da, Michael Lynch. All that time, Conlon had been secretly working for British intelligence. But that wasn't his only dark secret. Conlon also organised sordid sex parties deep in the Irish countryside, attended by underage, vulnerable girls and predatory, influential men. Conlon subsequently blackmailed these powerful figures to avoid exposure and prosecution, leaving him free to carry on his important work for British national security.

But weasel Conlon had kept one ace card up his sleeve ... evidence that implicated the brother of Conor Scanlon in paedophile activity. If

Conlon found himself in dire emergency, he'd use this dynamite material to shake down either the British authorities or the IRA ... maybe even both.

His sloppy murders of Valerie Gillespie and Melinda Marshall proved to be that dire emergency. Conlon had two things to fear. Firstly, the IRA took a dim view of 'volunteers' committing sex crimes, at least publicly. To prevent getting whacked, he told his IRA pal Michael Lynch about his smoking-gun evidence and indicated he'd be willing to do a deal directly with Conor Scanlon.

The second thing Conlon had to fear: prosecution by the British State. But Conlon knew how desperate the Brits were to force Scanlon to the table for peace talks. He gambled that the 'dark forces' who run Britain would give him anything he demanded in return for that game-changing footage.

What Conlon didn't know was that his old pal Michael Lynch had recently been 'turned' by British intelligence, ironically because of his presence at a number of Conlon's sex parties, captured on covert cameras. Neither man knew the other worked for the Brits or would ever admit it. Conlon believed he could use Michael to stall the IRA while agreeing a 'package' with the Brits. But the Brits had other ideas. Conlon had made the mistake of giving them the footage before he'd received his 'package'. He was suddenly of no value to them. Worse than that, his package would set them back millions.

They made sure Michael tracked down Conlon.

Knox then whacked Conlon, knowing Michael had no choice but to 'take the credit'. At a stroke, these ingenious spooks had eliminated the messy, costly burden of Conlon, boosted the standing of their other secret agent, Michael Lynch within the IRA and gained possession of the means to blackmail the IRA ... all for the price of a single bullet.

Epilogue

In December 1993, the British and Irish governments went public about their 'secret' peace talks, paving the way for the 1994 IRA ceasefire. That announcement pleased no one more than the fraught and war-fatigued Michael and Dolores Lynch from Clara, Co. Offaly.

Bernie Moss survived Jimmy's vicious knife attack, just. He sued the Met police, winning sufficient compensation to retire and live incognito. He now writes True Crime books under the pseudonym Dean S Sombrero and works as a consultant on British TV documentary series *Danny Dyer's Deadliest Men*.

Under Jimmy Reilly's terrazzo floor, forensics found blood belonging to Liz Little and Georgina Bell and the ball-peen hammer used to 'subdue' both women. Reilly was convicted of conspiracy to murder, manslaughter and money laundering and sentenced to sixteen years. His daughter, Barbara, currently runs his empire.

The Forensic Science Service discovered that Reilly and his dodgy labs had indeed isolated the single metallic chemical compound in blood that attracts carnivores, giving it the official name: trans-45-epoxy (e)-2-decenal.

The Florentine Garden's terrazzo floor was seized by the Criminal Assets Bureau and re-housed in the British Museum.

Mortuary assistant Erika the Viking, aka Erika Ellstrom, was convicted of perverting the course of justice and sentenced to seven years. She refused to speak during the entire judicial process.

Fintan Lynch's string of exclusives about Jimmy Reilly's downfall secured him the UK Press Gazette's coveted Reporter of the Year and Scoop of the Year awards. His book about Jimmy, *Life of Reilly*, made it onto the *Sunday Times'* bestseller list.

'Tammy' relocated to Seattle and used her £20,000 reward for the conviction of Reilly to buy a cocktail bar, which she renamed 'The Princess Anne'.

The publishers hope that this book has given you enjoyable reading. Large Print Books are especially designed to be as easy to see and hold as possible. If you wish a complete list of our books please ask at your local library or write directly to:

Magna Large Print Books
Magna House, Long Preston,
Skipton, North Yorkshire.
BD23 4ND

This Large Print Book for the partially sighted, who cannot read normal print, is published under the auspices of

THE ULVERSCROFT FOUNDATION